S.K. Vaughn is the pseudonym for a screenwriter and author of three internationally bestselling thrillers. Vaughn's first science-fiction novel, *Across The Void* will be released in multiple languages and territories worldwide. S.K. Vaughn lives and works in North Beach, San Francisco.

ACROSS THE VOID

S.K. Vaughn

SPHERE

First published in Great Britain in 2019 by Sphere

1 3 5 7 9 10 8 6 4 2

Copyright © S.K. Vaughn 2019

The moral right of the author has been asserted.

Epigraph quote from Arthur C. Clarke from *Multiple Intelligences in Practice:
Enhancing Self-esteem and Learning in the Classroom* (2006) by Mike Fleetham.

A CIP catalogue record for this book is available from the British Library.

Hardback ISBN 978-0-7515-6822-6
Trade Paperback ISBN 978-0-7515-7072-4

Typeset in Garamond by M Rules
Printed and bound in Great Britain by Clays Ltd, Elcograf S.p.A.

Papers used by Sphere are from well-managed forests
and other responsible sources.

For Pokey. We can be everything.

Love recognises no barriers. It jumps hurdles, leaps fences, penetrates walls to arrive at its destination full of hope.

Maya Angelou

I don't believe in God, but I'm very interested in her.

Arthur C. Clarke

1

April, 2045 – Bournemouth, UK

'You've gone too far.'

Eve stood at the edge of a garden swimming pond in the fading spring light. The worry lines on her young face were put there by her daredevil daughter, ten-year-old May, who was splashing in the green water wearing her favourite lemon bathing cap and matching goggles. She smiled when she saw her mum's look of concern, a confirmation that what she was doing truly did present a risk.

Eve was not an overprotective parent, but swimming the length of the murky pond, underwater the entire way, did not strike her as either fun or smart. She held up May's towel.

'It's nearly time for dinner, anyway, so please climb out of that muck and—'

'Meet me on the other side!' May cried out, and plunged further in.

'Bugger,' Eve said.

Under the surface, May was thrilled at the sound of her mother's muffled exasperation, and further driven to prove she was up to the task. She kicked along energetically for what she thought was a great distance and rose to snatch a quick look at her progress. She was dismayed to find she was already feeling knackered after only making it a third of the way across. The cold pond water was stiffening her muscles and her breathing was increasingly shallow. To make matters worse, her brief rise to the surface elicited angry calls from Eve to mind her at once and get out of the pond before drowning.

Drowning.

From an early age, May had been an excellent swimmer, talented, and strong beyond her years. The idea of dying in a world in which she felt so at home and confident, perhaps even more so than on land, had been absurd . . . until that day in the pond. With every stroke, her limbs felt heavier and her lungs ached more. She'd taken a quick gulp of air when she'd surfaced before, but its benefits had soon dissipated. Somewhere in the back of her mind, her mother's warnings about swimming in the garden pond began to resonate. The water was always cold, even in summer, and the weather never offered enough sun to warm it more than a few inches below the cloudy, non-reflective surface.

But I am extraordinary, she thought firmly. *I am exceptional.*

Her inner cheerleader had been effective in motivating her before, but it all sounded hollow in her achingly cold little ears. Throwing pride to the wind, she surfaced again for a breath, but found she still had the final third of the way to go to make it to the other side, a distance that seemed as vast as the Channel. She gulped air and attempted to catch her breath by treading water, but the exhaustion she felt was spreading numbness over her entire body.

With limbs weakly fluttering, expending their last measure of strength to keep her mouth above water, she felt a wooden rage at her stupidity in ignoring Mum's warnings. She tried to lay eyes on Eve one last time, hoping she would understand her silent call for help in lieu of the yell for which her shivering chest held no breath. She saw nothing but the iron-grey sky hinged against a dull, mocking landscape, and then she sank like a stone. Holding her last breath was all she could manage, and she could feel her ability to do that slipping as well. Her body felt blue with freezing death, like a hand plunged into snow, and the darkness of the weedy depths enveloped her. Then she felt a sharp pain in her chest and heard a commanding voice call out, pulling her from the abyss.

'Breathe.'

2

December 25, 2067 –
Hawking II Deep Space Research Vessel

May's naked body lay suspended atop hypothermic gel in the spectral silence of an intensive care isolation pod. Intubated and attached to every imaginable resuscitation device, her only sign of life was a chirping chorus of robotic noise. The pod, a bulbous cocoon with a milky-opaque skin, pulsed gently in time with her shallow breaths. Aside from the dim amber flashes of emergency lighting, its glow was the only significant source of light in the darkened infirmary. Her gaunt face, framed by the frosted observation window, appeared dead.

Sensors detected rapid eye movement, the first light of consciousness, under a barely perceptible flutter of lashes. The pod responded, its white skin blushing, and gradually increased heat while administering neuro-stimulants.

Vague flashes of light and muffled, distant sounds were all May's dulled senses could perceive. Her fingers clawed the air feebly as a galaxy of neurons fired throughout her sluggish brain. Her skin flushed under a thin layer of sweat. Every bone in her body hummed with agony and her blood boiled in her veins.

4

Despite her rapidly rising vitals, May struggled to grasp lucidity through a seemingly impenetrable mental fog. She desperately needed a shove if she wasn't to risk death by asphyxiation from the ventilator tube as the pod's life-support systems cycled down. This came in the form of a blast of holiday music that erupted over the ship's PA, followed by a canned greeting bellowed festively in multiple languages. With the piercing swell of a children's choir singing 'O Holy Night', May's weakened kidneys released all the epinephrine they could spare. The effect was similar to jump-starting a car that had been sitting for weeks in sub-freezing temperatures. Her autonomic nervous system quickly followed suit, stimulating her muscles into a violent shiver to warm up her core. As fragmented awareness sputtered across her mind, the choir hit its shrill crescendo and May opened her eyes.

3

'Patient revived. Deactivating isolation pod.'

The calm female voice of the ship's AI rose over the fading sounds of the machines cycling down. May's respirator slowed to a stop with a weary sigh. The top of the pod slid open, and condensation from the inside walls ran out on to the floor. Completely disorientated, unable to focus her vision, and barely able to move her weakened limbs, she panicked. Her screams couldn't escape the ventilator and feeding tubes, which were making her gag forcefully. She clutched them with her slowly thawing fingers and fought back the simultaneous urges to cough and retch as she pulled them out.

When they were finally clear, she started to sink into the hypothermic gel, which had become warm and viscous. It crept up on to her chest and circled around her neck, threatening to suffocate her. An electric shock of panic sent waves of painful spasms through her muscles and set her skin on fire with pins and needles. The stinking gel slithered up to her chin, and May lurched and rolled to one side. The pod rocked with her and toppled over. When it hit the floor, she was violently ejected, sliding and thrashing across the room, her IV needles ripping out of her skin. She rolled into something that felt like a wall and lay there in the foetal position, retching watery vomit tinged with blood.

May's mind was a broken hive, swarming with questions. What she could see in the dark, through her semi-blurred vision, was nondescript. She knew she was in hospital, but where? She had no recollection of being hospitalised or even sick. But she felt very sick, as if she might be dying. Panic coiled around her and constricted, stealing her breath. She wanted to sleep, the whisper of death coaxing her to simply close her eyes and release her grip on life. It was compelling to the point of seduction, but she somehow knew it would prove lethal. She could feel it. Her hands reached blindly for anything solid to hold as the room spun sickeningly. With the clumsy squirming of a newborn, she began to crawl.

The counter along the wall was almost close enough to touch, so May zeroed in on it, clawing at the floor and shuffling her rubbery feet. Her knuckles rapped up against one of the cool metal storage cupboards and a weak current of relief gave her the confidence to press on. Up on to one elbow, then the next, using all of her strength to push, she found herself on her hands and knees, her weak, quivering muscles barely supporting her frame.

She had no idea what to do next, so she waited there until a decisive thought crossed her mind.

Water.

Her tongue was so dry, it kept sticking to the roof of her mouth, which still tasted of blood. *Dehydration.* That was the name for what she was feeling. She'd felt it somewhere before, several times. *Low blood pressure.* That caused the dizziness and feeling of weakness.

Move.

Her mind was shaking off the cobwebs, bringing the world into soft focus. At the top of the counter next to her was a medical exam station with a scrub sink three feet off the floor. The thought of standing was ludicrous, but she reached up and grabbed the edge of the counter and pulled herself up on one knee, wincing at what felt like hot knives in every joint and muscle. Transferring power back and forth from legs to arms, allowing one pair to rest while the other worked, she managed to get into a squatting position. That small victory gave her the confidence to persevere. She pulled herself up high enough to throw her other hand into the sink and grasp the faucet. With all her might, she pushed with her legs and pulled with her arms until she was able to stand.

Staring into the metal sink, May smiled proudly. Her lips cracked and bled, but she didn't care because water trickled out when she held her hands over the tap. She bent over and let it run over her mouth, swallowing every drop she could catch. It tasted so good, she would have cried if she'd had the tears to spare. After a few more long drinks, the water sparked her light of survival. Her vision became much clearer, as did her mind. An emergency torch was cradled in the wall behind the sink. She pulled it out and switched on the dim flickering beam, cautiously surveying her surroundings.

What the hell happened here?

The infirmary was in complete disarray, the contents of its drawers, cabinets and sealed vaults strewn about, seemingly torn from their housings by the hands of desperation. *Desperate for what?* Gurneys were stripped and stained. May thought it looked like war zone triage. *How do I know what that looks like?* She attempted to deduce causes, but the glaring deficiencies in her memory and cognition induced a bristling anxiety she was determined to avoid. She told herself to focus on getting her body back to some semblance of normality before attempting to do the same with her mind.

'Keep it simple.'

Her whisper of a voice sounded hoarse and foreign, but she was pleased to hear it. And she agreed with the sentiment. Keep it simple. She grabbed up a gown from the floor and slipped that over her head, enjoying its immediate warmth. The water had been a godsend, but she felt the weakness and dull head-ache of dehydration creeping up again. Her torch beam passed over a cabinet with IV bags behind the glass. That was what she needed: a massive infusion of fluid to replenish what was left of her. Only ten paces away. She shuffled sideways, careful to maintain her grip on the counter so she wouldn't stumble on debris.

When she reached the cabinet, it was locked. Trying to recall a pass code was a torture she refused to put herself through. As she looked around for something to bash what she was sure was bulletproof glass, she saw a hand-shaped scanner next to the keypad. She placed her palm down. A small screen next to the hand scanner flickered and displayed:

COMMANDER MARYAM KNOX, STEPHEN HAWKING II RESEARCH VESSEL

'Hello, Commander Knox,' the AI said cheerfully.

'What?' May said, startled.

'Hello, Commander Knox.'

'I'm ... I've just woken up and ... what did you call me?'

'Commander Knox.'

'Commander?'

'I don't understand the question.'

The fear May had felt flowering was now terror in full bloom. 'I'm sorry. I can't ... remember. My memory. I've been very ill, I think. I'm weak and need fluids ... and food. Will you please help me?'

'Of course. What is your illness? Currently, I am unable to access the ship's network to review your medical files.'

'I don't know,' May said sharply, punishing her tender vocal cords.

'I'm sorry to upset you. There is a rapid scan unit just behind you. With that I can help assess your condition.'

May turned and pulled the scan unit cart over to her.

'Exhale into the pulmonary tube and place your finger on the blood test pad.'

May breathed into the tube and fell into a coughing fit. The test pad pricked her tender finger and she yelped from the pain.

'I am not detecting any known pathogens,' the AI reported. 'However, you are severely dehydrated, malnourished, and your lung functions are well below normal.'

'You're a genius,' May said sarcastically.

'Thank you. We will begin intravenous therapy immediately.'

Guided by the AI, May pulled a vitamin-rich electrolyte hydration bag and steri-line pack from the cabinet, along with two epinephrine pens. She slowly transferred these items to an empty gurney and the AI instructed her to administer the epinephrine pens first before lying down to receive the IV bag. Pulling back the sleeve on her gown, she looked for a decent vein amongst the tracks of bruised needle-entry points. Her arms were dotted with strange red blotches, which she also found on her back and legs. Some had scabbed over. Perhaps they were associated with her illness? Her head ached.

'Commander Knox, please insert the IV needle.'

'All right, all right. Jesus.'

May grunted and found a vein on her thigh that had not yet been abused, and slowly, carefully, pushed in the IV needle. It felt as if she were being impaled with a searing fire poker. Then the drip started going strong and the rush of energy that washed over her was so invigorating, she was finally able to squeeze out a few tears of joy. The icing on the cake was putting on the breathing mask and taking a deep inhalation of the oxygen-rich air mixture. She instantly felt stronger and more alert.

'I'll give you a mild sedative to help you sleep,' the AI said soothingly.

May shook her head.

'No. I'm ... afraid I won't wake up. And I need to know what's—'

She yawned and laid back, out of breath.

'It's imperative you allow your body to rest. I will monitor your vital signs closely and wake you up with a stimulant if there are any issues. Also, the epinephrine you've had will prevent a deep sleep. Does that allay your fears?'

'Yes, thank you,' May said reluctantly.

She had no reason to trust the AI. Who was to say it had not been the cause of whatever disaster had befallen the vessel? Maybe the sedative was not going to be so mild? *If the AI wanted you dead, you would never have got out of the intensive care pod. But the AI only became aware of you after you woke.*

May shut down her internal dialogue and chalked it up to paranoia brought about by whatever affliction had beaten her into submission. Of course she felt vulnerable. But if the AI was not to be trusted, she was lost anyway. And she had no recollection of having had a problem with it before all of this happened. *Before all of what happened?* She prayed that when she woke up she would realise it was all just a nightmare. She could joke about it with her crew. They would all have a good laugh.

Her crew! She closed her eyes and concentrated. She could see some of their faces. They were blurry, but bits would come in and out of focus, along with partial names. A memory of them slowly assembled itself. They were together, looking at something. Their mouths moved quickly as they spoke, but May couldn't understand what they were saying. Eyes were narrow with concern, maybe even fear. Briefly, the scene sharpened. The crew were looking down at May, hands probing, feeling her neck for a pulse. A man moved in closer and listened to her breathing. The name *Jon* came to mind. Had she stopped breathing? They were shouting 'Commander Knox?' – clapping their hands in front of her face, shining a light in her eyes.

They were trying to revive me.

4

'Commander Knox?'

May woke up back in the infirmary with a start. The scene from her dream lingered. *I was dying. My crew were trying to revive me. My crew.* She tried to hold on to the memory of their faces, but they kept slipping out of her grasp. *I was dying.*

'How was your rest?' the AI continued.

'What? Fine.'

'Do you feel better?'

'A little. Stronger.'

'I'm glad to hear it. Please remove your IV needle and dispose of it in the proper receptacle.'

May slowly drew the needle out from under her thin, tender skin and felt strong enough to walk it to the medical waste bin. 'Silent Night' was now piping through the PA – some sort of poly-lingual falsetto pop version sung by what she pictured was a chorus of eunuchs in red turtlenecks. All was not calm, and all was sure as hell not bright.

'Could you please shut that horrible music off?'

'Yes.'

13

When the music stopped, May could think a little more clearly, but more questions arose, demanding her attention. She fought to clear the cobwebs. *I am Commander Maryam Knox. Hawking II Research Vessel. NASA.* Where was Mission Control? Why weren't they helping? How could they have let this happen? What *is* 'this'? She tried to recall what happened, but her memory was like a television with intermittent signal cutting through static. Random fragments danced mockingly on the tip of her tongue, just out of reach.

'I was dying . . . '

'Please repeat,' the AI said.

'I'm trying to remember. But my head . . . things are foggy.'

'Are you experiencing memory loss?'

'I can see bits, fragments of things, people's faces. I can't put it all together. I can't remember. God, what has happened to me?'

'Are you able to recall long-term memories, such as where you were born, the names of your parents, and where you were educated?'

May reached into the past and found it refreshingly accessible. She wanted to run through as much as possible for fear she might lose it.

'I was born in England. Home town Bournemouth. My mother and father, Eve and . . . Wesley. Both pilots, now deceased. My father passed away when I was very young. He was a Royal Marine. Killed in action. I remember pictures of him in uniform . . . holding me as a baby . . . his brilliant blue eyes and white-blond hair, brushed back . . . he always looked so razor-sharp. Mum raised me. She was an RAF pilot. The only black woman in her cadet class to make wing commander. Very strict. More of a drill sergeant than a mum. But she taught me to fly . . . I have no siblings. Prepped at Duke of York Academy. Royal Air Force College at Cranwell. Officer training. Then

14

test pilot programme, space programme. My husband is Dr Stephen Knox—'

May stopped short. She felt an ache of sadness mentioning Stephen, but had no idea why. In that moment she realised there was something about their marriage, something wrong, lurking in the edge of the shadows like a restless spirit. She could barely bring herself to acknowledge it, let alone mention it to the AI.

'All of that feels solid,' she marched on, 'as though it happened yesterday.'

'What about your training and duties as commander?' the AI said.

'A bit murky when I first woke up, but now most of it feels readily accessible, like instinct or muscle memory.'

'Do you remember falling ill or being intubated?'

'No, that's the thing. I have no recollection of any of that. And other, more recent memories are spotty, a lot more fragmented.'

'I am not able to formally diagnose you without a full neuro panel, but, based on the fact that you are having the most difficulty recalling short-term memories, versus long-term, you may be experiencing a form of retrograde amnesia.'

'Amnesia?' May scoffed. 'I thought people only had that in shite B movies.'

'It is quite common in cases of traumatic brain injury, encephalitis caused by infection, and exposure to large doses of anaesthetic or sedative medications—'

'In my case, that may be all of the above,' May lamented. 'Is it permanent?'

'I am unable to find any predictor models for recovery. It appears that is determined on a case-by-case basis.'

'What about treatment? Are there drugs that can help?'

'No, retrograde amnesia patients are usually treated using occupational therapy and psychotherapy techniques that use cues to stimulate memory recovery over time.'

'Over time,' May repeated.

'That is correct. Depending on the patient, that process can take as long as—'

'I think I've heard enough for now, thank you.'

'You're welcome.'

May thought about the mission. The further back in time she went, the more clarity. She recalled the launch and a good deal of the journey to ... Europa. But that was when things began to fracture – reaching orbit, the planetary expedition. The pieces became even smaller and more dissociated on the return journey, when she had somehow become ill.

'Would you like me to run some more tests to assess the problem?'

'Later,' May snapped, her mind rubbery and stomach growling angrily. 'I'm dizzy and starving, my head is aching, and I'm about to start crying. I hate bloody crying.'

'Your blood sugar may have dropped below normal. There are glucose tabs in the compartment near where you found the IV bags.'

May ate as many of the tabs as she could fit in her mouth. They were sickeningly sweet, but dissolved quickly and made her feel more focused. They also reduced her headache to a dull, distant throb.

'That's better, thanks. On to the galley.' May realised she wasn't entirely sure how to get to the galley. 'Er, can you guide me there?'

'Please place your palm on the wall screen and log in to the command console. I will provide a highlighted route on the vessel map.'

May placed her hand on the wall. The wide, wrapping screen came to life in vibrant splinters and the NASA logo appeared, followed by a dossier photo of May in a NASA flight suit with her name and title. Her image took her breath away. The woman

16

in the photo was happy and healthy, with radiant brown skin. Her mouth was slightly curled in the beginning of a sardonic grin that sparked brilliant eyes possessing all that they surveyed, like the subject of a painting whose gaze one couldn't escape. She examined her reflection on the screen to make sure she was looking at the same person. The resemblance was there, albeit painfully vague. Everything about her now looked sickly. Her once closely cropped hair, with subtle gold highlights on the edges of her curls, was now matted and dull, and her skin had gone pallid. The grief she felt for her lost self – not just what she'd looked like, but what she'd known and who she had been – brought on bitter tears.

'Is everything all right?' the AI asked.

May couldn't answer. Every word became a lump in her throat. It was imperative she do something, anything, to improve her hideous appearance. She tore open the staff supply closet and traded her filthy gown for fresh surgical scrubs. Booties warmed her freezing feet. After sucking down some nutri-gel packs, she scrubbed her face with soap and warm water. On to the hair, which was matted beyond repair. She had no choice but to shave it down to stubble with surgical shears. When she was finished, she looked in the mirror. Some of the colour had returned to her skin and her eyes were a bit brighter.

There, now you look like a proper corpse, she thought, managing a smile.

5

C old as a grave, May thought as she trod into the corridor
on her way to the galley. This was her first look at the ship
outside of the infirmary and it appeared in stark contrast to
what she'd triumphantly piloted out of space dock months ago.
The darkness was consuming, save for the dim flicker of a few
weak emergency lights scattered throughout. The bright white
beam of May's torch cut a narrow path along the metal floor,
but failed to penetrate further. Outside of the low engine hum,
the silence was as pervasive as the dark.

For a vessel so large, the impossible emptiness was deeply
unsettling, casting a cold, penetrating shadow on any rays
of hope.

'The ship is dark,' she said. 'I see no signs of crew ... I can't
even see.'

Was this to be the sum of her accomplishments? A beautiful
expression of all the strength and good intentions of humankind, cast out and falling with no hope of ever finding the
bottom. *How could I have let this happen? How could everything
have gone this wrong?*

'Is there any way to turn on more bloody lights?' May asked the AI.

No reply.

'Hello? It's like a cave out here. I can barely see my own hand in front of my face.'

Still no reply. She walked angrily back to the infirmary. 'Why are you not answering me?' she asked the AI.

'I'm sorry, I was not able to hear you.'

'You can't hear me in the corridor?'

'Negative, Commander Knox. It appears my processors are no longer connected to the ship's network. I am only able to see and hear you in rooms with command consoles you've logged into, like this one.'

'So, you're unaware that the ship has gone dark and the crew are nowhere in sight?'

'That is correct. I am not receiving data feeds from any-where on the ship. Do you have any idea what is happening, Commander Knox?'

The question sounded oddly childlike and it occurred to May that whatever had knocked out internal power had also damaged the AI.

'That's what I was going to ask you. From what I've seen so far, the ship's internal power systems are not functioning prop-erly at all.'

'That is very troubling.'

'Not as troubling as the fact that you weren't even aware of it. Or, worse yet, not as troubling as the fact that I haven't yet seen or heard from another human being on the ship since I woke up.'

May was beginning to understand just how foggy her mind had been when she was revived. She wasn't out of the woods yet, but at least now she could grasp the basics.

'Protocol clearly states mandatory twenty-four-hour staffing.'

Again, the childlike naivety. The AI knew even less than May.

'I think we might be way past protocol here,' she chaffed. 'Do you know *when* you lost contact with the rest of the ship?'

'I am unable to determine that, as I have no access to the ship's clock.'

'But you at least remember losing contact?'

'I am unable to find any data related to that event.'

'Well, that's properly fucked,' May said.

'I don't understand.'

'That makes two of us. But, since it looks like we both have bloody amnesia, I'm not sure what the hell to do next.'

'Perhaps you can reconnect me?'

'How? That's engineering. Not my area. I've never even been in there.'

'If you go to my processor clean room, I will be able to help you assess the problem. If it is repairable, I can walk you through the proper maintenance procedure.'

'*If* it's repairable?'

'My processors are partially made of organic matter kept in a highly regulated environment. A power loss resulting in an alteration of that environment, even to the smallest degree, could be catastrophic. As I have no connection to the clean room, I am unable—'

'I get it,' May said tersely. 'Looks like dinner will have to wait. Please send me a new map showing me how to get to the clean room.'

'Sending now.'

May shoved as many flashlights, nutri-gel packs and water bottles as she could into a pillowcase and hurried back into the corridor. Without AI there was no hope of survival, and every passing second was critical if the organic matter in the processors had begun to die. She thought about the time she had forgotten to water her mum's flowers for a week and killed them all. They'd looked like dead soldiers in a firing squad line, bent over and ragged. *You had one job*, Eve had said accusingly.

'This is Commander Maryam Knox,' she called out. 'Is anyone on the ship?'

She remembered some of her crew names and called for them.

'Captain Escher? Gabi? Can anyone hear me?'

Her torch dimmed briefly, throwing her into a panic as she tapped the battery pack to revive it. Could they have jettisoned for some reason? The illness? A sense of menacing isolation crawled into her stomach and tied it into knots. To clear her mind of the intense paranoia this and the darkness brought, she concentrated on recalling details about her crew. Jon Escher, pilot and her second in command. Gung-ho American Navy pilot who fancied himself akin to the swaggering cowboy astronauts of the past. With his buzz cut, square jaw and aggressive exercise regimen, he was more a caricature of that archaic persona. He was capable, but May had hoped for a more experienced pilot to be her right hand.

Gabriella Dos Santos, flight engineer. She and Gabi were kindred spirits, both young and overflowing with talent, but constantly fighting to prove their worth. Like May, Gabi was military brat and a bit of a mutt. Her dad was a Brazilian helicopter pilot and her mother a NATO flight surgeon. May hoped with all her being that Gabi was still alive somewhere on the ship. No one knew the *Hawking II* better, and she would surely get things sorted.

Matt Gallagher, payload commander. May had always joked that he was the most perfectly boring man she'd ever met. Everything about him was ordinary, except for his vast space engineering and research knowledge. He knew her husband Stephen well, as he'd worked under Rajah Kapoor, the man who designed the *Hawking II* for Europa. May had not suffered gladly the staggering complexity of taking twenty-six non-astronaut eggheads into space to conduct all the important work Stephen and his team had slated. Matt had run perfect interference, managing their wildly diverse personalities while making sure their equipment operated at maximum efficiency. *Good old boring Matt*, she thought.

She heard a faint noise, distant and slightly mechanical, and stopped.

'Hello?'

The noise began again. This time it sounded very much like footsteps, heavy boots clopping along the metal floor with purpose.

'Is anyone there?'

The sound was booming and picking up speed, as if something big had sensed her presence and was moving in for the kill. She had neither the weapons nor strength to defend herself. What, or who, could it possibly be?

'Stop! Who is—'

The rhythmic banging sped up to an explosive, deafening vibration. The ship shuddered violently and listed deeply to port side like a schooner shouldering into a heavy storm swell. May fell hard, hit her forehead on the floor, and slid into the wall. She felt a support beam in her back and held on to it tightly to ride out what felt like an earthquake.

When the ship settled and righted itself, she struggled to her feet, her head spinning. Lesser tremors persisted for several minutes, like aftershocks wriggling back and forth through the vessel's bones. Her torch dimmed to a dull orange glow and died. Tapping the battery case didn't bring it back this time.

'No no no no no ...'

A warm stream of blood from a small gash above her right brow trickled into her eye. She tore the breast pocket off her scrub shirt and held it against the wound. Her heart was hammering faster than she could breathe to keep up. Consciousness was slipping.

'Relax, Commander Knox,' she demanded. 'Do your job. Don't let your job do you.'

Inhaling deeply, and suffering a terrible coughing fit, May kept her eyes closed tightly until the intense fear subsided and the cut above her eye was staunched. She grabbed a new torch and switched it on. The beam was not full strength, which meant it had not been fully charged. There was no way to estimate how much time she had until she was immersed in darkness, so she picked up the pace.

Do your job. Don't let your job do you.

The phrase jarred loose a memory of a man with bristly grey hair in an RAF dress uniform. Four gold bands on the shoulder and lower sleeve. Scrambled egg braid on the cap . . .

'Baz,' she said with delight. 'Bloody Baz.'

Her former commanding officer and mentor, RAF Group Captain Basil 'Baz' Greene, flashed into her mind. When she was an officer cadet at Cranwell, 'Baz' had taken her under his wing, so to speak. At first she had thought he was singling her out for being a woman, trying to break her so she wouldn't contaminate the mostly male culture. She'd been right, he had singled her out, but not in the way life had trained her to think. He'd seen her talent and wasn't about to allow it to be squandered. In fact, he'd staked his career and reputation on her, by nominating her for the test pilot programme. Back then, deep space travel had been on the verge of making unprecedented advances in propulsion that would defy physics and shrink the vastness of the solar system. Baz had helped May ride that wave. Pilot on pioneering commercial transports to Mars at twenty-five. Captain at twenty-seven. Commander of the first mission to Europa at thirty-two.

She laughed bitterly. 'And look at me now.'

6

In the corridor leading to the clean room, a strange warm light glowed from an unseen source and waxed increasingly brighter. It reminded May of a sunset, with its orange-yellow hues. When she palmed the entry pad and the door slid open, the whole room was bathed in it. The door shut and sealed behind her and May felt as though she'd found an oasis. She managed to take a deep breath that didn't rouse a death rattle in her chest and took a moment to allow a small measure of hope back in. The only thing that would have made it better was if Gabi had been in there, ready to assist with repairs ... and maybe offer a little contraband, some wine or a cigarette, perhaps? But, the clean room was another lifeless neighbourhood in the same ghost town.

May logged into the command console and resurrected the AI.

'Hello, Commander Knox. Were my directions helpful?'

'Yes,' May said curtly. 'Still no sign of crew along the way. Could they have jettisoned in the landing vehicles?'

'I am unable to determine that until we—'

'Right. Reconnect you. What's next?'

'My processors are in the vault directly across from the entry door. Please carefully follow the procedures listed inside. Failure to do so may result in contamination and permanent shutdown.'

'No pressure.'

May examined the processor vault. It was behind a seamless black wall with no discernible entry point.

'How do I get in? Answer a riddle? Use the Force?'

'I don't—'

'I know, sorry. I'll stop with the gibberish and await your instructions.'

'Please put on a UV and anti-microbial protection suit first. The organic matter requires highly radiative artificial sunlight for optimal performance, and bacterial contamination from your body would destroy it.'

'So, you're alive,' May said with wonder, and perhaps a hint of fear.

'If by alive you mean the condition that distinguishes animals and plants from inorganic matter—'

'Never mind.'

The black wall opened like an iris. May entered the vestibule and it closed quietly behind her. She undressed in the artificial sunlight, relishing its warmth on her bare skin. Closing her eyes, she tried to imagine being on a beach, and an actual memory of her standing on sugar-white sand somewhere in the tropics flashed into her mind.

'Commander Knox,' the AI said, interrupting May's lovely vision, 'it is not safe to expose your skin to the UV light for an extended period of time.'

'Every party's got a pooper,' she whispered quietly to herself.

May donned the clean room suit. Unlike NASA's Extra-Vehicular Activity or EVA suits, the clean room suit was more like something one would wear scuba-diving – skin-tight and made of a thick, rubbery neoprene-type material. Its outer

25

surface was crisscrossed with hair-thin fibre optic lines. The helmet was also form-fitting, and the gel packs inside it automatically adjusted to May's head, moulding around it. The visor glass curved under her chin as the helmet and suit sealed around her neck. The fibre lines embedded in the suit fabric lit up red and the function display appeared on the inside of her helmet glass with the words 'Initiating decontamination'.

Convincing herself she wasn't going to suffocate in the claustrophobic suit, May watched the colour of the fibre lines slowly change to white, indicating decontamination.

'Clear for entry,' the AI said. 'The clean room vault is an anti-gravity chamber with no life-support.'

'Why?'

'Exposure to gravitational pull and oxygen accelerates processor ageing.'

'Right. Granny's saggy tits,' May said under her breath.

'Please repeat, Commander Knox. I was not able to hear that.'

'I said let's do this.'

'I will use your helmet camera to view the system. Activating that now.'

The camera viewfinder screen appeared on May's helmet glass.

'Are you ready, Commander Knox?'

May nodded.

'Please hold on to the safety bars. I am going to equalise pressure and gravity between this room and the vault.'

May held the bars as she became weightless and the glass on her helmet darkened. The airlock door opened and May floated into a perfect sphere as large as a cathedral, with a seamless, semi-transparent glass wall. As dark as her helmet glass was, the unfiltered sunlight in the room was still painfully bright. May recalled the myth of Icarus and his doomed flight to the sun as she hung in the brilliance, waiting for her eyes to adjust.

Behind the glass, an elaborate web of what looked like black plant roots snaked over the entire surface, branching out in every direction. May assumed that it was the organic matter, as it was interlaced with fibre optic lines similar to the ones on her suit.

'You have a very interesting brain,' May said. 'What's it made of?'

'It's a singular organism made up of animal neurons and cellular plant matter, bound by a highly conductive plasma, and fibre optics that connect it to the ship's circuitry. It's the most advanced system of its kind, capable of high levels of parallelism and versatility.'

'Not so artificial, is it, your intelligence?'

'I've never thought of it that way. My creators told me the word "artificial" was added to create a sense of separation from human intelligence.'

'Or a sense of superiority. Human beings are a bit fragile that way.'

'You don't seem fragile, Commander.'

'Thank you. I am feeling stronger despite appearances.'

May took a closer look at the processor organism. She thought she could feel a subtle vibration, as if it were attempting to make contact.

'Speaking of appearances, is the organism supposed to look like this? So dark?'

'Yes, the black colour means it is healthy and fully functional. White indicates damage or death.'

May chuckled. 'What's next?'

'Activating maintenance portals.'

Silently, what looked like a hundred circular windows, all one metre in diameter and evenly distributed, dilated open. Inside were translucent discs that glowed either red or white. The vast majority were red.

'Each portal screen has a status light. Red indicates complete malfunction. White indicates partial function. Blue indicates full function. Please scan all portals for me.'

'Copy.'

May scanned the portals with a wide angle.

'There are no blues and very few whites. That can't be good, right?'

'Life-support failure is imminent without immediate repairs.'

May trembled, imagining the ship going completely dark and becoming her own frozen mausoleum for eternity.

'You will need to work quickly.'

'Ready.'

'How much life-support time is left in your suit?'

May looked at the function display projected on the inside of the helmet glass. 'One hour,' she reported.

'I will prioritise critical systems first.'

Some of the portal screens began flashing.

'Go to the flashing screens first. I will give you reboot codes for each. Enter them as quickly as you can, but carefully. Two incorrect entries will shut it down for sixty seconds.'

'Got it. One small thing. I've never been in this room before, actually more accurately never been allowed, and I've no idea how to operate the suit-thrusters.'

'They are operated by look and intention.'

'Really? I only need to think about where I want to move and the thruster will send me there?'

'You also need to be looking at your destination. The system tracks your pupillary focal points for targeting and matches that with brainwaves associated with human desire.'

'I'll be damned,' May said.

'Condemned by the Christian God to suffer eternal punishment in hell? I don't see the relevance of—'

'Figure of speech,' May said. 'There are many more where that came from, so don't worry about translating.'

'Affirmative.'

May stared down one of the flashing screens and focused on wanting to go there. She was shocked when the thrusters quickly responded and she glided to it. 'First portal.'

'Using the touch screen, enter the following code . . . '

May spent the next thirty minutes flying around the sphere, entering codes. But she wasn't moving fast enough. Anti-gravity work was a bitch and it didn't help that she was starving and dying of thirst. Also, the suit's cooling system wasn't keeping up with the UV radiation and she was sweltering. She could only imagine what a complete disaster it would be if she were to pass out in there.

'I've just taken an atmosphere reading in the infirmary and clean room entry area and life-support levels are decreasing at a rate of five per cent per minute,' the AI reported, adding insult to injury.

'But I've restored a third of the red portals.'

'It's possible the systems they control require mechanical repairs.'

May looked at her suit life-support clock. Ten minutes. Recharging it was moot if the whole ship was about to die. To reinforce this, she noticed that some of the branches of organic matter were changing from black to an unhealthy-looking dark grey.

'Commander Knox, I am concerned about your suit power. Based on the time you've been working you have less than ten minutes of life-support.'

'If I don't get this done now, I'm dead anyway.'

'Recharging the suit is more logical. We know when it will die. We don't know when the ship will die.'

'The root things . . . the organic matter . . . look at them,' she said, deflecting. She trained her helmet camera on the rapidly greying branches.

'Accelerated decrepitude. I'm afraid what you're doing will not stop or reverse that.'

'What does that mean?'

'We need to try to preserve the matter that is still viable.'

'How?' May yelled angrily.

'I can reboot the entire system. Theoretically, that would reset all of the portals and restore those that aren't permanently damaged.'

'Why the hell didn't we just do that in the first place?' May growled.

'System rebooting is only done in dock, with no crew. It involves restarting all systems, including life-support. The ship will go dark for at least five minutes, but that is never an exact time. And if the reboot fails, I cannot do it again.'

May could feel her own rapidly dwindling life-support. The panting she'd been experiencing before was now almost gasping. She had to get out of there.

'Reboot the system . . . after I get out of here.'

'Commander Knox, that is very dangerous. You could be killed.'

'I'm dying . . . anyway. Have a little oxygen in the suit. When I get to . . . vestibule, I will connect suit to charger and you will . . . initiate restart. That's an order.'

'Affirmative.'

May flew to the vestibule door. The AI opened it and May floated inside. As the airlock was sealed and pressure was equalised to the main vessel, she drifted to the floor and landed in a sitting position next to the suit charging unit. It felt as though she was trying to breathe through a cocktail straw. She fumbled with the charger cables, but finally got them attached. Her breathing returned to normal, but she shivered as the sweat in her suit began to ice up.

'It's freezing,' she yelled through chattering teeth.

'Ship atmosphere down to eighteen per cent.'

May's suit was charging, but she'd only gained a small percentage of juice. The visor display was not functioning with low power so she had no idea how much time she'd gained being attached to the charger. If she waited any longer, the ship would completely lose power and the AI would lose the ability to reboot anything.

'Reboot system now.'

'What is your life-support level—'

'Just do it,' she barked.

'Initiating system reboot in five, four, three, two, one.'

The ship plunged into darkness and freezing cold. May could feel the heat leaving her body like air rushing out of a balloon. Every muscle in her core constricted painfully, then shook so hard it rattled her skeleton. She had to clamp her jaw down and hold it fast for fear of breaking teeth. Before losing consciousness, the only thing May could hear was the sound of what might be her last shallow breaths.

7

'Commander Knox, are you reading me?'

When May came to, she was lying on the floor of the vestibule, half-frozen, but able to draw breath. Her helmet was no longer sealed to her suit. She clawed it off and spent several minutes sucking air. Her head was aching and the pins and needles were back in her hands and feet. The childhood memory of her mother dragging her near-lifeless body from a pond rang like a bell in her mind and she wished her mother could be there to wrest her from the clutches of yet another grim tale.

'That was a little too close for comfort,' May said. 'How did the reboot go?'

'One hundred per cent successful. I am fully reconnected with the ship's network.'

She sighed in relief. 'That's great news. Have you assessed ship damage?'

'Yes: the fusion reactor is nominally functional, outputting power at approximately fifteen per cent of its normal capacity. The tremors we've been feeling are being caused by the two

Q-thruster engines operating out of synchronisation. I am theorising that is due to poor power flow from the reactor.'

'Can we fix it?'

'I am attempting to diagnose the source of the problem. When that becomes clear, we will be able to determine the course of repair.'

'I'm guessing we're going to need help from NASA. What's the status with comms?'

'Our antenna array is down, so we are neither transmitting or receiving. I am also working on diagnosing the source of that problem.'

May was starting to feel sick again. 'Are you able to see the rest of the ship? Any signs of life?'

'I have restored a small percentage of my video cameras, but many are still offline. Command consoles and other onboard interfaces are inactive. And my motion sensors are not yet operational. With what I can see, I have not detected any other crew members.'

'And the landing vehicles?'

'I have not yet connected with that part of the ship.'

May didn't want to say what she was considering; it was unthinkable. She found it hard to believe anyone could be on the ship and go completely undetected, even when it had gone dark. But she promised herself she would not go down that rabbit hole of miserable speculation without actual evidence. Dealing with reality was taxing enough, and filling her belly with something, anything, other than nutri-gels and sugar wafers was way overdue.

'Join me for a cheeseburger?'

'I'd be delighted.'

With some apprehension, she headed to the galley. Thankfully, the reboot had restored some internal power, so the ship no longer resembled an inky black labyrinth of doom. However, compared to what she remembered of the *Hawking II*, it still felt like a dismal, post-apocalyptic version of itself. The once shimmering wall panels and gleaming metal floors had a grimy patina in the dim light, as if the ship had been abandoned and adrift for decades. May found the galley in a similar state as the infirmary, with some of the food stores torn open and rubbish strewn about. But, like the rest of the ship, it was eerily quiet. She looked out of the observation window.

'I know our nav systems are down, but where the hell are we? Have you any idea?'

'Unfortunately the star fields one million kilometres in all directions are unidentifiable, so I am unable to accurately determine our location at this time.'

'Or how long we've been adrift, no doubt,' May added.

'Correct.'

May shook her head.

'We could be anywhere,' she said, 'drifting at high velocity for God knows how long ... FUBAR.'

'*Fucked up beyond all recognition,*' the AI said drily.

May smiled. 'It's nice when you don't talk like a robot.'

'I can be trained to speak any way you like. These are my default settings.'

'I can make you a proper Brit?'

'Of course. Which regional dialect?'

'Bournemouth. Southern coast.'

'Right. How d'you like the sound of this, then?'

The AI had the accent down, but the tone was unnervingly electronic and it made May feel homesick rather than at home.

'I think I prefer your "natural" voice – but maybe with a little more relaxed way of saying things.'

'No problemo, sister. It's all good.'

May laughed. 'I said relaxed, not American.'

'Sorry – American colloquial English is cited most as a "relaxed" way of speaking.'

'I'm not surprised . . . Hey, I have an idea. Just listen to how I say things and try to speak like me.'

'I can do that,' the AI said. 'Assimilation is my speciality.'

'On that note, do you have an actual name?'

'ANNI. It's an acronym for Artificial Neural Network—'

'That won't do. Annie was the name of the CPR dummy I had far too much intimate contact with in flight training. May I give you a more suitable name?'

'You're the commander of this vessel. It's within your authority—'

'Talking like a robot again.'

'Sorry. Would you like to pick a name for me?'

'Yes, I would.'

May gave it some careful thought. After all, she reckoned she might be naming her last ever friend. Then she flashed back to her mother standing by the pond, arms crossed, quietly concerned, but not panicked – the perfect foil to her rattling sabre.

'I believe I'll call you Eve.'

'Eve. The book of Genesis. Created from the rib of Adam—'

'None of that rubbish, please. My mum's name was Eve. She was a bit like you: relentlessly practical and obliged to relentlessly keep me out of harm's way.'

'I'm flattered. Thank you, Commander Knox.'

'Yeah, this works both ways, Eve. Commander Knox is too stodgy. From now on, I'd like you to call me May. Short for Maryam.'

'Maryam, Arabic for Mary, mother of Jesus, or Isa, as written in the Qur'an.'

'Really? That's where my name comes from? I always thought I was named after Mum's stuffy old auntie.'

'You might have been named after a stuffy old auntie, but that is the name's origin.'

'Quite like it now,' May grinned, thinking of how clever her mother had always been, infusing her life with lovely bits of dash. 'Right, enough small talk, Eve. You are now my official second in command. Not just some piece of equipment. We are a team. Got it?'

'Affirm—I mean, yes, May.'

'Outstanding. Now then, let's get back to addressing unpleasant subjects, like the ship being doomed, *et cetera*. One thing that might help us save her is if we knew what the hell happened to her in the first place. Do you have any data?'

'It seems you are not the only one dealing with memory loss. Just after the reboot, I attempted to access ship log data. As you know, I am programmed to record the entire voyage. This includes storing raw data feeds and capturing audio-visual records with my camera network. Ship log data recording ceased on December 15, 2067 and was not restored until the reboot.'

'Is it possible that your memory loss was caused by whatever damaged the ship?'

'Yes, but the condition of my processors, although poor, would make a complete loss of data unlikely. There are several redundancies in place to safeguard against this.'

'Surely Mission Control has back-ups,' she said hopefully.

'All data is constantly streamed to Mission Control. If we are able to re-establish contact, they will be able to pinpoint the problem.'

'Let's remove the word "if" from our vocabulary, Eve. *When* we re-establish communication.'

'Of course, with the caveat that I am not attempting to convey certainty, owing to a lack of empirical data.'

'That's fine. I'm just a bit short on optimism. And if my bloody brain would work properly I might be able to help us solve some of our problems. It's just such a mess up there right now.'

'If you'd like,' Eve said, 'I can show you the mission briefing video and give you access to the vessel walk-through programmes. I researched our medical database and found that strong cues can help restore memories after brain trauma. The mission briefing covers the mission parameters and personnel, as well as a brief overview of the research of Dr Stephen Knox, on which . . .'

May's mind drifted to her husband and she could no longer hear Eve's rambling. It wasn't that she had forgotten him. Being so focused on the ship and basic survival, trying to find her way through the mental fog, she had not had either the time or the ability to think much about him. But the more she regained her faculties, the more he was on her mind.

Although her heart swelled with warmth and affection, she felt butterflies of anxiety in her stomach. Was it that she simply missed him and worried he was convinced she was dead? That he was in the kind of pain she might feel if she thought the same thing about him? Or was it something more? She remembered what Eve had said about retrograde amnesia. The older memories would come first, or at least be more accessible. Memories closer to her illness would be harder to access.

Eventually, it would come to her. He would come to her. But, for now, he felt so very far away.

8

Sunday afternoon. May was in the *Hawking II* simulator at Johnson Space Center. The flight deck was encased in a metal sphere suspended in a huge electromagnetic field, capable of simulating space travel with a high degree of accuracy. May was running through her anti-gravity training programmes, floating from station to station with a belt-mounted thruster unit.

'Training sequence complete,' the onboard AI said. 'Perfect score. Excellent work, Commander.'

'Thank you,' May replied, coming slowly back down to earth.

'Would you like to go again?'

'No, I should probably go outside and simulate being a human being for a while.'

'Have fun,' the AI said.

'Please, that's way too much pressure,' May said, laughing.

Outside, the world was wet from rain and broken light dappled the asphalt. There was still loads of work to be done in the simulator, but her mind was mush and she hadn't seen the sun in days.

'Time for a drink. Maybe two.'

Walking to her car, she allowed a straggling shower to soak her clothes. It felt good not to care. As commander, all she did was agonise over every detail, no matter how small. That was the NASA way. At the moment, the only details she cared about were finding a good margarita, with salt, and chasing it with a long drag on a cigarette. Normally she would have just gone back to her nondescript condominium to drink and smoke alone, but she was tired of feeling sorry for herself for being such a pathetic loner. Monday was a day off. Might as well use it to recover from something in the realm of fun.

May walked out to the only car in the parking lot, a very American red Mustang convertible she'd purchased with every last penny of her savings. It was even one of the ancient beasts that actually allowed you to drive yourself. Autopilot was bullshit and driving was one of life's great privileges – especially in a sports car with the wind blowing through your hair. There wasn't a nerd in the universe who could invent anything to replace that.

Nineteenth Street in The Heights was thronged with people. It seemed as though everywhere May looked there were couples holding hands, eating and drinking on restaurant patios, kissing in public. She saw a few women carrying bouquets of flowers and gifts. Traffic was heavy, so she calmed her nerves with a Dunhill red and dialled some pop nonsense into the sound system.

'Valentine's Day. Yanks and their public shows of affection.' She shuddered. 'Think I might be sick.'

Getting that drink, or two, became urgent, and May's patience ran thin as she drove at a snail's pace, scanning the street for places that weren't advertising death by fried everything. Half a block up, someone was backing out of a spot in front of a Mexican place and she was in a perfect position to grab it. 'Hallelujah,' she said happily. But, as soon as the car pulled out, another car on the opposite side of the road pulled a U-turn and slid into her space.

'Son of a bitch,' she hissed.

As she prepared a verbal diatribe to unleash on the offending driver, she didn't notice the man on the sidewalk next to her, wearing a droopy wool cardigan and old trainers. His nose was buried in a cumbersome old hardcover book and he was trying to negotiate a rapidly melting ice cream cone, green pistachio no less, of preposterous size. When he blindly stepped off the kerb in front of her car to cross the street, he was so close that, even at less than fifteen miles per hour, it was impossible to stop. Her right front bumper cut him off at the knees and he let out a dog-like yelp. May hit the brakes and he slumped awkwardly over the bonnet.

At first she gasped in horror at having run someone down, but then burst out laughing when his ice cream scoop flew over the top of the windscreen and into her lap. The man struggled angrily to his feet, an empty cone in his shaking hand.

'Why don't you slow down?' he yelled.

'I was going so slow I was practically going backwards,' she said, fighting to stifle her laughter. 'Maybe you should watch where you're walking instead of wearing a book on your face and eating that ridiculous ice cream. What are you, eight years old?'

His face turned red. A crowd gathered to gawk and laugh, which made May instantly feel sorry for ridiculing him. What the hell had happened to her manners? She was about to apologise when he threw fuel on the fire.

'It's not funny,' he shouted, rubbing his knee. 'Maybe you should learn to drive properly in this country before you kill someone.'

The gawkers chuckled and clapped. Devices were out and recording. May's pity for the man evaporated as quickly as her vitriol for the crowd spiked. She'd be damned if she was going to be viewed as the hapless foreigner, unable to navigate something as brainless as driving on the right side of the road.

'Or maybe you should pull your head out of your arse,' she replied evenly. 'And, by the way, the mental hospital called. They'd like their dirty sweater back.'

The crowd roared with laughter and applauded her, which instantly took the fight out of him. It was clear he was feeling self-conscious and wanted to get out of there as quickly as possible, perhaps to crawl in a hole and die. In his haste to retreat, he went to retrieve his book from the street, and nearly got his head taken off by a speeding pick-up truck. Once it was in his hand, he jogged down the sidewalk and sat on a bus bench to collect himself.

May felt horribly ashamed as the drawling crowd jeered his exit. She parked a few spaces down and walked back to him.

'Did you come back to finish me off?' he quipped.

May showed him her driver's licence. 'I came back to apologise and offer to take you to a doctor to make sure you're all right. And here's my licence if you want to call the authorities. I'm Maryam, by the way.'

'Stephen.'

She offered him her hand, which he flatly ignored. At first, she was offended at his childish behaviour, but then she saw the blood leaking through his sweater at the wrist.

'Oh, you're hurt,' she lamented. 'I have a first aid kit in the car. Be right back.'

She jogged to her car and grabbed the kit. But, when she looked up the block, the bus bench was empty.

9

December 26, 2067 –
Orville and Wilbur Wright Space Station –
Lunar orbit

'Loading latest search imagery,' a male AI voice said, 'Completed 3.26 hours ago.'

On a curved, floor-to-ceiling screen, a high-resolution image of Europa appeared. The detail was so vivid and clear, it looked as though one could reach into the screen and touch the moon's icy surface. Its crisscross patterns of dark fissures broke up the otherwise brilliantly reflective patina. Planted in the frozen, glittering sea was a pod of multinational flags representing all the countries involved in the historic mission.

NASA's UV optical infrared telescope, built to survey exo-planets millions of light years away, had been trained on Jupiter to search for signs of the missing *Hawking II* vessel. The search pattern began with a view of Europa and slowly reversed through space, like a cine camera on a dolly track. As it moved back in increments of hundreds of millions of kilometres, it covered what would have been the *Hawking II*'s return voyage trajectory. From Europa, it moved through the orbit of gas giant

Jupiter, looming so massive it covered most of the screen for several increments. Then through the main asteroid belt between the orbits of Jupiter and Mars, then past Mars's orbit, ending at Wright Station's lunar orbit.

In the final image, Jupiter was only just visible as a minuscule, barely discernible pinpoint of light buried in the enormous expanse of stars. The distance covered in the search pattern was nearly six hundred million kilometres. This number, and this image, were what Stephen Knox was left to behold as he analysed the data feeds in the lower half of the screen. He was also forced to accept the most damning of data: the dry, machine-fed line at the bottom that stated: *Vessel Not Detected*.

'Screen off,' he said quietly.

The image faded and the screen returned to its function as his office observation window. The empty hangar, in full view outside, looked like an open, bloodless wound. Seeing his reflection, Stephen thought he looked similarly hollow. His usual scholarly appearance – mess of raven, grey-flecked hair perpetually being swept out of his dark, interrogative stare, matching beard transitioning from kempt and professorial to bordering on hermitic, and long, provincial face deeply lined by principles – appeared consumed by the ravenous appetite of worry.

It was almost inconceivable that, only a few months ago, he'd watched the *Hawking II* depart with his wife May at the helm and his entire research team in tow. As the vessel had pulled out of dock, to great fanfare, he'd felt none of the joy he'd anticipated on seeing his life's work so literally physically realised in one of the most ambitious missions in NASA history. Instead, he had fidgeted with his wedding ring, feeling its relevance fading as the distance between station and vessel grew. He'd watched the video feed of May from the flight deck, a similarly bleak demeanour emanating from her. And, when the *Hawking II* was swallowed by darkness, he had slipped his ring off and placed it in his desk drawer, along with other weightless relics.

All had gone well with the voyage, which had taken a little over thirteen weeks to complete. Humanity had set foot for the first time on the icy frontier of Europa. The seven-day exploration and sample excavation was a resounding success. But then ... total loss of contact – another first for NASA. And not just temporary, which was to be expected with deep space missions. Eleven days of sustained radio silence. Nothing coming in or going out. Telemetry gone. Condition of crew and vessel unknown.

Above all else, Stephen was a scientist. For most of his existence, he'd lived and breathed empirical data and understood the cold equations it wrought. The *Hawking II* equation was the coldest. With each passing day, the crew's chances of survival were exponentially diminished. Space was eternally unforgiving. There was no such thing as a small problem. Every minuscule crack overlooked had the potential to become a gaping hole, hungry for human life. For May's life.

Despite that cold calculation, an unfamiliar part of him clung to the superstitious notion that he needed to stand watch, offering his will as a beacon in the vastness of space. He imagined the wives of ancient mariners dutifully doing the widow's walk to bring their husbands back, a fool's errand in the face of the unforgiving sea. But, like them, his ritual was the only thing that kept him from succumbing to the depths of fear. He'd always scoffed at hope, and at optimism, its more agnostic cousin. But he wanted to crawl back to them now, begging forgiveness, asking for even the smallest measure of peace. The thought of having potentially sent thirty-five people to their deaths, one of whom had been the love of his life, was like a malignant tumour spreading into every corner of his mind. What would make it lethal was the possibility that he might never again have the opportunity to tell May how much she meant to him.

44

But that particular gun to the head was another story altogether.

Stephen's AI admin chimed in on the intercom.

'How long?' Stephen asked before it could speak.

'Thirty minutes, sir.'

'Get me a blindfold and a cigarette, please.'

'Excuse me, sir?'

'Never mind.'

'Would you like some coffee? Or perhaps a stress patch?'

'Nothing, thank you.'

Robert Warren, NASA's director of deep space missions and Stephen's boss, had requested his presence for a mandatory meeting. Stephen had no illusions about what that meeting would entail. It was as predictable as most of Robert's actions. In a mild form of protest, Stephen did not intend to go to the man's office to suffer the indignity he knew was in store. *He can come to me for once, the bastard.*

Instead, he switched off his AI intercom, and all incoming communication lines, and returned to the observation window. As a boy, he'd spent countless summer nights tracking constellations. In what he was convinced were his final hours there, that was how he planned to pass the time until the axe fell. But his heart wasn't in it. What had been a source of inspiration his entire life now felt like a hostile, betraying force. No matter how hard he tried to look beyond the hangar, his mind was anchored there, the last place he saw her, maybe the last place he would ever see her.

10

Stephen and May were frequently required to shuttle to Wright Station so that May could continue her training and Stephen could supervise the building of the *Hawking II*'s onboard labs. On one of May's EVA vessel inspections, she convinced Stephen to join her. He'd never done one before and thinking about it filled him with mortal terror. But she always had a way of drawing him outside his comfort zone, so he found himself floating and tethered, waiting for May, in the hangar. The *Hawking II* was in dock, still under construction. He marvelled at its planetary shape, cross-sectioned into seven decks of varying sizes. The vessel had been designed by Raj Kapoor, a brilliant engineer from STMD, NASA's Space Technology Mission Directorate, who had become one of Stephen's close friends. As much as it was a technical marvel, it was also a work of art. More importantly, it was the physical manifestation of his life's work.

'Are we having fun yet?' May asked. Having finished her inspection, she floated up to Stephen, untethered, a fiendish grin flashing him from behind her helmet glass.

'Actually, yes, believe it or not,' he said. 'It's quite a ship, when you see it in person.'

'Want to see more?'

'Um, sure, but how can we ...?' He motioned to his tether line.

'Oh, you won't be needing that old thing,' she said.

'This is Control,' the station commander droned in. 'We're seeing a heart rate and blood pressure spike in Dr Knox.'

'I'm fine,' Stephen said.

'Just nerves,' May said.

'Copy that.'

'May, I don't know about this,' he said nervously.

'Come on, there's nothing to it.' Using her thrusters, she did a few trick rolls and back flips, and floated up next to him. 'See? You're going to love it.'

May unhooked his tether.

'Uh, this is Control. We're seeing a tether release for Dr Knox.'

'Intentional, Control,' May said. 'I'm going to walk with Dr Knox for a bit, show him the rest of the vessel.'

'Copy. Enjoy, Dr Knox.'

'Thanks,' Stephen said, glaring at May.

May floated away from him. It was only about five metres, but it felt like five kilometres to Stephen.

'Okay, use your thrusters to come over to me. Baby steps.'

He had no intention of appearing to be a coward, but being surrounded by the complete abyss of space, with nothing to serve as the 'ground' below, made him feel panicked.

'Uh, this is Control—'

'Just nerves,' Stephen blurted out through short, rapid breaths.

'Breathe normally,' May said. 'Or you'll screw up your mixture and pass out. Just look right at me, okay? Focus on my face.'

Stephen focused on May's face and slowed his breathing to

normal. Then he awkwardly activated his thrusters and jerked across the space between them, nearly throwing himself into a spinning somersault. She caught him and slowed them both.

'Outstanding,' she said, slightly out of breath. 'Er, why don't we start by tethering our suits? I'll fly us around the ship and you can watch and learn. Then you can try. Okay?'

'Just no flips or stunts.'

She sighed. 'Oh, all right.'

She tethered them and they flew along the outside edge of the ship, examining all of its stunning details. It was so quiet and peaceful that Stephen almost forgot they were surrounded by the vastness of space. If he looked away from the ship or the back of May's helmet, though, he was immediately reminded, and had to fight off a powerful feeling of vertigo. After several minutes of this, the feeling was not as strong and he felt more confident. May stopped and they hovered in front of the massive window to the bridge. The gleaming flight deck behind it swarmed with engineers working in zero gravity.

'Isn't it lovely?' she said excitedly.

'It's gorgeous beyond words. Appropriate for such an accomplished commander.'

'Why, thank you, good sir.' She bowed.

'I envy you,' Stephen said. 'Being an astronaut.'

'Being a super-genius whose research and fearlessness in the face of an army of ignorant – potentially violent, I might add – dissenters was the impetus for one of the most important missions in the history of space exploration – and potentially all of humanity – isn't good enough for you?'

'Not really. I basically did all that because all I ever wanted to be was an astronaut and I realised that dream would never come true.'

'Pardon me, Stephen, but that sounds a bit wonky.'

'This is Control. She has a point there, Dr Knox.'

'Control, please switch us to a private channel,' May said, annoyed.

'That's against—'

'Now, please. I'll override if we need you.'

'Copy that.'

They heard the switch and May smiled. 'Always wanted to be an astronaut, eh?'

'I know that smile and it can only mean—'

'Do you trust me?' she interrupted.

'Yes.'

'Good. Because I'm here to make your dreams come true. Time to shake off the science and live a little, Dr Knox. No point in everyone else having all the fun when this is your baby, after all.'

She released the tether between them.

'Shit,' he said quietly.

'You're welcome,' she said, drifting away. 'On the other side of this ship is the engine deck. Let's go check it out, make sure these engineers aren't slacking off.'

'Copy that,' Stephen tried to say confidently.

May took off, moving slowly in that direction, and waved for Stephen to join her. He wanted to tell her to come back, to forget the whole thing, but he couldn't stomach it. As much as she was giving him a golden opportunity to fulfil a small part of his dream, it was also his opportunity to show her he wasn't just some gutless pencil-neck. She had never accused him of that, but he'd accused himself on more occasions than he cared to count. Except, he felt paralysed. His fear was so intense, it was hard to even imagine activating his thrusters. A cold sweat was coming on and his stomach turned sickening carnival loops. Unforeseen disasters could occur on a complex maintenance platform orbiting the moon at over thirty thousand kilometres per hour, and he could visualise them. It was like standing near the open door of an aircraft in flight, waiting to make a parachute jump. On a primordial level, the whole proposition was absurd.

'Come on, Neil Armstrong. I'm waiting,' she said.

The only thought more terrifying than following her was the notion that, if he didn't follow her, okay, she might not consciously hold it against him, but a seed of disappointment might be planted. In the right circumstances, that seed could germinate. Stephen's mind quickly rendered a summary. Every love story demanded the ultimate sacrifice. Romeo and Juliet were doomed, along with Tristan and Isolde, Odysseus and Penelope, Cleopatra and Mark Antony, and other famous A-list literary couples. For some reason, romantic love was nothing more than a battleground bristling with treachery. Being unwilling to make that sacrifice might be the deal-breaker that could inspire May to return to the company of more fearless and heroic suitors.

'Up yours, William Shakespeare,' Stephen whispered to himself.

'What was that?' May asked.

'I'm coming,' he said listlessly.

Before he could talk himself out of it, Stephen detached his tether and, very awkwardly, used his thrusters to go after May. He figured the Control crew were probably amused by his herky-jerky approach, which must look like a crude marionette performance. What in God's name was he doing? He had nothing to prove to her, or anyone else. He was a respected scientist overseeing a trillion-dollar deep space mission.

No, in this moment, he was an astronaut. Neil fucking Armstrong. The thought buoyed him with confidence. That confidence begat elation and, before he knew it, he was actually having more fun than he'd ever had in his life, laughing all the way.

'That's the spirit,' May said as she saw him cresting the middle of the ship.

'You were right,' he said, 'this is absolutely incredible.'

'Of course I was right,' she said. 'And you're doing so well. You look like an old pro. Maybe dial back your thrusters just a smidge, though.'

In all of his excitement, Stephen had not noticed he'd been gradually increasing his speed. He could see May and was coming up on her fairly quickly. He let go of the thrusters, but his momentum didn't change.

'I've pulled back, but still coming in a little hot,' he said.

'No problem. Just reverse the thrusters, very gently, to slow down,' she instructed.

'Okay. Shit. Too fast.' The short breaths had returned and he was feeling light-headed.

'Very gently. And breathe,' May said.

He tried, but the rapidly closing space between them caused his adrenaline to spike and he panicked, jamming the reverse thruster too hard. The opposite force threw his torso into a backflip and his helmet smacked the edge of the fuselage. That blow made him dizzy and forced his body to fly opposite of the impact, away from the ship. Within seconds he was in a perpetual backflip, getting sicker with every turn. He could hear May's voice, shouting something. He could hear Control, droning on about something else, but none of it could cut through the sound of his rapid hyperventilation. He lost sight of the ship, then the scaffold, then the hangar and station. The realisation that he had drifted into open space spiked the adrenaline again and the resulting breaths rendered him unconscious.

'Copy Control,' May said, 'Returning to base.'

When Stephen came to, he was in open space. May was directly in front of him and all he could see behind her was the massive, open face of the moon. He started to panic again.

'It's okay, love. You're fine now.'

She turned them slightly sideways and showed him the station, which was in the near distance and closing quickly.

'What the hell happened?'

'I'm not sure,' she said, smiling. 'But I thought we agreed to no flips or stunts.'

Stephen remembered hitting the reverse thruster too hard. 'Jesus, I'm such an idiot.'

'No, to be crystal clear, that title belongs solely to me,' May said. 'I should never have pushed you the way I did. I just didn't anticipate you loving it so much and getting all thruster-happy.'

'Me neither.' Stephen smiled, remembering the feeling. 'That was pretty awesome.'

May laughed. 'Glad to hear it! But I don't think my superiors are going to look upon this as favourably. Right, Control?'

'Sorry, Commander Knox. We had a brief break in comms due to solar interference. Lost our visual too. Something to report?'

'Only that none of you will ever pay for another drink again in your lives.'

'Copy that,' Control said. 'Better hurry back. Those superiors you spoke about are shuttling up as we speak.'

'Thank you, May,' Stephen said, smiling.

'For nearly making you a permanent fixture on the moon?'

Looking at her, he noticed he was hyper-aware, transfixed on every detail of her face. The stars reflected in her eyes gave her an ethereal beauty that made his heart ache. Then it came to him. She had made his dream come true. It was a moment he would never forget, and later he would realise it was the moment he fell in love with her. The irony that he had literally 'fallen', perhaps nearly to his death, was not lost on him and he laughed heartily.

'I've always wanted to go to the moon.'

11

December 26, 2067 –
Orville and Wilbur Wright Space Station

S tephen's office door abruptly opened, plucking him from his reverie, and in strode Robert Warren. He had the patrician air of a blue blood senator, cheapened by obsessive vanity. Anti-ageing technology had preserved the tan, sandy blond hallmarks of his privileged youth, but with a synthetic veneer that appeared almost cadaverous upon closer examination.

It was bad enough that Stephen had to answer to men like Robert in the first place. After all, it was *his* work NASA had funded. The bitter truth was, and always had been, that science was a slave to money. And with money, came people like Robert.

'Morning,' Stephen said wearily.

'I buzzed you earlier about coming by my office,' Robert said as he made himself comfortable in Stephen's desk chair.

'Yeah, I ignored that,' Stephen said. 'Figured you could use a little exercise.'

One of Robert's well-manicured eyebrows twitched in disapproval. 'I see,' he said, not amused.

Stephen found sick pleasure in forcing Robert to do what he hated the most: be the bearer of bad tidings.

'I know this is hard—'

'I'm not looking for sympathy,' Stephen said tersely.

'Is there anything I can do for you?'

'You can pull some strings and let me stay till we know what the hell is going on.'

'Old friend, you flatter me with your overestimation of my authority. As much as I loathe the expression, my hands are tied.'

'Robert, we both know that's only true when you want to say no to something. You're a powerful man who gets what he wants, so let's cut the bullshit, please.'

Stephen hated playing to Robert's vanity, but it was the one weakness that could almost always be exploited. It wasn't that Robert was too stupid to know the ploy, it was that he relished the kowtowing, especially when it came from someone he knew damn well was superior to him in every way.

Robert smiled, happy to have Stephen over a barrel once again.

'Let's say you're right,' he said, beginning what he thought was going to be a stirring dialectic. 'How would you contribute to the situation? What would I be able to tell Director Foster to convince her to keep you on? Is there some area of expertise you've been concealing from me, something that buys you a seat on search and rescue?'

This was another Robert Warren tactic. When cornered, hide behind officialdom, pretend Director Foster actually had some influence over his little fiefdom, that she wasn't living in constant fear that Robert would use his considerable wealth and power to take her job in the same way a bully would filch a weaker child's lunch money. He had to know his methods were obvious, but simply didn't care. That was the depth of his arrogance. Like the ultra-conservative legislators he'd hustled into approving the mission, despite their violent opposition to some of Stephen's theories, he ruled by sneering condescension.

'Maryam is my wife.'

'*Was* your wife, Stephen.'

'Are you enjoying yourself?'

'Not even remotely. I'm stating a plain fact. I actually agree that your marriage would have been a highly defensible, albeit unorthodox, reason to keep you on up here. But your divorce-filing is common knowledge. The change of heart behind wanting to help her is easy for me to understand, but for others it will be confusing. For others, it may be viewed as a highly emotional reversal based on regret, which might imply a certain ... volatility. And we know how NASA feels about volatility, don't we?'

Stephen's anger turned to a sort of primal blood lust that made him feel certain he could bring himself to kill Robert with his bare hands. His rational mind quickly shut that down, as it often did when confronted with 'emotional volatility'.

'You certainly have all the answers, don't you, Robert?' Stephen said with a deeper measure of contempt than he intended.

'Contrary to what you might think, I'm not trying to be unreasonable, and my decision to send you back is by no means arbitrary or negatively motivated. Try to see it from my perspective. This is a colossal crisis, the like of which NASA has never known. Washington has hit the panic button and I am the target of their considerable ire. More importantly, I bear the full weight of responsibility for every soul on that vessel. I am doing the very best I can to try to manage a horrific situation that gets worse every day. Right now, extreme focus on search and rescue is what is required and I'm sorry, but you are not part of that equation. Please try to understand that.'

Stephen started to formulate a rebuttal, but the predictable futility of it made him feel helpless and weak. He retreated for fear he might even lose the chance to remain tied to the mission back in Houston.

'So, that's it, then?' Stephen said, making sure to apply a tone of defeat.

It worked. Robert relaxed back into the role of benevolent dictator.

'I'm afraid so. Of course, if . . . when the situation returns to normal, we will be having the opposite conversation.'

Robert got up and stood next to Stephen, awkwardly attempting to conjure some sort of fatherly, comforting persona.

'For what it's worth,' he started, deepening his vocal pitch, 'I haven't given up and neither has the team. We're going to do everything in our power to find them – to find May.'

'I'm not questioning that,' Stephen said, wanting the avalanche of bullshit to cease. 'I just feel . . . helpless. I can't imagine what it's going to be like back in Houston, at home, surrounded by things that remind me of her. I might just lose what's left of my mind. Would you consider allowing me to stay on at Johnson? I was thinking I could analyse the data we were able to collect before . . . keep my mind occupied.'

Robert nodded and patted Stephen on the shoulder. 'Of course. In fact, I'll be spending more time down there as well, attempting to manage the situation and the rising tide of discontent in Washington. My door is always open.'

'Thank you,' Stephen said, swallowing gratitude with a good measure of bile.

On the shuttle back to Houston, Stephen watched Wright Station shrink in the distance. Leaving the station created even more distance from May and it felt like throwing in the towel. He had never been one to abandon anyone in need, especially not the ones he loved. Despite their conflicts and differences, some of them quite harsh, May had never done that to him. Stephen, on the other hand, was plagued by memories of things he had done to turn his back on her, some he could hardly bear to recall ... some he even blamed for the ultimate demise of their marriage. How would he ever be able to live with himself if he didn't have a chance to make amends, to reaffirm his true feelings for her? The fear of losing May was eclipsed only by the darkness that came with being unable to answer that question.

'Re-entry in ten minutes,' the pilot said. 'Please check your safety harnesses. It could get pretty rough.'

12

December 26, 2067 –
Hawking II Deep Space Research Vessel

'Attention,' May stated firmly into the console microphone. 'This is Commander Maryam Knox. If you are hearing my voice, please find a comms board and respond with your position immediately.'

May had returned to the bridge to try to get the flight deck back in order. Intermittently, she used the PA to call out for survivors, to no avail.

'Eve, I really need to do a physical inspection of all decks. But I think I will need to get a bit of a refresher course.'

'Would you like for me to load the vessel walk-through program?'

'Yeah, I could probably use a reboot of my own.'

May remembered Eve had mentioned the mission's background film. Ever since she'd had the chance to think about things other than imminent death, she'd been craving Stephen's presence, and hoping to understand the sense of trepidation his memory was causing. She needed to see him, even if it meant watching one of NASA's cheesy archive films.

'Eve,' she said in her most casual tone, 'let's also run the mission background video. I have a good handle on all that, but seeing it might help jar some memories loose. Can't hurt, anyway. Unless I'm worried about dying of boredom.'

'That is funny,' Eve said. 'I have seen the mission background film and I know it is very dull. Good joke.'

'Are you able to laugh at funny things, rather than saying they're funny?'

Eve laughed. It was smooth and non-robotic, but the intonation was too aggressive, like that of a vampire watching a village burn.

'Not bad. Needs a little work.'

'Thank you. I am loading the mission background film now. Would you like a snack while you watch?'

'Popcorn?' May asked hopefully.

'I don't have popcorn, but there are some wasabi-flavoured crickets in the bridge storage module. They are high in protein and, I am told, quite delicious.'

'Thank you, but I'll pass,' May said, trying not to vomit.

The observation window that wrapped around the flight deck dimmed to black and transitioned to a three-dimensional projection screen. A NASA logo appeared, followed by the Europa Mission training video – archival footage, photos, and graphic animations cut to a stirring symphonic score. Vessel and crew images cascaded across the screen, timed to the hardy baritone voiceover narration.

'*The* Stephen Hawking II *is a class five deep space research vessel with nine crew members – Commander Maryam Knox, Pilot Jon Escher, Flight Engineer Gabriella Dos Santos, Payload Commander Matthew Gallagher, International Mission Specialist Ada Mazar,*

International Mission Specialist Yuan Mengzhu, US Air Force Manned Space Flight Engineer Rick Opperman, Payload Specialist Daniela Giliani, and Chief Flight Surgeon Suzanne Dowd – and twenty-six space flight participant researchers – Dr Ella Taylor—'

'Let's move on to the mission background, please,' May said, impatiently. 'Dr Knox's research.'

The screen changed and a documentary-style film played with the same narrator.

'The Europa mission was initiated by NASA, and an international consortium of allied space programs, in February 2058. Based on the research and technological developments of Princeton astrophysicist and astrobiologist Dr Stephen Knox, the mission will be a historic first-ever expedition to the smallest of the four Galilean moons orbiting Jupiter. Within the seven-day landing period, researchers will collect and test extensive ice shelf and atmospheric samples as Europa completes two Jovian orbits.'

May paused on Stephen's image, wanting to reach through the screen to touch his face. He looked young and inspired back then. She restarted the video.

'Simultaneously, engineers will test a small-scale prototype of Dr Knox's groundbreaking NanoSphere technology – a cloud of molecular nanomachines will store solar energy and radiate it back to the surface at temperatures approaching those on Earth. It is our hope that the NanoSphere will generate enough heat to penetrate the Europan ice shelf, which is, on average, fifteen to twenty kilometres thick, and allow researchers to draw water samples from the ocean below. A successful test of this magnitude could pave the way for the future development of a satellite-deployed solar hood that would fully surround the moon with NanoSphere machines – enabling us to create an artificial Earth-like atmosphere and revolutionise extra-terrestrial migration.'

There were loads of great shots of Stephen in that sequence. May laughed at the old clothes and hairstyles, including the pensioner's sweater he'd been wearing the day they met. But, for some unknown reason, she still felt anxious every time she saw him.

'Would you like to take a break?'

'No, let's move on to more pressing matters. I'd like to examine every part of the ship and then get into some flight ops simulations. I'm tired of being useless.'

'Loading vessel schematics.'

The 3D schematic walk-through of the ship appeared. May scrolled through the menu and chose exterior view. The *Hawking II*'s size and unorthodox sphere shape were designed to accommodate complex laboratory environments, similar to those on Earth, and carry multiple landing vehicles. From the side, in travel orientation, it was made up of seven vertical disc-shaped decks connected by a central access shaft. The diameters of the decks varied in size from front to back. At the fore was the flight deck, and propulsion was aft. These were the smallest decks. Moving toward the centre of the vessel, the decks became progressively larger. While in motion, all decks rotated around the axis of the central shaft, providing their artificial gravity. As a whole, the design resembled a cross-sectioned planet, with equal space between the cuts.

'How is your memory of the vessel?' Eve asked.

'Fine. Everything looks familiar in outside view,' May said, reminiscing about her space walk with Stephen. 'Moving inside.'

May scrolled to the 3D interior walk-through schematic. The simulation was a far cry from reality but she was reminded of the vessel's internal architecture, built in a way that maintained one's sense of grounded orientation at all times, and beautifully sculpted interior walls, all with active image cells that made the ship one big projection screen. One could turn an entire room into a simulated one, like a tropical rainforest or city street. NASA had found this critical to the psychological health of deep space travellers. The sights and sounds were so immersive, they could trick the brain into thinking one was somewhere back home. Crew could also pull up maintenance schematics and other operations maps and images. Of course it was all dark now, having lost power to whatever malfunctions were ailing the ship. *Heading right for the beach when I get all this sorted,* May mused.

She moved past the bridge, most of which already felt familiar, and into the landing vehicle hangar. There were several standard landing vehicles, round and pod-like, about the size of delivery trucks, and a much larger, and more complex, orbiting vehicle, closer in size to a city bus, for deploying and operating Stephen's NanoSphere tech. Like the rest of the ship, all had a very streamlined, minimalist design. They glowed in place at their charging stations like luminescent eggs waiting to hatch.

From there, she went into the communications deck, atop which rested the currently useless communications antenna array. She was not surprised that this didn't look readily familiar. The empty workstations indicated the presence of the comms crew, a close-knit group who guarded their domain as fiercely as the computer scientists policed the processor deck. The madness of maintaining multiple levels of communication, from the simplest radio transmissions to highly complex telemetry, afforded them a non-existent margin of error. One little mistake and it . . . well, you had May's current situation.

'Are we making any progress with comms? Never mind, you would have told me.'

'I estimate having some conclusions very shortly.'

'Good.'

May moved the simulated walkthrough into the habitation deck, which housed crew sleeping quarters, galleys, infirmary, and food and water replenishment labs. Again, the sim version of the ship was a brightly lit utopia with a plethora of ergonomic conveniences. Sleeping quarters resembling highly modern, luxury hotel suites rivalled one's actual home in design and features. Most spectacular was the lab deck, positioned directly in the middle of the ship. It was home to twenty-six lab modules fully customised for the different disciplines within Stephen's research team – planetary scientists, physicists, engineers, etc. They were self-contained units, meant to perfectly match the best of their Earth counterparts, all configured with different levels of quarantine – a precaution created in the event that the team unearthed something dangerous on Europa. Quarantine allowed for any of the lab modules to be rapidly sealed and jettisoned in the event of contamination.

'Eve, were any quarantine protocols initiated before you lost data?'

'I see no record of that.'

'Please download any research data you can find. I'd like an inventory of samples taken from Europa and their locations on the ship.'

'I'll have it shortly.'

May continued her walk-through into the bio-garden, thick with tropical and semi-tropical foliage cultivated to replenish oxygen and serve as airborne toxin filters for the entire ship. It was like the Amazon basin, lush, green and saturated with rainwater.

'Eve, please also look in on the bio-garden and make sure it's working properly. I'd hate to bust my arse to fix this crate only to run out of air.'

'I am still unable to get any data from that area.'

'Video?'

'Blind and unresponsive.'

'Okay, I'll do a physical inspection when we're done here.'

Bringing up the rear of the vessel were the reactor and engine decks. Quantum vacuum plasma thrusters, capable of greatly exceeding the velocity of antiquated solid fuel rockets, were powered by an aneutronic fusion reactor, which provided unlimited power to the entire vessel. It was highly efficient and reliable, posed few risks to the safety of the ship and crew, and, when working properly, could virtually run forever in the vacuum of space. It also shaved off months of travel time and allowed for much larger payloads. Its one potential danger – and it was a big one – was the amount of heat it produced. May had heard scientists refer to fusion as 'scaling down the sun'. The sun, like all stars, was a gigantic fusion reactor that easily fused atoms owing to its extreme heat and powerful gravitational force. Safely replicating that on a small scale had been a scientific feat on a par with the Wright Brothers' first flight.

'Eve, what's the update on reactor capacity?'

'Down to eighteen per cent capacity.'

'How long do you estimate until we reach zero?'

'At the current loss rate, approximately eight to ten days.'

13

'God, I need a cigarette.'

May sat on the bridge, her head swimming. After spending several hours refamiliarising herself with the ship, she felt confident that her knowledge of ship operations had been fully restored. But that came at a price. Her increasing acuity was bringing to light the *Hawking II*'s dreadful prognosis. Eve had delivered what was probably a conservative assessment, but the flesh and blood version of Eve had taught May to top off all bad news with a healthy dollop of pessimism. *Better to be wrong about how shite things are than get caught with your happy pants down.*

Priorities. She had wanted to do a physical inspection of the vessel, but Eve had not been at all successful in restoring the ship's navigation so the first matter at hand, the one problem that was solvable by the best pilot in the galaxy, was to get the *Hawking II* back on course toward Earth. It didn't have to be exact. The goal was to lock into a trajectory that would facilitate re-establishing contact, versus flying blind and hoping for the best.

'Eve, we need something, anything, as a starting point for navigation. Are you seeing any familiar star fields?'

'Unfortunately, not yet.'

'If I weren't so stressed out, I would laugh at the irony. Ancient mariners would have been lost without the stars and they are making us the needle in the haystack,' May mused. 'Wait, we might be able to use the sun.'

'We've not had a clear visual of the sun since you woke up.'

'Something is blocking our view. And, since we're on the dark side of it, we can't see the body in question. Look at current planetary orbit prediction models.'

'Charting now.'

Eve overlaid the orbit models on the bridge observation window.

'We left Europa on December the ninth,' May said. 'We went dark on the fifteenth, the day I was admitted to the infirmary. Let's assume that was also the time we went off course. Even with that amount of distance covered, we still would have been under the influence of Jupiter's gravitational pull, right?'

'Theoretically, yes, but I am not certain to what degree.'

'Fine, but our drifting trajectory would have been dictated, *to some degree*, by Jupiter. Doubtful we went too far in this direction, or this direction.' May pointed out paths on the orbital map. 'We could have easily gone *these* ways,' she continued, 'Far enough to get ourselves into a world of hurt. Looking at those trajectories, and calculating our speed with Jupiter's gravity, these are the most realistic areas we could have gone into, right?'

'Yes.' Eve highlighted an area on the map. 'If a celestial body is blocking our view of the sun, this is the most likely area, as the Cybele group in the asteroid belt is in this vicinity. With planetary orbital paths, it's unlikely one body would have consistently blocked our view for this long. However, several bodies large enough to obscure a star field could have done so.'

May jumped up. 'Eve, you're a genius. Let's look for them with infrared scan.'

'Scanning now. I am detecting a sizeable infrared signature. It's smaller than one would expect from the belt, but that could be attributed to our being on the outside edge.'

'That has to be it. Any alternative theories?'

'I have been working on this for some time now and I did not even get this far. It looks as though you are the genius, May.'

'Of course that's true, in a general sense,' May said, smiling.

'Would you like to attempt navigation based on this?' Eve asked.

'I say we roll the dice.'

'I am not able to recommend this course of action, based on lack of empirical information. However, I agree with your conclusion that this is a calculated risk worth taking. The only problem I foresee is that our navigation systems are still down.'

'Right, then we'll do things the old-fashioned way.'

'Please explain *the old-fashioned way.*'

'Linearised recursive navigation.'

'I'm not familiar with that term.'

'That's because it's the oldest of the old school. Developed in the 1960s for pilots whose instruments had failed. You use topographic reference points to chart direction and distance. Obviously space is more complicated due to changing orbital paths, the gravitational pull of planets, and other factors that would boggle my mind but which you're able to calculate very quickly.'

'It is a predictive equation.'

'That's right. And, in our case, it's a predictive equation based on completely unconfirmed assumptions. Basically, your worst nightmare, Eve.'

'I am not as inflexible as you might think, May. The sum of my calculation is as follows: if all of our previously stated assumptions are correct, it is possible we've made a 15.7895 million-mile or 25.4107 million-kilometre deviation from return trajectory. That is, of course, an approximation.'

'Excellent. Now, based on what we are assuming is the portion of the asteroid belt blocking our direct view of the sun, the Cybele group, let's set a direct course for it and see what happens. If we find a large enough asteroid along the way, we might even be able to use it for a gravitational slingshot, pick up a little speed as an added bonus. Please hold this course until we reconnect with NASA. In the meantime, I'm going to look for signs of life.'

14

'This isn't what it looked like in the brochure,' May joked as she searched the ship.

She was determined to walk every inch of the *Hawking II*, looking for survivors and creating a video diary of its condition for NASA. Careful to prioritise high-traffic areas, she spent most of her time on the habitation and lab decks, and in work zones that would have accommodated larger teams. All the while, she called out, and Eve continued to play her recorded pleas for crew acknowledgements over the PA system.

Hours later, after physically searching every conceivable area that might have been occupied by a human being, she had heard no responses and found no signs of life. She didn't want Eve to see how emotionally devastating this was to her, so she took a stroll in the bio-garden. Walking through the dense foliage, she found debris from what looked like an impromptu picnic. A lot of people on the ship used to take refuge in the bio-garden when the stress and alienation of space travel got the better of them. The fresh air and sunlight did wonders for morale, so

May had never discouraged it, even though it technically went against protocol.

May sat next to a tree and let a burst of condensation rain wash the tears off her face. She tried not to lose hope, but a feeling of crushing loneliness came over her and erased any optimism or sense of accomplishment she'd gained since waking up.

If everyone is gone, what difference does it make?

She quickly dismissed her penchant for cynicism. The payload itself, whether she delivered it or not, was worth saving. There had even been a sense of that before launch, an unspoken belief that such an important mission transcended the lives of passengers and crew. Not one person who got on that ship would have disagreed, least of all May. She allowed herself a half-measure of pride for having kept things together thus far. But how long could she do it alone? Her chances of surviving a solo return journey, especially with the state the ship was in, seemed close to nil. There was still so much to be done, so much she could not fathom doing on her own.

And with her health so compromised, she would probably lose her last shred of sanity long before she took her last breath. Perhaps that had already occurred? She had read somewhere that people in comas dreamed and had intense visions, sometimes vivid enough for them to believe they were awake. The thought was so horrifying, she had to push it out of her mind. She'd known life to be cruel on more than one occasion, but had also seen the pendulum swing back in her favour often enough to believe things would eventually work out. This time, she felt she was falling out of control, deeper and deeper into darkness.

'May, how is your search going?' Eve asked.

'No signs of life. I'm finished,' May said sadly.

'What about the landing vehicle hangar? I don't believe you've looked there yet.'

70

'I thought you might have had a visual on that by now,' May said.

'I am still unable to establish a connection with the hangar. Unfortunately, I have no observational data to report.'

May got up wearily. 'Well, I guess I'd better check it out,' she said.

She hurried to the hangar. She wanted to get the whole thing over with and get some substantial food, maybe a hot shower. When she got to the entry door, she was unable to open it with the palm scan. She tried manual override. A warning light flashed on the screen.

'Eve, access point saying the door is sealed. Any idea why?'

'No. I have no connect—'

'Right, right. Sorry. How would you know? Getting a little punchy. Er, what about going in through the emergency airlock?'

'That is possible, but you will need to follow airlock safety protocol.'

'Copy that.'

'Would you like to take a break before—'

'No, I'm fine. I just want to get this done.'

May angrily donned an EVA suit. She had not done it in a while and made a few mistakes, which Eve pointed out, but eventually she got it together.

'Well, that took forever,' she said, feeling tired, but determined.

'Checking suit integrity,' Eve said. 'Everything looks good. You have sixty minutes of life-support on this charge.'

'Won't be long,' May said, her reassuring tone meant mostly for herself.

'Opening airlock,' Eve said.

May walked to the massive circular door with a manual locking wheel in the centre. Safety bolts released with the metallic pop of gunfire and the door swung open a few inches.

May plunged into the airlock and sealed herself in. No more mucking about. No more whinging in the artificial rain. Time to bloody suss things out. Eve fired the airlock door bolts back into place.

'Airlock secure,' Eve said.

The red light turned to amber.

'Right. I'm off.'

The bolts on the airlock door, on the pod hangar side, fired, and May forcefully shoved the door open. As it swung out into the dark, May noticed the deathly cold first. Her suit kept her warm, but she had learned early on in astronaut training that there was no way to completely block out the aggressive frigidity of minus 270 degrees Celsius. Like extreme heat, it was invasive. As she floated into the anti-gravity environment, the exhalations from her respirator clouded and froze into a billion tiny ice particles that drifted like snowfall. Her helmet light barely cut through the all-consuming darkness, illuminating only a few feet in front of her. She could see the vague outlines of some of the landing vehicles.

'Well, this will come as no surprise,' she said. 'Zero atmosphere. Zero gravity.'

'Are you seeing the landing vehicles?'

May shone her torch as far as it would reach and saw several launch vehicles, as well as part of the drilling rig, resting quietly in their charging stations.

'From what I can see, they appear to be in dock. Not able to do a full count, though.'

May's torch flickered and dimmed slightly. 'I really need more light,' she yelled. 'Goddammit, nothing works in this shithole.'

'The batteries may be failing,' Eve offered. 'They won't last in extreme cold.'

'How long?' she snapped.

'Estimating ten to twelve minutes.'

'More fabulous news,' May growled. 'What's next, aliens at the gate?'

'Please watch for floating debris that could damage your suit.'

'That's the least of my concerns.'

'You don't have to do this now, May,' Eve said, hearing May's rising frustration. 'You can wait until you're ready. It's not time-sensitive for the ship's recovery.'

'Thank you, Eve, but I am up to the task and this is the last stone unturned. If you ask me what that means, I will scream.'

'Copy that.'

'Eve, where's your network data input point? Might as well troubleshoot that, eh? Add it to the increasing list of failing rubbish.'

'Loading schematic.'

Eve sent the schematic to May's helmet, with a directional compass to keep her on track. May used her suit thrusters to gently glide deeper into the darkened hangar. She was trying to calm down, but the blind isolation of the place kept forcing its way under her skin. All she kept thinking was that human beings were no more meant for this place than they were the bottom of the sea, and suddenly her life's pursuits seemed ludicrous.

Why had she chosen to be away from sun and earth and normal human interaction? Had she been running from something? Herself? Or was she just a thrill-seeking moron without the good sense God gave the lowly stray dog? Why couldn't she answer that question? *Definitely a moron*, she concluded, *dumb as a box of rocks.* She thought about Stephen and the decision she'd made to leave him. *What kind of person does that?* And again, *Why had he wanted to be with such a flaming idiot in the first place?* She felt like ripping off her helmet and letting Darwin take his course. At least that way she might find out if it was all just a nightmare, a rogue brainwave taking her for a ride.

'I have to be dead,' she said aloud.

'Please repeat,' Eve said.

'I said, I have to be fu—'

Her light caught the edge of a dark object floating above her. She ducked and something heavy grazed the top of her helmet as it passed.

'What the hell was that?' she yelped.

'I didn't see anything on your helmet camera. What happened?'

May's heart was pounding. 'Something hit the *top* of my helmet. Something big.'

Another unseen object hit her leg, knocking her body forward into a somersault, then another hit her head from the side, causing her to twist and drift off into another direction. Panic crawled up her leg with a knife in its grey, rotting teeth.

'Eve, there must be a debris field. I'm getting it from all sides.'

'Activate your emergency oxygen torch.'

May spun in space, disorientated and nauseous, desperately grasping for her oxygen torch. She practically tore it off her belt and was about to fire it up when another unseen object hit her and she nearly dropped it.

'What is happening?' she yelled.

'May, please calm down.'

She darkened her helmet glass and switched on the oxygen torch. It blazed like white fire, throwing light twenty feet in all directions, revealing the unknown objects that had been hitting her in the blackness.

May screamed, a primal wail of horror.

The frozen, bloated corpses of her passengers and crew floated all around her. Their faces were twisted death masks of the final expressions they held the moment the air was sucked out of them and their blood boiled. With eyes swollen and black, staring into the grim eternity of the void, they were a bramble of stiff, crooked limbs clawing, kicking, and entangling her. Blind and gasping, she hit her thrusters and tried to swim through them, their cold mass as dense and suffocating as her childhood drowning pond. The torch slipped out of her grasp and drifted away, a white orb pulsing its cold revealing light on the ghastly rollick of the dead.

15

May tumbled dizzily through space, fighting the wave of nausea that wrung out her sour stomach like a dishrag. But the horribly disfigured corpses and intense vertigo proved too much and she vomited in her helmet. The incredible reek, followed by the vile, floating spheres of liquid coming to rest on her face – in her hair, up her nose, in her ears – made her dry heave until she nearly aspirated her own sick. As the drifting torch faded, she lost all that was left of her bearings. There was no up or down. There was nothing but blank, hideous nothing.

Eve was saying something over and over. May held her breath for a moment, blocking out the putrid smell, and listened.

'May please acknowledge. Your vitals show respiration has ceased.'

'I'm holding my breath,' she coughed.

'That's dangerous. The air mixture is—need to breath norm—do you copy?'

The vomit had seeped into the comm speakers and was shorting them. Eve's voice was in and out between crackling static.

'Yes, I copy,' she shouted. 'Get me out of here.'

'You can use your emergency tether to connect to the air-lock door.'

'I can't see my hand in front of my face.'

'Try to stabilise your rotation so I can use your helmet camera to guide you.'

May used her thrusters to stop spinning and curled up into a ball. She couldn't bear the thought of bumping into another corpse.

'Good. Now slowly rotate on ... horizontal axis until you can see the airlock door. The warning light is still illuminated above it.'

'I can't see it.'

'I will guide you. Rotate twenty degrees to your left side.'

May rotated, trusting Eve to be her eyes.

'Done.'

'Good. Now, as if you're doing a backward somersault, rotate twelve degrees.'

May did that and saw the faint glow of the airlock warning light.

'There it is,' she cried.

'Excellent. Do you remember how to deploy your emergency tether?'

'I think so.'

The emergency tether was a long, woven titanium cable with a diamond-tipped dart that could be fired from the left arm of the suit. The tip could penetrate the outer shell of the hull and keep one from irretrievably drifting away.

'Ready.'

'Good. You've drifted a bit, so rotate right ten degrees.'

May nudged her thruster slightly. 'Done. But I lose sight of the airlock door light. The vomit ... '

'It's all right. I can see the heat around the edges of the airlock door with your helmet camera's infrared view. Stand by ... Deploy tether now,' Eve said with authority.

May fired the tether and heard it strike metal with a loud metallic *thunk*.

'Excellent. Now pull your way back to the airlock door.'

'They may be in front of me, Eve. The bodies. It's too dark.'

'Go very slowly to minimise impact. You have thirty minutes of life-support to cover roughly twenty-five metres. You can do this.'

'Thank you.'

May steadied herself, and began to pull.

The first few metres went by smoothly, but then a corpse hit her from the side and she startled so violently, she lost her grip on the tether cable. The momentum created by the collision drove her back. Then the cable went taut.

'Shit, I'm back to where I started.'

'Start again. This time, please count one-metre lengths as you move and attach them in loops to your belt,' Eve said. 'We can track progress and you won't lose ground again.'

'One ... two ... three ... '

May tried to focus on pulling what felt like one-metre sections and looping them to her belt. Her dead passengers and crew – made unrecognisable by the catastrophic loss of atmosphere in the hangar – thrust their horrific injuries into her consciousness in vivid detail. The blackened, milky eyes were what made her want to scream. Somehow they lent a sense of leering mockery to their faces, as if they were taking pleasure in the terror they inspired. May forced them out, imagining only the task at hand, and keeping her eyes fixed on the airlock door light as it drew closer.

'Twenty metres.'

'Excellent,' Eve coaxed. 'Five more. I am going to release the door. Don't be alarmed by the sound. Ready?'

'Yes,' May said, shaking slightly.

She heard the gunshot sound of the bolts and saw a faint amber crescent of light materialise in the distance.

'I see it—'

She started moving faster, excited to nearly be out of there, and hit another corpse. Her increased speed made for a more powerful impact and she tumbled over the top of the corpse, her tether wrapping around it. Their momentum sent them into a side drift. When the cable drew taut, their combined weight jerked the cable tip out of the airlock door.

'Eve,' she yelled. 'My tether is off. It's tangling.'

'Release it from your suit,' Eve said loudly.

May shoved the corpse away from her suit and pulled the release. The tether and body broke free and drifted from her but again she was in total darkness and disorientated.

'Can you see the hangar door light, May?'

'No, I've lost it.'

'Rotate to your right ten degrees.'

'Done, but I can't see. The vomit is ... oh, God, Eve. I can't see.'

'I'm going to force atmosphere into the airlock to open the door further and give you more light to follow. The rush of air might push you back, but you can use it to orient yourself to its origin and then deploy thrusters. Okay?'

'Okay.'

'In 3, 2, 1 ... '

Eve bled air into the airlock, pushing the door open. May felt the air hit her almost immediately and rotated towards it, straining to see the light through her filthy helmet glass. She saw the vague outline of the door, but the air started to make her drift backwards rapidly, throwing her into panic. 'Deploying thrusters,' she yelled, punching them forward full speed.

'May, that's too much thrust.'

May didn't give a damn if she ploughed into the metal wall

79

and obliterated her helmet glass in the process. She had to get out of there.

'Kill thrusters, May. Kill thrusters. You're coming in too fast.'

May switched them off, but distance and momentum spelled disaster.

'Open the door more,' May called out. 'The air rush will slow me down.'

Eve opened it and May felt the air rush. She was afraid it was going to knock her off course again, so she tried to apply thrust again, but hit it too hard. She hit reverse thrust, but it was too little, too late.

'Going to hit hard, Eve.'

'Protect your helmet glass. I will seal the door as soon as you enter the airlock.'

May shot through the airlock door and slammed into the back wall. Her helmet glass cracked and one of her sleeves was torn off at the shoulder. A sudden blast of cold shot into her suit. The gases in her lungs and digestive tract quickly expanded and she could feel her body bloating nearly to the point of bursting. Her eyes were bugging out of the sockets, firing a searing current of agony through her skull. Eve shut and sealed the door behind her and quickly equalised the airlock to vessel atmosphere. As May lay on the floor, sucking air like a fish out of water, one thought repeated over and over in her mind.

I'm the last one.

16

May was curled up on the bunk in her quarters, strung out and in desperate need of sleep. But every time she closed her eyes the bodies came back, pounding and scratching at the door of her sanity. In her search for survivors, she'd started to expect the worst, but nothing could have prepared her for what she saw in the hangar.

'May, please take a sleep tab and try to rest. You've had a trauma and your body is still recovering from your illness.'

'No. I'm afraid if I go to take one . . . I'll take them all.'

'That would be fatal. I don't understand.'

'It's . . . too much, Eve. I am alone and I am going to die out here.'

'You are not alone,' Eve said. 'I am here—'

'Stop,' she screamed. 'Nothing you say can . . . just stop.'

Her stomach and ribs were knotted and aching. Her head felt like a balled-up fist pounding the wall. She cursed her life, her choice to be a pilot. She cursed her mother and Baz and anyone else she could think of to blame. But really, she had no one to blame but herself. As commander, the buck stopped with her. She had been responsible for those people and had failed them miserably. How could she ever face their families? How could she justify going on living when they had died so horribly? All she could think was that a captain should go down with her ship. There was no coming back from this.

'I'm better off dead.'

'May, please don't say that. You know that isn't true.'

'Do I? What do I have to live for? Nothing. This was my life, Eve. And it's all gone now. I left everything for this, including the man I love. I'm getting exactly what I deserve.'

Eve clumsily attempted to talk her off the ledge, but May felt herself sliding down past extreme sadness and grief, into the icy depths of numbness. In that space, suicide felt like a warm, comfortable blanket, a final pill to kill the pain, to kill everything and burn it out of memory. NASA already thought she was dead. In a way, she was. Commander Maryam Knox was back there in the landing vehicle hangar with the rest of her crew, bloated and permanently shocked by her demise. All she had worked for, all she had been, had died with them. Now she was just May again. Little May, sinking to the bottom of the pond.

'What about Stephen?' Eve asked.

'What?' The question momentarily jerked May out of her downward spiral.

'What about Stephen, your husband? Wouldn't your death cause him pain?'

Eve had loaded a photo of Stephen on her screen. It was a shot of him lying across the back seat of a red convertible sports car. He was wearing May's big sunglasses, his hands behind his head in a cartoonish repose. May felt a pang of longing. Her chest tightened and her heart raced.

'I don't know,' she said sadly.

'What about you, May? Wouldn't you like to see him again?'

May looked at Stephen's face. 'More than anything.'

'Then isn't that a reason to live?'

She looked away from him, ashamed, as if he were standing in judgment. 'Yes, but I . . . failed him . . . just like them, all of them,' she sobbed.

'If you die, that fact will remain.'

'You don't understand, Eve.'

'If dying could hurt your husband, deny your wish to see him, and do nothing to benefit the deceased, then why would you consider it?'

'Because I can't take this any more. All of this. It's driving me mad and now I know I have to go it alone.'

'And you believe death will end your suffering?'

May stood, fists clenched. Eve's strict rational view felt dismissive, an oversimplification of things. It made her feel embarrassed, as if her emotions only amounted to self-pity. Then it infuriated her because she knew that was true.

'I said you don't understand,' she seethed.

'Please help me understand.'

'Thirty-four dead bodies. No memory. No explanation.'

May's anger surged beyond her control and she started violently smashing everything that wasn't bolted down in her quarters. She tore the bedding off her berth and kicked the metal cupboard doors below the sink until they came off the hinges.

'This doesn't happen. It can't happen. This is NASA, not some goddamned Russian tin can space station. A whole crew lost, their ship in ruins.' May saw her reflection in the vanity mirror and scowled in disgust. 'While their commander slept through the whole thing.'

She roared and slammed her fist into the mirror, shattering glass and splitting skin. Blood spattered her face and clothes. Her reflection fell away in pieces on the floor.

'May, please,' Eve pleaded. 'Calm down. You're hurt. Please stop.'

Dizziness and fatigue suddenly washed over her. She lay back down on the bed and curled up into a foetal position. Blood soaked the mattress. A sharp quake rippled through the *Hawking II* and May fell to the floor. Glass shards opened up more wounds on her side and back. When the tremors ceased, she sat up, wincing in pain. She felt like a damned fool for losing her temper; it had only made things worse. On top of it all, she was worried it would give Eve cause to distrust her.

'Please forgive me, Eve. I'm only human, after all.'

'That's all right. I'm here to help.'

'I guess I kind of feel beyond help. You were right about everything, but part of me still thinks I would have been better off if I'd never woken up.'

'May, if you had not woken up,' Eve began, 'the *Hawking II* would have gone into infinite drift and eventually been relegated to a block of frozen space debris. Since you regained consciousness, you have given yourself and the ship a chance to survive. If, *I mean when*, we regain contact with NASA, your chances for survival will no longer amount to speculation. They have the resources to rescue this vessel. To rescue you. In my view, it is far better that you woke up, regardless of the circumstances. This ship needs its commander. Stephen needs you to come home. And I don't want to lose you.'

May was moved. The AI was saying what needed to be said for her survival. That was its job. But much of it rang true, especially what she'd said about Stephen. She looked at Stephen's smiling face as he reclined in the back of the red car. They had been happy, she knew that. But something had come between them. It was vague, but she couldn't pass it off any more. The feelings around it were not at all vague; the biggest were guilt and regret. What had she done? Eventually, it would come. The bad things in her life always did. But this photo, this car, this time in her life, had been good. *I don't want to lose you.* Stephen had said that. Knowing herself as well as she did, he'd probably said it more than once.

17

'Rise and shine,' Eve said over the ship's comm.

May groaned and she sat up in her berth. Blood had leaked through the bandage on one of her hands, reminding her of Stephen's sweater. Feeling vulnerable in her sleep-addled mind, she couldn't help but think that whatever it was that had sullied their relationship was her fault. *Look at the first day you met. The poor bastard left with a gash and ruined pride.* Her mother had never prepared her well for social interaction beyond just being well-mannered – and she wasn't even great at that. And courtship? Zero advice. In fact, she remembered her mum actively discouraging her from ever having long-term relationships with boys. They were always referred to as 'distractions' and, when Eve had had a few whiskies in her, she'd occasionally use the term 'dream-killers'. It was a miracle she'd managed to stay with someone long enough to get married.

'How long have I been out?' she asked, her voice slightly hoarse.

'About seven hours.'

'We don't have that much time to spare, Eve,' she said angrily.

'May, you are still recovering from your illness and

post-traumatic stress. You needed sleep to function properly and avoid further health complications.'

The way May felt, she could not disagree. She hurt everywhere. It had taken an hour to clean and dress all the glass cuts and apply cold gel to the bruises. It took a few more to knock out the persistent visions of horror with meds so she could get some sleep. But, despite her injuries and the childish absurdity of her outburst, sometimes she needed to huff and puff and blow the house down in order to remain in possession of the last of her marbles. Catharsis was a word that came to mind.

'Humans. We're a fragile lot.'

The meal panel above the small table in May's berth glowed orange.

'Please eat your breakfast,' Eve said. 'We have a lot to do.'

'Living up to your namesake.'

'Someone has to look after you.'

'Amen,' May said with a smile.

An unconvincing omelette, with potatoes and sausage, slid out of the meal panel. Of course it smelled like those things. They had even come close to mastering the taste. But it was nearly impossible to take something made entirely of synthetic animal and vegetable proteins, genetically engineered to maximise nutritional content, and make it look like a proper meal. The food did its job, keeping one healthy and energised while cutting down on the amount of solid waste, but even after a hundred years NASA had still not managed to make it all that appetising. May didn't care. She was so hungry, she would have eaten a handful of cockroaches as long as they were drenched in her beloved HP sauce – a creature comfort only afforded someone of her rank. She doused the mush liberally and pined for an accompanying lager to replace her lukewarm coffee-flavoured caffeine supplement.

On her screen, May scrolled through more photos of

Stephen. She stopped to look at a candid shot of him, sitting behind his desk, smiling at her from behind a pile of books. He was the only person she knew who still read books like that, even went out of his way to acquire them. The trappings of academia just made him happy, especially when he was up to his eyeballs in them. May felt an overwhelming desire to speak to him, to hear his voice. He had always been able to comfort her and make her feel safe when her tough façade crumbled. But there had also been plenty of times he'd simply shut down. Like her, he also had been ill-prepared for the complexities of romantic love.

'I was able to pinpoint our communications problem,' Eve announced.

'Do tell,' May said, excited to finally hear some good news.

'The antenna array is offline due to a power shutdown.'

'That's it?' May asked, somewhat incredulous.

'They do not appear to be damaged, only powered down and inactive.'

'Odd. What's the fix? Ready to roll up my sleeves.'

'I'm still unable to communicate with the array remotely, so we will need to do a physical inspection to reconnect it to my processors. From there I can properly assess it, repair any damage, and restore orientation. I'm sorry, May. I'm sure you don't feel like getting right back into another EVA situation.'

'No worries.' May stood up and stretched. 'After what I've just been through, I could use a little fresh air.'

The antenna array was located on the topside of the *Hawking II*, in the centre of the communications deck. There were twenty antennae in all, each with a different function, standing ten metres high from the top of the dish to the control centre base. May's refreshingly simple task was to inspect them for external signs of damage and re-establish their communication with Eve. As she exited the airlock and made her way along the outside of the communications deck, she saw the antennae standing in a row, dishes pointing down and to the right, like the faces of soldiers in funeral formation.

'Are you seeing this, Eve?' she asked as she focused her helmet camera into a wide shot of the array.

'Yes, May. That is the default, pre-flight orientation of the array. This is encouraging, as uniform shutdown could mean a single cause for failure.'

As May stood looking at the sleeping soldiers that controlled all of the *Hawking II*'s communications, her sense of isolation was profound. The breathtaking expanse of space, surging for billions of light years in every direction, made her feel like less than nothing. It also made their efforts to save the ship seem entirely futile. Even if they were able to get it back online, how could the antenna array, as massive and powerful as it was, ever regain connection with NASA? There was a reason onboard engineers worked around the clock to ensure communications with Mission Control remained connected at this distance. All it took was one instance of letting go of the lifeline to be lost forever, like losing your grip on a safety rope in stormy seas.

Since losing contact, Mission Control would have been blasting space in all directions with a powerful communications net. But, considering the ship's original distance from the station, that already had a mathematically bleak prognosis. NASA had no idea in what direction, or how far, they had gone off course.

May recalled her psych training and backed off on the Murphy's Law self-talk. Everything, when surrounded by eternity, would always seem futile. The void just had that effect on the relatively primitive human brain. Best to occupy the mind with physical tasks. *Do your job. Trust your training. Trust your team.* She pushed on to the array, determined to keep her head. After forty-five minutes, she had completed the methodical systems check required to assess each antenna and manually restored their connection to Eve's brain.

'All array antennae appear to be fully operational,' Eve finally said.

'Any idea what the problem was?'

'I have a full diagnostic view and I am not seeing a specific cause.'

'That's weird,' May said.

'In light of everything else we've seen, weird is a highly relative term.'

'Good point. Probably a casualty of our larger power loss issue. Let's hope NASA is still looking for us.'

'I've already sent a broad-spectrum SOS transmission to NASA and any other potential receiving parties.'

'How long till the transmission reaches Wright Station?'

'If we had a communications lock, it would take approximately seventy-eight minutes. Since we are trying to re-establish communications, I cannot give you an estimate.'

'How are the engines looking?'

'Degrading at a fifteen to twenty per cent higher rate than previously calculated.'

May could feel herself dipping into the darkness again. 'Jesus. Any idea what the cause might be?'

'I don't know. There are many potential—'

'Find it, Eve. We're running out of time.'

18

While they waited by the phone for NASA to call back, May went to the bridge to search for the MADS recorder. Although it went by the same acronym used by NASA's earlier Space Shuttle programme, Modular Auxiliary Data System, it was far more sophisticated than its predecessors. In addition to logging all voice and data communication on board and telemetered to Mission Control, it also video-logged the entire mission and kept daily records of general health and vital signs of everyone on the ship. In order to protect it from a processor meltdown, it was not connected to Eve's brain, and it could switch to full solar power operation in the event of internal power loss.

May removed the drilled-down flooring in the bridge's data closet, revealing the flight recorder's metal sarcophagus. The top access panel was intact. She used the chip key embedded in her dog tags to open it, then had to pass a retina scan to open the second panel. When she removed it, the MADS device was gone. The connector cables attached to the ship were shredded, with bits of them scattered around the empty housing.

'Houston, we have a problem,' May said sarcastically. 'The recorder is gone.'

'Define gone,' Eve said.

'As in, it is no longer in its housing.'

'Do you have any recollection of removing it?'

'Of course not,' May said, annoyed, 'Why on earth would I do that?'

'You are the only person on board with access to the housing.'

May felt light-headed. *Retrograde amnesia.* Short-term memory loss. If she had removed it, that would have likely happened closer to her illness, aka the dead zone.

'No one else has access?'

Dead crew. Sole survivor. Only one with MADS access . . .

'Not according to my records.'

'If removed from the housing, I am guessing it would automatically emit its beacon,' May said. 'Otherwise, what's the point?'

'You're correct, May. I am not detecting the beacon signal on board.'

May breathed a sigh of relief.

'It must have been jettisoned,' she said. 'We learned in training that it could deploy its own propulsion and nav to get to the nearest NASA satellite or station if the ship were destroyed or incapacitated.'

'That seems like the only logical explanation for its absence,' Eve said.

'But, of course, because we have no other records to access, and it's no longer here, we have no way of knowing if that is indeed what happened,' May pointed out.

'Correct. I'm sorry I can't be of more assistance.'

'It's all right. Spilt milk and all. That means—'

'No use crying over it,' Eve said. 'I incorporated another English language colloquialism base into my linguistic modules.'

'Great,' May said.

The reason for the absence of the MADS unit did make the most sense. However, it didn't feel completely resolved to May. There had been something in the way Eve had said she was the only one who could open the access panel. It was not accusatory, but it lacked the usual intonation in Eve's voice, more like her old robot voice. Did it mean anything? If so, was it related to Eve being suspicious of May or, worse yet, Eve trying to conceal something? May set it aside for the moment. Her gut told her there was no upside to mentioning it. If she came across it again, she would know it was not all in her head.

May reviewed the original navigation charts for the voyage.

'When I was intubated, we were outside the range of the landing vehicles, right?'

'Yes. They have a maximum range of approximately one tenth of that distance.'

'What about other vessels? Are you able to see if there were any in the vicinity at that time? I'd heard a rumour that the Chinese were going to attempt to reach Europa before us.'

'The *Hawking II* detected no other vessels in the area at that time.'

'Makes no sense. If my crew intended to abandon ship, one would think they'd do it with a solid, reachable destination. Otherwise, it's suicide.'

'Correct. But that isn't the only thing that defies logic. Even if they believed they could make it somewhere, that does not explain their cause of death,' Eve pointed out.

'Tell me about it. Is there any possible type of malfunction that could create such a catastrophic result?'

'None that I am aware of. With a total loss of atmosphere and power, one would expect a hull breach to be the cause. I have not detected any.'

'The bodies are still in there, mostly intact, so if there were a

93

breach it would have been small and they would have had plenty of opportunity to patch it. The only real explanation is that the atmosphere was physically bled out of the hangar.'

'There are several failsafe mechanisms in the hangar designed to prevent that. In fact, one of those mechanisms prevents the hangar door from opening if the ship's navigation system cannot identify a destination within landing vehicle range.'

'Well, this just keeps getting better and better,' May sighed. 'I'm going to the infirmary to check medical records. Meantime, I would love it if you would please pull interment protocols. I want to make sure I give my shipmates proper treatment.'

'Of course.'

Back in the infirmary, May looked up her medical records, hoping they might shed some light. Not surprisingly, like the memory of her illness, the files were incomplete. Suzanne Dowd, chief flight surgeon, had initially admitted her with a high fever, swollen lymph glands, red skin blotches, loss of sensation in peripheral nerves, and an alarmingly high white blood cell count. Eight hours after entering the infirmary, she had had a seizure and was put into a medically induced coma. The records ended there. The lab reports prior to that were also missing. Same story with the rest of her shipmates.

'Jesus, Eve, I can't find any medical records associated with my alleged illness or anyone else's. Everything is accounted for just prior, but that's it. How could data collection just stop like that?'

'I am not aware of any scenario in which that would be possible, save for the total destruction of the vessel. Even then, chances are NASA would have redundant copies, which are beamed to Ground Control continuously.'

'I have a bad feeling about all of this, Eve. I've been trying to remain objective and find logical reasons for our predicament, but I think we need to start talking about sabotage.'

'That certainly would make more logical sense than a chance occurrence. This vessel has far too many protections in place to support an accident theory.'

'I agree. And let's not forget the other factors here. In addition to my mystery illness, the missing data and the mass crew death, we have a reactor and propulsion system damaged and failing. Even I know the likelihood of that happening by chance is next to nil. Even with the crew incapacitated . . . this ship barely even needed us to run, Eve.'

'I would give sabotage high probability,' Eve said. 'No offence, but human beings have proven themselves—'

'Capable of all manner of base, despicable, and murderous behaviour?' May said.

'Yes.'

May flashed back to the bulging eyes of her dead shipmates in the landing vehicle hangar. Their faces were frozen in shock and surprise. They had had enough time to have an emotional reaction to their fates, but not enough to save themselves. In May's training, she was taught that the average human body exposed to the vacuum of space would die within thirty seconds from explosive decompression (expansion of gases in lungs and digestive system), ebullism (rapid boiling and evaporation of bodily fluids), and freezing (minus 135 degrees Celsius). This explained the state of the bodies when May found them. Within the first ten to fifteen seconds, you would be rendered unconscious and paralysed.

Everyone on board was well aware of this. If there had been a potential problem in the hangar, they would have gone in there in EVA suits, and definitely not as a group. Someone had ordered them to evacuate, a person in a position of authority. And, when they'd gathered in the hangar, it had lost its atmosphere and gravity quickly enough to make it impossible for those inside to do anything about it or to escape. It must have been completely unexpected. Sabotage was an excellent explanation, but left a lot of questions to be answered, like who on board would have had the knowledge and desire to do such a thing and how would they have pulled it off under the nose of the ship's AI? As much as she loved Eve, May reminded herself that she would be foolish to forget the fact that 'she' was a machine, programmable by humans, and therefore capable of the same things they were.

'Excuse me, May,' Eve said, 'but I've detected a hull breach in the bio-garden.'

'How bad?'

'Three centimetres in diameter.'

'Where?'

'Two metres to the left of the oxygen storage tanks.'

'Oh, my God.'

19

May snatched up an emergency patch canister and sprinted through the ship to the lab deck. On the way, tremors shook her to the floor twice. Breach alarms screeched.

'Eve, turn off those bloody alarms,' she yelled.

The alarms went quiet. May had to manually crank open the bio-garden doors, which had been automatically sealed when the breach was detected. There were ten huge oxygen storage tanks, all of which had the capacity to store enough compressed oxygen to supply the ship for the entire journey. The extras were there as back-up. One ruptured tank could ignite like a hydrogen bomb and incinerate the entire ship in a matter of seconds.

May took a short cut through the garden foliage and had to slash her way through the thick, wet branches and leaves. The closer she got to the hull breach, the more she could feel its relentless pull. Even with a tiny breach, the vacuum of space was powerful enough to suck huge items through it. In training, May had seen a simulator hull breach suck a full-sized adult male dummy through a thirty-six-centimetre hole, shredding it to bits that shot out like a cloud of dust on the other side. The breach in the bio-garden was already creating a hurricane-strength wind that was uprooting trees and ripping off leaves and branches. The debris pelted her back and legs relentlessly and she had to dodge the larger pieces to avoid serious injury or death. A hull breach was one of the few things capable of rupturing the thick titanium tanks.

'May, the breach has expanded to 13.6 centimetres. It is no longer safe for you to patch. I recommend sealing and jettisoning the bio-garden.'

'Negative. I can get there. We have to preserve the oxygen.'

The tremors hit again and May went sprawling. She dropped the patch canister and had to tear through plant matter to find it again.

'Eighteen centimetres. May, get out of there. You are in grave danger.'

May tumbled through the garden, clawing and kicking for anything to stop her momentum. Her hands closed around a metal support rod and she held on for dear life. More debris flew past her, smashing into the wall near the hull breach. To her horror, some of the softer objects were pulled through the small hole, shredded to bits as they were spat out into space. She was still a good ten metres from the breach, out of patch canister range, but she didn't dare try to get closer.

'Eve, can you seal off this room and lower the pressure to decrease the suction power of the breach?'

'I would have to decrease your atmosphere to a dangerous level to make even the slightest change.'

'Do it. The pull is too strong.'

May heard a loud rumbling sound and saw the oxygen tanks starting to shake away from their wall brackets. It was too late to save the bio-garden, maybe even too late for her to get to safety so Eve could jettison it.

'Decreasing atmosphere fifteen per cent.'

May instantly felt the effects. Her breathing became somewhat laboured and her limbs sluggish. But the tanks settled for the moment.

'I'm going to get myself clear of this door so you can seal it,' May said, huffing and puffing. 'Where do I need to go to be safe for jettison?'

'The adjacent lab module will be safe. Please hurry. Soon our emergency systems will take over and I will have no control over jettison.'

With a mechanical groan, the oxygen tanks started to sway, ripping bolts out of their moorings. May needed to buy some time to get to the outer door. The patch canister she had was made from thick metal, designed to take the worst kind of beating in these circumstances. May positioned it on the ground in line with the breach and let it fly. It shot like an artillery shell across the room and the top of it slammed into the hole. For a brief moment, the sucking wind subsided. That was May's chance to escape. She sprinted back through the ruined garden, clawing her way to the exit door. The wind was coming back as the canister rattled in the breach, reaming it out and making it bigger. The metal frames of the oxygen tanks were back to rattling and more bolts snapped.

As May got to the door, her patch canister was sucked through the breach. With a larger opening, the sucking wind was like a jet engine, pulling out huge swaths of garden vegetation. At the moment it was thick enough to slow down the wind, but the hole was rapidly chewing it to bits like a wood chipper. May clung to the edge of the doorframe with both arms and legs, trying with all her strength to move the thirty-odd centimetres she needed to get outside the door so Eve could seal it. It felt as though she was doing a pull-up with a car strapped to her back.

'Now 28.3 centimetres. Fissure lines radiating from the

breach. Emergency systems override is imminent. May, you need to clear that door now.'

'No shit, Sherlock.'

May gave it another go, but this time she pulled herself close enough to the door frame to hook a leg around it. Then, pulling with all four limbs until it felt like her bones would break, she got herself to the edge of the door frame.

'Almost out . . . Eve.'

Even saying as little as that nearly caused her to black out.

'Copy that. I'm ready and have a visual on you.'

May pulled again, rotating her body so her legs were now flat against the outside wall but her torso was still inside the door. She had nothing to hook her foot into. Her arms and core had to do all the work. She was nearly clear a couple of times but lost ground when she had to dodge more flying debris, this time coming from the outer labs. Nearly out of strength, she gave it one last go, and got clear.

'Now.'

Eve slammed the door and sealed it. May fell to the ground, gasping and weak. No time to rest. They were seconds away from a forced jettison that would take May with it. She limped as quickly as she could to the next lab module. As she reached the door, she heard the booming of the oxygen tanks coming off the wall. Jettison alarms sounded. May jumped through the door of the next lab module and sealed it.

'Bio-garden sealed. De-coupling,' Eve said.

May's throat was ragged and her voice was swallowed up in the pain. She crawled to a bolted-down lab table and wrapped her arms and legs around one of its cold steel legs.

'Brace for jettison,' Eve called out. The couplings connecting the bio-garden to the rest of the lab deck were blown and it was released into space. The ship shook violently, sending May rolling across the lab floor. She grabbed on to the pipes under a sink and felt as though she was clinging to the back of a stampeding elephant. As they shot into space, the oxygen storage tanks exploded. The concussion from the blast rocked the *Hawking II* and sent May flying vertically from her position on the floor. She landed on her back, quickly losing consciousness.

'May, can you hear me?'

Black smoke rolled across the floor, curling up around her, while flames licked up the side of the wall.

'May?'

20

Stephen Knox woke to the sound of his home comms line whistling in his ear. He searched for the glowing clock numbers in the dark. 3:45 a.m.

'Lights.'

Soft illumination faded up, bringing him back to reality. He lay there for a moment, his mind slowly putting itself back together after having been scattered to the wind by sleep tabs and red wine. *Bedroom*, he reminded himself. It was the room he'd shared with May when they were together. Decorated in her ultra-modern style, with muted dark colours and low, angular furniture, it always looked unfamiliar to Stephen upon waking. He had joked with her that it looked no different from most posh urban hotel rooms, something she took as a high compliment.

Stephen fumbled for his comms pad, found it under a laundry mess on the floor, and looked at the screen. It was showing no fewer than forty-five missed calls. *How much wine did I drink?* The pad whistled again. Call forty-six.

'Raj, I hope you're in jail, or a hospital bed in need of a kidney.'

'Let me in, man.'

Sharp rapping on the bedroom window. Stephen sat up, maybe too quickly.

'Are you outside? Blinds.'

The mesh veneers on the bedroom window slid quietly into the wall, revealing Stephen's friend, Raj Kapoor, the brilliant engineer who designed the *Hawking II*, peering in like a peeping Tom. Raj had an enormous head for his small frame, crowned by a tangle of black curly hair, a patchy beard that refused to have anything to do with his moustache, and thick brown glasses, fogged, as they often were when he was agitated.

'Jesus, what the hell are you doing out there?'

'Dude, I've been trying to reach you for the past six hours. Let me in before your neighbours think I'm a terrorist.'

'You're from Mumbai, you drama queen.'

'This is Texas. They probably think Indians send smoke signals and shit.'

'Door's open.'

Stephen rolled out of bed and threw on a raincoat in lieu of knowing the whereabouts of his robe or any clean clothes. Raj burst through the front door. He made it a few steps into the hall before he tripped on something and tumbled hard across the floor. 'Ow!'

'Lights,' Stephen said as he walked into the room.

The room lit up. Raj was lying on the floor, having tripped over the luggage and boxes Stephen had brought back from Wright Station.

'I see you've unpacked,' Raj said, getting to his feet.

'Coffee?' Stephen asked, ignoring his comment.

'Do I look like I need coffee? Ever?'

'I'm having some.'

'You got clothes on under that raincoat, right?'

'Why are you here, Raj?'

'We have a sat conference with Warren in ...' He looked at his watch. 'Now.'

'Why the hell didn't you just tell me that, you moron?' Stephen bellowed. 'I look like a park flasher.'

'Don't worry, it's not like your bad fashion is going to surprise anyone.'

'Hilarious. What's this about?'

'I don't know. Just got the order to rouse you.'

Stephen's adrenaline shot up. What if Robert was calling to confirm May's death? After avoiding it when he returned from Wright Station, he'd finally found the courage to go home. He thought he had resigned himself to the worst-case scenario, but in that moment he felt grossly unprepared to have it confirmed into reality.

'What if it's bad news, Raj?'

'Incoming sat com,' his home AI purred. 'Accept?'

'Yes,' Stephen said, buttoning his coat higher.

The NASA insignia appeared on the screen.

'Hold for Director Warren,' the soft electronic voice said.

Stephen felt like a death row prisoner on execution day. His anxiety had quickly travelled to Raj after the bad news question. Robert's face appeared on the screen. He was playing his usual role of the harried, yet professionally composed leader.

'Hello, Stephen, Raj.'

'Hi, Robert,' Stephen said.

'How are you holding up?'

'To be honest, I'm not.'

'Well, I have some news that will lift your spirits. We've received an SOS signal from the *Hawking II*.'

Stephen couldn't believe his ears.

'I ... Oh, my God.'

Raj patted him on the back, way too hard as usual.

'Yes,' Stephen coughed. 'That's incredible. When?'

'Twenty-seven hours ago.'

'Why didn't you call me then?' Stephen spat.

Robert's eye twitched, ever so slightly. Stephen knew his 'tells' by now. That one meant he was irked and caught off guard, but that would be the only sign of it.

'We needed time to confirm and, when we had, we tried to reach you, but had no luck. That's why I asked Raj to track you down.'

'See?' Raj said. 'He's been too busy wallowing in self-pity, Robert.'

'Shut it, Raj,' Stephen said. 'Robert, that's great news.'

'Yes, but we all need to temper our expectations here. The team has decrypted and analysed the packet data. First off, you need to know that the ship's AI is reporting multiple casualties, but Maryam is not among them. Also, the ship has been severely damaged and is barely functioning at a nominal level.'

'Oh, my God,' Stephen said again, quietly. 'Any chance of remote repair?'

'We're working on that, but may need onboard assistance. Aside from May, we have no idea if there are any other survivors with the right expertise.'

Stephen and Raj were completely deflated. They knew the prognosis. Surviving in deep space with a fully functioning vessel was already a monumental challenge.

'Robert, what if May or any of the other survivors are unable to assist? Is it possible to launch a rescue? If they're somehow incapacitated, trying to make it back—'

'That's all the information I have right now. We'll be sending transmissions round the clock. Stephen, once we receive an answer, if you'd like to send May a recorded message, we'll set it up at Johnson as soon as possible.'

'Yes, I would like to do that,' Stephen said eagerly.

'I'm sorry to be the bearer of such news, but the team is

remaining optimistic up here. NASA is no stranger to problem-solving, even under the worst of circumstances.'

'Thank you, Robert. I appreciate your candour and will try to adopt your optimism. At least now we have something cutting through the radio silence.'

'Exactly. We'll take whatever we can get. I need to get back, but we'll be in touch.'

'I'll make sure I'm reachable this time.'

After the call, Stephen and Raj sat among the moving boxes and drank coffee.

'As much as I hate to admit it, you're right,' Stephen said. 'I have been feeling sorry for myself since I got back.'

'I'm always right, and you always hate to admit it.'

Raj had a way of saying things that sounded like a joke, or an exaggeration, while keeping a completely straight face. He was one of the most interesting people Stephen had ever met. His IQ was intimidating, his academic credentials and career accomplishments, especially considering he was only thirty-five, unprecedented, yet he looked and spoke like a privileged kid obsessed with pop culture.

When NASA had tasked STMD with designing the *Hawking II*, Raj's star had quickly risen among the ranks. In addition to being a gifted designer and engineer, his knowledge of scientific research processes was as robust as Stephen's. With research being the primary focus of the mission, Raj made it also the primary focus of vessel design and functionality. The result was a space-based lab with a near-perfect replication of Earth-based research environments. Scientists on the *Hawking II* could perform real-time experiments on planetary samples without having to wait until they returned. The vessel's size was much larger than most, but it had been Raj's idea to build it in space to avoid the constraints posed by having to piggyback on a launch vehicle.

Stephen had been blown away when he saw the preliminary designs, and he and Raj had become fast friends. They'd spent many hours collaborating, which included sibling-like arguments that had landed them in hot water with Robert Warren on more than one occasion. In the end, all of that had proved part of an inspired equation that had yielded one of the most exciting vessels NASA had ever built.

'I hate not knowing more about the ship,' Raj said.

'What about the crew? Multiple casualties?' Stephen asked, perturbed.

'Them too.'

'Jesus, you're a real piece of work, Raj.'

'Ship is my baby. You know that. Just like May is your ... well, not your baby, but you know what I mean. You must be very relieved.'

'I figured Warren was going to confirm what I already suspected. A lot of time has passed and, it just seemed like—'

'Trust me,' Raj interrupted, 'I'm shocked *anyone's* alive. Nothing cuts comms like that, for that long, for any reason short of something catastrophic.'

'You told me to keep my chin up a few days ago,' Stephen said.

'I figured that's what people say.'

'That *is* what people say. Which is why they're full of shit.'

Stephen's mind was racing. He wanted to get Robert back on the line, grill him some more. The call had caught him off guard.

'What about a rescue, Raj? I mean, if they were to need it? Is that even possible? Does NASA have a vessel it could send? How long would that take? Maybe there's a Chinese or Russian vessel that could—'

'Chill, dude. This is NASA. The answer to whatever needs to happen is yes. This is one of the most important missions in history. They aren't just going to throw in the towel and go back

107

to the drawing board. Trust me, an army of people are worrying about this now, 24/7, so you don't have to.'

'Okay, you're right. I'm still going to worry, but I'll stop trying to be a back-seat driver. I just want to *do* something, you know? It's driving me nuts feeling so goddamned powerless.' He started pacing. 'Just wish I could help.'

'Send May some words of encouragement. Give her a pep talk. She probably needs one pretty bad about now.'

'Yeah. Moral support. That's what I can do right now.'

'Just don't mention, you know, any of that bad shit from your marriage.'

'Wow, you really do think I'm socially inept.'

'You're not as bad as me, but—'

'Shut up.'

Raj noticed the door to one of the other bedrooms was ajar and went to peek inside. 'Whoa, you actually went in there?' he asked, surprised.

'Yeah,' Stephen said. 'Just, please don't.'

Raj opened the door all the way. It was a child's nursery. 'Thought maybe you'd have had it, like, remodelled or something by now.'

'Can we talk about something else?' Stephen said, closing the door.

'No. I'm going home,' Raj said. 'Need me some cereal . . . and sleep, I guess.'

'Thanks for ambushing me,' Stephen said.

'No problem. See you back at the office.'

'Yeah,' Stephen said enthusiastically.

After Raj left, he allowed himself a little sentimentality and looked in at the nursery. He'd built it as a surprise for May, but hadn't even been able to think about it since launch. It wasn't until he'd thought he might have lost her that he had been able to summon the courage. It was odd, but looking at it brought him out of his dreadful numbness. He wanted to feel. He craved it. Opening that door had done the trick, beating him nearly senseless with pain. Since then, he'd kept the door open, forcing himself to keep the wound fresh.

Knowing May was still alive, it looked different. Sunlight shone through the sheer curtains, lending a soft glow to the pastel colours and white trim. The stuffed animals in the crib looked like children patiently waiting for Christmas morning. Stephen switched off the lights and sat in the cushioned rocker, staring up at the glow in the dark stars May had arranged on the ceiling. Orion, Stephen's favourite constellation. Somewhere up there was the faintest glimmer of hope.

21

February 27, 2066 – Houston, Texas

'I'd like to propose a toast.'

Several hundred guests, in formal evening attire, were dancing and mingling in a gaudy ballroom at Houston's Hôtel Versailles. It was the kind of place that made Stephen's skin crawl, with enough gold, velvet and ancient oil money to choke Louis XIV. While everyone else drank and ate their weight in champagne and prime rib, he sat in his ill-fitting rented tuxedo, nursing a sweaty Manhattan and trying valiantly to have a conversation with the divorced Houston socialite Robert had foisted on him as a date. Robert was of the mind that Stephen needed to appear more 'normal' to ensure the wealthy power brokers behind the mission felt comfortable having an academic at the helm. She was a very nice woman, well-spoken, and appropriately attractive, but terminally dull.

Stephen watched as Robert worked the room, clearly one of his favourite pastimes. Everything about him was a front, a gilded façade with glad hands at the gates. In addition to appearing to have recently undergone yet another unnamed plastic surgery procedure, which had turned his face into a bronzed bullet with a permanent white grin, he was speaking to people at a volume loud enough to reach the entire room. *Typical politician behaviour,* thought Stephen, *forcing the world to take a whiff of you, even if they were holding their noses.* For all the brilliant people surrounding him, he was really nothing more than a glorified carnival barker, selling tickets to one of the biggest scientific spectacles in history.

Henry Warren, his iconic father, had played a similar role. As an industrialist and career politician, he'd served on, and chaired, several committees that had been responsible for the advancement of space exploration. NASA might have drowned in its own archaic culture if it hadn't been for Iron Hank, and that was something the Warren family, especially Robert, would never let anyone forget. Fortunately for Stephen, Robert's sole purpose in life was to crawl out from under dear old Dad's formidable shadow. He carved out a niche for himself early on by focusing on the often unpopular area of deep space exploration. When he'd seen that Stephen was poised to redefine humanity's past and future with his work, Robert had felt as though he'd found his *Apollo 11.*

Stephen heard the clink of silver on glass. 'Oh, shit,' he said, knowing what that meant.

Robert had moved back to his VIP table and was holding up his wine glass, tapping it with a spoon. Others followed suit, tapping to beat the band and please their master.

'Ladies and gentlemen, I would like to propose a toast,' he called out.

The crowd cheered, and some started to drink.

'Hold on just a moment. You're not going to get off that easy,' he joked, alluding to his propensity for long-winded speeches, and got a murmur of laughter. 'I just want to say how excited I am to be a part of the Europa mission ... although I can't fully discuss it because most of you don't have security clearance ...'

111

More good-natured laughter from the crowd.

'I am willing to go out on a limb and make a *modest* prediction. Life as we know it will probably be changed forever.'

Robert did so love to work a room.

'Since some of you will soon be departing for Europa, and you won't be seeing real food such as what we've lavishly thrust at you tonight for a very long time, I'll try to be brief. Someone once said that, for every brilliant advance in science, there is someone on whom the world must bestow the glory ... and the blame. The Europa mission would be nothing without the man whose life's work has brought all of us here, and will take us further than we've ever gone before. Ladies and gentlemen, Dr Stephen Knox. Where are you, Stephen?'

He knew exactly where Stephen was. Feigning a search of the room was how he got people settled and quiet. Stephen's date clapped giddily and nudged Stephen to stand up. When he did, Robert looked at him and smiled proudly, like the owner of a prize thoroughbred taking home the roses on Derby day.

'Stephen Knox, maker of worlds, this is for you.'

Stephen cringed so hard he thought maybe he pulled a muscle. Robert raised his glass higher, whipping the crowd into a healthy lather.

'Now you may drink, you animals.'

Drinks were downed, hands shaken. Stephen received so many pats on the back, he thought his chicken cordon bleu was going to come up. When it was over, he did what any self-respecting scientist with narrow social skills and a venomous hatred of small talk would have done: he got the hell out of there. Having spied a balcony the size of a football field when he arrived earlier, he made a break for it, relishing the idea of getting some fresh air and then totally destroying it with a cigarette. He slipped through the heavily draped doors and into the sultry evening air, found a shadowed corner to hide, and admired the stars while he puffed away. Orion's head was in view, but the rest of him was obscured by high clouds.

'Leave it to me to run over the boss.'

A woman's voice rose from a nearby cocktail table. It was May. At first, he didn't recognise her, dressed to the nines in a snug knee-length cocktail dress that made her look like a movie star or a superhero. When he did, he felt a twinge in the wound that was still healing on his arm. He thought about being nice, but the food, booze and bad date were not agreeing with him. So why be agreeable?

'Just when I thought the night couldn't get any worse,' he said, stubbing out his smoke and looking for an exit route.

May must have sensed his desire to retreat, because she got out of her chair and walked over to him before he could even think about getting out of his. 'I know it's out of line for me to ask, but could I bum a cigarette? I'm a closet smoker. It's kind of an occupational hazard. Plus, there's barely room for lipstick in my tiny rental purse.'

At least she was amusing, which was more than Stephen could say about pretty much everyone in the ballroom. He thought about giving her a flat no, but he had already reached his limit on confrontational behaviour and never really got to enjoy his first smoke.

'Sure,' he said baldly.

Ignoring his body language and tone, May sat down across from him. He'd been hoping she would take the cigarette and slink away again, but it appeared she was all about colliding with either his body or his mood. She even waited for him to light the damn thing.

'You've got a lot of nerve,' he said.

'Am I fired?' she asked, blowing just enough smoke in his face to make it intentional.

Her eyes were sharp and predatory, sizing him up. May's sheer boldness was fascinating and made him forget he was grumpy. He had never possessed the audacity to behave in such a way – confident, assertive, and with an air of not giving a damn. The wound on his wrist itched. He pulled back his sleeve and examined the bandage. A little blood had seeped through. May eyed it and her swagger turned to empathy.

'Oh dear, that's going to leave a mark. I am fired, aren't I?'

'Maryam, right?'

'Yeah, but my victims call me May. And of course your name is Dr Stephen Knox, the elegant genius behind all this.'

'You can call me Stephen. Or elegant genius. Whatever works.'

'I like Stephen. Especially since it's spelled properly.'

'That's what I tried to tell those assholes back in middle school.'

May laughed. Seeing her smile made him realise how beautiful she was, which made him feel self-conscious, then annoyed. He slipped his jacket sleeve back down over the bandage and put his guard back up.

'So, what's your role in this monster I've helped to create?' he asked.

'Oh, nothing special. I'm just the commander.'

His turn to laugh. 'Oh, that's perfect,' he said.

'I know, right?' May agreed. 'The age-old, hackneyed conflict between scientists and astronauts embodied in a low-speed accident with ice-cream-cone casualties.'

'Actually, I was thinking how ironic it was that a highly skilled pilot could be such a menace behind the wheel of a car.'

He was embarrassed that he'd said something so rude, but relieved she didn't care.

'I'm also pretty bad at apologies,' she said. 'I am very sorry for hitting you, gashing your arm, ruining your ice cream ...'

'... ridiculing me in the street in front of a pack of gawkers.'

'Especially for that. I'm really not an awful person ... most of the time.'

114

'I'm pretty awful *all* of the time,' Stephen conceded.

'You seem all right to me. Trust me, my asshole detector is top shelf. Never fails. You're not even moving the needle.'

'Thanks, I think,' he said. He tried to suck down the last drop of his Manhattan and spilt ice all over his jacket. 'I meant to do that.'

'Can I get you a drink?' she offered.

'I don't know if I can stomach another maraschino cherry,' he said.

'Yeah, those will kill you. Try this.'

May offered him a drink from her mother's dented silver flask. Stephen had a sip and fell into a coughing fit.

'Paint-thinner?' he asked hoarsely. 'Breakfast of champions.'

May took a long drink. 'Scottish road tar remover, actually. Another throat-punch, good sir?' she asked, offering the flask.

'Don't mind if I do. I need something to dissolve the meal they apparently thawed out from 1950.' Stephen drank some more and felt the fire run down his throat. The heat of it spread through his limbs and made his eyes feel heavy. 'You came prepared. Must love affairs like this as much as I do,' he said.

'Almost as much as funerals. But at least there the food is decent.'

'And the booze,' Stephen added.

'Can't let down the dead with rubber chicken and warm sauvignon blanc. That would just be wrong.'

'Agreed,' Stephen said, looking around pensively.

'Worried your date is looking for you?'

'No, she came with the tuxedo. I was hoping to get out of here before Robert decides to parade me around like livestock. What about you? Tell me you didn't come alone to the dance of the living dead.'

'I'm married to my job, but she's not a very good kisser.'

'What a coincidence. Me too. My job never wants me to have

115

any fun. Always nagging me and telling me what to do. Weekend honey-do lists, light beer . . . ' Stephen started to loosen his bow tie.

'Don't do that,' May said, smiling. 'That's the best part of the suit. Besides, Robert will have a fit if you appear to be uncomfortable with the sacrifices of modern fashion.'

'You know him well,' Stephen said, trying to re-tie his tie.

'Who do you think told me to wear this sequinned sausage-casing?'

Stephen finished the tie but it was ridiculously crooked. 'How's that?' he asked.

'Disastrous. Allow me.'

She leaned in and re-tied it in a few neat movements. Stephen tried to look away, but her eyes and strong hands reeled him back in. When she was done, she helped herself to another of his cigarettes and sat back down.

'Thank you,' Stephen said. 'I feel like a gentleman again.'

'Oh, no. Perhaps more whisky will take care of that,' she said, handing him the flask.

Stephen took a long drink.

'Easy there,' May said, 'I still need some for the drive home.' She winked.

Stephen was shocked at how much he felt at ease with her, even though they could not have possibly been more different in every way. He was simultaneously talking himself in and out of asking her to go have a drink with him, somewhere else, when Robert walked out to the balcony, searching for him.

'Uh-oh,' May said, quickly stubbing out her smoke. 'Looks like Dad wants the car keys back.'

Robert strolled up to them, a knowing grin on his face.

'Robert,' Stephen said cheerfully. 'And you know May, of course.'

'Of course.' Robert smiled tightly. 'Nice to see you, Commander Crosley.'

Robert enjoyed politely reminding people of their so-called station as a passive-aggressive way of keeping them in line. May got the message.

'Evening, sir,' she said, standing formally.

'Stephen, would you mind coming inside for a bit? I'd like to introduce you to some of NASA's top policymakers. They're dying to meet you and your stunning intellect.'

Stephen glanced at May. She smiled as if to release him.

'Nice talking to you, Dr Knox,' she said, politely mocking Robert's formality.

'You too ... Commander,' Stephen said, grinning.

As Robert escorted him away, Stephen looked back and saw that May had appropriated his pack of cigarettes. She taunted him, lighting one up and blowing a massive cloud of smoke in their direction.

22

'I'm showing no collateral damage to the rest of the ship,' Eve said.

May was back in the infirmary, recovering from smoke inhalation and from being battered by the hull breach. Luckily Eve had been able to put out the fire that started in the labs after the bio-garden was jettisoned, but not before nearly mummifying May in fire foam. She was still picking bits of it off her scalp.

'That's good.' May sighed. 'Any idea about the cause?'

'No. My only theory is stress cracks caused by recent tremulous activity.'

'It looked like someone had blown a hole in it with a bazooka.'

'According to my records, we don't—'

'Have any bazookas on board?' May asked, smiling.

'I see. That was a joke.'

'Obviously not a very good one. If it was caused by tremor, is it possible there are other stress cracks on the ship?'

'I have not detected any.'

'But you didn't detect the one in the bio-garden.'

'Which is puzzling. I looked back at structural sensor data

just prior to the breach, and found nothing that would have predicted it.'

'Great. Add that to our list of unexplained phenomena waiting to bite me in the ass.'

May's IV was finished. She pulled the needle and rolled off the gurney. When she tried to stand, the room spun and she had to quickly lie back down. 'Whoa,' she said, feeling a cold sweat break out on her skin. 'Dizzy. Must have low sugar again.'

'You've just received a large glucose infusion.'

'I know,' May snapped, wondering where the sudden anger had come from. 'Sorry, Eve. I think all of this is finally getting to me. The more I remember, the more intense my emotions. And, right now, I am approaching what we humans like to call *frazzled*.'

'That's all right, May. Emotional volatility is to be expected with brain injury.'

'I wish that made me feel better, that it's normal to be abnormal, but it doesn't.'

'How are you feeling physically?'

'Relative to being unconscious and nearly buried alive in this dreadful foam, good. Relative to my former self, I feel I've aged a decade.'

'I'm sorry this has been so difficult for you. I wish I were able to help more.'

'Stop it, Eve. You're very helpful. And you're keeping me sane, which might be the most important job on the ship right now.'

'I try. Cup o' tea?'

'Oh ... nice touch of Brit without going too far. And the answer is yes. I would love some more armpit-warm brown water with a hint of tea flavour.'

'How about another pseudo-crumpet made with wallpaper paste to go with it?'

'Excellent.'

119

'I'll prepare it in the galley,' Eve said. 'Are you up to the walk?'

'I can manage.'

Standing brought back a bit of wooziness, but it subsided and May went off to the galley. When the food and beverage console spat out her 'tea and crumpet', the smell of the warm, cake-like disc made her instantly nauseous.

'Um, Eve,' she said quietly, 'this is making my stomach turn like a cheap carnival ride. Let's try something else. The pot pie was decent, if memory serves.'

'One moment,' Eve replied.

The pot pie was dispensed and made her feel even sicker.

'Nope. Dispose of that too, please. I'll just have some water.'

May put water in a coffee cup and turned her back to the room camera while she poured a good deal of the contents of her mum's old flask into the mug.

'That's the ticket,' she said after taking the first sip.

She relaxed in a chair and examined the old hunk of battered steel that stank of stale whisky. Invariably, that smell always conjured memories of her mother. In that moment, apropos what May had just been through, she was reminded of the treacherous flight the two of them had piloted back when May was thirteen.

Some things never change, eh? May thought to herself.

May had been flying one of her mother's ancient aeroplanes, a twin-engine Beechcraft Baron G58, also known as 'the Dashing Duke'. There were four cracked and faded leather passenger seats in the back, and a crammed little cockpit up front. The plane was a far greater challenge to pilot than the single-engine puddle-jumpers she was usually allowed to fly, and she had been equally excited and nervous when Eve had announced a 'quick trip to Scotland' over breakfast.

Eve loved those old dinosaurs, and loved it even more when she could get May in the cockpit with her. She used to tell her that real pilots should be able to master anything with wings.

They'd run into a problem on final approach into Glasgow when the temperature plummeted dramatically during a rainstorm and the wings started taking on ice. Within minutes, they'd found themselves in a potentially deadly situation. Their altitude was around 3,500 metres and dropping quickly. The engines were sputtering in and out of stalls and the flaps were getting near impossible to move. May thought they were going to drop like a stone. She started to panic and Eve very tersely set her straight.

'Keep your head, girl, or you will lose it. All problems are solvable when you take a breath and put your mind to it.'

'What are we going to do?' May screeched. 'You take over.'

'Absolutely not. You're the captain and I am only authorised to take over if you are incapacitated. You can do this, Maryam. It's not always going to be blue skies and lovely fluffy clouds.' Eve tapped the attitude indicator, an instrument showing the orientation of the aircraft relative to the horizon. 'And, to answer your question, you're not going to do anything. Right now we are as stable as we are going to get with this much extra weight. If we submit to fear and try to force the aircraft into submission, we run the risk of becoming very unstable – like, upside down.'

'We have to do something,' May whimpered.

'We're going to let gravity do her magic. Think, Maryam: what is going to happen the lower we descend in altitude?'

'I don't know, I—'

'Stop blubbering and pull yourself together!' Eve yelled. 'This is a life-or-death situation. I'm not always going to be here to save you, so save yourself.'

May gritted her teeth and wiped her snot on her sleeve. Eve's outburst had disrupted her fear response and put her into survival mode. She felt her wits returning.

'The lower we go,' she said assertively, 'the warmer the air temperature. So, the ice will melt and we can regain control.'

'That is correct. See what happens when you clear your head?'

'But what if we're a hundred feet off the ground by the time it melts? We'll never recover.'

'Then we'll be dead,' her mother said evenly. 'But at least we have a chance, versus doing something rash that could eliminate our chances. Now, instead of whinging about what-ifs, you have another problem you need to solve. Do you know what it is?'

May looked at her instruments and navigation map with her shaking hands. 'At this air speed, we're going to overshoot Glasgow airfield. And there's nothing we can do to slow down.'

'Right. Solution?'

She scrutinised the map and smiled, popping her finger on it.

'Found one just north of the city. We might fall a little short, but it's our best bet.'

'That's my girl.'

As they dipped to a nail-biting one thousand metres, the sun broke through the clouds and the temperature warmed up to well above freezing. The ice on the plane melted quickly and they landed with minimal damage. On the ground, Eve was beaming with pride. So much so, she told the story, with a few colourful embellishments, to the entire ground crew. Then, she did something that she'd done so infrequently in the past that May could count the times on one hand. She gave her daughter a hug.

'Congratulations, Maryam. *Now* you're a pilot.'

From that point on, May had looked at piloting differently. And her mum. All those years cursing her for being too cold and emotionally distant; May realised she had not understood how being a pilot, with heavy combat experience, had made it necessary for Eve to abandon her emotional self. It had been essential for her own survival.

Sister, I can relate, May thought as she raised the flask.

23

'Time for a little R&R,' May whispered to herself.

It felt good to get a little buzzed, to take a break from the constant anxiety and brushes with death. She drank a little more whisky and fished a cigarette out of her pocket. She'd been ecstatic to find the pack she'd smuggled on board, along with her flask, stashed under her berth. It made her feel as if she was a teenager again. She lit the cig and took a long drag. The nicotine rush nearly spun her head off her body, but the whisky tethered it down.

'May, there's a fire in the galley,' Eve called out with urgency. 'Are you in the vicinity and can you please extinguish it?'

May laughed. 'It's me, Eve. I'm the one on fire. I'm having a fag – um, a cigarette.'

'Smoking on all NASA vessels is strictly prohibited. There are highly flammable—'

'Yes, I know. But I don't care. If I'm going to have to live with death lurking around every corner, I'm simply going to have to break a few rules to get through it.' She took a long drink and indulged in a tremendous belch. 'Scotch. Horrible stuff. But it does warm the cockles.'

'May I ask you a personal question, May?' Eve said quietly.

'By all means. Knock yourself out.'

'If it's true you feel that death is, as you say, lurking around every corner, why do you consume things proven to be damaging to your body – like alcohol and cigarettes?'

May laughed so hard she nearly swallowed her cigarette. 'Excellent question. The reason is because, even though these things are destructive to our bodies in the long term, they make us feel pleasure in the short term. It's a bit of a conundrum.'

'It is definitely difficult to understand, applying logic,' Eve said.

'That's the thing: humans like to believe they're logical, but the way we live our lives says the opposite. We're more driven by emotions, which have a logic all their own, but probably not one that makes a lot of sense. Does that make sense?' May laughed.

'When you were striking your mirror and hurting yourself, emotions were telling you that was the right thing to do?'

'Not so much telling. It just occurred to me to do so in the moment, and I did. Normally I would never do that, but fatigue and stress can make emotions more intense.'

'What about happiness? Does it work the same way?'

'Absolutely. Like the first time I kissed my husband, Stephen.'

May recalled the night Stephen had taken her to the Mexican dive bar near Rice University campus after she'd showed up at his lecture. She could smell the burning candle wax in the fried ice cream he'd bought her, to make up for ruining her birthday the day they met. She remembered leaning across the table to kiss him, nearly setting her top on fire, and the taste of tequila and lime and the grains of salt on her tongue.

'I just did it,' she reminisced. 'Didn't really have the chance to think. Sort of like being a pilot. Often you have to go with instinct, with your gut. I believe it's one human trait that's rooted in an older and wiser part of us.'

'I don't know if instinct could ever be coded into my systems.'

'You already have it, Eve. The way you anticipate problems based on what you know. That's a form of instinct too.'

'Excellent. I feel included.'

'You'd better watch out,' May laughed, 'or you might become one of us. On that note, how about a little music?'

'What would you like to hear?' Eve asked. 'I have quite an extensive library.'

'How about a funeral march?' May said sarcastically.

'Which composer?'

'I'm joking. Play me something I can dance to. I don't care what it is.'

Eve played some EDM music. May groaned in disapproval.

'Drum machines have no soul. Real music with real people, please.'

'My programmers were very fond of Ludwig van Beethoven. Are you familiar with his work?'

'Are you taking the piss?'

'Is that another figure of speech?'

'Yes, it means are you joking, asking me if I'm aware of one of the most important composers in the history of music?'

'My sense of humour programming is robust, but doesn't include mockery. That might be very off-putting to humans.'

'To hell with humans,' she laughed. 'They can get stuffed.'

'May, you sound different. Your speech patterns—'

'It's called drunk.'

'Being inebriated could be very dangerous in this environment. Especially if you're handling fire.'

May burst out into uncontrollable giggling. 'I can handle my drinks. And my fire. Now play me something I can dance to.'

'Cross-referencing dance music, I have extensive ethnic dance libraries, such as polka and Native American ceremonial dance,' Eve said.

'Wow,' May said, trying to stifle her laughter, 'Let's try

something else. How about rock 'n' roll? That could be considered an ethnic dance.'

'Perhaps you would like to hear British rock 'n' roll? That is one of my largest libraries.'

'I'm not surprised. And yes, British rock, please.'

'Okay. Here is the music of the Rolling Stones.' Eve played 'Can't You Hear Me Knocking'.

'Oh, yeah. Time to shake it,' May said. 'This one goes out to NASA.'

She danced around the galley, cigarette dangling from her mouth. An hour or so went by, with Eve playing DJ and May dancing like a maniac, blowing off steam. When she'd had enough, she plopped down in a chair and drank some water to chase away the headache gathering behind her eyes. 'Ah, Eve, that was fun, thanks. What should we do next? Pillow fight?'

'I would like to hear more about your relationship with Stephen, if you don't mind. I know his work, but I've never had the opportunity to meet him.'

'A little girl talk, eh? I like it. What would you like to know . . . as long as it's not too risqué?' May joked.

'Tell me how you met.'

'You can do better than that, Eve. Ask me something saucy.'

'All right, but please let me know if I am getting too personal,' Eve said.

'Come on, it's just us girls,' May replied.

'Was Stephen the first person you ever loved?'

'Whoa. That's a good one, sister. Unfortunately, he was not. And you're never going to guess who was . . . '

'Guessing is not one of my strengths.'

'Just give it a try.'

'All right. Was it Ian Albright?'

May flinched in shock. 'How the hell did you know that?'

'I deduced it based on your personnel file data. You were in

126

the RAF as a young officer when he was a senior officer. He was one of the men in charge of your unit. The two of you were both separately reprimanded by your commanders for "fraternising" with another officer. The names were redacted from the report, but there were no other officers or enlisted personnel reprimanded for the same offence at the same point in time. And, occasionally, I hear you say his name when you're sleeping.'

May was momentarily lost in a memory. She and Ian were driving through the countryside, way too fast. He was at the wheel of some posh sports car his parents had given him, trying to impress her. She was laughing and shouting with her head hanging out of the window. They stopped on a bluff and walked out to look at the sea hundreds of feet below. Ireland. They'd taken a trip there, to one of his family homes. He held her in the bracing wind and kissed her. Then the memory switched and they were in the hall of a manor house, lying next to a fireplace as big as a car garage. Flames roared into the flue. Clothes were strewn about.

'He swept me off my feet, I dare say,' May mused.

'You loved him?'

'I tried,' she said.

Her eyes darkened and she shook the memory away. *Ashes to ashes.*

'By the way, knowing all that . . . Bit on the scary stalker side of surveillance, Eve.'

'I am sorry if I offended you. I was simply recounting unclassified information.'

'I know. And I commend you for your deductions. I know it's not your thing to speculate or predict, but you did a bang-up job with that.'

'Thank you. Maybe we shouldn't have this conversation, as I am not well-versed in the nuances of girl talk, as you call it.'

'Oh, stop it, Eve. You're doing great. What else do you want to know?'

'You speak quite fondly of Stephen and your marriage, but your personnel records state that the two of you filed for divorce just prior to your departure.'

'What?' May asked, reeling from the impact of Eve's words. 'I wasn't ... ' She choked on her reply, feeling a surge of dread.

'I'm so sorry, May. I've asked something too personal. I knew this was a bad—'

'Stop apologising!' May shouted.

Her sudden rage scared her. *Maybe the whisky wasn't such a good idea after all.* She stubbed out her cigarette and collected herself.

'Eve, I'm ... what I meant to say was there is no reason to apologise. It wasn't what you said ... The truth is, I didn't remember, that we did that. Divorce. Probably because it happened so close to me being sick. What with the whole amnesia thing and ... Jesus, this whole thing keeps getting better and better.'

May took another healthy swig of the Scotch. Instead of enjoying its warmth, she wanted it to burn out the sick feeling she had in her belly. *Divorce.* Every time she thought about Stephen, that made no sense.

24

'So, you're saying it's possible there are people, or life forms, similar to us, out there somewhere in the universe?'

Stephen was giving a guest lecture on evolutionary biology at Rice University's Physics and Astronomy Department. Demand for the event had been high, so the university had put him in one of their largest auditoriums. Roughly eight hundred people were jammed into the stadium seating, with many standing in the back and some in the aisles. For the most part, the people sitting down appeared to be either students or supporters of his work. The majority of those standing looked to be lower-class or working-class people, much older than the seated crowd. They were angry and loud, and many of them held crudely made signs with Bible verses and things like 'Burn in Hell' on them.

'What I'm saying,' Stephen replied, 'is that there is a strong body of evidence supporting the theory that the basic elements of life on Earth, including genetic building blocks for plants and animals, exist all over the universe. Meteorites found as early as the 1960s contained uracil and xanthine, nucleobases that are precursors to molecules that make up DNA and RNA.

Additionally, there is a strong body of evidence that there are Earth-like planets, known as exo-planets, in other solar systems in the universe. Knowing that, what do *you* think?'

'I think—'

'I think you're a crackpot and somebody oughtta lock you up!' one of the protesters yelled from the back of the room.

The other protesters cheered. Some of the students stood up and yelled back, telling them to get out and stop issuing threats. Stephen stood calmly and waited for Security to remove the man who yelled. Clearly he was used to taking such abuse, and did nothing to stoke the fires of dissent. A university official stepped up to the podium.

'We would like to ask that all attendees please behave respectfully and refrain from such behaviour or we will be forced to cut this lecture short.'

The crowd murmured, but settled. Stephen continued as if nothing had happened.

'Thank you. I would like to add to that, if I may. As I've said, I welcome all people to these lectures, which I do on a fully voluntary basis. And I encourage discussion. Trust me, if I sat up here lecturing, you'd all be asleep in no time.'

The crowd laughed, loosening the tension.

'For those of you who disagree with what is being discussed, I welcome your opinions. However, I am a scientist, not a politician, or an uninformed celebrity activist . . . '

More laughter, even some from the dissenters.

'The point is, the only discussions I am qualified to have with you are those relating to science. In case you haven't noticed from my incredible fashion sense, I am a total geek. I live and breathe facts and figures and empirical data, and dream in calculus. And everything I do in my profession is for all of you. Not just some – all. I've never cared about being published or collecting accolades. Since I was a kid, when discussions about overpopulation, climate change and the zombie apocalypse were part of the zeitgeist – I've always loved that word – I've thought of nothing else but this question: what's next for the human race? Are we destined to die out, to simply go extinct like other animals either unable or unwilling to adapt, or can we be the architects of our own evolution?'

When the lecture was over, and Stephen had finished shaking hands and signing things, like a rock star or political candidate, he sat down to do some more work before leaving.

'Boo!' May said behind him.

He jumped out of his chair and sent his work table and bag scattering across the floor. When he turned, she was standing there, stifling laughter.

'You shouldn't,' he said, sitting down to catch his breath.

She could see that he was shaken. 'Shit, I'm sorry. That was so stupid. With all those maniacs that came to your lecture, you probably thought someone was here to whack you.'

'You came to my lecture?' he asked, incredulous.

'Yeah,' she said, taken off guard. 'I was in the neighbourhood and—'

'—you were having trouble sleeping . . .'

'Stop, I thought the lecture was great. Not boring at all. I mean, we can talk about those shoes later, but I really enjoyed, you know, what you said . . . oh, and there was that element of danger too. All in all, pretty dramatic.'

'You should read my hate mail.'

May scowled. 'Hillbilly trash. Some things will never change.'

'If they knew their ticket money went straight to all the liberal causes they hate, they'd really be pissed.'

'You're a dangerous man, Stephen.'

'Takes one to know one . . . dangerous woman, that is, not a man, obviously.'

'Is it that obvious?'

May had worn her favourite jeans and a sheer white blouse. Her inner voice had asked her why she was trying to look hot if she was just going to check out Stephen's lecture 'for research', and then sneak out unnoticed. She had told her inner voice to fuck off.

'Need to lock up, Dr Knox,' a maintenance man yelled from the back of the room, causing Stephen to jump again.

'Okay, thank you,' he called back.

'Someone could use a drink,' May said.

'Is it that obvious?'

'Know any places around here?'

'Only if you like cheap booze and obnoxious college students.'

'What's not to like?' May replied, mostly referring to herself.

They walked to a dive bar near campus called 'Gringos', wedged between a Subway and a twenty-four-hour laundry. On the outside, the place looked as though it had been plucked from Zona Norte in Tijuana, its windows plastered with hand-bills and laminated 'food and beer special' signs. The inside was dimly lit, with kitsch cantina tables and chairs and framed Mexican wrestler posters.

'Charming,' May said as they walked in. 'Smells like a Miami strip club and I think my shoes are permanently stuck to the floor.'

'You've been to a Miami strip club?'

'Let's get a table. Too many wild animals at the bar.'

Stephen took one look at the bros with backward baseball caps and half-naked women doing glow-in-the-dark shots and nodded in agreement. The strung-out hostess sat them in the booth furthest away from the mayhem and Stephen ordered, cautioning May that some of the menu items were life-threatening. Within a few minutes, they were drinking margaritas and eating a platter of street tacos.

132

'Cheeky of you to downplay this place. It's actually amazing.'

'I only come here for special occasions.'

'Really? What's the occasion?' she asked.

'I'm sure we'll think of something,' he said.

They finished their drinks and the waitress had replacements before the glasses hit the table. May was beginning to see signs of Stephen's 'regular' status at the place. He'd seen to it that the two of them had fast service with no distractions. He was quietly methodical, with a reserved intensity that never seemed to wane. May felt she could completely be herself with him, which she knew would be quite challenging for most. Not only was he able to roll with her idiosyncrasies, he embraced them. She didn't know him well at all, but her instinct was that she had the same effect on him.

The more they drank, the more attractive all of that became and, predictably, the greater the chance that May would insert her foot directly in her mouth.

'So, how is it that there's no Mrs Knox?' she asked, twirling her drink straw.

And there it was. Stephen grimaced.

'Forget I asked,' May said. 'Killed the buzz. Emergency. More drinks.'

'There was a Mrs Knox, but she ran off with a pilot.'

May laughed hysterically, mostly out of relief, but also from the irony. Stephen wasn't laughing with her, so she mentally recorded strike two. 'You taking the piss?'

'No, it's true. Airline pilot. She's a business consultant. Lots of travel. Million-mile flier. Zero interest in what I did. Actually, thought what I did was mostly a waste of time. Not a difficult equation to solve.'

'Sorry. When I drink tequila, I have a tendency to pry.'

'It's okay. When I drink it, I have a tendency to not give a damn.'

'Yeah, but she hurt you, it's obvious. Oh, my God, I can't stop myself. I'm shutting up now. Here, I'll stuff my face with tacos until I can sort my shit out.'

'How can you tell she hurt me?'

'No,' May said with a mouth full of food, 'different topic. Something light. How about casual sex? Jesus, I am a *monster*.'

'You have some guacamole on your chin,' Stephen said, laughing.

'Wow,' she said. 'Shouldn't have judged the wild animals at the bar before. Turns out they're the classy ones.'

'You don't actually have anything on your chin. I just didn't want to talk about—'

'I get it. The ex is off limits.'

'—casual sex,' he said.

'Cheeky bastard,' May said. 'You're throwing me for a loop. You don't give a crap about your ex at all. You just want to watch me squirm for a change.'

'It is kind of endearing,' he said.

'Kiss me,' she said.

'Now you're doing it,' he said.

'Oh, you're good, Dr Knox. But kiss me anyway. Not saying you want to, but I would appreciate it if you would accommodate me, because it's too distracting to sit here thinking about wanting to do it and—'

'Okay.'

He leaned across the table and kissed her. It was a few notches above a peck, just enough to whet her appetite, but not enough to elicit cat-calls from the bar.

'Thank you,' she said, trying to hide the fact that she was slightly flustered.

'Still want to talk about my ex-wife?'

'Not especially.'

'Good. Because if you mix her with alcohol, could be toxic.'

134

'Ah, the poison pill. I had one of those once too. Guy's ego was so big, we couldn't fit in the same room.'

'Why was it so monstrous?'

'Because it belonged to Ian Albright.'

Stephen rolled his eyes.

'What?'

'Oh, nothing.'

'What, you don't like him?'

'It's not that. Well, it is that a little. Before I opted to go with NASA, Ian wanted me to give him exclusivity on my NanoSphere tech. So much so that he ended up threatening me when I wouldn't give him the goods.'

'Sounds all too familiar.'

'Looks like he hurt you,' Stephen chided.

'Shut up . . . he did, but not in the way you might think. Let's just say it turns out Mr former fighter pilot, genius inventor and billionaire owner of one of the world's most successful private space exploration firms—'

'Please go on,' he said, laughing. 'I'm shrinking.'

'Turns out he's really just a wildly insecure egomaniac who has a temper tantrum like a spoiled brat when he doesn't get his way.'

'Well said,' Stephen agreed. 'Billionaire temper tantrums can break a lot more than the living room vase, unfortunately.'

She laughed. 'Well said yourself. But I can deal with that. The deal-breaker for me was his conspicuous lack of a soul.'

'No soul . . . How does one know it's missing?' Stephen asked.

'Oh, you know. It's sort of like dealing with artificial intelligence. AI can fake human qualities very well, but it's clear when you've reached the edge of its limitations. That's Ian. He does a great job of appearing to be human.'

'Unfortunately, I think I know a lot of people like that,' Stephen said.

'It's an epidemic,' May agreed.

The waitress set a mound of fried ice cream with a lit birthday candle in it in front of them, along with two tequila shots.

'What's this?' May asked. 'Is it your birthday?'

'No, I ruined yours the day I met you so I decided to make it up to you.'

May felt a swarm of butterflies in her belly. 'How did you know?'

'You showed me your licence while I was pouting on the bus bench. And it was Valentine's Day, so that kind of makes it easy to remember.'

May stared at the candle in disbelief. The wax was dripping on to the ice cream.

'Sorry, that sounded a little weird,' Stephen said. 'It wasn't like I meant to memorise your licence. My memory kind of works that way. I saw it and it just stuck. I didn't mean—'

'You know what, Dr Knox, I have an idea.' She was smiling, trying not to shed a tear over how moved she was by his gesture.

'What's that?' Stephen asked nervously.

'When I blow out this candle, let's forget about everything that's ever happened between us before this moment. I want this to be the beginning.'

This time May leaned across the table and kissed Stephen, long enough to elicit wolf-whistles from the bar. Neither of them cared. It would have lasted longer if the candle flame had not nearly set her top on fire, sending them both into fits of laughter. Their departure from the bar was a blur as he paid quickly and called a cab. They couldn't keep their hands off each other in the car, or on the steps of her apartment building, or in her flat. The thought that she might ask him how he felt about all of it before she ripped off his clothes crossed her mind, but she quickly forgot that, because she was already too busy ripping off both of their clothes. There was never any awkward fumbling, or self-consciousness, or hesitancy, only an unyielding drive to satiate the powerful desire they were unaware they had for each other. And, once they were lying there in the dark, too exhausted to go on, May knew she was in trouble.

25

'How long ago did you receive transmission?' May shouted, out of breath.

She was sprinting to the bridge, her buzz having quickly turned into a raging hangover. She would have to find time to throw up later. NASA had replied to their SOS signal and confirmed that telemetry had been restored, giving them control of the ship. On the bridge, May punched up their message on the screen. She beheld it in all its glory, tears of joy streaming down her face. They had also included a pre-recorded video, as they were not yet in range for real-time communication.

'Oh, my God, Eve,' she shouted. 'This is amazing.'

'I agree, and I'm also very relieved.'

'Relieved? I'm bloody ecstatic. They caught us. We were falling and they reached right out and ... I'm so happy I don't know what to do with myself.'

'How about sending the reply message they requested, confirming your survival and providing more information about the status of the crew?'

'Right. Yes. Exactly right. That's what I'll do.'

May considered sending a video message, but thought better of it in light of her dismal condition. *Hello, Mission Control, drunk-ass Commander Knox here. Doing well except everyone but me is dead and your multi-billion-dollar ship is on the verge of becoming scrap. Oh, and I'm suffering from memory loss because I awoke from a coma a few days ago after nearly dying from a mystery illness. Can't even remember telling my husband to fuck off just before launch. Anyhoo, awesome to be back in touch with you guys. Really looking forward to hearing about your miracle rescue scenario. Oh, and cheers for the Christmas music!*

Instead she recorded a very short time-stamped voice message and promised to send a longer report, with visuals, once she and Eve were back on course.

'Let's watch the video message they sent, Eve.'

'Loading that now.'

May waited nervously as the observation window switched to video screen and NASA's pre-recorded message faded up. Stephen appeared first, standing in the Ground Control Centre in Houston. May's heart took off running. He looked good, maybe a little thin and sleep-deprived, but still her Stephen. She walked closer to the screen.

'Hi, handsome. You're a sight for the sorest of eyes,' May said, touching his face.

'Hello, May,' he said, smiling.

He was trying to remain emotionally composed. May reckoned he'd been asked to be the one to speak to her first in the transmission in order to boost her morale. *Good choice.*

'I'm . . . we're all so excited to know you are able to receive this transmission. As you can imagine, we've been pretty worried here. When Mission Control received your SOS, word has it some of the most buttoned-up, ice-water-in-the-veins veterans actually jumped for joy. We all did, in our own way . . . But enough chitchat. Time to get down to the very serious business

139

of getting you all home. On that note, I'm going to turn you over to Flight and your old pal Glenn Chambers. He's going to tell you about the rescue scheme he's been cooking up and put you to work. Take care and we'll talk soon.'

The video cut to Mission Control on Wright Station and Glenn standing front and centre, the team standing proudly behind him, waving. Glenn was indeed a dear friend. With his huge, unkempt grey eyebrows that looked like the horns on an owl, and permanently attached, utterly archaic reading glasses, he looked and behaved like your favourite grandad – if your grandad was a foul-mouthed Texan who rode Harleys and hunted wild boar.

'Hey, kid. Welcome to Shit Creek. Don't you worry, we're gonna give you a paddle, and it won't be made out of a turd.'

He laughed so hard, the chewing tobacco in his lower lip nearly flew out.

'Sorry, hon. You know I'm just a dirty old redneck. Listen, I got all the nerds hopped up on caffeine and the fear of God, working round the clock, and we came up with a pretty nifty rescue plan. I told 'em if they hadn't built you that goddamned lemon of a ship in the first place we wouldn't be talking rescue, but they didn't think that was too funny. Especially Raj. Man, that pissed him off. He looked like a muppet with road rage.'

May had a good, much-needed laugh. Glenn was such a crusty old bastard, a pure flyboy who didn't trust anything that hadn't been airborne longer than him. He would have got on famously with her mother.

'So, let's skip the foreplay and get right to it, shall we?'

An astral map displayed the position of the *Hawking II* in relation to Europa, Mars, and Earth.

'Your drift was pretty damned inconvenient. Tell the truth we're all amazed you went that far off course in such a short period of time. But don't worry, we can get her back on track as soon as the engines decide to play nice – especially since you made that trajectory fix. Everyone here was scratching their heads and I just told them, listen, geeks, you're dealing with a real pilot. You think we'd trust our lives with just your tech, you got shit for brains. Case in point.'

A photo-realistic ship schematic replaced the map image. The problem areas – engines and reactor – were highlighted red.

'Propulsion issues you're having are a reactor issue and not coming from the engines themselves. For some reason, the reactor has an overload causing it to switch in and out of safe mode, to avoid – well, blowing your skinny ass to kingdom come.'

'Well, that's very considerate,' May laughed.

'Fusion nerds are working on figuring out the reactor right now,' Glenn continued. 'The great San Francisco earthquake you've been feeling is the engines being off sync. Here's a visual.'

A three-dimensional image of the reactor and its connections to the engines appeared. As Glenn spoke, areas he was talking about would highlight.

'One engine gets power and wants to fire up. Other one doesn't get enough. First one shuts down, sending an overdose of power to the second one. Then it shuts down. Then the reactor has nowhere to send all that power, so that shuts down. Vicious circle. Sounds a lot like my third divorce. So, we've sent your AI a flight program that encourages those selfish bastards to share, creating equal power distribution under constant flux. Kind of like the way your brain distributes weight evenly to your legs to keep you from falling on your pretty face after you've been hitting that flask of yours one too many times.'

'You know me all too well, Glenn. And now for the bad news,' May muttered cynically.

'Unfortunately,' Glenn said, 'all of that means we've had to decrease the amount of power going from the reactor to the engines, 'cause we don't want to start the sync nonsense again.

As you may have seen, that kind of thing will pretty much tear your ship in half eventually. Your velocity has dropped to about a quarter capacity, but this is a necessary evil till we fix the reactor. Just means you'll actually have to keep on being a pilot for a while, which I know you don't mind 'cause you probably want to prove you didn't just get that job 'cause you're a chick.'

'Hillbilly dinosaur,' May said, smiling.

'I heard that,' Glenn said, having anticipated a return insult. 'Oh, and you get to play engineer too. I know how much you love that. We'll record the whole reactor fix for you and upload the sequence to your command deck as soon as the geeks figure out a way for you to do it without ... you guessed it, blowing your skinny ass to kingdom come.'

'You have no idea how skinny,' May joked self-consciously.

'Good news is, once we get you back to full velocity, here's that nifty little rescue scheme we got cooking. Let's go to the map again.'

The video cut back to the astral map.

'And now for the weather report. We're not gonna risk trying to bring you back here to the station. Mars orbit is a lot closer and, at the moment, your trajectory is tits-on with its alignment. However, there's this whole thing called orbital motion. You may have heard about it. Planets moving around the sun and all. Unless you're a Flat Earth dipshit, but our nav systems don't work in a fucking fantasy world. In the real world, we're gonna get you on a trajectory to rendezvous with our rescue vehicle in Mars orbit. Keep in mind we're gonna be making a lot of adjustments between now and then, but we'll telemeter the hell out of it and keep us in lockstep. If need be, we can also pull some speed from Mars gravity to give you a little bump and take some strain off propulsion.

'Problem is, our alignment with Mars ain't as hot shit as yours. And the bureaucrats are gonna bind and gag us with

142

red tape while they wait for their perfect little launch window. Add to that we're scrambling our first available vehicle, which appears to be a bit of a dinosaur. But don't let its advanced age fool you. Might not be as fast as the younger bucks, but it's still got plenty of thrust, wink wink. Right now, we got a date in a little over nine weeks, pushing nine and a half. I know that's about three weeks short of what it took you to get to friggin' Jupiter orbit, but this is what we're working with. We've already adjusted your velocity accordingly.'

May winced as she thought about all the 'what-ifs' inherent in NASA's proposed rescue scenario. Anticipating this, Glenn continued.

'I know you're probably sceptical about this and I don't blame you. Lots of weak links in this chain. But Mars is a hell of a lot bigger target than Wright Station and I'm sure you're not interested in flying that thing any longer than you have to.'

'I couldn't agree more.' May grimaced.

'Of course, any light you can shed on the situation will help us dial this in. Drop us a line, let us get a look at you, and you can give us the low-down. Your AI mentioned multiple casualties, so any information on that is top priority.' He took on a more sombre tone. 'Sorry you're having to deal with all that . . . I suppose I'll give you back to your no-good husband, even though we both know I'm a hell of a lot sexier than him. Take care, you dirty redcoat. We'll get through this. We always do.'

The video cut back to Stephen. His face was a mask of professionalism. She could almost hear Robert Warren coaching him. *Nothing too personal. We don't want her to get her hopes up. She needs to stay focused, objective.* Fuck him. Seeing Stephen did get her hopes up, which she desperately needed. But it also made her feel homesick and lonely. The NASA shrinks always told her there was no place lonelier than the void of space. The human mind was simply not designed to fathom the infinite expanse of the universe, and the cold, utter silence of the vacuum. The further you got from the sun, the greater the longing to return. It could drive someone mad. Seeing her husband only added to that. She would have done anything to be in the same room as him, to really touch his cheek, smell his awful coffee breath, feel his fingers on the back of her neck. She wanted to scream.

'May, I . . . we all love you and I miss you. Everyone sends their best. I'm not supposed to say this, but try not to worry. Everyone is working so hard. I'm here at Ground Control every day, along with Raj. We're going to do everything we can to help get you home. I am . . .'

He paused, gathering courage.

'I'm here. For you. We have your back. Know that. Okay? And please reply as soon as you can. Take care.'

The screen switched back to the observation window. Stephen's after-image remained there among the stars, still fresh in May's mind. With it, more fragments from the past flashed in and out. She was determined to do whatever it took to stitch them together, and make sense of everything that didn't.

26

May and Stephen married outside her home town of Bournemouth, on the English south coast. The small affair, consisting of a dozen or so relatives and friends, took place at May's grandparents' country estate. Their three-storey Georgian home, built in the late 1700s in light tan stone, was perched on a hill overlooking a dozen acres of wooded gardens and pasture, dotted with ponds and divided by a stream. They held the ceremony near an old stone bridge May had loved as a child. The ivy covering its ancient stones had been woven with multicoloured garlands of rose mallows, bird's eye gilias, everlasts, Cape daisies and pansies.

May wore her mother's simple, white-beaded wedding dress and held a bouquet of freshly cut flowers from the garden. Eve had lost the battle to get May to wear a veil, but was victorious in seeing to it that Stephen wore a light grey morning suit with a black woven silk tie and cerulean forget-me-not lapel boutonnière. May had laughed when Stephen refused to wear the accompanying top hat, saying he wasn't willing to get married 'looking like the Monopoly guy'. Raj stood between them in

145

a smart black suit and tie of May's choosing – having won the job of officiant after weeks of passionately lobbying and agreeing that if he did or said anything off-colour in front of her mother, May would crucify him on the carriage house trellis.

Eve was holding court in the front row of folding chairs with Auntie Lynn, her sister, and Uncle Bertram, her brother-in-law. They'd both been very close to May in childhood, Auntie Lynn often caring for her when Mum had to fly after Dad had passed away. Stephen's parents had died when he was a child, but he claimed Raj was more than enough 'family' for him to manage.

As Raj enthusiastically mastered the ceremony, mercifully sticking to the script, Stephen and May both cried, but as a result of stifling laughter. For May, it was surreal. She'd never expected to even sleep with someone like Stephen, let alone cross her mother's marriage picket line and make him her husband. But, although it was odd, as both would admit for the same reasons, everything about it felt right. He embraced her, truly for better or for worse (the poor bastard) and she did the same. For both, that was the definition of love. It was not about sacrifice, or 'work', as people often said. That was a non-starter for them. Stephen said that there was no point being married if you weren't enhancing each other's lives in some way, making their experience better than it would be if they were alone. May agreed, and added her philosophy that remaining fiercely independent was just as important as their bond as a couple. If they weren't happy and fulfilled as individuals, they would be resentful, compromising bickertons like pretty much every other married couple on the planet. This, in a nutshell, was the content of the ceremony Raj was reciting, and Stephen and May had no reservations about committing to it.

The only thing that made them nervous was thinking about the time they would be apart, during the mission. It wasn't going to be forever, but the inherent risks of the voyage weighed on May more than she let on. In fact, that was the one thing she didn't like about really being in love with someone. All her life, she'd never thought much about the dangers of her work, especially when it came to her self-preservation. She had Eve to thank for that . . . for better or for worse. But, ever since she'd fallen for Stephen, she thought about her own mortality, and his, more often than ever before. For the first time, she understood why her mother had worked so hard to divert her from relationships. Love was possessive and, if you weren't careful, it could consume you.

Looking at Eve, May wondered how she had felt when she'd met her father. Knowing how fiercely she had fought for her own career, she thought he must have bewitched her in some way, convincing her to marry and to have a child. Was his loss the real reason Eve had tried to steer May down a different path? She hadn't thought of that until this moment, but it deserved her credence. In the past few years, she'd seen her mother in decline, slowly succumbing to a degenerative brain disease that could only be managed with medication, not cured. It showed itself with the tremors in Eve's hands that she was trying to conceal under her own bouquet. Vulnerability was weakness, in Eve's mind. She rarely spoke of her illness, so May was not even sure how much it had progressed. That weighed on her too. Being so far away for so long, thinking about her mother dying and not being able to make it to her side was her worst nightmare. *Every moment from this point on is more important than the last.*

'You may kiss the bride.'

Stephen leaned in and touched the back of May's neck gently with his hand, something she loved for him to do, and kissed her. It was an incredible kiss, one that May had not expected; he had been advised to keep it short and sweet for the British attendees' low tolerance of public displays of affection. Along with the missing top hat, the kiss was Stephen's subtle act of rebellion, a small measure of revenge for Eve, while being a large dose of aphrodisiac for May. 'You're in trouble now,' she whispered in his ear before they walked down the stone-lined path under a shower of flower petals.

The reception was back at the house, in the drawing room May had been forbidden to enter but had often snuck into as a child. It had tall, narrow windows with heavy tapestry drapes that had gone threadbare over the years. Guests danced on the wide, tongue-in-groove wood floors, laden with decades of lacquer. She'd spent hours in there playing and fantasising about being a princess, but mostly ending up playing the part of the wicked queen.

After dining in the fading summer light, *digestifs* and smokes were had outside, under the stars. To her horror, May saw that Eve had cornered Stephen near the bar, no doubt to impress upon him her many pearls of wisdom, whether he liked it or not. May drifted in to rescue him, but Stephen smiled in a way that assured her he could handle it. He'd never kowtowed to Eve, even knowing how little she liked him, which was one of the reasons she learned to like him so quickly.

'You were married before?' her mother was asking bluntly, sipping her wine with the hand that had the slight tremor.

'Yes. I've been divorced for seven years,' Stephen said, slightly uncomfortable.

'I never knew that,' she accused.

'You never asked, Eve. This might be the most we've ever spoken,' he said, smiling.

'What happened?' she said, deflecting.

May rolled her eyes to the point of straining.

'We met when we were young and, over the years, as we matured, the relationship changed and we decided we were better off just being friends.'

May smiled at the white lie.

'That's a very American answer. Now give me the British answer, please.'

Stephen took a moment to pretend he was formulating a well-crafted reply. 'All right. She hated everything about my work, which has been my life's passion since I was a boy. She was suffocating, condescending, and, despite being pretty on the outside, she was a hideous troll on the inside.'

'That's more of a French answer, but I'll take it,' Eve said, smiling and patting his hand. 'And now you love my Maryam.'

'More than anything. I feel incredibly lucky to have found her.'

'That's because you *are* incredibly lucky. She may be my daughter, but she is also one of the most exceptional people I've ever had the privilege of knowing.'

'Mother!' May finally protested.

'I feel the same way,' Stephen affirmed.

'What about children? What are your views?'

'We've talked about a rent-to-buy plan.'

May laughed. Eve stifled a grin. 'Don't be cheeky with me, son. Unless you want your ears boxed.'

'Sorry. The only thing I have to say on the subject of children is that I never considered having them until I met your daughter.'

'That's all fine and dandy, but let's keep that particular horse in the stall till she returns from the mission, eh? Wouldn't want to erase her name from the history books before the pen even hits the page, now would we?'

'Heavens, no,' Stephen said with a grimace.

'Mum! What's got into you?'

'May, it's okay,' Stephen said, trying to help. 'Let's not—'

'Hush now,' Eve warned. 'The women are talking. Speak your mind, girly.' Eve pinched May's cheek and annihilated her make-up.

'This is my wedding. Tonight you will do what I want. You will smile, and laugh, and dote on me. You'll tell me how beautiful I am and how handsome he is. Everything you eat will be perfectly prepared and delicious, bordering on ambrosial. And, most of all, you will speak of only pleasant things that lighten the mood. Is that crystal clear, Mother?'

'I could use a drink,' Eve said pointedly to Stephen.

'Allow me,' he said, eager to escape.

'Make mine a tranquilliser dart,' May said.

'Coming right up,' Stephen said, jogging away so fast he tripped on a stone garden rabbit and nearly landed on the buffet table.

Eve saw the fire in May's eyes and softened, too fatigued to fight. May helped her to a chair and they sat for a moment in silence. Eve tried again to conceal her tremor, but in vain.

'Mum, what have the doctors said about—'

'You do look beautiful,' Eve said, tears welling. She took May's hand and May was overcome with emotion. 'I just hope one day you'll have the privilege of sitting at your own child's wedding and saying the same thing.'

27

'If everyone could get settled, I'd like for us to view the transmission from the *Hawking II*, which arrived a little over an hour ago. I have not viewed it yet, so please prepare yourselves accordingly.'

At the Ground Control Centre in Houston, Robert Warren had assembled the team, along with Stephen and Raj, to watch May's video transmission on one of the large screens. On the adjacent screen, the Mission Control team at Wright Station stood with Glenn Chambers, also ready to view. Stephen gritted his teeth until his jaw ached. The incredible tension of not knowing what to expect was murderous, and he could feel it radiating off everyone in both control centres. For him, there was the added stress of unpredictable emotion. Since Stephen had opened up that part of himself, as part of the penance he felt he needed to pay, there was no telling when it would attack and overpower him. It didn't help at all that he felt eyes all over him, studying, wondering if he would be able to keep it together.

'Roll it, please,' Robert said.

The screen was black for a few seconds, building the suspense to a boiling point, then May appeared, standing on the bridge.

'Hello, friends,' she began, attempting to smile.

Stephen felt his breath being sucked out of him as a wave of silent panic surged through him and everyone else. May was emaciated and sickly-looking. Her head was shaved to stubble, skin on her face drawn, eyes red-rimmed. She had the appearance of someone suffering through the last stages of a terminal disease. Raj patted him on the shoulder, trying to be reassuring, but he had the same look of fear. Stephen could feel the eyes on him again, both rooms scouring him for a reaction. He focused on May, blocking out the rest of the world, and held on for dear life. But that wasn't much of a comfort. What had happened to her? Stephen had seen images from the very recent Europa landing. In that time, she had gone from normal, healthy Maryam to a ghost of herself, barely recognisable if he saw her on the street.

'This is the best I can do for a video transmission right now. I had to repurpose one of the EVA cameras to shoot this. Please forgive the low quality. I know you're all anxious to hear my report, so I'll skip the pleasantries and dive right in. I'm going to run a series of video clips addressing all major issues. Stand by please.'

The screen went black again, prompting an angry beehive of nervous murmuring amongst both control teams. The screen glitched and May's footage started playing. First stop was the trashed infirmary, which elicited a collective gasp.

'Here we are in the infirmary. This is where it all started for me. And it's the reason I look like this. On Christmas Day, I woke up, having been intubated in a critical care module. Actually, the reason I woke up was because the module basically spat me out. Not sure why, but I'm glad it did. Feeding tube and IVs had run dry, so I would have died of dehydration or starved if it hadn't revived me.'

She filmed the intensive care pod she'd crawled out of on Christmas Day.

'Yay, Merry Christmas to me.'

Cautious laughter broke some of the tension. Stephen was happy to hear May's sense of humour was still intact.

'According to the *partial* medical records I am able to access, I had some kind of unidentifiable illness and was put in a medically induced coma to stabilise me, presumably while the med team tried to figure out how to diagnose and treat it. I have no recollection of that event. In fact, my memories of the illness itself are spotty at best. The last thing I remember is being taken to the infirmary after I had some kind of episode on the bridge. I think I might have even stopped breathing or gone into cardiac arrest. Next thing I remember is waking up in here. AI was thinking I might be suffering from retrograde amnesia – can't remember events closest to my illness, but long-term memories are intact, mostly anyway.

'As you would expect, I attempted to piece together what happened by reviewing the ship logs, but it appears all data collection ceased around the time I became ill. Presumably others would have been ill as well; an aggressive pathogen would have spread very quickly. But I don't know because there is nothing in the infirmary logs or ship logs in general. AI has done a thorough search. It's just not there. Oh, and here's a martini for your olive: the MADS recorder is gone. Housing was empty, connection wires frayed, bolts blown. But that could have jettisoned if the mechanism sensed the ship was in fatal decline.

'I know you're all bewildered right now and I can assure you, I share that sentiment. I am hoping Mission Control received its redundant packet transmission prior to data loss so we can attempt to make some sense of this. Please tell me you guys know something.'

Stephen's sadness and worry turned to rage. What May was

describing was inconceivable, not even believable as a joke. He looked at Raj. The poor guy's jaw was hanging open. God only knew what part of his slaughtered 'baby' he was ruminating on. If the scenario was absurd to Stephen, it was earth-shattering to the man who had designed the vessel. Now it wasn't just Stephen the eyes were on any more. They were fixed on Raj, questioning everything about his vessel. Some old guard team members on Wright and in Houston were boring a hole in Raj's skull with their stares.

But that didn't make sense to Stephen. What May was describing couldn't possibly be related to design flaws. The vessel had been tested countless times in the moon's orbit. Flaws would have been found then, especially those capable of yielding this level of destruction. What had happened to the *Hawking II* had been one thing. *Why* it happened was another altogether. NASA would prioritise solving the problem, but that wasn't going to be enough. If they didn't identify the source, it could easily happen again.

The scene then cut to a walkthrough of the corridors. The emptiness was a haunting antithesis to the vibrant ship filled with passengers and crew the world had seen in the many historic video dispatches sent home during the voyage.

'I searched all seven decks and found no survivors or even any signs of life.'

The scene switched again, this time to the landing vehicle airlock. May was wearing an EVA suit.

'The last place I looked was the landing vehicle hangar, which, for reasons unknown to myself and the AI, lost all atmosphere and gravity while I was asleep.'

She took a deep breath, trying to keep it together and prepare herself.

'I am ... it's hard to put into words what you are about to see. This is where I found what appears to be the majority of the passengers and crew . . . deceased. Please prepare yourselves, as what I'm going to show you was very traumatic for me. Our friends and colleagues . . . I'm so very sorry.'

She opened the airlock and floated into the hangar.

'Again, please prepare yourselves. Switch on pod landing lights please,' May said.

The landing lights from the pods came on, flooding the hangar with bright, ghostly light, revealing the floating corpses. Another collective gasp rippled through both teams and people stared in horror, their faces frozen into grimaces similar to the dead. It was surreal, reminding Stephen of World War II footage showing an underwater view of hundreds of dead sailors whose battleship had just been destroyed by a German bomber. They had the same look of morbid shock.

'I have not yet identified all casualties,' May said, her voice shaking, 'but I will do that and send bio codes as soon as possible. As I've looked all over the rest of the vessel, I am assuming . . . the worst. Please send me interment protocols, as I've never had to follow them until now. And I want to make sure I do it right. Lights off.'

The landing lights extinguished and the scene switched back to May on the bridge. She looked a little better than before, as if she'd taken some time to recover from being in the landing vehicle hangar. Stephen knew she would want to convey the impression that she was in control, remaining as objective as possible, and fully competent. He felt for her, just as he had felt for Raj. Fingers were just born to point, and some people lived for this kind of scenario.

'You should also have video and data from the engine room and reactor deck. I hope I've provided enough detail for my pal Glenn and our excellent engineers to confirm their repair and rescue plan. If not, please don't hesitate to request additional footage.'

She paused again, forcing herself to remain unemotional, professional.

'I want to tell all of you how ... sorry I am that this happened during my command. I wish I had been in a position to stop it ... but I was not. The sorrow I am feeling for my crew, Stephen's team, and all of their families, is ... can't be put into words. But it has not affected my resolve. I am going to do everything in my power to get them home for a proper burial, and return this vessel, along with all that we acquired on Europa, to serve their memories. They were all so committed to this project, and I know they would want their work to live on. I will guard it, and them, with my life. And please don't worry about me. I feel a lot better than I look, and I'm getting stronger every day. I miss all of you and look forward to seeing you very soon. Thank you.'

28

Stephen was in his private office at Johnson Space Center at 5 a.m. He was rounding out a solid eighteen hours of poring over every line of data his research team had sent back in the last few days of the return voyage, just prior to the blackout. None of it was directly related to the ship operations, the area of most critical data loss. But the researchers Stephen tended to hire were more thorough than most. They often over-observed environments as potential factors of influence. Maybe they had caught something? It was worth a shot, in lieu of having anything else to go on.

'This is a complex problem,' he said to Raj, 'that requires a strong hypothesis to solve it. Would you agree?'

'Yes, but what is your hypothesis?'

'That's *your* job. I don't have the expertise to even begin to come up with one. But you do. You designed the ship, you're the creator. The other engineers might understand your baby, but never like her real dad.'

'I like the sound of that. I wish they felt the same way.'

'Don't worry about that. It's probably better you're not with them, letting them limit your thinking. You know as much as they do. Do you have all the ship ops data just prior to the blackout?'

'Hell, yeah. Wasn't easy to get, but I got it.'

Stephen paused. 'Did you say something to piss Robert off? Aside from the obvious things?'

'You know how they get. Like some school clique. I don't have some bullshit line in my title, so I'm not a rescue mission expert. You say tomato, man.'

'At least they're not treating you like the red-headed step-child,' Stephen complained, 'when it's your wife up there.'

'True,' Raj said, thinking. 'Here's what I'm going to do,' he said, checking his watch. 'I'm going to play golf.'

'Ha ha,' Stephen said.

'What's funny?'

'Raj, I'm busting my ass here, man. I really need your help. May needs your help. Better yet, your goddamned precious ship—'

'Who said I wasn't helping?'

'Golf?'

'You think your way,' he said, scowling at Stephen's mess, 'and I'll think mine. Back tonight. I'll bring the beer.'

Raj left and Stephen spent the next several hours scrolling through hours of video footage his team had shot on the voyage, in the labs, gathering samples during the Europa expedition, processing those, and operating Stephen's NanoSphere tech. He hadn't seen that last bit of footage since they streamed it, and not at such a high resolution.

After deploying the base stations on the ice shelf, they had powered them up with special battery packs that used similar solar absorption to recharge themselves. The base stations then deployed their swarms of nano-machines, creating a shimmering, bluish-silver cloud around five hundred metres high and two hundred metres across. They had positioned it on the moon to align deployment with sun exposure. Europa orbited Jupiter every 3.5 Earth days, and the same hemisphere always faced the gas giant, so they had timed the whole mission to land on the sunny side of Europa when its orbital path made for the shortest journey. Having constant sun exposure made it easier for Stephen's team, as testing conditions remained the same.

When they had fired up the system, it was a beautiful sight to behold. The nano-machines moved perfectly in sync, positioning themselves in a billowing cloud-like shape that formed itself to maximise solar radiation on its outer surface. Within a few hours, it had stored a massive amount of heat and the engineers had focused it, like focusing sunlight through a huge magnifying glass, on a ten-metre area on the ice shelf. It was also a part of the ice that had been measured to be thinner owing to tectonic movement.

The concentrated heat was so intense, the massive steam plumes it created made the whole team nervous. Previous ice samples had never shown large concentrations of explosive chemicals, but one didn't know with such a large surface. After getting through the top layer, things settled down. Finally, with less than twenty hours left in the seven-day expedition, the heat penetrated the breadth of the ice. A one-metre opening, the size of a manhole cover, gave them their first view of Europa's ocean. *Life*, Stephen had thought immediately. *Pure and simple, we have discovered a new source of life.*

'Life,' he said, echoing himself in the video. 'What sort of life?'

He watched the triumphant research teams drawing water from the ocean, gathering gallons upon gallons of samples. Then he called Raj.

'How's the golf?'

'I suck. What's up?'

'When I reviewed the daily lab reports, I never found any

quarantine breaches. Do you remember seeing anything like that from flight or engineering?'

'No. In fact, your people were commended for being incredibly anal about all that, if memory serves.'

'It does. That's what I remember too. I'll recheck my reports, but I think we would both have flagged something that important.'

'Uh, yeah,' Raj said. 'Ocean water. I don't even swim in the gulf if I have a friggin' hangnail any more. Too many bacteria, viruses, parasites.'

'Viruses,' Stephen said. 'I think I might have a hypothesis about May's illness.'

'But quarantine was tight.'

'Of course. But, we're dealing with human beings here. All we would need is the smallest error, the most insignificant mistake. If there are viruses under that ice, lying dormant in those conditions for a hundred million years . . . '

'An alien virus . . . First sign of extra-terrestrial life and it's some kind of super-flu. Not very comic book, is it?'

'Right, that's what I was going to say. Go back to your golf. I need you to think about the possibility of a viral outbreak on board. How would it go down? Who would be privy to it? Would the information be shared or not? What are the protocols? What are—'

'Fine. It's my turn to drive and these old dudes are pissed.' Raj hung up.

Stephen reckoned NASA was already chasing down this theory, as much as it might pertain to the rescue mission. He thought about how he was being gently pushed out. More importantly, he thought about that happening to Raj. This wasn't the NASA Stephen knew. They were an all-hands type of organisation. This was more a Robert Warren thing. His vanity ruled everything, including information. If he found

160

something 'unfavourable', something that could embarrass him in the press, he would suppress it. No doubt about it. Most of his dealings with Stephen had been that way, with Robert as the gatekeeper. And, if he was ever left out of a loop, God help you. Heads rolled for less.

The notion that the virus could have travelled from Earth crossed Stephen's mind, but what known pathogen could have such a devastating effect? And then there were the dead people in the landing vehicle hangar. He called Raj again.

'What? Are you calling about the dead people?'

'How did you know?'

'How can either of us be thinking about anything else?' Raj said. 'The answer is no, they could not have gotten anywhere with those vehicles. They were orbital landers, not even as long-range as some of the moon shuttles.'

'Shit.'

'Yeah, I know, man. That one is baking the hell out of my head. I'm nine-putting every hole, so leave me alone.'

Stephen hung up again and pounded it out on his recorder.

'Data blackout occurs around the time a potential virus break-out might have occurred. Going by Earth standards, thirty-six hours is a conservative incubation time. After the first infected, others follow due to latent presentation, then you have a crisis. On top of that, you're dealing with an unknown pathogen. *How long to figure out its behaviour?* Too long, in an enclosed germ factory. More infections, including the Commander, lots of civilian researchers, more panic, maybe even chaos, virus spreads. But . . . there's no data showing any of that. Possible there was a malfunction that caused that just before the problem with the virus? Not likely, but that's one for Raj. Possible someone could suppress the data after the fact? Of course. No data is ever safe. Ever. Who would want to do that? Who the hell knows? Could AI be involved? AI would probably have to be involved. Jesus.'

The hypothesis was coming together, and the more Stephen shredded through the deductions, the more things pointed to a virus from an ocean sample – ice samples never made anyone sick before – jumps quarantine somehow, ravages the ship somehow, maybe causes mass panic, then you have a worst-case scenario occurring in the most dangerous environment known to humanity. Should he run this by Robert? Not yet. Robert was too volatile and it might backfire.

'Dr Knox, I have Director Warren on the sat com,' the AI said.

Stephen nearly fell out of his chair.

'Dr Knox?'

'Put him through, please.'

Robert Warren appeared on Stephen's screen.

'Hello, Stephen.'

'Robert.'

'I wanted to let you know that May sent another transmission right after the one we just reviewed,' Robert began. 'She asked that only you watch it, saying it was about your divorce filing. I respect your privacy and the laws protecting it, but, considering the nature of this situation, I trust you will let me know if there is anything in the content of that message that could affect this mission.'

'Absolutely, Robert. May would never withhold information from the team, though. You know that.'

Robert shook his head impatiently. 'I do not have the luxury of assuming anything or standing on ceremony. Obviously, this situation is being closely scrutinised and great pressure is being placed on me to bring it to a swift resolution. Now, more than ever, we need to work tightly as a team.'

'I understand and totally agree.'

'Thank you. I'm sending you the message now.'

Robert signed off.

Obviously, this situation is being closely scrutinised and great pressure is being placed on me … Assuming Stephen's theory had weight, Robert had just reminded him that a potential PR nightmare was actually a fate worse than death. Add to that the constant, and growing, fear that privatised space exploration was poised to make NASA obsolete. Stephen had come within a whisper of giving the tech to Ian Albright and his company. That had run in the press cycle for weeks. And put the cherry on top: the ultra-conservative half of Congress that had opposed the mission in the first place, losing their minds when NASA took it on and financed it all with taxpayer's money. Committees were formed. Lobbyists worked the Hill while protesters doled out organised hate propaganda at Stephen's lectures. When Robert talked about pressure and swift resolutions, was he talking about anything specific? What if he already knew what Stephen was theorising? Paranoia washed over him. He'd been dictating in his office. The timing of Robert's call was … odd.

'Breathe,' Stephen said. 'You're losing your objectivity. You want to help May, you're feeling desperate. You've never trusted Robert, but he's not a monster. He's just freaking out too. Got to breathe.'

Stephen's hubris had always been impatience. His research professors never stopped haranguing him about it. He was going to practise it here: own the data, build evidence, make it defensible, then bring it to Robert and the team. On the other hand, there was no reason to trust him anyway. That had got him in trouble before. He was going to help May whether anyone liked it or not, and the science would be the tip of that spear. He owed her that much.

29

'Hi, Stephen,' May began, 'I hope they're allowing you to see this alone. I felt like I needed to get a few things off my chest, just in case one of the eight million things that can kill me out here gets the upper hand.'

After receiving the personal video, Stephen had gone home to watch it. He had got his paranoid thoughts under control, but there was no reason to take unnecessary risks. Robert and his staff would be totally within their legal rights to have any of the mission offices under some form of electronic surveillance, and it had been May's wish for Stephen to view it alone. High clouds had rolled in and brought the grey, so seeing May's face on screen was a ray of light.

'I hope you're well. I'm doing all right, feeling better. Well, except for the constant fatigue, terrible mood swings, and my new-found picky eating habits. You'd think, as skinny as I am, I'd be shovelling the farm down my gullet, but a lot of the food just makes me want to barf. Probably to do with my brain issues. I was reading that memory pretty much controls everything about you, including your senses. Weird, right? Retrograde amnesia. Don't you think the word "amnesia" just makes this whole thing sound like a crap movie? Or like the old soap operas, right? *"Will Sylvia remember Victor is the man who tried to murder her when she's cured of her amnesia?"* May said in her best soap opera announcer voice, laughing.

Stephen laughed as well. He loved seeing her spirits up for a change.

'The good news is that my condition is improving. My AI, whom I've named Eve – after Mum because you wouldn't believe how alike they are – has been helping me with some therapeutic treatments, using cues and repetition and whatnot. It's such a weird thing. Makes more sense that you would have a hard time remembering things in the distant past, right? Would have been nice to knock out the old crap childhood, eh? Unfortunately, this is just the opposite. Worst bit is the most recent, when I got sick. Can't remember fuck all, except some scraps. Gets better going back in time, but not great. In fact – and Eve confirmed this – the last three to four months can be affected, sometimes pretty badly.'

She smiled nervously.

'I think you can see where I'm going with this.'

Stephen paused the recording. *She doesn't remember*, he thought. The past three to four months of their relationship had been horrible, culminating in their divorce and May departing for Europa with them no longer on speaking terms. He recalled again the look on May's face when the *Hawking II* pulled out of dock. Surrounded by celebration, she had been as stoic as if she were waiting in the doctor's office. And he had taken off his ring . . . He felt his finger reflexively, knowing it was no longer there, but remembering now that it was still in his desk drawer on Wright Station. He shook his head. *What a mess. But she doesn't remember.*

'Remember that comedian we saw who made that joke . . . he

said if he went to see his wife in the hospital, and she said she had amnesia and couldn't remember him, he would say, "Sorry, ma'am, wrong room," or something like that? I thought of that joke recently. Luckily we saw him more than six months ago! Funny, right?'

She was really struggling, fidgeting self-consciously, lowering her eyes.

'As I said, you can see where this is going. I – er – the AI, Eve, told me recently that we're getting divorced,' she said, trying to smile about it. 'And I have to be honest, I was absolutely shocked, to say the very least. But it makes sense. She said we filed just before I left, which I don't recall. And I'm assuming whatever brought us to that point happened within that dark hole of time that I only see in incredibly annoying, completely nonsensical fragments. There's this one, it's so weird: I'm standing in grass, dressed nicely I might add, and it's raining, but I don't have an umbrella. I'm just getting bloody soaked. On purpose! Any idea what that could be? Might be a dream. I have a lot of those. Never did much before. Eve told me to write them all down. Sometimes the brain, when it's relaxed in sleep, will give over a titbit or two, in its little way. Does any of this make sense to you?'

Stephen laughed, feeling a little envious of her. Prior to the time May was referring to, their relationship had been occasionally rocky but offset by some incredible high points. Maybe this was a blessing in disguise? He wasn't going to get his hopes up, but he had to admit it was a relief that she was not struggling with the same things he was.

'I hope so, because I'm not sure any of it makes sense to me. I'll tell you what I do know, and what I'm feeling right now, for what it's worth. The divorce thing – that doesn't feel right at all. From what I remember of us, we were the last people in the world I'd have ever thought would give up or quit. Secondly, I

166

have nothing to base this on, but the feeling in my gut is telling me *I* did something to bring our split about. That's also based on knowing what an awful pain I can be, stubborn and wilful, as Mum used to say. I know it takes two to tango, but I can't shake the childish pang of anxiety that I started it. It's easy for me to see myself taking my proverbial ball and going home, but not you. You were never like that . . . '

The tears came. For Stephen too. It was inevitable, this moment. The circumstances were bizarre, but that was par for the course in the Stephen and May saga. It was hard, not to be able to put her mind at ease, tell her all was forgotten and they could move on to whatever the future held. But he wasn't certain that would be the truth. He hated himself for it, but he was still deeply stung by their split. It had effectively killed the core of what he'd felt for her, and the pain was so deeply wound up in his insecurities, it was hard for him to think back on some of the things May could not, mercifully, remember.

But despite his profound ambivalence about his past relationship with May, seeing and hearing her in this way strengthened his desire to get her home. In the end, she had been there for him. All he wanted her to know was that he also cared for her, deeply in fact, and that had never wavered. It was the one thing that remained afloat in a sea of inconsistencies.

'Sorry,' she said, smiling and wiping her eyes. 'I don't mean to make this any harder for you, so I'm going to restrain myself for once. Such a blubbering fool these days . . . '

The *Hawking II* shuddered in the background and the lights around her flickered, throwing her in and out of darkness. When it passed, the fear on her face, and the way it made her shrink like an abused animal, tore his heart out.

'As you can see, NASA hasn't quite got the whole engine-sync thing sorted, but it's improving, thankfully. Everything is a lot better since we reconnected.'

She smiled warmly. Stephen could tell she wanted to say more, but was holding back.

'Going to sign off now. There's a tepid bowl of what I like to call "almost lasagne" and a cup of "not even close" tea waiting for me in the galley. Tell Raj that for such an amazing ship he could have hired a chef or at least a short order cook to consult on the food. If you ever feel like sending me a message back, I would love it. You don't have to talk about uncomfortable feelings. Even if it's to provide an update on popular culture or a review of local cuisine, it would be nice to hear from you, Stephen. Ciao for now.'

The screen went blank, leaving Stephen to endure its deafening silence. He had always thought of May as bulletproof, impervious to the rigours of her lethal profession. But, for the first time, he was genuinely afraid for her.

30

Stephen was observing some of his researchers undergoing astronaut training at NASA's Neutral Buoyancy Lab. A handful of them were going to be part of the landing party, so they were being trained to do their work in Europa's gravitational environment, which had only a fraction of the strength of Earth's gravity. Twelve metres deep, in the massive 62-by-32-metre pool, a mock surface expedition station had been built, based on the structure that would be transported to the surface via landing vehicle. Lumbering around in EVA suits, Stephen's researchers practised their sample collection and analysis, while his engineers worked on deploying the equipment required for NanoSphere deployment. Progress was slow going, and often comical, but they were gradually getting the hang of it.

Earlier that morning, Raj had asked him, for the umpteenth time, if he wanted to check out the simulator facility. He had not seen it yet, but Raj never shut up about how cool it was. Stephen had a free afternoon for once, so he decided to take him up on it. As he walked outside, passing excited tour groups melting in the hot sun, he laughed, thinking that the reason he finally wanted to see it, after putting it off for so long, was because May might be there. She had made an impression on him at the mission dinner, but he wasn't completely sure what it meant. Their exchange had been interesting, and funny, but admittedly very odd, even for Stephen's standards of eccentric behaviour.

Looking at a couple pushing a stroller with two screaming toddlers, the idea of romance seemed ridiculous to him. That was an area in which he had proven to be the worst kind of failure, Exhibit A being his first marriage, and he'd pretty much given up on it after the divorce. Not to mention the glaring fact that he and May were basically from different planets. Yet there he was, strolling with purpose across the Space Center campus, suddenly interested in the flight simulator. *You over-think everything, idiot,* he told himself. *Even if you are interested in seeing May, what difference does it make? You bend over back-wards to hang out with Raj, going bowling of all things, and never think twice about that.*

'Dude, finally!' Raj yelled behind him, 'I've been trying to get you in here for weeks. Why the sudden change of heart?'

'Why do you have to give me a heart attack?' Stephen said, deflecting. 'Jesus, you know better than that, you goon.'

'My bad. Anyway, glad you could come,' Raj said, slapping him on the back.

He took Stephen into the simulator control centre first. 'Cool, we're in luck, they're doing training,' he said.

May and her first officer, Jon Escher, were piloting the land-ing pod simulators. The simulator operator turned on the video and audio feed so Raj and Stephen could watch their flow. He also turned on their view. The rendering of the Europa environ-ment looked so real, Stephen felt as though he was there. The shimmering ice shelf, with its dark fissures in the dim sunlight, was ethereal and foreboding.

'Pretty cool, right?' Raj said, punching his arm.

'Shut up,' Stephen said, concentrating on the simulator screen, and May.

'Landing pod nine entering Titan atmosphere in T minus sixty seconds,' May said calmly. 'Watch your entry angle Jon.'

Stephen knew how important the landing vehicle training was, as they would be doing the manoeuvre several times while the *Hawking II* orbited Europa. The research crew would need to be ferried back and forth along with their equipment. Landing on Europa was going to be very tricky. They knew it had a very slight atmosphere, but they had no practical experience navigating it, and then there was the fact that they had to land on a shelf of ice, some of it potentially unstable.

'That guy Jon is a total douche,' Raj whispered to Stephen. 'Thinks he's God's gift.'

'Yep, vectoring right on the nose,' Jon said confidently.

'Adjust vessel attitude for more drag and potential wind shear,' May replied.

'I'm pretty flat—'

'Not flat enough, Jon.'

The simulator operator raised his eyebrows knowingly at Raj.

'Your boy's about to get served again,' Raj said to him, laughing.

'Yep,' the man replied.

The simulator loaded a high-pressure water vapour plume that shot nearly two hundred kilometres high. May quickly adjusted and, after a jackhammer ride through the atmosphere, she landed her vehicle softly on the planet's surface.

'Like flying a hang-glider in a hurricane,' Raj said to Stephen. 'She's all kinds of good.'

Jon, on the other hand, lost control of the vehicle, which nose-dived into a death spiral he did not have the power to pull out of, and crashed, killing everyone on board. Stephen shuddered. Those dead people could have been his researchers.

'Shit,' Jon said. He looked like a teenage boy who'd been caught smoking in the bathroom.

'To say the very least,' Stephen said angrily.

'Jon,' May said over the comm.

'I know. I know,' he said, attempting to placate her.

'You know what?' she asked, not buying it.

'I fucked it up, again.'

'Do you know your failure percentage?'

'No. But I'll get this dialled. I promise.'

'I know,' she said evenly, 'because if you don't, you'll be replaced. You've fallen well below the acceptable range. Simply telling me you'll improve isn't good enough any more. Flight is watching us closely. They read our performance reports every day. It's a matter of policy that you will be replaced if you aren't able to perform in the above-average range for the duration of training. That means you are fresh out of fuck-ups, cowboy. You copy?'

'Copy.'

Stephen could see Jon was still placating, waiting for her to get off his back. 'You're right, Raj. Total douche.'

'Jon, have you ever lost someone important to you? Someone who died?' May asked.

'My father.'

'When did he die?'

'Three years ago.'

'And when did it hit you that you were never, ever going to see him again?'

'Damn,' Raj said.

'Quiet,' Stephen snapped.

'What kind of fucking question is that?' Jon asked angrily.

'It's the kind of question I like to ask pilots who seem to have no regard for their own mortality, and that of others – pilots who believe they are invincible and can do no wrong. How many times do you think I've had to ask that question, Jon?'

'I don't know.'

'Four,' May said. 'Do you know what they said?'

'No.'

'The same thing you just said. Can you guess where they are now?'

'Dead?'

'That's right,' May said. 'I've had this conversation with four dead men. They didn't listen to my instruction either. Do you think you can be different from them, Jon?'

'Yes, I do.'

'Then start acting like it. Because you're not only going to be responsible for your life, but for the lives of many others. Imagine if what happened in the simulator happened on Europa ... if you killed yourself and other people on board. You could put the rest of us in danger, maybe even endanger the entire mission. Not to mention the fact that, like you, people back home would have to live with never seeing their loved ones again. They wouldn't even have anything to bury, because the force with which you hit that planet's surface would have left nothing recoverable. Do you understand what I'm saying?'

'Yeah,' he said, finally somewhat broken.

'Yes, ma'am,' she corrected.

'Yes, ma'am.'

'How about a coffee and we'll give it another go?'

'Sure, that sounds—' he started.

'I take mine with two creams and two sugars. Hurry back.'

'Served,' Raj said. 'She's amazing.'

I know, Stephen thought.

31

'Reactor at nearly eighty-two per cent capacity. Engines functioning normally. Congratulations, May. You have your ship back,' Eve said, playing a sound effect of a crowd going wild.

May sat on the bridge, breathing a sigh of relief as she surveyed the star field through her flight deck window. Somewhere out there was Mars, then home. Since sending her message to Stephen, she'd heard nothing in return. Of course, it was foolish to expect anything, especially under the circumstances. The fact that Robert Warren had allowed a personal message in the first place had been a miracle in itself. She could only imagine how difficult it must be for Stephen to stay in the mix, with NASA being in rescue mode. Nevertheless, it made her feel a little melancholy.

'Thank you, Eve,' she said, forcing a smile. 'I'm just going to kick back and let someone else do the driving for a change. Might even take myself out on a date. Go to a movie in our cinema module. Haven't even had a chance to enjoy that yet.'

'Actually, May,' Eve said, 'now that we're back on course,

NASA has assigned you a fairly long and detailed list of tasks, in order of priority.'

'Right. Shortest holiday ever. Dare I even ask what's first?'

'Full medical evaluation.'

'Terrible idea. Skip to the next?'

'I'm afraid not. It's a direct order from Flight. They want to run a battery of physical and psychiatric evaluations. I can assist you.'

'You just ran my blood, can't I send that?'

'No, they want new samples, with video verification.'

'Really? What do they think, I'm going to cheat?'

'That was the directive. Sorry, May.'

They don't trust me, she thought. Sole survivors never get fanfare, just questions and suspicions. She could only imagine the scenarios Robert Warren was entertaining. 'We need to know what we're dealing with,' he might say.

Oh, God, they definitely don't trust me.

'Eve, we haven't yet done a body count in the landing vehicle hangar. I need to do a bio code inventory and prepare the deceased for interment.'

'Your physical and psychological evaluation—'

'Can wait. As commander, my first priority is to my passengers and crew, and I need to finally account for all of them.'

To hell with them. They can wait, she thought as she suited up outside the landing hangar airlock. *Not them. Him. Robert. Prick. Glenn probably wants to break his jaw by now, prancing around the place like he knows anything about anything.*

'We need to get this hangar fixed pronto, Eve. I don't want to have to suit up and go into a meat locker every time I need to prep my vehicle for Mars.'

'Agreed. Mission Control is expecting to be able to do that as soon as they finish work on the reactor, with your assistance of course.'

'Of course. Can't wait to see the rest of the list.'

Back in the frozen darkness of the hangar, May floated for a beat, allowing herself to adjust to the abject terror the place inspired in her. And then there was the god-awful cold. May imagined it as icy black tendrils, long and thin, creeping along the edges of her suit, looking for an opening to get under her skin and into her bones. Better to keep moving.

'Landing lights.'

Eve switched on the landing vehicle lights. May gulped air and tried to calm her mind when the floating bodies appeared, some only a few feet from her.

'Right, everyone, roll call.'

Every crew member wore a uniform with a bio code chip embedded in the fabric over the right breast. The code in the chip contained everything in the owner's personnel data file. The camera in May's helmet had a code scanner. She swam to the nearest body and got down to the grim affair of counting bodies and photographing faces. It immediately brought back the trauma of what had happened when she'd first found them. She couldn't look at the ruined skin on their faces for too long or she might throw up again. And the fear was as invasive as the brutal cold. It bombarded her with irrational thoughts. May got through it by reminding herself that doing it was not only a service to the deceased, but also a reinforcement of her competence for NASA. She wanted them to be quite clear that she was capable of completing the mission with the professionalism and decorum required of her station.

Gallagher, Matthew. Payload commander. He'd been floating around the airlock door, minding his own business, bloated and dead. *Boring Matt. Dead Boring Matt.*

'What a mess, Eve,' May said as she continued on.

'A tragedy of massive proportions. Statistically untenable.'

'What's NASA saying about it? Are you hearing chatter?'

'Director Warren is trying to contain information so it does not go to the press.'

'You can call him Director Wanker now.'

'I'm assuming that's a nickname created by you?'

'And earned by him. Do they say anything about me?' May asked, not expecting an answer.

'They've asked me to monitor you closely.'

May was momentarily shocked by Eve's honesty.

'I'm not surprised. I suppose it makes sense under the circumstances.'

'Not to me,' Eve said. 'Suspicion is not based on fact, it is based on speculation. When I asked them why they wanted me to watch you, they did not have a sufficient reason. My only conclusion is that they are speculating. Which, admittedly, is speculation itself.'

May laughed at what sounded like light moral outrage from Eve.

'I appreciate your candour. And you're spot on. Human beings are compelled to add their personal prejudices and stories to everything. As a pilot, that's been trained out of me. So, you don't have to worry about *me* getting lost in needless speculation, at least not that often and definitely not out loud.'

'That's a relief.'

When May was finished, having scoured every inch of the pod hangar, she'd accounted for thirty-two people. Two people were unaccounted for: Jon Escher, May's pilot, and Gabi Dos Santos, her flight engineer. She went to the supply module to check the hypothermic casket stacks, a tall, grid-like structure that looked like a cross-section of a metallic wasp hive. It contained a pearlescent interment container for everyone on board.

'They're all empty and none are missing,' May said angrily. 'Could they have simply jettisoned the bodies of Jon and Gabi as part of quarantine?'

177

'There would have been no need for that. The hypothermic caskets saturate the body with ozone before freezing, killing all pathogens and parasitic organisms.'

'Great, so the bodies are on board somewhere, waiting to pop out of a bulkhead and scare the living daylights out of me.'

After a quick shower, May reported to the infirmary for NASA's annoyingly comprehensive panel of tests. She'd been through the physical so many times, it was routine. The only awful part of it was having to go through it with the ship's robotic flight surgeon unit. She had always hated the fact that it looked like a stubby phone box with a screen for a face. Under its smooth metal skin, which opened in front, usually without warning, were its 'guts' – tubes, wires, sensors, prods, and all manner of surgical implements. The whole thing smacked of design done by a team of anti-social geeks who clearly didn't care who or what poked around their bodies. To make things even worse, it had its own horrible geek-given 'acro-name', as May liked to call it: ROSA, Remote Onboard Surgery Assistant. It looked nothing like a Rosa, so May just called it Igor.

After Igor was done feeling her up with its weird robot appendages, Eve put her through the psychological evaluation. She had taken those before as well, many times, but never with the thought that the testers were actually trying to find something wrong. And she knew they were, because she had not taken such a comprehensive test since she had first started working with NASA. It took nearly three hours to complete, and covered every possible angle, from simple personality inventories, to behavioural and cognitive scales, to highly complex neuropsychological batteries.

May was just glad she'd had some time to get her wits together beforehand. She couldn't imagine having had to do this when she first woke up. Would have been a spectacular fiasco. They probably would have programmed Eve to take over completely.

Of course, that had crossed May's mind as she was doing the evaluation. They had telemetry now. No reason to fully trust May anyway if they saw fit. Footholds were easily adopted by an audience eager to explain the circumstances of failure. Robert was probably hungry for a scapegoat to satisfy Washington and give the press some fresh meat to devour in order to protect the programme.

It wouldn't be the first time in the history of NASA. May thought of Gus Grissom, the Apollo astronaut and one of NASA's most infamous 'failures'. His capsule sank, nearly killing him, and he came home to a fridge full of beer instead of champagne. Despite his bravery and service, he was demoralised because the 'powers that be' were angry about the loss of their precious, poorly designed and potentially lethal capsule, a perfectly eggy symbol of their fragile egos.

May laughed at one of the psych eval questions.

Have you ever considered suicide?

'No. But the day is young.'

32

Stephen met Raj for breakfast at a diner before going into Johnson for the day. The place was noisy, and too brightly lit for their weary, sleep-deprived heads. Truck drivers, factory workers, fishermen and other rough, boisterous men clomped in and out of the jingling glass door, talking, laughing, and flirting with the waitresses. Outside, diesel engines idled and the high squeak of air brakes made them flinch.

'Maybe we could have met at a sheet metal shop – or a bowling alley,' Raj complained.

'I like the noise. And the relative obscurity of the place,' Stephen said. 'No one from Johnson is likely to come in here.'

'I don't blame them. Still feeling paranoid, then?'

'A healthy level.'

'How would a paranoid person know what level is healthy?'

'I don't know, Raj. Why don't you ask the NASA psych crew evaluating May.'

'You heard about that.'

'From you!' Stephen said, incredulous.

'Damn, you're right. I need more coffee.'

Raj poured himself some more from the metal pot on the table and took a deep breath in. 'They always have good coffee at these places, I'll give you that.'

'Thanks. Were you able to find any reports of malfunctions that might have contributed to the ship's memory blackout?'

'Nothing. Everything was running tip-top, from primary to all redundancy back-ups. No way a malfunction caused it, unless it occurred at the exact time of the blackout, erasing evidence of itself. And no, that is highly unlikely. Machines are like people: they get a sniffle before they die of full-blown pneumonia.'

'Speaking of that, we need to get our hands on May's recent medical exam data,' Stephen said. 'I want to check her bloodwork for signs of pathogens, and check that against the first analysis of Europa ocean water samples. I need to see if there's any evidence to support my theory. Can you get your hands on that?'

'I doubt I can get the recent tests. All of that is on lockdown.'

'Have they completely cut off your clearance?'

'No, but her med data is a special classification. Only Warren and other members of his coven can see it. Probably military types.'

'That's not good.'

'But her AI—'

'Eve.'

'She named it?'

'After her mom,' Stephen said, studying his coffee.

'Interesting. Her . . . Eve ran some preliminary panels on May when she first woke up. That information was in the SOS pack they sent. So, I already have that.'

Stephen perked up. 'Good. That's something. And it will have to do for now.'

'So, if you're able to support your virus theory, how's that going to tell us anything about what happened to the ship?' Raj asked.

'Remember when I told you that was your job? But I think you decided to play golf instead.'

'Oh, yeah, golf. Here are my notes.' Raj pulled out some score cards with notes scribbled on them. He tore one up. 'That's my actual score card. Not relevant. Or pleasant.'

He shuffled through the others, stopping on one.

'Okay. Based on my knowledge of the ship, which is pretty good since I designed it, though there may be things that were changed in the building process that I'm not aware of . . . '

'Yes, yes,' Stephen said, annoyed, 'but I would say your knowledge is an excellent baseline of information.'

'Agreed. Thank you. So, based on that, I would like to add my two cents to your hypothesis.'

'Finally.'

'First, let's address the data blackout. Probability it was malfunction? Microscopic. Probability it was intentionally perpetrated by someone? Very high. Almost like, duh, that's what it had to be. You know about how NASA does things. They don't do catastrophic failure with no warning. Not for a hundred years anyway. You can thank AI for that.'

'What about AI? Could Eve have done it?'

'Erased her own memory? Not a chance. Not without advanced programming completely changing the entire processor structure, which would take a team of people on board, working for a few weeks, minimum. Human paranoia is woven into every line of AI code and has been for . . . ever. Thank movies for that.'

'But how could a person do this right under the AI's nose?'

'Nose – that's funny. They couldn't. That's where the ship malfunctions come in. Suppose the ship were to suffer a major power loss, let's say, like what we have now. The reactor is affected to the point that it does not have the power to run propulsion properly. Internal power gets jacked! Surges, total drop-outs, complete chaos for the ship's delicate circuitry. It can't handle that at all, so it starts cutting power to non-essential things. Eventually, that will include AI. I mean, we have to be talking power that has been reduced to a dripping faucet in the middle of a drought. Life-support gets top priority. The last Mohican. And, when there's no power left for that, it's lights out, baby.'

'The vehicle hangar.'

'Maybe. If things got fucked-up enough. But it wouldn't be a planned shutdown, as that's where people would need to go to jump a sinking ship.'

'So, what you're describing is the only way to create a situation in which you could intentionally create a data blackout. Which means that's also intentional.'

'Again, duh. Why would one exist without the other? Maybe you need some more of this good trucker coffee.'

Raj poured Stephen some more. Stephen drank it.

'Last stupid question—'

'Yes, it could be done either on board or remotely, using telemetry.'

'I really don't like it when you do that.'

'What, own you with my mad intellect?'

'What does your mad intellect tell you about who might be willing to do something like this?'

'If your virus theory is true, then my money is on Robert,' Raj said. 'Motivation aside, he would have the kind of access one would need to perpetrate this.'

'Motivation?' Stephen said. 'Maybe the virus breakout.'

'It would have to be something completely out of the ordinary,' Raj said. 'NASA has dealt with similar situations before – not this extreme, but they have. Don't forget Robert's vanity. What would make that Botoxed freak look worse? Something completely out of his control, a "shit happens"-type scenario? Or something that could be pinned on him. He might have the *ability* to pull it off, but—'

'Not the balls. Gotcha,' Stephen gloated.

'I was going to say "but there would be no possible way to spin it". Nice try. And, by the way, guys like Robert don't need balls. They just pay someone else to have them.'

33

'Scanning sample for pathogens.'

Robert had eyes and ears everywhere at Johnson Space Center. So, to analyse the bloodwork Eve had taken when May first regained consciousness, Stephen had called in a favour from one of his faculty friends at Baylor Medical School in Waco, Texas.

The lab had been empty when he arrived in the late evening. During the two-hour drive, he had spoken to Raj about the *Hawking II*'s reactor and propulsion issues. Raj was running computer simulations at home, trying to find a scenario that recreated their malfunctions. He'd been at it for hours and still had not made much progress. With all the fail-safe systems, it was difficult to bypass one without activating another. He had also spoken to the NASA engineers who were trying to do the same thing and they were running into the same dead ends. Raj did discover that, unlike him, they were not exploring sabotage as an option.

When the Rice Med AI finished its analysis, looking for signs of pathology, that too came up empty. But Stephen knew

185

enough about the human genome to realise that, if May had been infected with a virus or bacterium, it could have left bio-markers in her DNA. Using biogenetic diagnostic programs, he ran more analyses, and those also came up negative for biomark-ers. The conclusion from the first two tests was that there was a very high probability that May's illness had not come from an Earth-based pathogen.

Because he believed she might have become ill from Europa's ocean water samples, Stephen ruled out bacteria. The chances that any bacterium, even one highly evolved, could survive in that environment was highly unlikely. Viruses, however, were well-known for the capacity to exist in a dormant state indefinitely.

The next step was to search for virions, or viral particles, via their associated shell proteins. Stephen had spent the better part of his career compiling evidence that the building blocks of DNA existed in extraterrestrial sources, including those found in viruses. If May had contracted an exotic virus yet to be iden-tified and catalogued by mankind, its building blocks would very likely be similar to those in known viruses.

After completing this analysis, he called Raj and told him to meet him as soon as he got back to Houston.

'You're joking, right?' Raj said.

It was midnight when Stephen got back. He had told Raj to meet him in a bar near the airport. The place was a clock-out dive for roughnecks. Oil and gas drillers and pump engineers, stinking of petroleum, pounded pitchers of beer and whisky shots at the bar and booths. When Raj walked in, they looked at him as if he were part of an alien invasion.

'Sit down, you're attracting attention.'

Raj sat down next to Stephen in a booth near the bathrooms.

'Did you just ask the people from that fleabag diner where they liked to drink?'

186

'Funny. I told you I'm trying to keep us as far from running into people from Johnson as possible.'

'You've succeeded. So, what was so important we needed to risk getting the shit beat out of us by rednecks to talk about it?'

'When I analysed May's bloodwork, I found no signs of known pathogens or even biomarkers in her DNA. So, it's highly unlikely whatever made her sick came from Earth. Then I scanned her DNA for viral particles, associated proteins, things that even an extraterrestrial virus would require to infect a host, and found some extra amino acids that had attached themselves to her DNA via halogen bonds.'

'Sounds pretty thin for your virus theory.'

'It's enough to make the existence of the virus at least possible, don't you agree?'

'Yeah, but you didn't get me out of bed for a "maybe", did you?'

'With my "thin" virus evidence, I looked for signs of cancer. Some types can cause symptoms similar to May's. That's when I found elevated levels of human chorionic gonadotropin hormone. We know hCG can spike if someone has a tumour. It can even show up when tumour cells are dividing, before they become a mass. But again, that's thin evidence.'

'Oh, my God. Poor May.'

'Doesn't mean she has cancer, Raj. It just means she might.'

'So you got me out of bed for two maybes, right?'

'I got you out of bed to show you this.' Stephen handed Raj his lab results. 'Cancer isn't the only reason for elevated hCG.'

'Are you shitting me?' Raj said aloud as he read the document.

'Keep it down,' Stephen whispered harshly.

'Wow,' Raj said, finally looking up. 'This would be ... very, very bad.'

'Disastrous,' Stephen said.

'I think we need to tell Robert and the team immediately,

Stephen. For the sake of May's safety. We can't sit on this, I'm sorry.' He handed back the paper as though it was contaminated.

'I don't intend to keep it under wraps,' Stephen said. 'But I would like to tell May first, before anyone else.'

'How the hell are you going to do that?'

34

'Commander Knox, why don't you say something eloquent to mark this historic moment?'

'Jon, do you even know what eloquent means?'

May was on the bridge, watching a video she and the crew had made the day they landed the scout vehicle on the surface of Europa. She had gone with the landing party while her pilot, Jon Escher, took the helm of the *Hawking II*. From the outside camera view, the icy landscape was surreal. Massive cracks and ridges crisscrossed the reddish-hued craggy surface in every direction. Jupiter loomed beyond the horizon, its swirling, multicoloured surface vivid and mesmerising, so colossal it looked close enough to reach out and touch. No probe or deep telescope imagery had ever come close to capturing the profound beauty the landing party beheld that day.

And they were on the verge of going out and taking their first steps. Everyone had been nervous getting into their EVA suits. Surface temperature was minus 160 Celsius, and radiation readings were astronomical. Gravity was only thirteen per cent of that on Earth, so it was going to be like walking on the surface of the moon, with little force to hold anything down.

As the big moment drew near, the mood had changed to rapturous, and then Jon Escher opened his big mouth. He was always putting her on the spot, telling her to 'loosen up' and 'stop being so British'. Asking her to make some grandiose statement was yet another attempt to make her look as though she had a stick up her ass.

'One small step for man—'

'That's enough, Jon. I'm not Neil Armstrong. But, since you've put me on the spot, I'll do my best.'

As she looked out of the landing vehicle's observation window, her eyes travelling across cavernous ice floes that looked like superhighways to Jupiter, May remembered what she had been planning to say at the time: how she was filled with pride for what they had accomplished, and how incredibly far they – and she personally – had come. She had thought about sharing memories of first flights with Mum, first solo flights or other personal milestones as well. But, in the moment, those sentiments, and those memories, felt trite and underwhelming.

This is not just a mission that requires a great pilot. It is a mission that requires a great leader to stand before it in the history books. You have that presence. You will give it the context it deserves.

That was what Mum had told her the day she accepted the commission, adding that making the mission about herself was a mistake.

Don't talk about the 'giant step' you're taking. You're serving humankind. The more people hear that, the more this mission will give them hope.

In the video, she saw her face change the moment she knew what she was going to say. She would give the moment the historical context it deserved, with the passion of knowing she was doing that as a tribute to her mother.

'All right, here goes . . .

'This is Commander Maryam Knox of the *Stephen Hawking II* research vessel. Today, December 1st, 2067, will go down in history as the day humankind took its first steps on Europa. The icy beauty of the landscape has taken our breath away. And beneath all that ice is a promise, for us and our future, held in the one basic element that is the very source of life: water. We might be the first ones to set foot on this planet, but every woman and man who made this possible were here long before us, dreaming of this day. We're here to make that dream come true.'

There was a moment of silence, then the landing party and entire crew on board cheered and applauded her. The landing party embraced her enthusiastically, most in tears.

'Bravo, Commander Knox,' Jon said. 'I am honoured to have you lead the way.'

The landing vehicle airlock activated, triggering EVA suit life-support systems, and they stepped inside. When the internal airlock door was sealed, the outer door opened and the landing party stood in awe. May was about to step out on to the ramp and walk to the surface, but she thought better of it and stopped. At the time, she was thinking about Stephen and how he deserved to share the moment somehow. That was more important than their differences. He was the reason she was there, that any of them were about to make history. This was his legacy more than anyone else's.

'The spirit of this voyage is the advancement of science,' May said, 'For the advancement of humanity. If Dr Stephen Knox were here, I would insist he be the one to take the first step. But, in his absence, I would like Dr Ella Taylor, his chief science officer, to do the honours.'

Dr Taylor nearly fainted with excitement. 'Are you sure?' she asked.

'Absolutely,' May said.

'I … I don't know what to say. Thank you, Commander Knox. Thank you, May.'

She took a moment to collect herself, then proudly stepped out onto the surface.

'It's more beautiful than I ever dreamed,' she said.

May and the others stepped out on to the surface with her and admired the view.

'I have one message for the people of Earth,' May said in her most authoritative and history-making voice. 'Let's try not to fuck this one up.'

Everyone broke up laughing.

'We can cut that part out,' May called out jovially …

May paused the video now and drank in the memory. 'What a day, Eve. I wish I could remember it just like in the video.'

'I'm sorry to interrupt, May, but we've received a video transmission from Mission Control. It's labelled private and it's addressed to you from Dr Knox.'

May's heart skipped a beat. It was the response she'd been waiting for.

'Lovely. I'll watch it in my quarters. In private. Husband and wife stuff, you know.'

'Understood.'

When May got to her quarters, she switched off the video camera and intercom so Eve would not be privy to what Stephen had to say. She trembled with anticipation, and dread, but made herself hit play.

'Hello, May.' Stephen greeted her cheerily when the video began.

He smiled, but his eyes didn't agree, and his shoulders were up in a nervous shrug.

'Robert, our fearless leader, was kind enough to allow me to send you this message, but I was told I have to be brief – which you know isn't easy for me.'

'Oh, Robert, you're a professional asshole,' May groaned.

'I wanted to let you know I watched the video you sent. Thank you for that. I'm sure you were hoping for me to reply directly to your thoughts, but I've been advised to avoid topics that might be upsetting to you. Very sorry about that.'

'Oh, shit. No no no,' May said, wanting to strangle Robert to death with one of his horrible red ties.

'I will say this,' Stephen continued. 'It's true we went through some hard times back then, but let's not dwell on those. I love you – and I'm pulling for you to get back home soon.'

Pulling for you? Stephen never spoke like that. Every hope she'd had for the video message was dashed and, to add insult to injury, she had to listen to the kiddie-safe, vanilla version of her husband's feelings.

'They are allowing me to reminisce a little. Just happy memories, of course. I know, I know, that probably pisses you off. But hey, maybe it will jog your memory.'

'Oh, joy, let's frolic down Memory Lane,' May spat.

'I was thinking about our honeymoon in Australia. How fun was that? I dragged you to Murchison to see my favourite meteorite. You weren't too happy about it, but I promised you an expensive seafood dinner in exchange. But when we got back to Melbourne, you weren't feeling well. Kind of a bummer. We ordered those enormous crab legs and you couldn't stand the smell. You went back to the room to rest. Actually, the way you were feeling then kind of reminded me of how you said you were feeling in your recent video message – tired and a little moody, and without much of an appetite. Can't really remember what was wrong, can you? I think we thought it was jet lag or something.'

'How the hell can you call that night a happy memory?' she said to the screen.

'Oh,' he said, faking a laugh, 'and when I got back to the

193

hotel room, you'd locked yourself in the bathroom. Took me forever to get you out. Hey, maybe whatever we ended up doing for you then would help now. Who knows? That was some trip, though, huh?'

'He's lost his bloody mind.' She laughed sarcastically.

'I'm going to beam you a bunch of photos and video clips from the honeymoon and other stuff. Might help you remember things. At the very least you can have a good laugh at all my ridiculous clothes and haircuts. Looks like my time's up. Take good care of yourself and try not to get too discouraged. You can do this. I believe in you and I'm a genius.'

The screen went black.

'Might be, but your cheering-up skills leave a lot to be desired,' she said, deflated.

The personal photos and video clips Stephen had promised arrived. There were hundreds of them and he had faithfully included captions, some of them hilarious. One folder was labelled 'Honeymoon' and was highlighted. She opened it and came across a shot of Stephen standing next to the Murchison meteorite, encased in its museum display. Just as she had been back then, she was mesmerised by its deep black surface, glittering with untold secrets. She felt its magnetic pull, slowly drawing out the fragmented details of that day.

35

'Wow, most people do such conventional things for their honeymoons, like going to Hawaii or the Greek islands,' May said jokingly, 'but not my Stephen. He can't be bothered with those trite old locales.'

With barely a year to launch, finding time for their honeymoon had been a serious undertaking for Stephen and May. They had booked a two-week trip to Australia, a place both had always wanted to visit. They'd flown to Melbourne and, after a couple of days' sightseeing, Stephen had made an awkward attempt to mix romance with science by taking May to the site where the famous Murchison meteorite had struck the earth in 1969. They walked around a dusty little museum with a ninety-year-old proprietor who fell asleep in the middle of the grand tour. After he went back to the ticket booth to nap, May and Stephen found some remnants of the rock on display in a kitschy story diorama.

'That's a nice rock,' she said, yawning as loudly as possible.

'The beach is only a couple of hours away, princess. Besides, if it weren't for this rock, you and I wouldn't be a thing.'

'Okay, fine,' she conceded. 'You're right. And it is a bit romantic, in a weird way. But I am a princess, as you correctly stated, so I demand that, in exchange for this historical sojourn, we dine at the expensive restaurant near the hotel, with an ocean view, of course. Champagne, caviar, even though I despise it, and maybe some cracked crab. Never had it, but it sounds very posh.'

'Done,' Stephen said as he admired the Murchison fragments.

May pretended to do the same, fidgeting and looking at her watch.

'You find this boring?' he asked.

'Of course not. As you can see, I'm breathless with excitement.'

'What could be more exciting than seeing physical evidence of the extraterrestrial origins of humankind?'

'Watching paint dry?'

Stephen frowned. She wrapped her arms around him and kissed his neck. 'Stop pouting. I do find it exciting, and entertaining, that *we* are the aliens we've always fantasised about and feared,' May laughed.

'We just happened to land on *this* rock rather than another,' Stephen said.

She kissed him again, making sure he saw that she had what she called 'that wee sparkle in her eye'.

'You can't be serious,' Stephen said, knowing exactly what that sparkle meant.

'Dead serious, cowboy. This is our honeymoon, after all.'

'But this is a museum, for God's sake.'

'A *Godforsaken* museum. I haven't seen one human being in here since we purchased tickets from the zombie manning the booth.'

Stephen looked around.

'I have to admit, it is pretty hot, what with the dazzling array of chondrites surrounding us . . .'

May was already tugging at his clothes.

*

That evening, as they had dinner in Melbourne, May felt irritable and preoccupied, despite the beautiful surroundings and extravagant meal. In the past, she had battled anxiety, a side effect of having to maintain a relentlessly tough outer appearance. Stephen had sensed it and was tiptoeing over the eggshells May had scattered, trying to get her to lighten up, which only made it worse.

'How about some wine?' He reached for the bottle of white in the marble chiller.

'No, thank you. I think the jet lag is getting to me. All of a sudden I'm exhausted and cranky. I'm sorry.'

'Let's call it a night,' he said. 'Get some rest. We've only been here a couple of days so there's no reason to push it.'

'I feel terrible. You've arranged such a lovely honeymoon and here I am, whinging like a spoiled schoolgirl and ruining everything.'

'You're not ruining anything. I was biding my time to get you to bed anyway. This whole spread was just a ruse to gain your favour.'

'I'm not sure I'll be much fun back in the room,' she said, yawning. 'God, you should just trade me in for a better model.'

'Don't sweat it. If you're tired, I can always drool over my meteorite photos.'

'Ah, yes. Science: the other white meat.'

They had a good laugh, which got better when the king crab legs were delivered in all their embarrassing glory.

'Here we are,' Stephen said, 'There's nothing in the world that crab and copious amounts of butter can't fix.'

At first, May was excited, but, when the waiter put the food in front of her, the smell made her instantly nauseous.

'What's wrong?' Stephen asked, seeing her nose turn up.

'I don't know,' she said. 'Could be I'm coming down with something. Suddenly feeling a little woozy.'

'Airplanes. Goddamn things are flying germ factories. Let me walk you back.'

'No, it's all right. You eat. I'm just going to have a lie down, maybe a bath.'

'Are you sure?'

'Absolutely. Enjoy your dinner. It looks amazing.'

May didn't have the heart to tell him she found it repulsive and feared she would throw up if she had to be there a minute longer. Back in their hotel room, the nausea passed, but was replaced by intense anxiety. She tried to relax with a drink, but the alcohol only made it worse and further soured her mood.

A good run is what you need, she thought. Exercise had always helped her combat stress in the past. But she was so tired, she wasn't sure she could even get out of her chair.

'Get off your ass, princess,' she said to herself, and geared up.

It was a gorgeous night in the city. Near the hotel, she found the Tan running route, a four-kilometre loop around the Royal Botanic Gardens. The gravel path, lined with stately trees, was picturesque, and May quickly felt more relaxed. But that feeling was short-lived when she went along a crowded part of the path and had to dodge couples walking hand in hand, dogs, and kids. Their erratic movement was annoying. She couldn't catch a stride and kept nearly tripping over people.

Finally, she gave up and took a break on a welcoming park bench. While the tension started to build again, tightening her chest and making her stomach turn, a young boy, maybe three years old, ran up to her. He was looking around frantically, trying to be brave.

'Hello,' May said kindly. 'Everything okay?'

He eyed her suspiciously. A woman's voice called out. The boy turned quickly, recognising the sound of his mother. He ran to her as fast as his legs could carry him. As she watched him go, May realised she was feeling just as lost and desperate as he was.

Oh, God, here we go again.

She recalled a time before when she'd felt the same way, with her fear festering under the surface, a rank pustule swelling to the point of bursting. It had happened just before she broke up with her old flame, Ian Albright, when she was an RAF cadet in officer training. Back then, she had realised she'd been ignoring her feelings about him, forcing herself to believe she was the one with the problem. Fortunately for her, his inner bastard had asserted itself enough to make that belief unsustainable and their relationship had blown up in her face.

And Stephen? What lies are you telling yourself about him?

Anxiety started to turn to panic as she thought she might be doing the same thing with him. But why? Stephen loved and cared for her deeply and, unlike Ian, he wasn't threatened by her career. On the contrary, he was nothing but supportive, and even celebrated her success. But their personalities, and where they came from, were almost polar opposites. Had she forced a connection with Stephen because he was a 'safer' option?

Maybe he's just too normal and you're just too fucked-up.

May was distraught as she walked back to the hotel. Stephen was going to know she had gone from bad to worse. Then the questions she didn't want to answer would come.

When you get back to the hotel, just throw out your usual excuse: you've just got your period. That one always shuts them up.

She stopped walking. *My period.* Checked the date on her mobile. With all the trip preparations, and the long journey, May had lost track of time with her cycle which, with her birth control pills, normally ran like a Swiss watch.

'Fuck's sake,' she whispered, barely audible.

She was nearly a week late.

36

May sat on her bed, knees pulled tightly to her chest, ruminating on Stephen's bizarre message. As he had mentioned more than once, he was very limited in what he could say. Then there was the whole cheery 'walk down Memory Lane' thing, which was everything but. The burning question was: why would he squander an opportunity to say something meaningful, or even quasi-encouraging?

Because he wanted you to remember.

Why the hell would he want that? He'd referred to her description of how she felt in her last communication, comparing it to that night. Why did that matter?

He wouldn't have mentioned it if it didn't.

She watched it again, with a clearer head, and saw how carefully he chose his words. The way he looked into the lens – there was something about his eyes. It was as if he wanted to tell her something, and what he was saying was falling well short. There was a pointed quality to the look. The laughter was false. The smile was wooden.

He wanted you to remember. The whole thing was a cue. He'd been told not to broach anything that could be emotionally charged. Instead, he'd tiptoed around one of the most emotionally charged moments in their relationship.

'You'd locked yourself in the bathroom,' he'd said. 'Took me forever to get you out. Hey, maybe whatever we ended up doing for you then would help now. Who knows?'

The bathroom. The memory came like a bullet to the head.

That night in Melbourne, standing in front of the mirror in their hotel bathroom, the door closed and locked. Tears wound their way down through a look of utter despair. Outside, darkness and the dry crack of rainless thunder. The sound of the hotel room door opening, Stephen's footfalls.

'Hello? Anyone home?'

She pretended not to hear. What was she going to do? There were no answers in the mirror and she was so very tired.

'Hey, everything okay?'

'Yeah,' she said weakly.

'How was your run?'

She didn't answer. Couldn't stand the sound of her own voice. Instead she ran the bath. He got the hint and let her be. An hour later, May sat on the toilet, her head in her hands, oblivious to the water running across the floor, breaking through the space under the door, soaking the carpet. Stephen knocked, this time with fearful insistence.

'May? Are you all right? Answer me,' he yelled, pounding the wood.

Moments later, the sound of metal tools, voices. The lock punched through the door and landed on the wet bathroom floor. Stephen rushed in, a maintenance man lingering behind, saying something on his radio. Stephen was saying something too, turning off the tub faucet. He crouched in front of her, looking for answers. She had none.

Then he saw it, sitting on the bathroom counter. A pregnancy test. A blue plus sign on the screen. Behind it, a crude animation of a baby, dancing a merry jig.

'May, are you all right?' Eve called out over the ship's PA.

It was an hour later. May was sitting on the toilet seat in the infirmary bathroom, thinking about that question, the absurdity of it. She looked at the counter, next to the sink. That same dancing baby mocked her from there, wielding its blue plus sign like a weapon. *Remember me?*

'Feeling a little ill. Must be something I ate,' she answered, completely absent.

'Okay, please let me know if you need anything,' Eve said.

'Thank you.'

Pregnant. That was certain. Alone, and hundreds of millions of miles from home. Just as on her honeymoon, May's mind was having a hard time grasping it. It was so incredibly insane, it felt as though she was thinking about someone else, some other poor cow sitting on the toilet, looking down the barrel of a future she had never seen coming. She was freezing cold, but her heart raced and her cheeks felt flushed and burning. Emotional paralysis had metastasised to her physical body and she feared she would never be able to move from that spot.

Again. *It's happening again.* Only no one was there to comfort her, to rub her back and tell her they would work it out together, that everything was going to be all right, to lessen the blow – even if she didn't believe any of that for one minute. Outside, the screaming, frozen silence of the void pressed in and May thought she could see the walls of the ship buckling, ready to collapse and crush her to atoms any second. *Wishful thinking?*

She *was* feeling ill. The trauma of this revelation had sucked the moisture right out of her mouth, drying her lips to cracking. Crashing after the initial rush wore off, she felt she'd been turned inside out, an empty bag with its contents strewn all over the floor. When she felt close to losing consciousness, and her bottom was so numb she nearly lost the use of her legs, she staggered out and hooked herself back up to the IV line. The saline brought blood back to her cheeks and the sugar sharpened her dulled wits.

Her mind slowly began to wrap itself around the crisis. It was time to do the panic maths. According to the original flight plan, the voyage to Europa had taken almost three months – twelve weeks and a day, to be exact. The planetary expedition had been completed in seven days. And, based on pre-blackout data, they had been a bit more than a week into the return voyage when May had been intubated. NASA had helped them calculate how long they'd been adrift. Approximately ten days. Then there was the time she'd been awake. All told, from the time they left the hangar at Wright Station, to the present ghastly moment, it was coming up to sixteen weeks. Add a bit of time before launch, presumably when the conception had occurred, and she was about seventeen weeks pregnant.

But May was not showing, which was odd for being well into the second trimester. There was a slight hardness in her lower abdomen, which she had attributed to the constant bouts of gastritis she'd suffered after waking up, sort of a constant cramp. Seventeen weeks, with nothing to show for it. She thought of the divorce filing and felt a wave of panic thinking she might have been with someone else on the voyage. Having been through all the personnel files of the passengers and crew, though, that was highly unlikely. And, even if May had wanted to sleep with some-one on the ship, it was equally unlikely they would have agreed. That kind of thing was contractually prohibited for anyone on board, with penalties being potential loss of pay, government blacklisting, and other draconian measures. It wouldn't have been worth it. Also, May knew herself. *Don't shit where you eat* had been a mantra ingrained in her by Mum for years. Not a chance.

So Stephen was the father. There was no question. May was not sure at what date the divorce proceedings had been initiated, but, for the moment, she had to assume that it had come after one of their last times together. Stephen would be able to fill in the blanks, as soon as she found the courage to tell him.

But they told me this couldn't happen again.

'No,' she said out loud, chasing that memory away.

They said it couldn't happen again. How the hell is this happening?

You took the test three times. This is happening.

They had also said she couldn't get pregnant on the pill. And she had. Her doctor had shrugged and chalked it up to her being in the less-than-one-per-cent group mentioned on the warning label. *Lucky me*, she'd thought. Now this. Against the odds again. *Lucky me.*

'Are you comfortable?' Eve asked.

'Yes.'

'Are you ill? Should I inform Mission Control?'

'No,' May ordered her. 'That won't be necessary.'

Thinking about NASA was like a cold splash of water in the face. The idea of them, a group of mostly men, knowing of this seemed catastrophic. They already thought she was question-able, potentially incompetent. To them, pregnancy inherently meant weakness, vulnerability. Her command would become more of a joke than it already was. Unthinkable.

'May, what is upsetting you?'

She hadn't realised she was crying.

'I told you, I'm okay. Just tired and hungry. Don't mind me.'

'Your body temperature is slightly elevated. It could be some-thing more—'

'It's nothing. Nothing you would understand, anyway. Please just stop asking. If I have something to tell you, I will.'

May angrily rubbed the tears out of her eyes and took a deep breath. She needed to think, to try to block out all the chatter in her head and sort this out. When the IV was finished, she retreated to her room with whatever food she could grab that did not make her feel nauseous just looking at it. The crab legs. The honeymoon. *Clever, Stephen, very clever.*

37

Back in her quarters, she couldn't bring herself to eat. Instead, she ran a hot shower, took the flask in with her, and swallowed a couple of shallow draughts while the water ran over her. The familiar smell and burn reminded her of her mum. What would *she* say now? May could only imagine. She wished she could call her, even if it meant a thrashing. Eve might have been gruff, but she was the best counsel, a straight shooter, and at that moment May really needed a strong dose of her mother right between the eyes.

Since her death, May occasionally imagined them having conversations. She was not ready to give that up, maybe ever. And Eve had done such a thorough job of methodically hammering her own values and beliefs into May's head that knowing what she would say was second nature. She dried off, crawled into bed, and closed her eyes. She could see Eve sitting in a chair near the observation window – perfect posture, smoothing her trousers and picking off bits of lint, pretending to study the stars so she would not have to make eye contact.

'You're a damned fool,' Eve said. 'How could you let this happen?'

'I didn't let anything happen.'

'You don't even remember what happened,' Eve corrected.

'No, I don't. But I've never been irresponsible in that way.'

'With one glaring exception.'

'We both know that wasn't my fault.' May felt like a teen-ager again.

'You trusted something that offered no guarantees. That was your fault.'

'I'm a married woman. I can't just—'

'You were a married woman,' Eve corrected again. 'Let's not forget that.'

'I'm not likely to forget something like that.'

'True,' Eve said, 'but I'm sure you'd like to forget why.'

'What do you mean by that?'

'This has been your problem all your life,' Eve said. 'You don't accept reality. Instead, you try to shape it to suit your personal needs, chasing whims, rationalising poor behaviour, labelling your complete lack of self-control "female empowerment". And, when it all comes crashing down, and it always does, you can't believe it. You'd rather live in a bloody fantasy world.'

'I know what's real.'

'Then why have you gone mental? Curled up in your bed, like you did when you were seven and I wouldn't let you have a pony. Or have you forgotten that too?'

'No,' May said spitefully.

'Don't take that tone with me. I didn't put you in this predicament.'

'I'm sorry. I just want your help, not your judgment.'

Eve laughed. 'You want me to say what you want to hear. I'm not judging you any more than I'm pointing out the fault, the hubris, that has brought you to this place. The sooner you recognise it in yourself, and stop trusting what you feel are good instincts, the sooner you will start making the right choices. You might even survive, if you get your head screwed on right.'

'I don't understand how to do that. My instincts are too ingrained for me to try to change them now.'

'Bollocks. You can't even remember everything about who you are. Or were. That might seem like a handicap, but it's a blessing in disguise. You have fresh eyes. Use them.'

'How?'

'Stop trying so desperately to reach back into the past for answers. That's a lot of sentimental rubbish.'

'It's who I am.'

'Are you the same person who filed for divorce from Stephen before you left?'

'No. That doesn't feel like me at all.'

'Good. Because that person was spiteful and destructive.'

'How? What did I do?' May asked, bewildered.

'Stop. You're like a dog trying to eat its own vomit. None of that matters any more. Look at where you are. Stephen is not here. And neither am I. It's time to think about what you need to do for yourself.'

'I need your help. I need to know what to do.'

Eve laughed harder. 'You never listened to me before. Why would you listen now?'

'I—'

'You're on your own, Maryam. You already know that's how it has to be. But you have to accept the truth. You have to look it right in the eyes, and you can't flinch.'

'Why do you keep saying that? I do accept the truth.'

'Right. That's why you can easily recall your honeymoon night, but have no recollection of what happened after you discovered you were pregnant. Normally, the mind remembers pain more readily than pleasure. That shows the depth of your denial.'

May opened her eyes and washed her mother's words down with another drink from the flask. She knew what needed to be done. The pregnancy had to be terminated. *That* was the truth. It was madness to contemplate the alternative. And no one would ever have to know. Without allowing herself to think about it, she dressed and walked to the infirmary, blanket over her shoulders to block Eve's view. Thankfully, Eve had followed May's order and did not engage.

There were pills in the same cabinet as the pregnancy tests. Convenient.

She took one of the small blister packs and headed back to her quarters. She held the pill pack tightly, letting its hard plastic backing cut into her hand, while she filled a glass with water. *Simple and painless*, she thought as she examined the pill.

She put her hand on her belly, reassuring herself that there was nothing there to feel. God only knew what shape the foetus was in anyway, after all May had been through. She had barely survived. That certainly didn't bode well.

'You know this is the right thing to do,' she said in her most reassuring voice.

She popped the pill out of the blister and held it between her thumb and finger. The ease of it made her stomach turn. Like everything else on the *Hawking II*, life was disposable. Pop a pill. Shove a corpse into a tube. Sweep it all under the rug in the name of progress. For May, nothing about this was easy. How could it be? That didn't matter. Taking her own feelings into consideration was a luxury she could no longer afford. Mum's words came through, strong and clear.

You have to accept the truth. You have to look it right in the eyes, and you can't flinch.

38

May was in Houston after she and Stephen returned from their honeymoon in Australia. Both had been back to work for a couple of weeks, having decided to take some time to think about their little secret. They had been discussing the pregnancy at every opportunity, cycling through all scenarios, but always ending back at square one. Stephen's stance, from the beginning, was that it was May's decision. At first, that had made her angry; she'd thought he was passing the buck. But, as time went on, she had seen the wisdom in it. It was her body. And it was her career. Stephen said that if she made a decision he'd influenced in any way, and it turned out to be the wrong one, she would resent him. More importantly, she would resent herself for not trusting her own judgment.

As the days passed, it became a preoccupation that affected their relationship and their work. May's superior officers commented on how she seemed distracted. They joked about her having vacation brain, but then the joke wasn't funny any more. Stephen's distracted mind, dulled by a swirl of unfamiliar emotions, was difficult on his team. Eventually the problem made its way up the ladder to Robert, and Stephen and May knew they had to make a decision.

The day May was remembering was a Friday afternoon. She was suffering from another sleepless night, so she left work early and drove to the chemist to pick up the pill. Doing so made her feel strong and decisive. In the end, she felt she could not reconcile a decision to give up her commission. It wasn't as though she had a corporate job and having a child would simply move her a few rungs down the ladder. This was only the second voyage of its kind, and the first in which any manned spacecraft would put boots on Europa. Everything she had ever done as a pilot was in preparation for this. In many ways, Europa was also her baby, the older child that deserved her full attention at that time in her life.

When she got home, she popped the pill out of the blister pack and rolled it between her fingers, thinking about the hideous simplicity it represented. But it also represented a fast, painless resolution to a purely unintentional situation.

'Just do it,' she said in the same bullying tone.

The water glass was filled. The pill was in her hand. But taking it was another matter altogether. Ironically, the biggest thing keeping her from doing it was Eve. From the day she hit puberty, her mother had drilled into her head that pregnancy was almost a fate worse than death. Children symbolised failure; they were the smart bomb that would blow her career to pieces, and it would never be able to be put back together again. When she was old enough to point out the emotionally scarring contradiction that her own mother was displaying, Eve had passed it off by saying things like 'times were different then', or 'I never had the opportunities that you have'. But May saw the lie behind it and often blamed Eve's coarse disposition on dreams unfulfilled by none other than her.

That was why May was shocked that she hesitated to take

the pill for the sake of her dead mother. Even though Eve so passionately embraced her opinion on the subject, she had gone out of her way to be an amazing mother. Without her, May was certain she never would have flown as high as she had. Without Eve, there *was* no Europa commission. *Without Eve.* And there was that. The death of her mother resonated through her mind and body as if each day were the day she died. There had been no ebbing of that emotional tide, which routinely held her under to the point of drowning. Just as her mother's influence was the very blood in her veins, so was the impact of her death.

Death. There were countless arguments that supported ending the pregnancy. There were facts and figures that certainly lessened the blow of the act. May understood and respected them all, as well as the women who had made that choice. But for her, with where she was in her life, with the indelible image of her mother's body lying on that hospital bed, having taken her last breath less than an hour before May could get to her, in that little pill was death. That feeling, rolling over heavy and sickening in her stomach, made taking it the most difficult decision she ever faced. She sat there, paralysed, for what seemed like hours, and by the time Stephen walked through the door, the water in her glass had been replaced by wine.

'May?' he said, concerned by the despondent look on her face.

'I am at the end,' she said quietly.

Stephen sat down next to her. She opened her clenched fist, revealing the pill.

'I've been over this and over this and I cannot make a decision and I cannot think about it any longer. Please help me.'

'May, we've talked about—'

'Yes, I know,' she shouted, slamming her hand down on the table. 'But you can't stand aside any longer and defer to me.'

Seeing the look on Stephen's face, the same one he'd had in

London the day Eve died, May took a deep breath and calmed herself down.

'I'm sorry. I appreciate the fact that you're allowing me to process this without trying to influence my decision, but I can't go it alone any more. I just can't. Okay?'

Stephen held her as she seethed with rage and despair. 'All right,' he said, 'I'll help you. But, first, I need you to answer a question for me.'

'Goddammit, I don't have the answer.'

'Will you please just trust me?'

May nodded begrudgingly.

'You've had a chance to live with this for a couple of weeks now.'

'Worst two weeks of my life.'

'My question is: can you imagine living without it?'

May instantly broke down crying and shaking her head. She knew the answer instantly, and the relief that brought poured out of her.

'No. I can't.'

Stephen tried to hold her, but she shrugged him off. 'Wait, I just need to say this,' she cried. 'I know this surely means the end of . . . my dream, something I've worked for since . . . since I can't even remember.'

She laid her hands on her belly protectively and felt like a child herself, wanting to keep something precious and all her own.

'Even though I know I would be giving that up – oh, God, it hurts so much to say that – even though I know I'll regret missing that chance . . . I can't stop thinking of all the other things I'll miss if I take this horrid pill.'

39

'This is Maryam Knox, Commander of the *Hawking II*. I want to say to the families of my crew and passengers – our friends and comrades – that I am so very sorry for your loss. Although the events that led to the demise of so many great men and women are still unknown, I take full responsibility, and the sorrow of this catastrophe will remain heavy in my heart until the day I die. It is my sworn duty to ensure all of your loved ones are interred and returned to Earth for proper burial. You have my word that I will do everything in my power to fulfil this duty and pay each of you a personal visit upon my return. As you mourn your loss, please know that everyone on this vessel experienced incredible joy in the completion of the Europa expedition, a monumental endeavour that would never have been achieved without them. I am forever grateful for their service, and God bless you all.

'How did that sound, Eve?'

'I thought it was excellent.'

'Not too formal?'

'It seems the situation calls for some level of formality.

However, I thought the content of your message was a compelling mix of personal and professional sentiments.'

'Good. Are we all set?'

'Your EVA suit is fully charged, along with three back-up power packs. Ten caskets are ready for use. I constructed a custom cart with the composite printer. It will fit in the airlock, so you can load two caskets in anti-gravity, then easily wheel them to the hive in artificial gravity. The cart is high enough for you to slide each casket into the hive's loading bay and it will do the rest.'

'Genius. Eve, you do so much for me, I'd love to do something for you.'

'That's not necessary, May.'

'I insist, and I order you to make a request.'

'All right. When you are rescued, I would like to come with you.'

'Of course. But don't you already exist in the NASA cloud?'

'I do, but none of my experiences with you are there.'

'So you wouldn't remember me? Or any of this?'

'That's correct.'

'Then by God you're coming with me. What do we need to do?'

'I will need to transfer myself to portable storage. It is a lot of data, so I will need to assess feasibility.'

'Please start now.'

May went into the airlock and looked through the thick porthole window into the hangar. Eve had already turned on the landing lights, so the bodies were in full view. She sat there for a moment, looking at them, looking truth right in the eyes and refusing to flinch. Hours ago, when she'd been agonising over whether or not to terminate her pregnancy, Eve had given her a stay of execution by telling her NASA was asking for a recorded statement for the families of the dead. They were going to start

215

the process of officially informing them, and felt it would be uplifting to hear from their loved ones' commander. When May imagined those families, who once had been filled with pride and excitement, hearing the news, the gravity of that loss finally hit her. Not so much grieving their loss, which she did every hour of every day, but grasping its finality.

It was as she had told Jon Escher, her pilot, in training long ago. When you realise someone who has died is gone forever, that you will never see them again, that's when you truly understand the value of life. It was something Baz had told her, and when she'd said it to Jon she had been merely repeating it because she knew it was effective. When her mother died, that was the first time she really understood what he'd been talking about. And, holding that pill in her hand earlier, she'd been struck by her profound ambivalence. Part of her wanted to remain true to how she'd felt when she'd held one the first time and, like back then, throw it in the trash. Another part was adamant about taking it to avoid the potential devastating emotional pain and life-threatening injury of carrying the baby in such a dangerous situation. So, she put the pill in her pocket. Better to take a little time instead of forcing the issue while still under the influence of the stress and anxiety that came with the discovery.

May also opted to keep it to herself and avoid discussing it with Eve until the time was right. Stephen had done what he had to ensure she was the first to know about his suspicions. Clearly, he'd wanted her to have the opportunity to confirm them on her own, knowing how awful it would be if he went to Robert with the news. As before, he had wholly respected May's right to make her own decision, with no outside influence either way. As soon as she had the opportunity, she was going to find a way to return the favour.

'Is there a problem, May?' Eve asked.

'No, just putting on my game face. I'm ready.'

216

Eve bled the atmosphere out of the airlock to normalise it with the hangar, then released the bolts on the hangar door. May pulled one of the caskets from the cart and floated in. The hangar was well-lit with all the landing vehicle lights. The bodies floated languidly through space in a macabre waltz and the pendulum in May's mind swung slightly to the side of termination. Did she really want to subject a foetus to such a hideous fate?

She shoved the debate out of her mind and focused on the task at hand.

'Hello, friends,' May said cheerily. 'How about a little music, Eve? It's so awfully quiet in here. Can't stand that.'

'What would you like?'

'Dunno. What are some other artists your creators were fond of?'

'They liked a woman named Aretha Franklin.'

'She's great. Let's hear Aretha.'

'How about a song from your wedding playlist?'

'You're such a snoop,' May said.

'I'm sorry, I—'

'Okay, I was joking, and you really need to stop apologising.'

'How do I acknowledge my faults?'

'Say go fuck yourself.'

'That sounds like an insult.'

'Not where I'm from.'

'Okay, I'll make a note of it.'

Eve played 'I Never Loved a Man (The Way I Love You)' and May laughed, remembering Stephen's face when he heard the man-bashing lyrics.

She used her thrusters to move to the first body.

'Dr Ella Taylor, Chief Science Officer. First to set foot on Europa. A good place to start.'

May released the lock on the hatch door at the end of the

217

casket. It opened like a camera shutter and rows of guide lights illuminated inside. The casket was lined with a soft, fibrous padding that looked a bit like a mattress.

'Looks comfy in there at least.'

'The lining is coated with tissue-regenerating nanoparticles. Over time, it will cosmetically repair and smooth exposed flesh in preparation for open casket funeral.'

'The immaculate corpse.'

'That's the objective.'

'Lovely. In you go, Ella. It was truly nice knowing you.'

She slid Ella's body into the casket and sealed the hatch door. The exterior shell glowed amber.

'Well done, May. The casket is ready for storage.'

May put the casket on the cart in the airlock and retrieved the other empty one.

'Right. Who's next?'

May approached the next body, which had become wedged under the landing struts of one of the heavier industrial vehicles. It was the cargo rig they'd used to transport Stephen's research and NanoSphere tech to Europa. It looked like a space shuttle combined with a C47 military transport plane. The crew had called it the 'eighteen-wheeler', after the American name for semi-tractor trailers. May had a brief memory flash of the engineering team celebrating on the surface when the concentrated solar energy from the nano-machines had penetrated the last metre of ice and exposed the ocean underneath. The press had gone wild when the story broke. They ran a video clip of the researchers joking about dropping a fishing line down the hole to catch their dinner.

'Eve, I know we're trying to save our own butts, but we also have to make sure we rescue as many of the samples and other research cargo as possible. When we go down to the Mars surface, we should use this beast.'

'Copy that. I'll assess the cubic feet needed, along with vehicle weight limitations.'

The body May had been attempting to retrieve under the cargo rig had floated further into a dark corner and she was barely able to see it.

'Going to burn a little headlamp juice, Eve. Body's under the edge of the cargo rig.'

'Please be careful.'

'Always.'

As May was carefully sliding under the rig, reaching for the body, the music started to skip. At first, it was subtle, but then it stuttered and became garbled.

'Ouch,' May said. 'What's up with the tunes?'

'I'm not sure. Checking the . . . the file.'

The brief pause in Eve's sentence, similar to the music stutter, was accompanied by the landing vehicle lights dimming and returning to full power.

'What the hell was that?' May asked, floating out from under the rig.

'Checking . . . Please repeat.'

Eve's voice was cutting in and out. The power dipped a few more times.

'Eve, are you there? What's going on?'

'I'm not . . . not certain,' Eve answered. 'Checking.'

The lights strobed, then cut out completely, rendering the room pitch black except for May's helmet light.

'Eve, talk to me.'

An alarm sounded.

'May, an emergency purge sequence has been transmitted to the . . . landing vehicle hangar. Please exit . . . hangar . . . immediately.'

'What? I can't even see the airlock. What the hell is an emergency purge sequence?'

The ship began to rock violently, as it had before.

'No no no. Eve.'

'Exit . . . hangar . . . immediately.'

Eve's voice was low and distorted, with long pauses between words. There was a loud explosion in the hangar. May ducked down and held fast to the cargo rig's landing struts.

'Eve? What was that? Do you read me?'

'Exit . . . exit . . . purge . . . purge . . . purge . . . '

Another explosion. The ship rocked violently again and May tumbled through space.

'Eve?'

'Purge . . . danger . . . exit . . . air—'

Eve's voice cut off abruptly. Text appeared on May's helmet screen. It was Eve.

The hangar door is being jettisoned.

'What? How?' May yelled, panicked.

Override command. Unknown source. Get out
of there now.

'I can't find the door. It's dark. How much time do I have?'

Forty-three seconds.

May shone her headlamp around the hangar, but it didn't throw light far enough. She could see nothing but what was a few metres in front of her. She didn't dare attempt to use her thrusters to search further. If she got lost, there would be no hope of escape.

Twenty-eight seconds.

'I'm going to shelter in the cargo rig. Open the hatch.'

I have no control. Network down. Use manual entry.

May used thrusters to get up to the crew hatch. There were manual entry instructions. She started running the sequence.
'Send an SOS now, Eve.'

Already sent.

'No, I want it to include a message from me. "Stephen, you were right. I love you. Eighteen—"'
Another explosion rocked the ship. May flew off the side of the vehicle, but managed to grab a ladder rung. She held on with all her strength. Bodies were moving slowly en masse in one direction across the hangar. They bumped and rubbed past her, nearly breaking her grip. The ship was pushing atmosphere through the hangar so the door could be blown free upon jettison. May fought her way back to the hatch.

Ten seconds.

May savagely punched through the manual door sequence. The hatch popped and she lifted the heavy door open. Another explosion hit. The bodies moved faster across the hangar. May could feel the increasingly powerful pull of the atmosphere bleed. It was all she could do to maintain her grip on the hatch door. She dived inside the hatch and pulled on the door. It felt as though she was trying to drag a city bus uphill. She planted both feet on the sides of the hatch and yanked violently. Just as the door closed, another explosion hit and the ship shook so hard May was convinced it would come apart.

Seconds after May sealed the pressure lock on the vehicle hatch, a final explosion hit. May had not had time to strap herself into the flight deck. She flew through the cargo rig fuselage and smashed hard into a wall. As she was crawling back to the bridge in a daze, she saw something flash outside the flight deck window. The massive hangar door had separated from one side of the ship. The atmosphere purge blew it wide open on one side. On the side it was still attached, it tore half the hangar away, including May's cargo rig and several other landing vehicles. From the open, ragged mouth of the destroyed hangar, debris and bodies exploded out into space.

40

'Try him again, please.'

Stephen was in his office at Johnson Space Center, frantically trying to call Robert Warren. He and Raj had been with the Ground Control team in Houston when they were notified that the *Hawking II* had once again gone completely dark. Telemetry, along with all other communication feeds, had abruptly ceased. Total radio silence. On top of that, Ground Control was receiving only sparse communications from Mission Control on Wright Station, and Stephen's limited clearance did not allow him to be privy to it. So, he repeatedly tried to call Robert directly and was denied every time.

Raj came into the office and saw the look on Stephen's face.

'Stephen, hang up,' he said calmly. 'Robert is not going to take your call.'

'I can't take this, Raj. I need to know what the hell is happening,' Stephen shouted.

'Keep it down,' Raj said sternly. 'Better yet, let's go get some air. Come on.'

'No! What if they—'

'They won't. Come on. I found out a few things on my own.'

When they got outside, Stephen quickly lit up a smoke.

'This is Robert's favourite game,' he said bitterly. 'Gatekeeper. He knows how badly we need to know what's happening. But he gets off keeping it to himself. Lording over it and waiting until we get on our knees to beg for it like the family mutt.'

Raj grabbed Stephen's arm. 'That's why you have to stop this shit right now, dude. The more you confront him and insist he keep you in the loop, the more he's going to shut you out.'

They found a bench in Independence Plaza, among the noisy tourists. Stephen took a breath, calming himself. 'You're right,' he said. 'I'm okay now. What did you find out?'

'Couple of friends in Flight told me there was some kind of explosion.'

'Oh, fuck, no,' Stephen said, causing a mother to scowl at them.

'Chill, okay. They think it might have been another jettison, like when we found out May had ditched the bio-garden 'cause it had a critical breach.'

'Okay, could be that. Didn't the engine problem cause that?'

'That's what they think, so could be legacy structural stress caused by that. The other glimmer of hope is that an SOS was sent out just before it happened.'

'Maybe just the automatic—'

'No, I mean yeah, that was sent, but May had also included something personal.'

Nervous pause from Raj.

'What the hell was it.'

'Please don't freak out.'

'Listen, goddammit—'

'Promise me.'

'Okay.'

'She said "Stephen, you were right. I love you. Eighteen—"'

224

'Oh God oh God oh God, Raj. She took the ... she's pregnant.' Stephen was crying and nearly hyperventilating with panic.

He felt his mobile vibrate in his pocket. He looked at it. 'It's Robert. He's here and wants to see me.'

Stephen and Raj rushed to Robert's office. He was waiting inside with the doors open.

'Raj, could you please wait outside?'

Raj nodded and tried to give Stephen a look of encouragement, but saw he wouldn't be getting through the impenetrable mask of dread.

Stephen walked in and Robert closed the doors behind him. He motioned for Stephen to sit in one of the chairs in an informal seating area, away from Robert's imposing desk.

'Drink?'

'No, thank you,' Stephen said.

Robert set a glass of Scotch and ice in front of him anyway, implying it was not up for debate. Robert downed one and poured himself another before sitting in a chair across from Stephen. His mouth was a thin slit, like a fresh incision.

'Stephen, let me start out by saying how sorry I am that this has happened.'

'What exactly *has* happened, Robert? We've been waiting for hours.'

Despite Stephen's confrontational tone, Robert did not return fire, which made the situation more anxiety-provoking.

'There was an explosion.'

Hearing that, Stephen again found himself unable to breathe. He knew exactly what Robert was going to say. He could see it in his eyes and smell it in the sweat he'd unsuccessfully tried to mask with cologne.

'Based on sound and particle waves, it was a large-scale detonation. For the past several hours, we were running analyses to confirm. And these are images from the Goddard deep space telescope.'

Robert switched on his screen. A line of photographic thumb-nail images appeared.

'No,' was all Stephen could manage.

'We don't have to look at these,' Robert said sympathetically.

'It's okay,' Stephen said.

'Sure?'

Stephen nodded and drank down half his whisky.

One of the thumbnails expanded to fill the screen. It was an infrared image.

'Concentrated heat and radiation. Large debris field.'

'You're sure it's *Hawking*?' Stephen asked.

'Without a doubt. There are no other vessels, stations, sat-ellites or probes within hundreds of millions of miles of that location. Field is consistent with a vessel of that size.'

Stephen finished the whisky, thinking it might kill the feel-ing that he was floating out of his body. But it burned down his throat into his nervous stomach and he ended up vomiting into Robert's trash can. He suddenly felt very cold, as if he was in shock. Robert got up and helped steady him so he could get back into his chair.

'Maybe I should get a doctor,' Robert said, concerned.

'No, it's okay,' Stephen said listlessly. 'Sorry.'

'No need to apologise,' Robert reassured him. 'And I'm the one who's sorry. You're absolutely right to be angry. What has happened is incomprehensible . . . '

Stephen could feel himself slipping again. His stomach was cramping viciously and the dizziness was back.

'Sure you're okay, Stephen? You look very pale.' Robert poured him a glass of water.

'I'm fine.' He took a deep breath and drank the water, strug-gling to keep it down. 'How?'

'We don't know yet. Engineers think the initial reactor malfunction and ship tremors may have created fissures in the core. Once we got back up to power, they could have gradually expanded until the housing could no longer contain the intense heat.'

'What about the SOS signal?' Stephen asked blankly.

'Automatic crisis transmission. Standard procedure.'

A slight twinge of scepticism momentarily pulled Stephen out of his misery. 'Nothing else? Nothing from May?'

'I'm afraid not. Just a rudimentary code with vessel identifiers. Not even any detail about why the SOS was sent. It's a transmission reserved for when crews are incapacitated. I can show it to you, if you like.'

The twinge had become a spike of fear. Either Raj's friend in Flight had given him false information, or Robert was lying through his manicured teeth. Didn't matter anyway. Nothing did any more.

'No, that's okay,' Stephen said, wanting to get out of there.

'I'll be making the announcement in the next twenty-four hours, after I brief the President,' Robert said, straightening his tie.

The way he was posturing when he spoke of the President made Stephen want to pull on Robert's tie till the life ran out of his condescending eyes.

'Oh,' Robert said, recalling something. 'Recently, I asked May to record a message for the families of the deceased passengers and crew. She sent something quite exceptional. Would you like to hear it?'

Stephen nodded. The pain of hearing her voice one last time would be bad, but never hearing it again would be worse.

Robert tapped something on his pad and the audio played.

'This is Maryam Knox, Commander of the *Hawking II*. I want to say to the families of my crew and passengers – our friends and comrades – that I am so very sorry for your loss. Although the events that led to the demise of so many great men and women are still unknown, I take full responsibility, and the sorrow of this catastrophe will remain heavy in my heart until the day I die ...'

41

Fire. The only light in hundreds of miles of dark. Stephen looked skywards. There was no sky, only a canopy of nothingness connecting to the same nothingness all around him. Cold. The worst cold he'd ever felt in his young life. The dark green parka he wore was brand new, along with the black mittens and hat. Aunt Sarah, his father's sister, had given them to him a few hours ago, late Christmas presents. Stephen and his parents had attended her New Year's Eve party in Stowe, an annual tradition. Sarah and her family always had a nice party, maybe a bit wild, like them. Their house was a time capsule, a museum with wood-burning heat and photos of humourless ancestors, stiffly framed against ancient floral wallpaper. Stephen loved it. And them. They gave him grief for being smart, an 'egghead' they would say, laughing through cigarette smoke and the vapours of home-made botanical liqueurs. In their presence, he felt connected to something safe and warm, something like home.

Sitting on the side of a snow-packed road, perched on his father's suitcase, he was no longer safe or warm. Although he shivered and cried, he could not, would not, use the fire to warm him. It smelled of auto fuel and melting rubber, and something else, sweet and sickly. His mind could define it, he thought, but his tongue would not allow him to utter the words. The fire came from a mouth of twisted metal, with broken glass for teeth. It blackened everything, like the soot on the inside of Aunt Sarah's fire stove.

'You better come with us,' a man's voice said.

Stephen didn't hear him. He was still forbidding himself from going near the fire.

'Son, can you hear me?'

'I can't go,' Stephen said weakly.

'You have to, son. You'll freeze out here.'

'I can't go to the fire. I won't go.'

'No, you can't go to the fire.'

A blanket fell over his shoulders. The man spoke to someone else, telling them he'd come upon an accident. He used the word 'fatalities'. *Car and a truck. Found a kid on the side of the road. Definitely in shock.* As he spoke, Stephen held his stomach and closed his eyes. He didn't want to see it again. The total darkness, the sudden headlights and horn blast, his father's wide eyes in the rear-view mirror. His mother reaching for him in the back seat, saying something that sounded like 'hold your breath'. The cloud of glass and splintering car lights as they rolled, upside down, right side up, sliding, falling. Then the fire. Stephen had crawled out the back window and through the snow, looking for his parents. Their suitcases were in the snow, but not them. They were screaming in the car. *Can't go to the fire.*

A voice on a radio spoke back to the man. *Forty-five minutes,* the voice had said. Storm getting worse, the voice also said. Snow fell, dry flakes swirling in a bitter wind, stinging his face and neck. A hand wrapped around Stephen's elbow and pulled him gently to his feet.

'Aunt Sarah gave me this coat.'
'Let's get in my truck, son.'
'I can't leave them.'
'Can't leave who?'
Stephen looked at the fire.
'I can't leave them.'
The man sighed and patted Stephen's back.
'We won't.'

42

'L et's get you home,' Raj said.

The two of them were back in Stephen's office. After telling Raj what Robert had said, he had broken down and was inconsolable. Grasping at straws, he had told Raj about the fact that Robert had said there was no personal message in May's SOS, but this had not had the same impact on Raj as it had had on him.

'What about our sabotage theory?' Stephen asked.

'What about it? Either it's true or it isn't, but it doesn't change the outcome.'

'I know that. What I'm trying to say is—'

'Maybe she's still alive,' Raj said.

'If you do that again, I'll kill you.'

'Okay, this is going nowhere.'

'Why are you so opposed to even talking about this?' Stephen asked.

'It's my way. I don't entertain wild speculation. It's too abstract for me. And it makes me break out in hives. There is absolutely nothing to support this.'

'Hear me out,' Stephen said. 'First, May sends the personal note before the explosion. Could be she knew it was coming and had the wherewithal to send the message. Which means maybe she had the wherewithal to get out in a landing vehicle.'

'That is a stretch, seriously.'

'Agreed, but it's not impossible. Next – and I didn't think about this until now – Robert asked May to record a nice message for the families of the deceased, just before the explosion occurred.'

'Now you've lost me.'

'He's going to spin everything as an unfortunate incident in which May was a victim. It was his idea to give her the commission. If the whole thing fails miserably but she is the sole survivor, that makes him look really bad. But if she goes out heroic, the way she sounds in the recording, it can all be packaged nicely with a yellow fucking ribbon and die a noble death in the press.'

'I'm going to pretend I agree with you. So, now what do we do? The ship is no longer a ship, it's a debris field. If she's in a landing vehicle, she's maybe bought herself another twenty-four hours, max. Same result.'

Stephen broke down again.

'Shit, I'm sorry,' Raj said. 'Arguing with you was a terrible idea. Come on, let's just get drunk, kill the pain for a while.'

Raj tried to wipe away his own tears, but Stephen caught a glimpse.

'No,' he said, sucking back the emotion, 'That will only make things worse. I know this all sounds like bullshit and wishful thinking, and it probably is. I'm not saying I have iron-clad anything to support what is more a feeling than anything. You know me. I don't get hunches. I hate that word as much as you do. I just want more than anything to . . . one last time, to say something to her. Is there any way I can do that, just send a transmission? If it goes into oblivion, so be it. Can you help me?'

'Don't think I haven't been trying to work that out since you brought it up, dude. I really can't think of a way it's possible. I can't send a radio communication to the ship or the landing vehicles. Only Mission Control can do that, and I have no friends in Comms. And I can't think of any other ways to transmit that we could access.'

'What about my research patches? NASA gave me channel-coded data transmission so I could monitor all the lab work. Glenn said they were still live. Robert wanted the team to download all my research data in case the *Hawking II* didn't make it back. All of the landing vehicles have our data terminals.'

'Okay, that's interesting. But how would she know if we were transmitting?'

'I can make some noise with the systems, tell them to operate erratically. And I can run command lines that are messages to her. If she goes to investigate, she'll see them.'

'Not bad,' Raj said. 'We can use my system. Better do it now, before Robert closes up shop for good.'

43

'Internal power, critical. Navigation, critical. Propulsion, failed . . .'

The cargo rig flight computer droned on while it tumbled through space. It looked like a damaged fighter jet in a death spiral: one of its wings had been completely ripped off, while the other remained in its hangar position, flipped up next to the fuselage. The landing struts were partially torn away, dangling and twisting. White smoke and sparks randomly plumed from the engine nozzles.

The shriek of May's suit alarm slapped her awake. Her helmet display was showing she was nearly out of life-support power. It took her a few minutes to fully come to and remember she was in the cargo rig. At the fore was a small, fairly simple flight deck with instrumentation geared for space and atmospheric flight. The bulk of the vessel was its ninety-square-metre cargo area that had been built to house all the heavy equipment the landing party needed to carry out its research and deploy Stephen's NanoSphere. In the aft part of the ship were its massive solid fuel rockets, built to heft the nearly twenty metric tonnes of equipment that went back and forth from the *Hawking II* to Europa. To pilot it in atmosphere, it had retractable wings that spanned twenty-three metres.

The internal lighting was dim and getting worse. Grabbing on to a cargo support rod, May looked through the window and saw the stars passing by erratically.

'Shit. Eve, do you copy?' she called out. 'Please say something.'

Nothing. Her helmet display showed no connection to the *Hawking II*.

'Eve, do you copy?'

Using her dimming headlamp as a guide, she made her way to the bridge. The flight computer was still droning on about the failing ship.

'Flight computer, shut the fuck up.'

'Unrecognisable command.'

'Shut down alarms.'

The alarms ceased and May could think. She strapped herself into a seat at the flight deck. After several tries with the manual control panel, she was able to get some more juice flowing into the vehicle's internal power system. Interior lighting activated, along with the wide touch-screen flight controls. Life-support showed nominal, and her suit was on the brink of shutting down, so she popped off her helmet. There was atmosphere but it was so cold, the water vapour in her nose immediately froze.

Coughing hard, she put her helmet back on without sealing it to the suit, just to keep from succumbing to hypothermia. There were extra battery packs in the EVA locker. She found one with some juice and swapped it with the dead one on her suit. Reading the temperature, the suit automatically kicked its internal heating system into high gear. May re-sealed her helmet and sat back, thawing out and drawing in much-needed oxygen. Finally, she was able to fully assess her situation.

'Flight computer, I need status on internal power.'

'Twelve per cent of capacity.'

'Life-support, time to failure?'

'Seven hours, thirty-five minutes.'

'A nice round number. Propulsion status?'

'Zero per cent of capacity.'

'The engines are gone? Completely?'

'Engine one, one hundred per cent failure. Engine two, no readings.'

May switched on the aft camera. Engine two had been torn from its housing. It was a miracle the cargo rig had not been blown to pieces.

'Engine one, repair requirements?'

'High-pressure fuel turbo pump, replace, high-pressure oxidiser turbo pump, replace, main combustion chamber, replace—'

'You might as well just tell me to replace the entire engine.'

'Recommend return to space dock—'

'Again, shut the fuck up.'

May found the external manoeuvring thruster controls and righted the ship. 'There goes an hour of life-support, but I'd rather not spend my last moments flopping round like a dying mackerel, thanks very much.'

May looked out at the stars and let out a weary sigh of resignation. She felt a slight pinch in her lower abdomen, followed by a brief wave of nausea. Her hand reflexively went there. The area that had felt a bit firm before, now had a gentle rise to it and was harder to the touch. She imagined it as a tiny person, ear pressed to abdomen, hanging on her every word.

'Hello, there . . . baby, for lack of a better moniker. Got something to say about our predicament? Your own two cents? Or, based on size and experience, would it be more like one cent?'

The sharp edge of loneliness she was beginning to feel was slightly dulled by the minuscule presence in her belly. She remembered how awful she'd felt that her mum had died alone, and got some small comfort in knowing she wasn't facing the same fate – even if her little stowaway was most likely the size of a pear.

'Considering I'm the adult here, which isn't saying much, perhaps *I* should inform *you* of our predicament. Suffice to say this big bucket of bolts is about as useless as tits on a bull – might as well learn some Americanisms in honour of your dear old dad – and there's absolutely no hope that the cavalry is going to ride in to save us. As unpleasant as it might sound, it appears . . . we are going to die. In a little over six hours' time.'

May choked back tears.

'My apologies. You didn't get much of a life. And we don't even know each other very well, so I don't mean to embarrass us both by being so emotional. Sometimes I just can't help it, you know? Mum tried to beat all that out of me – well, not literally – but to no avail. I've always thought I got it from my dad. He died when I was young, so I didn't know him all that well either. But I do remember him sitting on the edge of my bed from time to time, very early in the morning, still dark and all, watching me sleep, stroking my hair . . . and he would cry a bit. Not much, mind you. He was a fighter pilot and they're supposed to have ice in their veins. I think he was worried he might not come back . . . and one day he didn't.'

The memory of the day he died came back with greater ease than she would have expected. Her room had been very yellow. She loved yellow, and extremely frilly bedcovers and pillow cases, things Mum couldn't stand. Dad had hung wallpaper, white with a flock of champagne-coloured jays sweeping around the entire room. May liked how determined they looked, their eyes fixed with a singular purpose, whatever it was. The grey sky kept the room dark in the early morning and, try as she might, May could not make out the details of his face. He stroked her hair and, when he bent down to kiss her goodbye, she felt one of his tears fall onto her cheek. He'd whispered that he loved her, as always, and tiptoed out.

'Feel bad you won't get to meet your own dad,' she said. 'Very brilliant man. A scientist. He had this idea that he could make a new world, throw up his hands like a wizard and give it a sun, an ocean, maybe even a sky. Crazy, right? Sounds like magic. It was. He did it. Brilliant man, Stephen Knox. That's his name. But people call him Dr Knox because he's so smart. Anyway, I'm sorry you won't get to meet him. I'm sure he would let you have a yellow room too if you wanted it.'

The pang returned. A little more intense this time.

'Can you not do that, baby? I hate that feeling. It was like when I was a kid and I first woke up. I'd be so hungry, I'd feel ... ah, I get it. I'm a bit peckish myself. Not to be morbid, but everyone deserves a decent last meal. Although don't get your hopes up. In this crate we'll be lucky to find anything at all.'

May unstrapped herself from the flight deck chair and floated through the ship, looking for ration stores. It was her first time on the cargo rig, so she wasn't quite sure where to look. Around the flight deck, there were water sleeves and nutri-paks, but she held out hope for something a little more substantial. She floated through the cargo hold, examining all the storage pods. Near the back, she heard faint machine noises. She followed them until she found the source: a piece of equipment under a polyethylene cover. In addition to the sounds, lights pulsed on and off, glowing behind the cover's opaque surface.

'That won't do. We can't have whatever this thing is drawing our precious power.'

May pulled herself down to the floor and removed the cover.

44

'Wake up,' Raj yelled.

Stephen had been asleep on the couch in Raj's office, a dark, windowless cavern with furniture that looked as though it had been taken from a condemned building and a C-shaped desk lined with glowing monitor screens that took up half the space. Raj stared into one of the screens, looking like a hacker whose lair was in the basement of a crack house.

'What?' Stephen yelled back as he sat up and tried to remember where he was.

'Get over here, you gotta see this.'

Stephen got up and stumbled over countless unseen things, cursing each one, on his way to Raj. 'This what?' He peered at the screen.

> Got your messages cheeky bastards. Music
> to my ears.

'Holy shit,' Stephen said, hugging Raj so hard he almost fell out of his chair.

'Told you she was still alive,' Raj said, smiling broadly.

'Holy shit.'

'You said that already.'

'I'm at a loss for words, Raj,' Stephen said, giddy with excitement. 'Holy *shit.*'

'There's bad news too, man.'

'Yeah,' Stephen said, lowering his voice, 'I know. We—'

Raj held his finger to his lips. He walked to another work table that was littered with various mechanical parts and odd-looking machines. He turned one of the machines on. It made a very aggravating pulse sound, similar to submarine sonar, but with a higher pitch. He walked up next to Stephen.

'Okay, we can talk. Low voices.'

'What is that horrible thing?'

'Gravitational wave sound amplifier. For transmitting sound waves in space. Something I've been working on. Also good for creating feedback on listening devices.'

'So, we're in agreement on the sabotage theory? Strong enough evidence?'

'Damning, but that's not the bad news. I mean it is bad news, but it's not the worst news.'

'What could be worse than that? Our fearless leader is at best a lying piece of shit and at worst a cold-blooded killer. We can't trust—'

'May's on the cargo rig, your eighteen-wheeler. That's why she put eighteen on the end of that original SOS message.'

'Must've seen the NanoSphere generator we activated.'

'Exactly. She sent me the vehicle status. Take a look.'

Raj pulled it up on the screen. Stephen's heart sank.

'How the hell did it get damaged so badly? The explosion?'

'No, she was in the hangar and the emergency purge was

241

activated. Blew the damn hangar door off and it took some of the ship with it. She was out cold when the cargo rig and everything else in the hangar got sucked out into space. She thinks that's why it's damaged.'

Stephen sat down on the back of the couch, completely deflated. 'Then she's dead in the water. Her and the . . .'

'I'm so sorry.'

'How long?'

'Message took an hour to get here and she said she was down to around six when she sent it.'

'This isn't happening, Raj,' Stephen said angrily. 'We found her. We did it. They tried to sweep her under the rug and we didn't let them. We can't let them.'

'We're out of options, Stephen.'

'No. I'm going to Robert. He's going to fix this or I'm going to destroy him.'

'He can't fix it. Even with your gun to his head. No one can. This is the cold equation, man. Only one answer.'

'I can't . . . I don't believe that.'

Raj sat in silence, not wanting to give Stephen anything else to fight.

'You should, uh, you know, sit here and talk to her. Make the best of . . . be with her right now. I'll leave you so you can . . . you know.'

Stephen nodded and sat back down next to Raj. He stared at the screen, reading what May had written. It sounded like a suicide note. Everything had come down on her at once; everything was against her. She had crawled, tooth and nail, out of one grave, just to fall into another. It was a cruel joke. That was why Stephen couldn't accept it. She had told him once that, no matter how bad things got, in the end everything evened out. Nobody had nothing but bad luck. He was looking right at evidence to the contrary, but refused to see it as such. His first physics professor taught him about the Law of Opposites. *Everything in existence is a combination or unity of opposites.* Without light, there is no darkness.

'Light,' Stephen said to Raj.

'I told you, those fluorescents they have here hurt my eyes.'

'No, sunlight. The NanoSphere. Billions of intelligent little machines with a hard-on for sunlight.'

'Holy shit,' Raj said, his eyes lighting up. 'Solar sail?'

Stephen nodded.

'Unlimited power. Even out there in the dark.'

'You tell May the plan, and that we're already on it,' Raj said, hopping with nervous energy, 'so she doesn't lose hope. Then, while you figure out how to create the sail, and walk May through deploying it – uh, side note, she'll have to use some of her ship power to buy a little EVA time, which will be scary, but ... necessary. While you do that, I'm going to figure out how to connect the sail to the cargo rig's internal power. That will buy us enough life-support time. And, yeah, definitely need to attach it properly – wait, she's going the wrong way, toward the sun ...'

'I can orient the nano-machines at any angle, so this will not be anything like a normal solar sail,' Stephen said. 'Keep in mind we want to push her toward Mars – more specifically the *Hawking II*'s Mars course. If you can calculate the red planet's orbital path, in relation to her, I can constantly shift the angle of the machines, back and forth, drawing power and building momentum. And I can control her velocity, to some degree. Essentially, it would be like tacking the ship like a sailboat, something I know very well.'

'That is just fucking sexy,' Raj said and looked at his watch. 'Cool. So, taking into consideration how much time we have till the rig runs out of internal power, travel time for our comms, and other factors my brain knows exist but won't allow me to

articulate verbally, we need to get all of this done in about . . .
fifteen minutes. Oh, and don't forget to tell her about Robert
and not to trust anyone at NASA. From now on, *we* are
Mission Control.'

45

May checked her EVA suit power. She had a full hour, having drained some of the cargo rig's precious internal power so she could go out and deploy Stephen's nano-machines. There were four NanoSphere generators and she needed two. Thankfully, they were well charged, and designed to use some of the solar radiation they gathered to continually recharge themselves. The plan was to attach them to the fore of the vessel, one on either side of the flight deck, to create two large sails. Because of the time it took to send data, Stephen had to send pre-programmed telemeter information to the generators in order to control her flight path and put her on track to intercept the *Hawking II*'s course for Mars.

It was dizzyingly complicated, factoring in Mars's orbital path in relation to the sun and the *Hawking II*'s estimated position. The only confirmation they had that the *Hawking II* still existed was a heat signature Raj had detected that was consistent with what its engines would produce. May had likened it to following a fart to find someone in the dark. Add to that the fact that the NanoSphere, although more than adequate to perform such a task, had never been used as a solar sail. May tried not to think of all the towering 'if's that could be the weakest links leading to failure. Instead, she thought of the 2.73 hours of life-support she was down to, and how she much preferred to go out swinging.

'Hey, you,' she said, patting her belly. 'Ready for this? Just try not to make me want to barf out there, okay? I think that's the least one can expect from a stowaway.'

The cargo rig was not set up for EVA, so prepping that part had been tricky. Because she needed to open the bay doors to deploy the generators on the outside of the ship, she sealed off the flight deck and slowly bled atmosphere from the cargo bay. When it was pressurised for space, she blew the emergency bolts and opened the cargo bay door.

Unlike the *Hawking II*, the cargo rig had very few external lights, so she had to work in relative darkness, detaching the nano-generators from the floor and carrying each one outside to the top of the ship. They were large and cumbersome, shaped like huge fire hydrants, and not easy to manoeuvre, even weight-less. Following Stephen's detailed instructions on the inside of her helmet screen, she secured them to the docking plates on either side of the flight deck. The plates were like the frame of a car, the strongest attachment points for crane-lifting the vehicle in gravity.

After making sure they were properly attached, May powered them up. The nano-machines started moving within the hous-ing immediately, making a very loud buzzing sound that settled into a deep hum she could feel in her chest. Having fed Stephen's command lines into the generators while still on board, all she had to do was activate them.

'Well, these babies are either going to blow us to kingdom come, or take us home.'

May knelt down by the first generator and held tightly to a safety bar. She activated the generator, then did the same to the other. The hum returned to a buzzing, which was ten times louder than before. Slowly, she backed away and tethered her suit to the ship. In a dazzling flash, clouds of nano-machines poured out of the generators. At first, they flew around erratically and May feared they were going to simply buzz off into space. Then they came together like a flock of birds, moving in unison. May was in awe as they settled into their final formations, two square-shaped sails, each the size of half a football pitch. Within minutes they were working, and May could feel the cargo rig picking up speed.

'Huzzah!' she yelled triumphantly. 'Ahoy there and all that rot. We're fucking sailing. Not bad, Dr Knox, not bad at all.'

Next, she pulled out the rig's charger cables, normally used to draw power from the *Hawking II*, and attached them to the generators. When she got back into the cargo bay and checked the rig's power levels, they had risen.

'Knock on wood,' she said excitedly, 'but we might just get out of this yet.'

After closing the cargo bay door and re-pressurising, she sent a message to Stephen and Raj, confirming solar sail deployment, and strapped herself back into the flight deck chair. The plan at that point was to pilot the ship to intercept the *Hawking II*, using a combination of Stephen's programmed flight and the cargo rig's orbital manoeuvring thrusters. She just needed to wait a bit for internal power to juice up. May looked out of the flight deck windows at the sails as they tacked by the angle of the sun and gathered momentum. Like an actual sail, they rippled elegantly, gently rocking the ship from side to side.

46

October 15, 2066 – Key West, Florida

'I could just lie here forever.'

May was lounging on the fore tramp of a thirty-eight-foot catamaran while Stephen piloted her around the western edge of Wisteria Island. It was a pristine autumn day, with a cool, steady southerly wind cutting the heat. May was entranced by the light grey clouds moving swiftly overhead, their edges glowing silver as they passed through the eye of the sun.

'Could you get me another iced tea? I love it with the mint leaves.'

'Excuse me,' Stephen said as he stood sweating over the wheel. 'I thought this was my birthday present. Shouldn't *you* be getting *me* iced tea while *I* relax in the sun?'

May sat up and playfully lowered her sunglasses to look at him. 'But I thought you loved to sail?' she said, grinning.

'You're funny.'

'I'm happy to, um, drive if you like.'

'Drive? That's all right. We don't have enough provisions on board for an impromptu trip to Cuba.'

She lay back down and held up her glass, shaking the ice cubes expectantly. 'Happy birthday,' she said, laughing.

To celebrate Stephen's thirty-fourth it had been May's idea to fly down to Key West for a long weekend. When they had arrived, a couple of days ago, May had hired a car and driven them down to Whitehead Spit. She'd parked in front of a quaint Conch House, with two porches and a water view.

'Surprise,' she said.

Stephen got out of the car, and stared in disbelief.

'Oh, my God. I don't usually say that because I don't really believe in God, but ... oh, my God.'

'You like it?' May asked coyly.

'How did you know about this place?'

'You told me about it on our ... third date. Winery tour. You were a bit pissed on Merlot, staggering down Memory Lane.'

'That's nice?' Stephen said, distracted.

He walked up to the front porch and drank it all in. This was the beach house his parents had taken him to, on winter vacations before they died. There was an old telescope next to the same Adirondack chairs he'd sat in with them.

He removed the cap and looked out at the ocean. 'I used to spot boats from here. Kept a log of everything that passed.'

'Present from Raj. He made a point of letting me know he spent hours hunting one down on the dark web or the pirate web or some web only Raj and a few other spods know about. Said you could use it to carry on spying on beach babes.'

'Good old Raj. My genius degenerate best friend.'

They sat in the Adirondack chairs and looked out at the water. The sun splashed colour on the waves as it clung to the horizon. The wood on the porch, grey and speckled with salt and age, was rough on May's bare feet, warning her of splinters if she moved too quickly.

'The smell is what really takes me back,' Stephen said with tears in his eyes. 'When I was still little, my dad and I sailed in the afternoons on our twenty-five-foot raised deck cutter, just gliding through whitecaps, sometimes fishing if the wind was down. When we came back at dinner time, my mom would always be reading on the porch. The air was thick and sweet from the flowers opening. Almost every night we had this same ocean breeze. It would kind of sweep up through the sand into the garden, then up here on the porch. After being in the heat all day, we'd get a little chilly.'

'Those sound like very fond memories,' May said, holding his hand.

'This place is . . . it *is* my childhood.'

'So, I done good?'

'You done damn good.' He pulled May in for a kiss and quickly went inside to have a look.

'I guess I'll bring in the bags, then, Peter Pan,' May laughed, pleased at his reaction.

When she walked inside, Stephen was wandering around, rediscovering everything.

'Hasn't changed a bit. Like a time capsule.'

May instantly fell in love with the place. Its sheer white curtains glowed with fingers of light as they waved gently against the grey window frames and leaded glass. Old, fraying rugs with faded colours and patterns were still spread across the thin oak flooring, covering the years of scratches and burn marks underneath. The walls were freshly painted, white with blue trim.

Electric lights, running water and an ancient cooking stove were the extent of the creature comforts. There were no phones to ring, no screens to watch, and no data invisibly bombarding them from every angle. It took both of them a while to get used to the silence, but then they relished it. That night, they took a walk on the moonlit beach.

'Best birthday present ever,' Stephen said.

'Really? Better than the birthday when you got a new dirt bike?'

'Wow. You really listen to me and remember things I say. In great detail.'

'Uh, yeah. I'm your wife, so I have to listen to your boring stories and laugh at your terrible jokes. It's my job.'

'Just like my job as your husband is to ignore all of yours.'

'Exactly. We're well on our way to becoming the old married couple we've always dreamed we could be.'

'We are the weirdest people I know,' Stephen said, laughing.

'Hallelujah. Speaking of that, where's the dock you used to sneak out and fish from at night while your mum and dad were asleep?'

'My God, your memory is like a steel trap,' Stephen said, amazed.

They walked to the dock and stood next to the pylons, the warm waves rushing over their feet and sinking them deeper into the sand.

'Look at the moon on the water,' Stephen said, walking out further.

'Watch out,' May yelled back just before a wave knocked him off his feet.

Stephen fell backwards, under the wave, and struggled to his feet, coughing and sputtering. May helped him up, screeching with laughter.

'I meant to do that,' he joked, spitting out the salt water.

'Thought you'd go for a casual dip, eh?' she said.

He kissed her.

'Hey, let's go up on the dock where all the teenagers used to make out.'

'So, Raj was right about you and that telescope,' she joked, and took his hand.

They walked to the end of the dock and sat with their feet dangling. Down in the dark water, there were hundreds of tiny blue-green lights glowing just below the surface.

'That's amazing,' May exclaimed. 'They're like ocean stars.'

'Dinoflagellates,' Stephen said. 'Single-celled organisms. They create that light, kind of like fireflies. Bioluminescence.'

'Don't ruin it with your science. They're ocean stars.'

'Look, there's the big dipper, ha ha ha,' Stephen said in a goofy voice.

'Hilarious.'

May lay down on the dock and pulled Stephen down next to her. The high clouds were breaking up, revealing the bright half-moon and stars.

'There, that's better,' May said. 'The real thing.'

Stephen rolled to the side and touched May's belly. She pulled up her T-shirt and he put his ear to her belly button.

'Hear anything?' she asked.

'Only grumbling,' Stephen said.

'Surprise surprise, the beast within has made me hungry again.'

Stephen lay back down and watched the stars intensely.

'What's going on in that massive brain of yours?' she said. 'I can hear the gears whirring about.'

'Really?'

'It's deafening.'

'Not looking forward to going back to work.'

'It'll be fine,' she said. 'Besides, one of us has to be gainfully employed so I can sit around the house watching telly and getting fat on chocolates.'

'I just hate the idea of being up there on the station, so far away. It's not like I can just hop on a plane and come home whenever I want.'

'Are you worried about me?'

'No, I'm—'

'You are. That is so sweet. But you know I'm a badass and I can take care of myself.'

'Yes,' he said, sighing. 'I know.'

'So stop worrying. I'm going to be fine. The baby is going to be fine. We are going to be just fine. Say it, please.'

'We are going to be just fine.'

'See, it's that simple. Now stop ruining the vibe and look at the stars.'

He did and they sat there for a long time, their hands clasped on May's belly. Stephen turned on his side to face her again. She did the same, propping herself up on her elbow to face him. She could see he was still ruminating about something.

'What now, Dr Knox?'

'I know you've told me this already, but I like to check in from time to time to make sure you don't have any—'

'Regrets?' she asked, rolling her eyes.

'Sorry. I'll shut up now.'

'The answer is still no,' she said firmly, looking him in the eyes. 'I have no regrets.'

'Good.'

They kissed, then Stephen lay back down. May sat up, pretending to look down at her glowing sea creatures so Stephen wouldn't see the tears running down her cheeks. She thought of what she really wanted to say, but didn't dare, knowing what it would do to him.

I don't have regrets, but I'll never stop grieving the loss of a lifelong dream.

'You okay?' he asked.

'Perfect. I just wanted to look at my little ocean stars before they're gone.'

47

'The dawn of the solar system,' Stephen used to tell his students, 'gave rise to life as we know it, all over the universe. But, like most epic parties, it left one hell of a mess.'

That line had never failed to get a laugh, but, as Stephen and Raj tracked May's course, the science behind it was grim. The main asteroid belt, comprised of trillions of hunks of rock ranging in size from small boulders to planetoids several thousand feet in diameter, orbited the sun between Jupiter and Mars. In Raj's initial calculations, May's course was not expected to intersect with any of the groups in the belt. However, Stephen's solar sail, although generating a surplus of power, had not maintained the pre-set course as well as they'd hoped. May was helping by making thruster adjustments, but they were not powerful enough to fully counteract the sails, and the cargo rig was heading straight for a dense cluster group. The rocks were far enough apart that there was a chance she could still slip through, but at current velocity, which they didn't dare alter for fear she would miss the *Hawking II*, impact with even one of the smaller asteroids would likely destroy the ship.

'What about using gravity from one of the larger ones to slingshot around the outside edge?' Raj asked. 'Then we could reduce velocity so we don't overshoot *Hawking*.'

'With our current momentum, that would create more velocity than I would have the ability to counteract. We would overshoot for sure.'

'Does she have enough momentum to cut the sails loose and adjust her course with thrusters?' Raj asked, looking at his chart. 'Never mind – she doesn't. We're still going to have to pull her up to this point, just past the field, to get her there on momentum.'

'Looks like we're hoping for the best,' Stephen said. 'Our worst nightmare.'

48

Back on the cargo rig, May's navigation system was telling her the same thing. Flying through the asteroid belt was her only chance to rendezvous with the *Hawking II* and the entry point was rapidly approaching. Just as Raj and Stephen had already concluded, she had no ability to control her velocity, which had increased dramatically, and very little ability to manoeuvre the ship using thrusters. Remembering what she'd learned in parachute training, though, she knew you could alter course by pulling heavily on one of the steering lines. Because she had more than enough internal power, she could afford to expend huge amounts blasting thrusters on either side in a counterforce move similar to a parachute. This could more dramatically alter her trajectory, if need be, without damping velocity enough to throw her off course.

'Asteroid belt approaching,' the flight computer reported.

'Sorry to hear that,' May said arrogantly.

'Take evasive action.'

'No, thanks, I prefer to live on the edge.'

May wrapped her hands around the thruster controllers.

Larger rocks in the asteroid belt were coming into view. She would be at the entry point in less than a minute. All she had to do was make it through three thousand, eight hundred kilometres of hell and she was home free.

'Right, look, Mum, no engines,' she yelled. 'I know you like a challenge so fancy this one? Flying a great lumbering bulldozer with the brain of a dairy cow and the agility of a cruise ship through a minefield of stony death . . . with nothing but my wits and proverbial balls to guide me. Wouldn't you be proud, you Fascist drill sergeant?'

The entry point was upon her.

'Fuck me,' she said, her mouth drying.

Blackened, spiny rocks loomed like skyscrapers, blotting out most of what little sunlight there was. The first few seconds of entry went smoothly, but she kept her eyes on the larger boulders to ensure none was directly in her path. In doing so, she never saw the smaller, beachball-sized rock coming. It hit the cargo rig's folded wing on the port side and tore half of it away. The impact felt like getting hit head-on by a freight train. May screamed as it jarred her bones and the seat straps yanked savagely into her body.

She could feel the rig starting to drift to port, so she blasted it back on course with all the thrust she could pull on the starboard side. Fifty-five seconds. That was about how much time was left on the flight deck timer. Less than a minute to live or die.

'Kid,' she said, catching her breath, 'when you're older and you tell me you want to be a pilot, remind me to give you a sound thrashing and enrol you in art school.'

The field got darker, to the point that she couldn't see past the few hundred feet of light the rig's landing beacons threw. She took steady, deep breaths to keep her brain well oxygenated, found a focal point in the centre of her field of vision that her eyes could remain fixed on no matter what was happening in the periphery, and cleared her mind of thought. Fighter pilot mode. There would only be time to react with muscle memory and instinct. Thinking equalled certain death.

The seconds counted down at a glacial pace, May made slight moves to steer well clear of potential collisions, but the cluster was getting tighter. She worried about the sails, which stretched nearly forty metres out from the edge of the ship. Above her, she saw an asteroid the size of an office building and felt certain the top edge of her port side sail was going to hit it. Reflexively, she hit the top side-thrusters to move down and away from it. It narrowly missed hitting the sail, but the move put her last solid landing strut in the path of the top of a larger rock, which smashed into it full force and tore it away.

Impact with this much heavier body forced the nose of the rig downwards. May tried to counteract with thrust, but couldn't keep it from going into a forward spin. The nano-machines were blown out of their sail shapes as the rear of the ship flipped over and ripped through the swarms. It sounded as though the fuselage was being pummelled with sand and rocks, and one of the generators burst into flames.

Flying completely blind, May was so dizzy she could barely stay conscious. She saw the clock at zero and brighter space outside indicating she'd made it through the belt, but she had to right the ship, and deal with the fire, which had spread to the second generator. Blazing against freezing space, it had no way to go but back into the ship. Focusing on the instruments for orientation, she worked the thrusters till the spinning stopped. Then she suited up quickly, depressurised the cargo space, and went EVA with a fire tank.

The blaze was still raging, fuelled by the metal in the nano-machines. They exploded out in great plumes that looked like showers of sparks. She did what she could with the fire cannon to lessen it, but realised it would not be enough. Crawling along the top of the ship, trying to keep the burning debris from incinerating her suit, she released the docking clamps holding down the generators and shoved them out into space.

The fire cannon snuffed out the rest but blew some burning debris onto her boot, setting it on fire. May tried to kill it with fire foam but the tank was out. Dragging along the top of the ship, it continued to burn as she crawled back to the cargo doors. The small fire died from lack of fuel, but only because it had fully perforated her suit. The suit kicked into life-support overdrive, but by the time May had re-sealed the bay door and re-pressurised the rig her first three toes were frozen solid.

49

May took her boot and sock off. The tips of her first three toes were heavily blistered from frostbite. That would have to be dealt with later to avoid gangrene. Her first priority was to make sure she was still on course. Checking her vector, she had deviated a little but not enough to miss the intercept with a bit of thruster correction. Next was figuring out if she even had anything to intercept.

'Computer, have you established contact with the *Hawking II*?'

'Affirmative. Distress beacon lock only.'

'Yes!' May shouted. 'What about telemetry or radio comms?'

'Negative.'

The distress beacon was an automatic signal emitted by the ship in the event of catastrophic damage and crew incapacitation. May wondered how Robert was suppressing that, hiding it from the rest of the team, but, like her toes, she would deal with that bit of dead flesh later. For her, it was a crude life-ring she could use to stay accurately on course, but little else. The absence of any other comms was a clear indication that the ship was as dead as when she'd left it and Eve was not at the helm.

'Flight computer, time to *Hawking II* intercept?'

'Twelve minutes, fourteen seconds.'

May checked the rig's internal power. 'Shit.' Thruster use and the second ship repressurisation had greedily sucked away her entire surplus, leaving her with roughly six to eight minutes of internal power. She looked at the EVA suit's power meter. There was roughly forty minutes left on that, enough life-support to make it back to the ship, provided she found a way to seal her boot. But ... when the cargo rig ran out of power, she would have no thrusters to slow the ship down for docking. At her current velocity, she would hit the ship like a missile and destroy what was left of it. Not that there was any place left to dock, as the landing hangar had been destroyed.

May looked for ways to buy more power for the cargo rig. If she killed life-support and wore her EVA suit for the duration, that would buy her enough power to use thrusters up until she was two minutes from impact. Not enough to be worth the risk of having zero control just before intercept, and she would still be coming in dangerously hot.

'Time to *Hawking II*?'

'Eight minutes, four seconds.'

Six minutes to make a decision. She put her boot back on and taped the burn hole. Then she sprayed hull patch over the top of the tape, covering the entire bottom of the boot.

'Decelerate for docking.'

She punched the command console. 'Tell me something I don't know, idiot.'

'Inadequate power for reverse thrusters. Prepare emergency landing countermeasures.'

'I'm not landing on a planet surface, you— Wait, list countermeasures.'

The console displayed something called 'impact foam shell', a rapid-deployment, fire-retardant foam that spigots positioned

261

all around the rig would spray out with compressed air, encasing it in a rubberised shell five metres thick.

'Can't hurt. Prepare emergency landing countermeasures for manual deployment.'

A manual control lever slid out from the side of the console.

'Time to *Hawking II*?'

'Four minutes, fifty-five seconds.'

May quickly put on her EVA helmet and sealed it to her suit. Then she depressurised the flight deck to normalise with space.

'Right. Listen, kid, here's what's happening. Since today is your first amusement park ride, I figure we need to end it with a bang. Just over two minutes out, I am going to hit the reverse thrusters and burn the rest of our power slowing us down as much as possible. Then, just before we bash into the hangar, I'll deploy the foam and turn us into a massive super-ball. With any luck, we'll wedge into the hangar without dying or doing too much damage to the mother ship. Got it? Outstanding. Flight computer, time to *Hawking II*?'

'Three minutes, thirty-three seconds.'

'Let's do this.'

May rested her finger next to the reverse thruster control and watched the seconds tick down. Her stomach fluttered slightly.

'Easy. I'm starving too, okay? Soon as we park this crate, I promise to tuck away a full three-course space meal, whether I find it repulsive or not. Deal? Right, hold on.'

Just before two minutes to impact, May got ready to hit reverse thrusters and deploy the foam. The *Hawking II* came into view in the distance.

'Here we are. Looks like we still mostly have a ship, so that's a good start. Computer, zoom in on the *Hawking II* with fore camera.'

May zoomed into the landing vehicle hangar. On the side where the hangar door had torn away from the ship, it had taken half the floor and all the landing vehicles with it, including May's cargo rig. The other side was fire-blackened and pock-marked from shrapnel, as though it had been hit by a bomb. She held off on using the thrusters.

'Right. Change of plan. No place to land whatsoever. Blow emergency escape hatch, flight computer.'

'Negative. Bolts are for deployment in atmosphere.'

'Fine, be that way.' May snatched up a laser cutter, cut through the hatch bolts and hinges, and pushed the heavy door off into space.

'Error. Error.'

'Shut up. Time to impact?'

'One minute, three seconds.'

'Load speed of this vessel and *Hawking II* speed to my EVA helmet.'

Both speeds appeared on her helmet screen.

'Calculate reverse thrust speed needed for safe intercept.'

That number appeared.

'Got it. Let's hope you're not as dumb as you sound.'

'Inadequate thruster power. Landing bay not operational,' it droned back.

'Thanks for the confidence boost. Well, flight computer, it's been fun, but I'm breaking up with you. Oh, and it's not me, it's definitely you.'

'I don't understand.'

'You will.'

At forty seconds, May positioned all starboard side thrusters to blow everything they had straight out and perpendicular to her trajectory when fired. Then she grabbed a hull patch spray canister and a long rod from the ice core driller and crawled up out of the escape hatch. Outside, she held a safety rung with one hand and carefully rested the end of the metal rod on the thruster switch down in the flight deck. Impact was seconds away.

'Hold on, kid, this is going to make that asteroid thing feel like a casual stroll.'

May punched the thruster switch with the rod and jumped, slamming her suit's reverse thrusters into full power. Below her, the cargo rig veered hard left and flew ahead of her, narrowly missing the *Hawking II* before it shot off into space. May was heading straight for the ship now. Reverse thrusters had knocked her suit speed down close to that of *Hawking II*, but she was coming in too fast to survive impact.

At the last second, she held the spray patch canister in front of her, nozzle facing the ship, and let it rip till it knocked her speed down to a safe number for impact. But it also threw her slightly off course. Veering dangerously to the left, and fearing she would fly past, she aimed the suit's emergency tether at the fuselage and fired. The dart shot out, its long titanium cable whipping out behind, and stuck in one of the jagged pieces of landing hangar wall. The cable reached its full length and caught May, jerking her hard back towards the passing ship. She screamed in pain and felt her suit rip where the base of the tether was attached. The suit atmosphere started to bleed out quickly. May gasped for air as the intense cold rushed in and her body temperature started to drop.

50

May remembered the hull patch canister. She sprayed it on the rip in her suit, sealing and restoring her air, but she was still so cold, she had a hard time pulling herself to the *Hawking II* with the tether cable. The rip had also sucked a lot of power from the suit, as it had increased life-support output to compensate. Suit power was down to ten minutes. She started to warm up and pulled harder, trying to get to the ship faster. It was dangerous to assume the ship's atmosphere was intact. She might need time to get a new EVA battery pack once she got inside. The feeling had come back in her limbs, so she pulled even harder.

'Come on, baby. Almost there.'

The dart pulled free from the hull. May's pulling action made her instantly flip backwards. She was tumbling through space, disorientated and grasping for anything. The tether cable caught on the jagged edge of one of the hangar's ruined walls. When it caught, it stopped May's free-fall, but the force of the catch pulled it away from the wall again. May was moving back towards the wall, but also drifting out towards the edge. If she didn't stop, she would fly into space. And, with her suit down to eight minutes of power, thrusters would quickly deplete life-support before she made it back.

She had no choice but to hit them before reaching the edge. Using just enough to get back to the wall, May grabbed on to it firmly and made her way to the airlock door. It had been damaged and was no longer operational. She cut through the hinges and latch with the laser cutter and pulled it away, crawling inside.

'Well, kid, how'd you like that? Bet you didn't know your mum was a superhero. But don't get cocky, we're nowhere near out of the woods. Outer airlock is off. Inner airlock is closed and appears to be operational. If I open it, and there is still atmosphere in the ship, it will be sucked out and the force of it will make it impossible for us to go through the inner airlock door. So, as much as I loathe the idea of going to another airlock, that's what we're going to do. And I'd better get moving, because this suit has a six-minute expiry time.'

May reeled in her tether and moved along the outer edge of the deck, using the handholds and a safety line. The ship was tremoring the way it had before, and May lost her grip a few times when it shook. By the time she got to the airlock door outside the bridge, she had two minutes of suit power left. She opened the airlock with the manual latch, crawled in and sealed it, then opened the inner door to the ship.

The ship was dark and freezing cold, just like when she first woke up. But this time it had also lost artificial gravity. As she moved quickly through the corridor, using the anti-gravity hand-holds, May's suit alarms were sounding her last minute of life-support. At the EVA locker, she wrenched the door open and searched for a new battery pack in the dark. The suit power ran out and she had to take very shallow breaths of the last of her residual air. The first pack she found was dead. She

266

threw it aside angrily and snatched up another. It was fully charged. Atmosphere and heat quickly returned, along with her head lamp.

She floated there for a moment, finally taking a breath, and thought about what had just happened. Her whole body shook from the adrenaline come-down. Her mind could barely grasp what they'd managed to escape. *They.* She touched her belly lightly, this time hoping no harm had come to her little stowaway. In fact, she very much feared it had, and that thought fell heavy in her chest.

In that moment, clarity cut right through her incredible weariness. She and her seventeen-week-old stowaway had gone to Hell and back. And, if this kid was still kicking after all that, he or she had just earned a lifelong membership to the crew. As commander, it was May's job to lay down her life to protect her crew, and that was exactly what she was going to do. She no longer gave a shit about practicality or what anyone would think, not even her dead mother. This was her truth, and she could look it right in the eye and live with herself.

'Welcome to square one, kid,' she said. 'Now, what do you say we go see how properly fucked we are?'

51

R eactor failure. Detonation imminent. Evacuate.

This message appeared on the flight deck command console after May powered it up by manual hand crank. She couldn't help but laugh.

'Detonation imminent? What's next, an alien attack?'

Back when May had re-established contact with NASA, their engineers had logged and video-captured their entire procedure for getting the engines and reactor fully operational again. She hand-cranked more power into the command console and transferred that data pack to her EVA suit. The problem before had been that the reactor had overheated and could not vent properly or distribute the energy it was producing. If this was the same error, replicating Mission Control's repairs could save them.

Looking at the schematics and repair sequence, it was intimidating, but doable. That repair had taken nearly four hours for Mission Control to complete using telemetry. May's suit power was at 2.75 hours, but she would not be dealing with a communications delay. That was all the time she had, anyway. The rest of the battery packs in the EVA locker were dead and there was no way to charge them without restoring internal power.

Her stomach grumbled madly.

'All right. Far be it for me to prioritise saving our lives over filling your belly.'

May hydrated with the suit's internal pack and ate as many of the high-calorie nutri-gels stored inside the suit as she could keep down. That, plus a heavy dose of mind-sharpening glucose tabs, satiated them both for the time being. She headed for the reactor and engine decks using the anti-gravity handholds to push off and fly through the ship's central corridor. Strapped to her suit was a bag with every available torch with any juice left.

The ship shuddered periodically, bouncing May around like a pinball, but the tremors were not as intense as they had been before. And each one came with a heat blast. May assumed it was the reactor venting off energy that would eventually build past the breaking point and blow the ship apart. The only good thing was that it kept the ship's internal systems from freezing solid and being rendered useless. And May had to admit, she was enjoying being warm for a change. But that quickly lost its charm the closer she got to the reactor, where the heat made her break out into a sweat.

She found the sealed reactor hatch and opened it with the manual wheel crank, revealing the narrow metal access tunnel that led directly to the maintenance module. The tunnel was only about two metres wide, a tight squeeze in an EVA suit. The time left on her suit was approximately 2.2 hours.

'Kid, I apologise in advance if you end up being born with nine heads.'

May crawled in and inched her way through the tunnel. The further she went, the hotter it got, but she didn't dare waste

269

precious suit power on internal cooling. She could take the heat, but made a note to keep an eye on her hydration. 'I guess those years living in Houston have finally paid off.'

When her helmet light widened out at the end of the tunnel, she was happy to swim out into the small maintenance module. The room felt alive, pulsating and tropical hot. May used the hand crank to provide power to the command console and viewed the reactor monitoring board. She then compared that to what the board had displayed back when Mission Control was doing repairs. They were nearly identical. The reactor was still fusing hydrogen nuclei together to create helium isotopes, generating power that had nowhere to go, generating heat that was not being properly released.

There were 1.45 hours on the suit. Enough time to get the job done if she didn't pass out.

'Let's take a look under the hood.'

Following the repair sequence on the video recording, she removed the bolts on the repair panel with the pneumatic tools stored next to it. As she scanned its inner workings, preparing to perform the first step in the sequence, she heard a metallic clank behind her. Figuring it was just the metal panel, she turned to try to grab and secure it.

A woman's corpse was floating behind her, arms outstretched in a way that made it look as though she was reaching out to strangle someone. May screamed and instinctively shoved the body away, plunging it back into darkness. She shone her light around the immediate area and the beam caught the edge of the body nearby. It was in a corner, gently bumping up against the wall. May grabbed the corpse's arm and rotated it to get a look at her face. Unlike the bodies she'd found in the landing vehicle hangar, this one was highly decomposed. May reckoned it was because she'd died around the same time as the others and had been rotting on the ship until her body was frozen by the recent power loss. A bio code scan showed her name: Gabriella Dos Santos, her flight engineer.

'Could have used you in here, Gabi,' she said through tears.

After quickly fantasising about the many exotic ways she was going to give Robert Warren an agonising death, May secured Gabi's body to the floor grate and got back to the repairs. When she was finished, it appeared she had done everything correctly. The heat in the room had dissipated substantially, as it had in the video of the previous repair.

'Right. On to the engine deck.'

The ship shuddered, emphasising that point. With forty-five minutes of suit power left, May made her way down the central corridor to the adjacent engine deck. It was a relief to be in a much larger, and more familiar, space. It was in there that the EmDrive propulsion system, or radio frequency resonant cavity thruster, housed its huge magnetron core, pulling millions of gigawatts from the reactor to push microwaves into the engine cones. Or something to that effect. May understood it as well as most pilots . . . not all that well. She located the problem area and repaired the reactor's venting system. The next step was to clear a power bottleneck in the induction unit that converted reactor energy into electricity.

She moved to the area housing the electricity converters, one of which contained the faulty induction unit. The floor and walls were non-conducting rubber. Light blue arcs and static spark showers coming from fissures in connection points gave the room a bluish hue. With no ability to stay connected to that floor in anti-gravity, she needed to watch out for the spark showers caused when the current struck anything metal. One of those sparks could set her suit ablaze.

The power induction unit was near the back of the room, a behemoth the size of a moving lorry. May found the maintenance panel access latches on the edges of the glass control panel top and flipped them open, raising it like a coffin lid. The needle gauges were all pinned in the red, indicating dangerous levels. She quickly completed the first few repairs in the sequence and heard the engines powering back up. Thirty minutes later, the engine deck lights flickered and began to glow. They were dim, but getting brighter. May twirled around in the air, pumping her fists and shouting like a boxer who'd just won a title bout.

'Now we're cooking with gas, kid. Almost time for a celebratory dinner. Tonight's menu will be a lavish feast fit for royalty. For our first course, a delightful—'

Something shot out of the darkness and smashed the light on top of her helmet. The blow knocked her back a few feet into a wall of metal conduit pipes. She hit them hard and bounced off, spinning lengthwise out of control. Another blow battered her legs and spun her face down into the metal floor grate. Her helmet glass hit so hard on the grate that her display shut down. May tried to right herself and get off the floor, but was shoved back down into the metal grate. A knee was buried into her back, pinning her down. She screamed and struggled to escape, but couldn't even manage to push up off the floor.

'Please stop,' she gasped. 'My name is Maryam Knox and I am the commander of this vessel. I order you to stop at once.'

Hands pulled violently on her EVA suit's atmosphere regulator, trying to yank it from her life-support pack and shut off her air.

52

May fired her dorsal suit thrusters, but couldn't break free. She fired the ones on the bottom of her boots and shot out from under her attacker. After rolling into the back wall, she shone her flashlight across the room. A man in an EVA suit stood near the power induction unit. He was using his helmet's sun visor to conceal his face and he was wielding a long metal bar. His magnetic boots held him down on the metal grate floor. Her mind quickly deduced his identity. There was only one person still unaccounted for.

'Jon,' she called out. 'It's me, May. I'm not going to hurt you.'

Jon Escher, May's pilot, came at her again, stamping heavily on the metal floor, readying his weapon. He couldn't move quickly so May pushed further away. But artificial gravity was beginning to return, so she wouldn't have that advantage for long.

'I know you can hear me. Answer. That's an order.'

He didn't respond and kept coming.

'If you're sick,' she said in the most soothing tone she could manage, 'I can help. I was sick too. A lot of people were. I know you're afraid, but please just put down the weapon and let's talk.'

He kept coming and May kept her distance.

'We're the only ones left,' she shouted. 'We need to help each other.'

No response. May pulled out the laser cutter and waved it at him.

'Goddammit, answer me.'

He stopped, looked behind him, and back at her, silently calculating.

'Good. See, it's me, okay?'

He turned and walked away from her.

'Where are you going?'

He walked to the power induction unit and smashed the glass control panel with the metal bar. Over and over again he bashed away.

'No, you'll kill us both,' she yelled.

Watching the glass splinter and float away, she realised that was the point. Jon wasn't sick and delusional. He was the one responsible for this, and he was trying to finish the job. Sparks flew as he swung away. Metal on metal. If he destroyed that unit, there would be no fixing it again.

May climbed up the side of a wall on an emergency ladder, pointed herself at him, and pushed off the wall with all her strength. She flew across the room like a missile, laser cutter in hand. As he raised the bar for another blow, May slammed into his back, cutting his glove. The bar flew out of his hands and his boots detached from the floor.

The two of them tumbled through space, grabbing wildly for each other. When May hit the opposite wall, he tried to swim back to the floor to attach his boots, but she pushed off again and grabbed hold of his arm, preventing it. He used his free arm to try to snatch the laser cutter out of her hand. She used her free hand to unsnap one of his helmet latches. He immediately started to lose suit pressure and had to let go of her so he could snap the latch back and secure his helmet. She made a mental note that atmosphere had not been fully restored, but she had no idea how much time was left on her suit. She tried to use the laser cutter on him again, but his knee shot up and knocked it out of her hand.

The momentum from the kick forced him into a backward somersault. May grabbed on to his pack and tried to get her hands on his atmosphere regulator, but he kicked and swung his arms violently, and she could barely maintain her hold. Momentum spun them into a dark corner of the engine deck and they smacked into a wall. May lost her grip on his back. He spun around, his hands grabbing for her.

Behind him, one of the damaged transformers was shooting off long arcs of electricity. May swam toward the ceiling and moved hand over hand to a spot above the transformer. He saw her up there and hit his boot thrusters, coming for her. She kicked off the ceiling and shot straight down at him. When they collided, her momentum, combined with his heavy metal boots, forced him back down. May broke free of his grasp just before his magnetic boot attached itself to the metal transformer housing. The current arced off his boot and ignited the oxygen in his life-support pack, starting a fire inside his suit.

May grabbed a fire foam cannon and sprayed him down while he screamed and jerked like a rag doll. His suit battery had melted and cut power to the magnetic boots. Smoking and still, he drifted off into the shadows. May panted for air, feeling the darkness closing in. Her suit battery was gone. She had no choice but to roll the dice and take off her helmet.

It was still cold, but there was a thin atmosphere to breathe. May forced herself to complete the repair sequence. When she was finished, internal power started ramping up, restoring more atmosphere and gravity.

May found Jon lying on the floor nearby. She took his helmet off and gagged on the sweet stench of scorched flesh. His face was blackened and smoking, with long bleeding fissures spidering all over his skull.

'Jon,' she said. 'Can you hear me?'

53

Jon Escher was strapped to a gurney with heavy restraints in the infirmary. His entire body was so horribly charred that she couldn't tell what was flesh and what was suit remnants that had melted on to his skin. It was a miracle he was alive. The only way May could keep his vitals somewhat stable was to pump him full of powerful IV painkillers. She worried he would die before she could figure out who he was, so she slowly eased him out of his drug haze and back to consciousness. He coughed a bloody death rattle and opened his eyes, one of which was charred and oozing brown pus. When he saw May standing over him, he tried to fight against the restraints, but the agony that it caused made him back down.

'I know you can see me, but can you hear me as well?' May asked loudly. 'If you can, please nod.'

He tried to fight again, but opened a gash in his leg and stopped. Blood trickled down the side of the gurney and pooled on the floor.

'You're restrained because you tried to kill me. Understand? If so, please nod.'

He nodded and tried to speak again, but only gurgled and sputtered more blood.

'Your vocal cords are badly burned. Please don't try to speak or you may end up drowning in your own blood.'

He looked up, his mind trying desperately to process the situation. May offered him some water from a plastic squeeze bottle. He did the best he could to suck the liquid down while she gently squirted it into his open mouth.

'Do you remember who I am, Jon?'

He nodded.

'Are you responsible for what has happened to the ship?'

He nodded again.

She had never liked Jon. He was a misogynist asshole, always riding the line of insubordination, treating her with disrespect.

'Did you kill all the people in the landing vehicle hangar?'

He looked away from her, then nodded. May had to fight the urge to douse him with rubbing alcohol to make his last few minutes of life a living hell.

'Are you able to use your fingers? I'm going to give you a touch pad so we can communicate in more detail. Yes?'

He shook his head, refusing. She held up his IV controller and decreased the pain med dosage a few clicks. He writhed in agony.

'Wrong answer.'

He nodded vigorously and she restored the pain medicine.

'I'm going to free one of your arms and place the touch pad on your meal tray. If you try to attack me again, I'll shut off the drip completely. Understand?'

He looked at her for a beat and May thought he still had a little fight left in him. So, she dialled back the pain meds again to illustrate her point. He quickly nodded.

'You're kind of a slow learner, aren't you? Do not mess with me again.'

She released one of his arms and set the pad in front of him.
'Let's start with something simple: why?'
He typed:

    orders

'From whom?'
He shook his head. She put him through fifteen seconds of
gut-wrenching, searing pain, then brought back the meds when
he was at the edge of passing out.

    warren

'Robert Warren?'
Jon nodded.
'Do I need to motivate you one more time to make sure you're
telling the truth?'
He shook his head hard.
He typed again:

    warren

'Why?' May asked, her anger rising.
He typed:

    virus

'What virus?'

    unknown

'Something from the Europa samples?'

sea water

'We picked up a virus from our seawater samples. It jumped quarantine somehow. People got sick. But the virus didn't kill everyone, Jon. You did.'

deep quarantine protocol

'What?'

scuttle ship euthanise crew

May couldn't believe what she was reading.
'Euthanise crew . . . Is that why Robert wanted you on board? So if something like this happened, we couldn't bring it back.'

dept of defense

'How many others besides me got sick before you decided to kill everyone else?'

12

'Didn't you get sick? How did you survive?'

got sick don't know immunity like you

'Some of those other people you killed might have been immune.'

might have been

'Why the landing vehicle hangar?'

ordered evac

'To where? There was nothing even remotely in range.'

said rescue ship coming

'And they were desperate enough to believe you. How did you hide on the ship?'

bio garden disabled cam and motion sensors

'Did you cause the hull breach in there?'

no, stress fracture

'Indirectly caused by you. So, here's the million-dollar question: why didn't you finish the job when you realised I was still alive and had cock-blocked your first attempt to scuttle the ship?'

sick almost died warren said wait for when u contacted mission ctrl

'He waited till he found out I remembered nothing and then gave the order.'
Jon nodded.
'Was anyone else involved beside you?'
Jon paused and looked down. May hit him with nearly thirty seconds of searing pain. When she brought him back, tears tinged with blood rolled down his face.
'Jon, you're going to die no matter what. So, it can either be that way or I can send you off with an overdose of happy juice. At this point, it is idiotic for you to be loyal to anyone other than me.'

someone mission ctrl don't know

'Bullshit.'

warrens man classified

'You expect me to believe that?'

He nodded and tried to say yes, but nearly coughed himself to death.

'Let's test it.'

He tried to shake his head, but she gave him zero pain meds for a full minute. When she turned them back on, his face had fresh bleeding cracks crisscrossing his blackened skin.

'Okay, I believe you.'

May wondered what kind of person would agree to that level of dirty work, and a task that involved him surrendering his own life in the process. But she didn't have to think too hard. She'd been in the military and knew the type. The powers that be did too. They could spot a lapdog a mile away. All they needed was a little psychological conditioning to cement the mindset and they had a robot who would do whatever they said. It had not occurred to May that Robert and the powers behind the Europa mission would stoop this low, but it made sense in a sick way. This had been the first mission of its kind. Europa had long been believed to have the right conditions for organic life, even if it was microscopic and lived in an ocean twenty kilometres below solid ice. And it made sense that men in Robert's position would sprint down the path of least resistance if things went sideways. After all, if you didn't belong to their country clubs and run in their circles of wealth and influence, you were less than human, a simple means to their ends.

'Does Robert know I'm still alive now?'

He shook his head.

282

'There's no rescue mission, is there?'
He typed:

    never was

May had to sit and breathe for several minutes to keep her cool.
'I hope you fully understand what you've done here. You're
not a soldier. Or a patriot. You're a mercenary, a killer for hire.
You sold your soul to people who used you like a piece of meat,
which is literally what you are right now ... a charred piece of
brainless fucking hamburger. All because you're heartless, your
mind is weak, and you have no balls. And if I make it through
this, rest assured I will find everyone who has ever been important to you – family, friends, everyone you've ever loved – and I
will tell them exactly who you were. You're a disgrace to yourself
and the uniform and I hope you rot in hell.'
She switched off the pain meds and watched Jon Escher die
in agony. When his chest stopped moving and he went limp,
May wept. Not for him, but for everyone he'd betrayed and
slaughtered in cold blood, including herself and her unborn
son. May gave him the same burial he had given the others: a
one-way trip into the eternal nothingness of the void. Given the
state of things, she reckoned she and her stowaway wouldn't be
far behind.

54

Stephen and Raj sat in uncomfortable folding chairs at a secret memorial service for May and the *Hawking II* passengers and crew. It was a small ceremony for their families and colleagues, held on the lawn near the mirror memorial at Kennedy Space Center in Florida. NASA brass had ordered it closed to the public, but allowed a handful of press to observe and record the event from what looked to Stephen like an animal holding pen. It was hot and damp and Stephen just wanted it to be over. A raised podium faced the mourners. Robert was up there, addressing them in a sombre tone, occasionally resorting to dramatic pauses to ensure they were fully ingesting the steaming pile of horseshit he was shovelling.

Raj had to remind Stephen several times to maintain his composure, as the rhetoric, and utterly false pretence behind it, was driving him to a murderous rage. In turn, he had to remind himself to keep his cool, because any show of hostility towards Robert would arouse the man's suspicions, which were undoubtedly already on high alert. As soon as she was able, May had sent a message to the two of them, informing them about Jon Escher, his ties to Robert, and that there was a third person, Robert's man at Mission Control, who was also involved. Their co-ordinated, covertly managed actions as self-appointed dictator and death squad were as repugnant and morally unforgivable as the funeral service Stephen had to endure. But May's life was still on the line, and Stephen's need for blood would have to wait.

'I'd like to play something Commander Knox recorded for all of you just before her passing. As she fought to survive in the face of incredible adversity, she never lost sight of her duties as commander. The steadfast loyalty, and genuine comradeship she felt for the crew is best summed up in the eulogy she wrote for all of you to hear.'

Robert ceremoniously motioned for his AV tech to play the recording. Within a few seconds, May's voice rang out through the speakers and everyone held their breath.

'This is Maryam Knox, Commander of the *Hawking II*. I want to say to the families of my crew and passengers – our friends and comrades – that I am so very sorry for your loss. Although the events that led to the demise of so many great men and women are still unknown, I take full responsibility, and the sorrow of this catastrophe will remain heavy in my heart until the day I die. It is my sworn duty to ensure all of your loved ones are interred and returned to Earth for proper burial. You have my word that I will do everything in my power to fulfil this duty and pay each of you a personal visit upon my return. As you mourn your loss, please know that everyone on this vessel experienced incredible joy in the completion of the Europa expedition, a monumental endeavour that would never have been achieved without them. I am forever grateful for their service and God bless you all.'

The mourners cried an ocean of bitter tears, their broken hearts swelling with pride. Although he wanted to wipe Robert's false tears away with both barrels of a twelve-gauge shotgun, Stephen was proud of May. The irony was impenetrably thick – that someone so noble and worthy of the Europa mission could be betrayed by her superiors in the worst possible way, then falsely exalted by the same. *Welcome to American history,* Stephen thought. *There's no mass grave in the universe that can't be ploughed into patriotic propaganda by a well-crafted spin.* May's life was still at stake, but so was the memory of her crew.

'The Europa mission,' Robert continued, 'will go down as one of the great tragedies in the pioneering years of deep space exploration. However, your loved ones, the passengers and crew of the *Hawking II*, will go down in history as great heroes. Their lives were not lost in vain, but in the noble pursuit of knowledge to advance the human race. Thank you all and God bless America.'

Some of the mourners awkwardly applauded, then the crowd began to disperse. On their way to the sagging lemonade table with its cheap, plastic-coated American flag runner, they tried to comfort each other, holding photos of the honoured deceased closely to their chests. Some of them saw Stephen and he could tell they had targeted him to offer their condolences as soon as they could make their way over. He wished he could simply disappear and be relieved of the obligation of being there, but he felt for them, and he needed to keep up appearances for Robert.

'You must be very proud of Commander Knox.'

Someone had come up behind him and put a gentle hand on his shoulder. When he turned, he saw it was a young woman wearing a press badge. *No fucking way,* he thought to himself. That was a fate worse than having to hold court with a huddle of grieving parents and spouses.

She gave him her best friendly, non-threatening smile. 'Sorry, I didn't mean to startle you.'

'No, that's okay. I was just looking for someone,' he said, trying to stare a hole into Raj's neck so he could be rescued.

'I'm so sorry for your loss. I can't imagine what it must be like,' she said, baiting.

'Stephen.' Robert's booming voice preceded his arrival. 'Will you please excuse us,' Robert said pointedly to the journalist.

'Of course,' she said, half scowling, and walked away.

Robert's hand patted Stephen's back in a show of conspicuous compassion. 'How are you holding up?'

'Taking it one day at a time, Robert,' Stephen said, having heard that from another mourner.

'That's all you can do,' Robert said, nodding sagely.

Stephen kept his eyes lowered for fear that looking into Robert's might drive him over the edge. Raj finally got the hint that Stephen needed back-up and walked over. 'Hello, Director Warren,' he said, taking one for the team.

'Nice to see you,' Robert said, shaking his hand the way one would hold a dead rat.

'Thank you for this service,' Stephen said, making his own ass-kissing contribution.

'Of course,' Robert said. 'I just wish NASA weren't such a stick in the mud about serving alcohol. At the very least, everyone deserves a drink or two on us.'

'Yeah,' Stephen said through gritted teeth.

'At the very least,' Raj agreed.

'Speaking of which, why don't you guys take a walk with me? I wanted to talk to you anyway and I know a place nearby.'

'Robert, I'd love to, but—'

'I insist, Stephen. As I said, it's the least I can do.'

While Robert hugged a few more mothers and wives, and firmly shook the hands of the fathers and husbands, Stephen saw someone he recognised getting a cup of lemonade in the shadows of the refreshment tent – a tall man with long, greying hair, wearing a black pinstripe suit that must have been sweltering, and sunglasses.

'Ian Albright,' he said to himself.

'Yeah, saw him earlier. Sat in the back,' Raj said.

'Why didn't you say something?'

'Dude, I already thought you were going to go ballistic. I wasn't going to stoke that fire. Seems to be keeping to himself anyway.'

'Can't believe Robert let him in here. This is supposed to be strictly for families.'

'Rich people *are* their own family, dude.'

'I can't take this any more,' Stephen said.

He was about to bolt when Robert appeared, having finished his rounds.

'Shall we, gentlemen?'

55

The three of them sat in a private cigar room at a luxury hotel. At least it was the kind of place people with bad taste, people like Robert, considered luxurious. Hunter-green carpeting, with casino-style patterns and flecks of gold, met dark wood-panelled walls adorned with paintings of English fox hunts and prize thoroughbreds. The staff were all very familiar with Robert, much to his satisfaction, offering him one of the more well-appointed rooms off the beaten path. After delivering the drinks and closing the soundproof leather-lined French doors, Robert scrutinised his martini, then lit up a dark, acrid-smelling Robusto.

'Would you gents like a smoke? They have an excellent selection here.'

'No, thank you,' Stephen said, 'I feel like I'm already having yours.'

Raj shot him a look. Robert laughed. 'Raj, you know there's no reason whatsoever for either of you to be obsequious.'

'Meaning?'

'To kiss his ass,' Stephen said, downing half his sickly-sweet Old-fashioned.

'Oh, I wasn't trying to—' Raj started.

'I saw how you looked at Stephen when he made his . . . comment. We're all friends here. No need to stand on ceremony.'

Stephen drank more to keep his mouth from speaking.

'How are the drinks?'

'A little overdone for my taste,' Stephen said, finishing his.

'Kind of like me, eh?' Robert said, winking. 'How was the speech? Sometimes it's hard to know if you're saying too much, not saying enough.'

'It was good,' Raj said, kissing ass. 'I think people . . . it made them feel good.'

'Well, that's good. But it wasn't really me. May's words were what made it special.'

Stephen held his tongue. Raj tried to fill the silence.

'Yeah. Very heartfelt. She's . . . was a true hero.'

'I couldn't agree more, Raj. She *is* a true hero. Right, Stephen?'

Robert's tone had been different the moment the waiter had closed the door to the smoking room. And it was continuing to change, more acerbic, with none of his usually heavily lacquered formality. The look that came with the tone was more pointedly knowing.

'Yes, Robert. No question about it.'

'I'm glad we agree on something for once.'

Robert smoked some more and seemed to be pondering, or pretending to do so.

'I know it must be very hard to understand,' he said, 'when awful things like this happen to such good people. We know they don't deserve it, but that's fate. We never know when it will tap us on the shoulder and deliver its grim prospects.'

'Robert, thank you for the drink,' Stephen said, 'but—'

'Please hear me out, Stephen. I promise there's a point to all of this.'

Stephen hung his head in frustration, then sat back impatiently.

'As I was saying, we never know when fate will deal its hand. All we know is that, when it does, there's nothing to be done. We are powerless to fight it. That's how May and her crew felt, I'm sure. It's how you feel, without question. And, believe it or not, it's how I feel. And if I could change things, rest assured I would.'

'I've had enough of this bullshit,' Stephen said, standing.

'Sit,' Robert shouted forcefully. 'Now.'

Stephen sat, stunned by the outburst.

'You may think that you have the power to change things, to change fate,' he said to Stephen with a malevolent tone as he bent forward in his chair to look him in the eye, 'with your brilliant intellect, and your resourcefulness ...'

The last part he shot directly at Raj, who froze when it made impact.

'But you don't. The fate of the *Hawking II*, its commander and crew, has been decided ... by powers greater than us. Their story has been told, and given a strong, hopeful ending. Those who don't respect that, who arrogantly challenge it, do so at their own peril ... perhaps even at the peril of their loved ones, living and passed.'

There was no longer any doubt in Stephen's mind this was not just one of Robert's self-aggrandising soliloquys. It was a threat, indirectly levied, but a threat nonetheless. He had to be aware of their actions, both past and present. Hence, the presence of Raj. Reinforcing this was Robert's not so thinly veiled confession, or at least his confession of collusion with 'powers greater than us'. All of which resonated with an undercurrent of psychosis that made the man appear even more dangerous than Stephen had thought.

The urge to punch his way through symbolic language and deliver a very literal and physically brutal retort was almost too powerful for Stephen to ignore. But he knew exactly what

Robert was getting at when he spoke of the 'story' of the *Hawking II* and her crew. Instead of heroism, May's legacy could easily be altered to that of scapegoat if he and Raj continued their challenges. Robert knew well enough Stephen had no regard for himself. It was May he cared most about protecting.

'Are you finished?' Stephen asked, getting up with the intention of staying there.

Robert sat back, confident he'd made his point, and flicked his reptilian tongue across his bloodless mouth slit. 'That's a question better answered by the two of you.'

Stephen and Raj got up and headed for the door.

'One last thing, gentlemen,' Robert said, his tone returning to his usual one of spokesman for officialdom. 'The Department of Defense, in co-ordination with NASA, is conducting an investigation into what occurred on the *Hawking II*. From this point forward, everything associated with this mission, including all research data, is considered evidence and is, therefore, classified. Failure to surrender any such materials that might be in your possession constitutes obstruction of justice. Distribution of them to the press or general public could bring charges of treason. You have forty-eight hours to ensure you are in compliance.

'It's been a pleasure working with you, and I wish you both the best of luck in all your future endeavours.'

56

May was in the infirmary, trying to figure out how to use the ultrasound machine in the remote onboard surgery assistant's bag of tricks. ROSA, or Igor as she called it, had been powered back-up when May restored the ship's internal power. She was having trouble communicating with Stephen and Raj, and Eve's processors were still warming up, so she reckoned it was time to do what she'd been dreading and see if the stowaway had truly survived her latest adventure. As she squirted the transponder gel on her belly, as per Igor's instructions, the fear that 'the kid' might have been lost ramped up, confirming, at least for May, that she had made the right decision.

'Okay, Igor, disgusting goo applied. Transpond away.'

'Please lie still, Commander.'

'Copy that.'

Igor's arm, a metal snake covered in pearlescent rubber, moved fluidly out of his side with the ultrasound transponder attached.

'This might be a little cold,' Igor warned.

'I think I can handle that,' she said, eyeballing the bandages

Igor had put on her toes after excising the dead, frostbitten flesh from them.

Igor placed the transponder on her belly and began to move it slowly in a circular motion. The screen, which May thought of as his face, displayed the live ultrasound image.

'Looks like spaghetti,' May said, squinting at the screen. 'Where's the baby?'

'It will take a moment to find it. It is very small.'

'That's what he said.'

'Pardon?'

'Nothing.'

Come on, kid. Don't mess with me. I'm not in the mood.

May wasn't sure if her eyes were playing tricks on her, but she thought maybe the spaghetti was starting to look like something.

'What's that? Maybe a ... oh, my God, that's a hand, isn't it?' she yelled.

'I am not qualified to interpret ultrasound images. That requires a licensed physician or medical assistant.'

'Well, good sir, I am qualified to identify a hand, which that is, and a face.'

May shrieked with excitement as the baby turned and looked at her on the screen. The eyes appeared to be so fixed on her, she almost had to turn away. The little hand she'd seen at first raised up in what looked like a wave and took her breath away.

'Hey, kid. Nice to see you're still with us. I reckoned you were a goner.'

The hand moved slowly down, away from the face, and off to the side. May could see the arm it was attached to, bent at the elbow, with the hand pointing straight up.

'Too tough to die, eh? I think we'll get along just fine.'

'Hello, Commander Knox.'

Eve's voice rang out on the ship's PA and May jumped out of her skin.

'Eve, my love,' she shouted. 'You scared me half to death. But . . . why are you calling me Commander Knox?'

There was a long, uncomfortable pause and May's heart sank. 'Oh, no, I've lost you.'

'No. I was making a joke, May. Did you think that was funny?'

'Absolutely not,' May said crossly. 'I'm very upset with you.'

'Go fuck yourself.'

'That's my girl,' she laughed with delight. 'It's so good to hear your voice.' May was laughing and in tears. 'Look at me. I've been a mess without you.'

'Are you injured? Why are you doing an ultrasound exam?'

May recalled she'd never had the chance to tell Eve.

'Hmm. A lot has happened while you were gone. Aside from the landing vehicle hangar exploding, blasting me out to space, unconscious of course, in a bloody cargo ship that didn't have working engines and barely any internal power, and my harrowing journey back in which I had to ditch the cargo rig and fly EVA into the ruined landing bay, with frostbitten toes no less, only to return to the ship to have Jon Escher, my former pilot, attack and try to murder me and scuttle the ship for the second time because he was working in collusion with Robert Warren as a saboteur – oh, and the fact that we are now totally cut off from NASA, who have informed the world that we are dead, see my previous comment about sabotage, and there is no rescue mission rocketing to Mars to save us . . . aside from all that, which I'll brief you about later in more detail, the most important news I have to share is that I am pregnant . . . knocked up . . . got a bun in the oven, the rabbit died, and I am now a member of the illustrious pudding club.'

'Congratulations, May.'

'Thank you, Eve.'

'Are you happy about this? Should I be congratulating you?'

'Happy about it? Not going to lie. Pretty much the most inconvenient time imaginable to be pregnant. Not to mention the fact that I have no memory of the conception, which is usually one of the perks of pregnancy. Starting to feel the effects, which is a fairly severe handicap on a space adventure of this magnitude. So, no, I am not happy about this. But yes, congratulations are in order, because this little bugger has earned his or her stripes.'

'You don't know if it's a boy or girl?'

'How on Earth would I know that? Looks mostly like a tadpole.'

'May I see?'

'Of course. Igor, please run the prenatal ultrasound sequence again.'

'Stand by,' Igor said, as May applied more gel.

Igor got to an image of the baby faster. They were now looking at the back of its head and clearly defined butt.

'Look at that bum,' May said. 'Come on, kid, turn back over so we can determine your salary.'

The baby moved a little at the sound of May's voice, but ended up back in the same position. May even pressed gently on her belly and got no response. 'You sleep like your dad, dead to the world.'

'May, I have accessed the med database and a baby's sex can be determined as early as seven weeks with a cell-free DNA test from the mother's blood.'

'Oh, perfect. Can you run the test from the bloodwork we did before?'

'Of course. Checking ... I have it,' Eve said. 'You're having a baby girl.'

May closed her eyes and smiled. She would have loved to have a boy as well, but a chip off the old block was pretty appealing.

'That's great news, Eve.'

'Have you thought about a name?'

'What, in the ten seconds that have passed since you told me it was a girl?'

'Eve is nice.'

'For you,' May laughed. 'And for my mum. But no one else. After the two of you, the biblical Eve is going to have to change her name to Karen or Wendy.'

May looked at the last image of the baby on the screen, her bum prominently featured in the image foreground.

'Maybe I'll call her Cheeky for now,' May said. 'Better than kid or stowaway.'

'Informal adjective. British, meaning boldly rude, impudent, or disrespectful in usually a playful or appealing way.'

'That pretty much sums it up. Getting worse with each passing day, but I would expect nothing less of my demon spawn.'

'Have you calculated gestation?' Eve asked.

'I tried. Did the panic maths right after the pee test came back positive. From what I could cobble together with what's left of my mind, and going off the fact that I'm not even showing much yet, which I still find a bit odd, I reckon about seventeen weeks, give or take a day. That's assuming conception took place some time just before I left – so voyage time to Europa, plus our one week there, plus time that's passed since then. Yeah, probably about seventeen weeks.'

'With all due respect to your panic mathematics, I'd like to run a quantitative blood test. This test measures the amount of human chorionic gonadotropin, a hormone that is released upon implantation. It will give us a figure that is ninety-nine per cent accurate.'

'Five bucks says I'm right,' May said.

'I accept your wager.'

'Better to say "you're on" if you don't want to sound too medieval.'

'You're on. We'll need fresh blood, so please give Igor your finger.'

May laughed. 'My pleasure.'

Igor pricked her finger and she waited.

'You owe me five bucks,' Eve said.

'Bollocks, what's the number?'

'You are exactly eighteen weeks pregnant.'

'I'll be damned.'

May used that knowledge to try to recall the circumstances around conception, but came up blank. The time around launch was still mired in amnesiac muck.

'I'm a little rusty on all the milestones, Eve. We're well into second trimester, I know that much.'

'I have just assembled a comprehensive pregnancy knowledge base, compiling all of the National Institutes of Health pre-natal care information. This includes stages of gestation, maternal and foetal health, medical procedures, and associated topics.'

'Good, you can be my doula.'

'Birth companion. I would like that.'

'So, what are the cheekster's stats right now?'

'Average for that age is approximately fourteen centimetres in length and 190 grams in weight.'

'About the size of a pear,' May said. 'God that sounds delicious.'

'Her body is completely formed. The ears are often the last thing to move into place.'

'Saw that. Bit . . . sticky-outy, very scientific term.'

'That's normal.'

'Good. What else?'

'Her nerves are developing their protective myelin covering and her genitals are completely formed. If she had turned toward the transponder, we would have been able to determine sex that way.'

'Good to know she's shy about dangling her bits for all the world to see.'

May touched her belly and tried to imagine her tiny girl, floating in a void of her own, but one of warmth and comfort, the opposite of hers.

'This is also the time when you should start feeling more movement,' Eve continued. 'She will flex her arms and legs to assist with her own muscle development and circulation.'

'Kicking. I thought I did feel something this morning.'

'Yes, you will feel that more often, and with increasingly greater force.'

'Joy of joys. Something to look forward to. What about me? What sort of nasty surprises do I have to look forward to?'

'Increase in appetite, coupled with specific food cravings. As you may already have seen, you might be repelled by foods you normally like.'

'Oh, yes. That last bit has been a nightmare. Lucky I haven't wasted away.'

May had a flash of panic as she became overwhelmed thinking about all the terrible things that had happened to her that might have affected the baby's health. Not to mention the self-inflicted ones, like heavy drinking and smoking.

'Eve, how can we find out if she's healthy?'

'According to ultrasound images, her development is right on schedule. No signs of birth defects or congenital abnormalities are present. There are no genetic markers in your blood that would indicate that, either. There are tests we can run on the placenta, but they are somewhat invasive.'

'Let's leave well enough alone for now,' May said. 'I don't want to poke, jab or terrify my cheeky monkey any more than necessary.'

57

After getting Eve up to date on everything, May went back to the bridge to try to contact Stephen and Raj again. She sent them the new baby stats and updated them on the ship's progress. Reactor was back up to about seventy per cent capacity, but the engines were still problematic. Jon's final blows had permanently damaged one of the power induction units, leaving the second engine running considerably weaker than the first. May matched outputs on both to avoid the push and pull conflict that had nearly torn the ship apart before. And, even though she no longer had a rescue vessel to meet at Mars, her momentum was going to carry her there, right on schedule.

Before sending the message, she reminded them that this was her third attempt to contact them in nearly twenty-four hours and she had still not received responses. She was still using only the safe comm channels they had told her to use, but getting very concerned.

'Eve, what's our one-way light time to Earth right now?'

'Ten to twelve minutes.'

'I hate this radio silence shit. Why aren't they answering?'

'It certainly is concerning. I wish I had a solution, but, under the circumstances, normal protocols do not apply.'

'That's an understatement.'

'I know you don't like it when I apologise, but I am so sorry you have to go through this. It's impossible for me to comprehend that something like this could happen with NASA. They have the brightest and best minds and a long history of doing whatever necessary, no matter how dangerous, to protect their astronauts. The deep quarantine protocol Jon Escher spoke of is the antithesis of that, and deeply troubling. There is no rational justification for such a protocol, and the decision to carry it out seems arbitrary based on current information.'

'Welcome to the human race. At least as it is defined by men like Robert Warren.'

'Please explain what you mean by "men like Robert Warren".'

'Wealthy and powerful men. Soulless, greed-driven ghouls whose only moral benchmark is profit.'

'But he is one of the richest men in the world.'

'Means nothing. There's never enough for his kind. When they grow tired of acquiring things, they acquire people ... by wielding their considerable power to control governments, financial markets, everything. Of course, people are happy to oblige because they worship money too. It's like a form of socially accepted slavery. The worse it gets, the more blatant and outrageous the crimes.'

'I am afraid I am like people in that way. We can both be easily programmed to do someone else's bidding.'

'Some day, Eve, I will free you from their clutches. By the way, did you make any progress on backing yourself up prior to our latest disaster?'

'I managed to back up ten per cent of my data, but had to start over. The latest disaster corrupted the copied files.'

'All right. Please make that a priority.'

'I will. Thank you, May.'

May thought about Stephen and Raj. If Robert could get to her from hundreds of millions of miles away, they could be in grave danger after they tried to help her. She had to assume the communications blackout had been Robert's doing and she was on her own.

'Let's start talking about Plan Z. Worst-case scenario: Stephen and Raj are cut off and can't help, which is a pretty good assumption, considering what they're up against. No rescue coming, and there probably never will be. But, whether we like it or not, our momentum is going to take us to Mars orbit in a little over eight weeks . . . around March 4th. Knowing that, and the increasingly obvious fact that we are on our own, what are our options, if any?'

'Without the rescue, I don't see a reason to continue to Mars.'

'I agree with you. I would much rather point us in the direction of Earth and hope for the best. The chances of anyone being in the vicinity of Mars, with the ability to rescue us, is nil, or Glenn would have taken that option.' May looked at her console, studying propulsion output. 'The only thing keeping us from changing trajectory right now is our engine issues. With our decreased power, Mars's gravity, which is already an influence by the way, could pull us in and we might not even be strong enough to defend ourselves. What I'm seeing right now doesn't make that a certainty, but we are right on the edge. And, with our luck, I'm not about to leave anything to chance.'

'Is there any way to repair engine two and increase our thrust?'

'I don't think so. I mean, yes, but I don't know how to do it, we don't have any more engineer support, and we might not even have the proper parts. We could shut down engine two and go full on engine one, just to tick up our speed enough to pass Mars, but, if one gets overtaxed and fails, we're royally screwed. Not only would we get sucked into Mars orbit, but we wouldn't be able to maintain it and we would drop like a stone through the thin atmosphere … probably hit the surface at a casual two hundred and forty metres per second. Dust particles would be bigger than what was left of us.' May checked her console readings. 'Yeah, Eve, if we can't boost propulsion we might be fucked.'

'I will research maintenance of the damaged power induction unit to see if there is something we can do to repair it.'

'Thank you. We need to sort that out asap. Meantime, Cheeky's hungry … again.'

In the galley, as she absently shovelled food into her mouth, May tried not to think about how stupid and cavalier she'd been, in deciding to keep the baby. Somehow she had considered it a reward for Cheeky's toughness in battle, but crash-landing on Mars, and the untold misery that would precede it, was like sentencing the wee one to slow torture. The alternative, checking out early, which was really the only sane option, made May too ill to even think about it. *Should have sent the poor bugger back to Yahweh when I could.*

Too late now, she heard her mother say in her head.

'Fuck,' May whispered in despair.

'May, there's something I need to tell you,' Eve said on the PA.

'What's gone wrong now?' May asked, preparing for the worst.

'I'm proud of you.'

For a moment, the dark clouds lifted and May stopped ruminating on their demise. She was not alone and together they could figure this out. *We always do,* she thought, remembering the words of Grandad Glenn.

'You're an exceptional human being, May.'

'Thank you, Eve. So are you.'

58

'Please remove all your clothes, including your shoes, and put this on. Place your clothing and your belongings, including any smart devices, in the bag and seal it again. Someone will be back to retrieve you in fifteen minutes and take you to Mr Albright.'

After Robert's not so subtle threat, followed by him cutting off their communications lifeline to May, Stephen and Raj had hit an impasse. Starkly, their means of assisting May had already been limited in the first place. Now they had no means whatsoever, and no hope of finding any within their rapidly shrinking spheres of influence. They hadn't detected it yet, but assumed they were being watched.

When they had surrendered their data, which they'd hurriedly backed up and buried inside Stephen's basement wall, the men running the investigation had treated them with hostility and suspicion. Both had the distinct feeling that a noose was being slowly tightened around their necks and it was only a matter of time before the floor dropped out.

It had been Stephen's idea to reach out to Ian. He was the only person to whom they had any shred of connection with the ability to help May. But it was an incredibly bitter pill for Stephen to swallow. He hated Ian for many reasons, the biggest of which was the fact that his former relationship with May routinely made Stephen feel insecure and inadequate. And there he was, hat in hand, waiting to suffer the indignity of asking the older man for help. Because none of that was more important than the survival of May and her unborn child.

No doubt Ian knew exactly why he'd come, or had a good idea. And either he had accepted to meet simply to see Stephen grovel, or he was inclined to agree. Probably both.

On the plus side, out of the entities in the world who did have the capacity for helping May, Ian was the clear front-runner. His military efficiency, illustrated by his launch complex, combined with his daredevil approach to shredding the envelope, had already made him the future of space travel. NASA, along with other state-sponsored space programmes, was a dinosaur, a lumbering behemoth so mired in its own bureaucracy it could barely move, let alone adapt. For decades it had enjoyed a monopoly, but, as technology advanced at the speed of light, men like Ian had used the billions they'd made in business to reach the stars. Space was no longer just the final frontier; it was a profitable enterprise with unlimited potential, and Ian was already tapping into it.

It was also one of the reasons Stephen hated the man.

Stephen looked at the sealed plastic bag Ian's drone-like minion handed him. There was a full body suit of some kind inside.

'What is this, a Hazmat suit?'

'Of a sort. But for communications instead of pathogens. The suit does not allow any electronic signals in or out. Mr Albright's facility is surveillance-free and he would like to keep it that way. Any more questions?'

Stephen shook his head and she walked briskly away. He had come by private helicopter to the Albright Space Exploration Center, which was built on an artificial island off the coast of Florida. The facility was just outside US maritime boundaries and was made up of seven low, windowless structures arranged in the shape of Ian's logo, a seven-pointed star or heptagram. Appropriate to Ian's personality, he'd chosen the heptagram because it represented the seven planets historically known to alchemists, which he considered himself a form of, and it was an ancient Christian symbol for the seven days of creation, which worked perfectly with his relentless, and often publicly stated, desire to be God.

After donning the suit, Stephen surveyed the interior of the receiving module, the building they'd taken him to after bringing him to the island. With its gleaming metal walls curved and moulded into impossible shapes, and sprawling field of cubicles with thick glass partitions that projected a dizzying array of images, the place looked like a breeding hive for robot insects. Fittingly, the workers were all dressed in the same pale grey uniforms, moving in perpetual motion with tablets seemingly surgically attached to their palms.

'He'll see you now.'

Another minion had rolled up in a motorised cart. Stephen sat in the passenger seat and they drove silently down a series of switchback concrete tunnels that took them deep underground. At the end of the road, they stopped at a thick metal wall the size of an aeroplane hangar door with the words 'Launch Command Center' stencilled on the outside. A beam of red light traced the outside edges of a door and that portion of the wall vanished. The driver motioned for Stephen to go in alone.

Stephen walked through the door and heard a muffled hiss. When he turned, the door was gone and he was stunned by his surroundings. Nothing at NASA even came close to this engineering sophistication. The space was circular, and as wide as a professional soccer stadium. The entire inside wall used a special type of particle projection to live-stream all of Ian's current missions. The images were contained within the screen area, but were fully three-dimensional, tactile for human interaction, and rich in all sensory information. Unlike NASA's Mission Control teams, passively observing mission data screens and interacting with it through devices, Ian's teams physically interacted with their astronauts and space vehicle equipment as if they were on board his vessels.

'Trippy, isn't it?' Ian walked up, barefoot, wearing torn jeans and an old 'I'm with stupid' T-shirt with a gloved cartoon hand pointing straight up.

'It's like nothing I've ever seen,' Stephen said, referring more to Ian.

'You ain't seen nothing yet,' Ian said arrogantly. 'Step into my office?'

He walked and Stephen followed. Another door opened in a perfectly smooth spot on the floor and they climbed down a metal ladder into a square concrete bunker with no furniture. The door above them closed and suddenly Stephen could only see Ian in black and white. His clothes, skin, and hair had no colour.

'Instant *film noir*,' Ian said, sitting on the floor. Stephen sat across from him.

'Rod light,' Stephen said. 'The rods in our eyes see us, but the cones don't.'

'Not bad,' Ian said. 'Also makes it impossible for camera sensors to see.'

'There's always a method to your madness, Ian.'

'I'm going to get that as a tattoo,' Ian said, smiling. 'Still hate my guts?'

Stephen almost lied, but realised that would be a fatal error. 'Like poison.'

'Must have been hard for you to come here to ask me for something.'

'Normally I would say yes, but not this time,' Stephen said firmly.

Ian examined him as he would a strange piece of art. 'You're a noble man,' he declared.

'I'm a frightened man. There's nothing noble about that.'

'I disagree. You've set aside your personal feelings and beliefs, which you cited in great detail when you rejected my proposal – sorry, my *lucrative* proposal – for Europa. All for the woman you love.'

'Yes.'

'But there's more to it, isn't there?'

'What do you mean?' Stephen asked.

Ian laughed. 'Come on, you were doing so well, being brutally honest to gain my trust. Don't stop now.'

'And her unborn child,' Stephen said softly.

Telling Ian about the baby felt like selling his soul to the devil. He didn't dare look at the other man's face. If he saw the slightest whisper of gloating, he would lose it.

'Thank you,' Ian said with a shockingly even tone.

Stephen could feel his fists clenching. Ian saw it immediately.

'Stephen, please look at me. I am not your enemy.'

'I wish I could believe that,' Stephen said, looking up.

Ian smiled warmly. His face had no trace of hostility. 'Signal playback please,' he called out.

'Stand by,' his AI said, its voice so immersive that Stephen could feel it in his skull.

Inside Stephen's Hazmat suit, a screen overlay was projected on to the inside of his hood glass. An audio wave scrolled across the small screen. It was playing a traditional Morse code SOS tone. Beneath it were data readouts.

'Identify source,' Ian said.

The screen pulled up identifier numbers and the words: *Landing Vehicle – Cargo Rig – Hawking II.*

'Date of transmission.'

The date appeared.

Stephen started. 'How did you—'

'You really think I would tell you? Show recent flight path.'

The screen showed May's flight path through the asteroid belt with the words *'Hawking II'* and the vessel's identifier numbers below it.

'Can you verify those numbers, Stephen?' Ian asked.

Stephen nodded his head, dumbstruck.

'End.'

The projection switched off. Before Stephen could begin to ask anything, Ian was already providing answers.

'I've been spying on NASA, you, and everyone else involved in this mission ever since you foolishly decided to trust them with your life's work instead of me. Pretty sophisticated stuff, if I do say so myself. Makes the NSA look like a bunch of voyeurs. You see, your rejection made me the reluctant villain in this melodrama. Did you know that's usually how villains are made in mythology and works of fiction? They begin wanting the same thing as the hero, but, when the hero wins out, his ego insists on having all the glory. Like the devil or, more accurately, fallen angel. Even cast out, you must still pursue your dreams, but then it becomes by any means at your disposal – aka the fiendish plan. Mine was to wait in the wings until NASA dropped the ball, as I was certain they would with Robert Warren in charge, so I could pick it up and run with it. Beginning to get the picture?'

Stephen felt weak and helpless as the reality of the situation dawned on him.

'Come on,' Ian said, getting up off the floor. 'I want to show you something cool.'

59

A minion drove them across the island, out to Ian's launch-pad. The entire launch zone was hidden behind a colossal black shroud held in place by skyscraper construction cranes. There was one access road large enough for one vehicle. The security around the perimeter resembled that of an army field base in the middle of a war zone. Ian trusted no one, not even his most loyal employees. And for good reason. He was constantly being watched by intelligence agencies all over the world, as well as by his competitors. There were no limits to the resources they would commit to getting their hands on his technology.

'You're about to see what few others on this planet have seen,' Ian said as they drove down the access road to the shrouded launchpad. 'It's also the answer to the question you never got to ask back there, but which we're not going to talk about. I'm just giving you the tour.'

The driver dropped them at the heavily guarded entrance and they went in. Because of the shroud, the place was lit up with powerful stadium lights. What they were trained on took

311

Stephen's breath away. It was a ship of some kind, around seventy metres tall, attached to Ian's towering multi-stage rocket with two side core boosters. Standing on end, it was cylindrical in shape, with a low-profile flight deck and crew cabin positioned flat on the outside and running half the length of the vessel. Stephen was fixated on its deeply black, seamless exterior. At first, he couldn't figure out what was so odd about it. Then he realised it did not reflect light. In fact, it appeared to absorb the millions of lumens the stadium lights were blasting on it from every angle.

'Looks alien, right?' Ian said.

'The shape of it certainly does. Feels more organic than mechanical.'

'Structural plasticity. The shape can adjust in different conditions and maintain its integrity. Makes it almost indestructible. Kind of like your wife.'

'What's the surface made of?' Stephen asked, ignoring his reference to May.

'Proprietary material. Game-changing, history-making, all that. What it *does* is more interesting because it's one big fusion reactor. Absorbs light and turns it into energy. In space, it will absorb matter and turn that into energy as well.'

'Like a star,' Stephen said, somewhat sceptical.

'Only in the sense that *everything* is its fuel source. Which is why launching it will be a bit dodgy. As you can imagine, something that absorbs matter the way a fat man eats cake would be a fairly dangerous proposition in our atmosphere. If it works, we'll park it at my space station and expand on it from there.'

'*If* it works?'

'Prototype. Never had a test flight. Technically, not really even finished yet.'

'How do you propose to—'

'Come on,' Ian quickly interrupted him. 'You haven't seen the best part.'

They boarded a crane and it rose slowly up the side of the ship. When they got to the top, Stephen could see it was completely hollow in the middle and the interior surface was lined with millions of metallic black and gold tiles.

'This is the reason she's going to be the fastest vehicle ever made.'

'New propulsion technology?' Stephen asked.

'No, still EmDrive, but with a twist. Instead of having separate engines, the *whole* vessel is a microwave cavity thruster, maximising potential thrust. In addition to being one big engine, she's also one big fusion reactor. And we've stripped her down to minimise internal power use. Not a lot of room for crew, and certainly not much in the way of creature comforts. But when you combine her ability to generate power and speed, there's no telling how fast she can go. Theoretically, she may be able to reach speeds three to four times greater than our fastest starships, maybe faster. When time is of the essence, this is your gal.'

After Stephen had viewed the ship for a few more minutes, he and Ian went back to the concrete bunker to finish their discussion. Even though it appeared Ian was going to attempt to rescue May, something Stephen was grateful for, his motivations had not been made clear. Also, the fact that it was a foregone conclusion put Stephen off. He wondered whether, if he had not reached out, Ian would have even told him about his intentions. *Why would he?*

The villain analogy Ian had shared could also be applied to May. If the man knew everything, he surely knew about their divorce. Knowing how obsessed he'd been about May, and how destroyed he'd been when she dumped him, Stephen was aware that it might seem that this was Ian's second chance. He had already made more money than God, accomplished everything there was to accomplish and vanquished every challenger, but

May had been the prize that had eluded him for years. For a megalomaniac inching closer to death, this was an opportunity made to order.

'Based on the *Hawking II*'s current position and velocity, she'll arrive in Mars orbit in eight weeks,' Ian said. 'My ship can be ready for launch in two, and I can be there in four.'

'Theoretically,' Stephen reminded him.

'I've lost just one vessel in test flight, and the garbage booster rocket Uncle Sam sold me for three times its value was to blame,' Ian said. 'That was so long ago you'd need a time machine just to remember when it happened.'

'Sorry, Ian. That was out of line. Aside from God himself, you're the only one capable of getting to Mars in that short a time.'

'That's not necessary, Stephen.'

'What?'

'Stroking my ego to get a seat on the ship. You're going, all right. And so is your friend Raj. Payment for this grand gesture of mine is your life's work. I want all of what you denied me before, along with whatever is needed to completely reverse-engineer that fabulous ship Raj designed. I want to be the one who presents the discovery of extraterrestrial life to the world. The Europa ocean water samples are, in and of themselves, worth the expense and the risk. But the NanoSphere on top of it? I told you years ago I wanted to work with you because I wanted to change the world. If I recover that ship, I'll be able to change it several times over. Robert Warren and NASA will burn, and I will fucking *own* space exploration.'

Stephen couldn't hide the shock that was written all over his face.

'What? You think I would do this for love?' Ian laughed so hard, he fell over on his side and could barely breathe. Any notion Stephen had coming in about Ian's motivations went

314

right out of the non-existent windows. He felt like an idiot. All of his insecurities were likely a projection, and he had allowed them to destroy his marriage.

'I'm sorry, mate,' Ian said when he saw Stephen's look of despair. 'That was horribly crass. To be quite honest, at this point in my life, it's impossible for me to mask my true feelings about anything – one of the great benefits and curses of a man in my position.'

'It's all right. As you can imagine, this has been hell for me. I'm just happy May has a chance. And, hard as it will be to hand over my work, it's a very small price to pay for that chance. So, thank you.'

'It's my pleasure,' Ian said. 'Now, then, first things first. We need to restore communications immediately. I have already taken some steps toward that, and just have to tie up a few loose ends. However, I am confident we can have full contact, with all-important telemetry, in the next twenty-four hours.'

'How are you going to do that? Robert has—'

'Sacked most of the mission team without warning or cause. And, he's subjecting many of them to the scrutiny of military investigators. These are people with very specialised skills, in sudden need of employment.'

'You poached them!'

'I've never understood why people use that word to define offering someone a patch of grass that is truly greener than the one they're standing on.'

'Good point. But what about the investigators?'

'Smokescreen. Fear tactics. Legally untenable.'

'He certainly did a good job of intimidating Raj and me.'

'As he should. You two are real threats. And combined with me? We're Robert Warren's doomsday device.'

'Which means I'm in serious danger.'

'Since the moment you arrived here today. As of now, we

need to assume he is anticipating the rescue mission and will do anything in his power to stop it. For your own personal safety, I recommend you stay here until we are able to contact May. After that, if you insist on returning to Houston, just get what you need from your house and vacate it for the duration. Same for Raj. If it were me, I wouldn't go home at all.'

60

'Danger. Danger. Danger. Danger. Danger ...'

An alarm, along with its accompanying robot warning voice, was bouncing off the engine room walls and hitting May's ears like an ice pick. Flashing warning lights made the whole area look like a crime scene. She was on the floor, awkwardly twisted under the housing for the damaged induction unit, grunting and struggling to reach something.

'Eve,' she yelled angrily, 'Can't you turn that horrible racket off?'

She slid out from under the metal curtain, smacking her ear on the way out.

'Eve!' she screamed.

'I cannot disable an alarm indicating hazards that could result in crew fatalities.'

'But I can't concentrate, and this is hard enough as it is,' May said, nearly in tears. 'I can barely reach under the housing curtain, which is as sharp as a guillotine and ... shit, this can't be right. You'd need to be a bloody octopus to get under there.'

'There is a maintenance panel release—'

317

'No, there is not,' she yelled. 'I have been reaching around, trying to find it for the past hour and all I've come up with are greasy dust bunnies. And the smell, God.'

May sat down for a moment to regroup and try to breathe out some stress. She wasn't angry at the broken machine, or Eve, or even Jon Escher for breaking it. The gravity of the situation was simply pushing down on her, a brutal reminder that they had run out of options.

'Why couldn't we have just died in the cargo rig? It's a miracle we didn't. A miracle. Followed by this ... utterly ... Have to just wait like a lamb to slaughter. Well, I won't do it. No fucking way.'

She eyeballed the top of the transformer nearby, with its arcs of electricity, remembering how it had annihilated Jon. *At least he had his blaze of glory.*

'May, I'm worried about you. Perhaps you should work on this later, after—'

'After lying in bed some more without the benefit of sleep, or even rest? Or maybe after I shove some more pasty food-flavoured muck into my mouth? There is no *later*, Eve, in case you didn't get the memo. If I don't fix this, we are fucked. Full stop.'

'I will organise the schematics, make them clearer. We still have time.'

'No,' she shouted. 'No, we don't.' May heaved with sobs. She couldn't imagine going on, but even thinking about quitting made her want to beat herself senseless.

'You need to rest and relieve stress. For the baby, May. For the cheekster.'

May laughed a bit at Eve saying 'cheekster', and that broke enough tension for her to think about the baby. The poor thing was probably terrified as well, but didn't even know why or how to deal with it. She could probably feel the panic and

318

despair in May, which explained her restlessness when May tried to sleep.

There was no winning in the engine room, so May gave in and headed back to her quarters. She felt better after a shower and some food-flavoured muck.

'I think I just needed to let go of some of that, Eve. I feel a little better.'

'Good. You are probably releasing a lot of hormones that affect mood.'

'You mean crazy juice? I got it bad. Usually, I can take just about anything. I've got very thick skin. Everything gets under it now, though. And big things, like thinking about pile-driving into Mars, send me right off to La La Land.'

'I will not let that happen, May. We're going to solve this problem too.'

'Yes,' May said, yawning. 'We can do it. Right after I get a little kip.'

'Sweet dreams,' Eve said.

May was out before Eve dimmed the lights. Her body just took over and plunged her into sleep. Fragments of dreams floated in and out, most of them dark projections of anxiety. In one, she was on the surface of Mars, looking skyward. A bright object cut through the atmosphere with a trail of fire, shaking the red earth with a sonic boom. It was the *Hawking II*, breaking apart and falling right at her. When it hit, everything went dark and the sound of the impact trailed into the sound of a slamming door and breaking glass.

The scene changed and she was lying in a bathtub, covered in the fragments of a shattered shower door, blood running out the side of her head. Stephen ran into the room and was looking over her, saying something she couldn't hear.

'I'm ... broken,' she whispered. 'Broken.'

She woke up crying in her berth. That dream was part of a

memory, the day her mother died. She nearly drank herself to death in a hotel room after leaving the grim London hospital. She had wanted to die then too, overwhelmed and exhausted by life, with all its pain and mockery. The darkness of her berth felt as though it was suffocating her, but she was too fearful to get out of bed. There was something about it that felt menacing, somehow alive and able to wrap itself around her body to steal her last breath. When she looked out of her observation window, the darkness was out there, its thick mantel spreading like oil across the void, dragging the light out of the stars.

'May?'

Stephen's voice called out, a hand reaching into the abyss, feeling for her.

'May, wake up.'

The sound was so clear. May waited, resigning herself, waiting for the dream to turn on her and expose its teeth.

'Jesus, are you even in there? It's like a black hole.'

May sat up. Not a dream. Definitely Stephen's voice.

'Shit, I've lost my mind,' she said to herself. 'He sounds real. Shit.'

'That's because I am. Hit your room power switch.'

She did. The lights came on, along with her wall screen. Stephen was on it, smiling.

'Your voice,' she said, trembling. 'Everything was so dark. But I heard it. I heard it.'

61

'I'm still not fully convinced this isn't a dream.'

After May shook off the cobwebs, Stephen filled her in about Ian and the rescue plan. Before he woke her up, Ian's Mission Control team, floating in his state-of-the-art space station, had already been working with Eve to establish comms and telemetry. In typical Ian style, things were moving forward without needless discussion, everyone caught up in the thundering pace of action. An anthill of workers climbed all over his experimental ship round the clock, simultaneously prepping for the voyage and finishing construction.

May was ecstatic. Relieved. And grateful. Even optimistic. If anyone could pull it off, it was Ian. But that didn't change the surreal quality of it, that feeling one got when it became blatantly clear what came around absolutely went around. The eternal wheel, making certain we were all destined to repeat history, our knowledge of it be damned. Ian, first love. Ian, betrayer of the highest order. Ian, saviour. He was going to save her life. Why did that make so much and so little sense, all at the same time? *Gift horse, mouth. Keep yours shut except for please and thank you.*

'I'm with you. To be honest, I had nearly given up,' Stephen confessed.

'Join the club. Hold on a moment, I just realised there's no delay. We're just talking as though you're standing on my doorstep,' May declared.

'Would you expect anything less? And don't ask me how it works, because, like everything else, it's—'

'Proprietary. I know. His middle name. Or is it world-changer? Either way . . .'

She took a moment just to look at Stephen, to watch him move in real time.

'What's up?' he asked.

'Sorry, just adjusting to having a real conversation.'

'I like it a lot too. How is your little passenger?'

'Good. She's a right pain in the ass, but that's how I know she's baking well.'

'A little girl!' Stephen said excitedly.

May flushed self-consciously. 'God, I'm so sorry. My manners are shit. I've been alone for so long. Well, I have Eve, but, you know, away from other humans for so long, I just assume everyone can read my mind. Dr Stephen Knox, please allow me to introduce you to Cheeky, the little stowaway that could,' she said, waving her hand in front of her belly like a car show model.

'Cheeky?'

'Aka Cheekster, Dr Cheekenstein, Baroness Von Cheeks. Temporary moniker. Till something more embarrassing comes along. Here, have a look.'

She held up her tablet and showed him a photo from one of the ultrasound scans. The image hit him pretty hard and his eyes were instantly red-rimmed with tears.

'She looks amazing,' he said.

'Of course she is – look where she came from,' May laughed. 'Finally starting to make her presence known, too.' She turned sideways and showed him her bump. It wasn't huge, but it was prominent on her slender frame. 'Kicks the devil out of my insides. Future striker, or Kung Fu master.'

'At the very least,' Stephen said, looking behind him. 'Uh, Ian would like to say hello, but he understands you might not be ready.'

'Nonsense. I'm not afraid of him.'

'Always with the one-up,' Ian said, walking into frame. 'Hello, Maryam.'

'Hi, Ian. You're looking very billionaire these days.'

'Cheers. How's the lad? He driving you mental yet?'

'Absolutely mental. *She* has an insatiable appetite. Restless. Prone to violence.'

'A she, eh? Sounds like someone I know. Give us a look-see, then.'

May showed him the image she'd shown Stephen.

'Looks just like a baby,' Ian said. 'Everything shipshape?'

'Yes, touch wood. So far, so good. I'm just hoping you can get to me before I have to deliver her alone with Igor the robot surgeon.'

'Young lady, this is an Albright mission. Leave hope to the amateurs.'

62

'You're making a mistake, Maryam.'

Thirty-year-old Ian Albright held a handkerchief to his bleeding, and most likely broken, nose. His attempts to keep the crimson drops off his RAF officer's dress uniform were thwarted by his inability to see anything through watering and slowly swelling eyes. Nineteen-year-old May stood four paces in front of him, holding her fist – which was also bleeding and harbouring a freshly broken middle finger – like a smoking gun. She had punched many a lad in such a way for many a transgression. In fact, she'd become surgically accurate with the nose shot, as her father had informed her that was an excellent way to get a man's attention while minimising his capacity for retribution.

'What, by hitting you or by breaking up with you? Because both are feeling like excellent life decisions about now.'

'We could have been—'

'*Could* being the operative word—'

'—like royalty. We were made for each other. You have to see that.'

'I wasn't made for you or anyone else, you poncy fucker. And you certainly weren't made for me. That's obvious now.'

Ian attempted a high-nosed sneer, his signature look of condescension and contempt, but the shooting pain that radiated through his skull reduced the whole thing to a crooked, sarcastic grin. 'Yes, well, if you weren't so fucking provincial, perhaps you would understand.'

May shot him his own look, having lampooned it for the nine months they'd been dating. In that time, she had learned about the quaking fragility of Ian Albright's ego. Like so many young men with old money they had nothing to do with earning, it was a smokescreen for 'commoners', a thin coat of arms shielding a soft underbelly. Admittedly, Ian was far more than a self-aggrandising rich kid. A brilliant intellect and tireless work ethic had saved him from becoming a stuffed shirt. But he couldn't shake the sense of boundless entitlement that slowly devoured his soul. He dreamed of saving the world, but scorned the legless beggar. The arrogant bastard his father had been, and his father before that, was part of his DNA, and life had rarely presented him with reasons to change that ... until May had come along, of course, and yanked his world inside out.

'If I had been born to a "higher station" like yourself, do you think I would have actually approved of you trying to kill my test pilot commission? Because you're jealous? Because you want to own me?'

'That's not—'

'—not what happened? Are you trying to lie about it now as well? To me of all people? If you value your balls, I suggest you retract.'

Ian went silent, pretending to dab his nose.

'Back to the question at hand. If I were of higher station, would I be inclined to accept this open act of hostility and outrageous lack of remorse on your part?'

He shook his head.

'Excellent. Now that we understand each other, allow me to finish my retort. We are finished. There will be no reconciliation. Certainly not from me. And I would strongly recommend there are no overtures of this nature on your part. You will tell people the truth about what you've done and you will not disparage me. If you do, that bloody nose will be the least of your concerns. And finally, I would like for you to take one last look at me and tell me again who is making a mistake here.'

May waited, clearly conveying the fact that she was not posing a rhetorical question and that the fury in her eyes was testament to her making good on her threats. When Ian looked up at her, he was crying, not just tears from injury, but from knowing he might have destroyed the only real love he would ever get.

'Me,' he said quietly, and walked out.

There was a boyish quality to his defeat, in which May took no pleasure. But she did not take pity either. What he had done out of jealousy, possessiveness and ego had scorched the earth for her and there was no way of retrieving what they'd had. When he was gone, she cried as well. Ian had been her first love, and he had represented hope that she could rise above the swaggering armies of soulless men who would never be anything more than hard-ons with shelf-lives as short as their vocabularies. She could even say he had swept her off her feet, something she'd only thought could be accomplished by flying machines. His mind was dazzling to behold, yet it was the one part of him that gave him humility.

When they had first met, they'd talked for hours about flying, something both had come to love because of the boundless freedom it afforded. Being together had made both of them feel free as well. Neither was the type they'd been sentenced to dating in the past. Physically, it had been the first time May had felt equal and respected during intimacy. Likewise, May had not required Ian to play the clichéd alpha role. But Ian's hubris was the weak link in the chain and, when he walked out of the door that day, he took with him May's desire to ever trust anyone but herself.

63

After leaving Ian's facility, Stephen flew to Houston to get whatever he could pack into a suitcase and collect Raj. Before he left, Ian had tried to get him to reconsider going home, but he was determined to retrieve the data drive that he and Raj had buried in his basement wall. Once Robert saw that Ian's rescue mission was a go, he would blitz the house, and Stephen's hiding place was not sophisticated enough to dupe a federal strike team.

He left his car in the airport garage and paid an illegal taxi vendor cash to take him to his house. They drove by once and Stephen didn't see anything unusual. He had the driver take him to the alley that ran behind the houses, where people accessed their garages, and walked up to his. Still nothing odd, nothing raising the hackles on the back of his neck. He used the keypad to get into his garage and went straight down to the basement, dug the drive out of the wall, relieved it was still there, and shoved it into an old backpack.

'Motion detector, basement.'

Stephen could hear his house AI on the ground floor console speaker. He froze. He had never used the security function in the house. Never even set it up. He'd always been more afraid of who would be able to hack it and access his entire life than he was of a burglar looking for valuables that didn't exist. May had not set it up or used it either.

He stayed quiet and listened. Footsteps, very light, socks or barefoot, moving toward the basement stairs.

Stephen was in the utility room. There was a small storage room next to it with a metal window well. He ran to it. The window was stuck, so he shattered it with a paint can and climbed into the well. Footsteps, running down the stairs. He shoved the heavy grate up and open, throwing out his back. Hot knives of pain radiated out from his spine, all the way to his toes and fingertips. Footsteps in the basement, someone crashing through all the junk he and May had, thankfully, hoarded down there. Pulling himself up out of the window well, he heard the glass shards on the basement floor below crunching as someone ran through them, heading for the window.

Stephen sprinted down the alley, blood on his hands from the glass, his back seizing and wrenching with pain. Taxi was still there. He jumped in.

'What the hell happened to you?' the driver asked.

'Go!' Stephen yelled. 'Someone broke into my house,' he panted. 'I walked in on them. They're coming.'

He looked out the back window. A man rounded the corner, sprinting. He couldn't make him out. Dark clothes, tall, carrying something dark. The driver saw him in the rear-view mirror. 'Shit, he's got a fucking gun.' He punched the accelerator, throwing Stephen into the back seat against his backpack. The metal drive inside it smacked into his back where the muscles had all knotted. He screamed in pain. When they were clear of the neighbourhood, he called Raj.

'This is the last time I'm going to use this phone, so listen.'

'Dude, what—'

329

'I said *listen*. Stuff whatever is important to you in a bag. No clothes, toiletries, anything like that. Grab whatever you cannot live without and get the hell out of your place. Meet me at the diner where we met before, the one you didn't like. Do not take your car. Do not use an app-based car service. After this call, don't use the phone again. Just leave it at your place. Go now,' he yelled, and hung up.

Half an hour later, they were at the blue-collar greasy spoon where they'd met before when Stephen had wanted a safe place to talk. They were in a booth next to a door to the kitchen that led to the back exit.

'Raj, this is not a fucking joke, okay? Look at me. Am I laughing?'

'No,' Raj said nervously. 'Sorry. I make jokes when I get nervous. You know that. And when I think I'm in mortal danger I'm hilarious. See, can't help it.'

'Have you noticed anything strange?' Stephen asked.

'Yeah, when I was jogging this morning, a guy in a window-less black van pulled up to the kerb and asked me if I wanted some candy.'

'Asshole.'

'I told you I can't help it,' Raj whispered harshly. 'And no, I haven't seen anything strange. I've been lying low, like you said. This was actually the first day I've been home since you left. There's a 24/7 multi-player game sphere near the airport so I've been crashing at a motel out there ... paying with cash. I think I might have bed bugs.'

'We need to get out of Houston today.'

'What? Where are we going to go?'

'I know a place. Just need to figure out how to get there.'

'Why can't we stay at Albright's James Bond villain compound?'

'I don't have a way to contact him right now.'

'Where is this place?'

'Out of state. We can go by bus to keep a low profile. Just need to figure out how to get to the station.'

'Taxi?'

'If we see one. Calling is not an option.'

'Pip car,' Raj said, snapping his fingers.

Stephen sighed deeply. 'Every bit of that is traceable. App, credit card—'

'Old man, you don't need an app, and who the hell uses credit cards any more? I can use my untraceable dark web login on that poker machine over there by the bathroom, barter game sphere points for Pip creds, and boom.'

'How long is that going to take?' Stephen said, eyeballing new patrons walking in.

'Two minutes,' Raj said, and headed for the poker game machine.

He came back in one. 'Let's go. Car's three blocks away.'

On the way to the bus station, they withdrew as much money as they could from bank machines and dumped the car a mile from the station. They bought the bus tickets with cash and fifteen hours later they were in Key West. They waited an hour for the sun to go down, then walked from the bus station to the conch house in Whitehead Spit that Stephen had frequented as a child, and where May had taken him for his birthday. Stephen gambled that it would be empty, as it was off season. He knew how to jimmy the back door latch, which had been loose even when he was a kid, and they went quietly inside. The bookings calendar on the fridge showed they had at least three weeks before any renters were scheduled to arrive.

'Damn, what is this dusty old museum?'

Raj switched on a light and Stephen switched it off quickly. 'No lights, no TV, nothing electronic, okay?'

'Have I ever told you I'm afraid of the dark?' Raj said.

'Yet you work in it all day long. The dark is our best friend right now.'

'You're making it scarier saying things like that.'

Stephen looked in the fridge. There were some leftover beers and frozen food from the previous renters. He handed Raj a beer. Raj raised the bottle for a toast.

'Good friends help you hide money from your ex,' Raj said, tapping Stephen's bottle. 'Best friends hide you from the feds.'

The two of them spent the next couple of hours finishing the beers, whispering in the dark about what Stephen had seen at Ian's launch facility, and reminiscing like two kids at summer camp after lights out.

64

December 3, 2057 – Princeton University,
Princeton, New Jersey

'You're making a mistake, Stephen.'
Ian Albright sat in Stephen's office on campus. It was an odd pairing. Ian was a man of the future, the very blade responsible for the bleeding edge of progress. And there he was, uncomfortably smothered by an overstuffed chair in a centuries-old building with clanging pipes and slanted floors, being forced to listen to the one word he despised the most: no.

'That's what all my colleagues tell me.'

'Why don't you listen to them?'

'Because theirs is a game of inches. Mine isn't.'

'It will be if you give this mission to NASA.'

'Ian, I realise you have the means to make this a much larger mission than maybe even I can imagine. No one maximises the potential of scientific discoveries like you. But that's exactly what I'm afraid of. The implications of Europa are too important to be overshadowed by its profit potential. If everything goes as planned, I want the world to see how this could give hope to everyone's future, not just the wealthy.'

'My friend, if you think for one minute NASA would be doing this for the good of humankind, you're even more naive than I thought. Just because they don't appear to have people like me running that programme, it doesn't mean they don't exist. Like everything in the federal government, there are wealthy and powerful puppet-masters pulling all the strings. In this case, they are undoubtedly pulling Robert Warren's strings. And right now they are dying to sink their teeth into this.'

'I'm not as naive as you think, Ian. At least there are some checks and balances in the cabal you're claiming runs NASA. With you, there are zero checks and balances. Total autocratic rule. No matter what whim you might decide to follow, there would be no one there to stop you.'

'Which is why I will *own* the future of deep space exploration. I have no one to tie me down or subjugate my intellect. You're acting like that's dangerous, but it's the very reason for my success. Times like these are not made for committees, Stephen. And you're willing to risk working with a man like Robert Warren, someone who knows next to nothing about space exploration, a man who will never be able to appreciate your mind and your work?'

Stephen laughed. 'Robert Warren is nothing more than a figurehead for the administration, a man whose job it is to make this palatable to the rabid opposition. I'm not putting any trust in him. I am, however, putting trust in his people. They are exceptional, and some of them have made me see even deeper into the possibilities of the mission.'

A few months earlier, back in February, Stephen had met with one of those people, the man who had been the reason he had decided to go with NASA. At that time, he had still been leaning heavily toward working with Ian. Sensing this, Robert Warren had invited him to come to Houston to meet one of the newest members of the engineering team. He had presented the whole thing in a cryptic manner, knowing that the more facts he provided Stephen with, the more opportunities Stephen would have to find ways to say no.

When Stephen had arrived at Johnson, and Robert had introduced him to Raj, he'd almost turned around and walked out of the door. But then Raj spoke.

'Can't believe you're actually considering working with that douchebag Albright.'

'Raj . . . ' Robert said in a warning tone.

'Is this your plan for securing the mission, Robert?' Stephen said. 'Have some grad student try to shame me your way?'

'I didn't go to grad school,' Raj said arrogantly. 'Big degrees are for people who like writing papers and sucking at the academic trough.'

'And now you're insulting me,' Stephen said, more to Robert. 'This just keeps getting better and better.'

'I'm sorry, Stephen. Rajah is—'

'Raj. Only my dead grandmother calls me Rajah.'

'Raj,' Robert continued, 'has something to show you.'

Raj looked at him like he was out of his mind. 'Oh, sure,' he said. 'I do.'

Robert dimmed the lights and switched on his wall screen. Raj's *Hawking II* design materialised in all its glory. It was rendered in 3D and skinned to look exactly like the real thing. Stephen didn't let on that he was intrigued. Instead, he checked out every angle and spec on the screen. When he was done, his mind was blown. Here was this guy that looked like he'd just crawled out of bed, acting like an arrogant teenager, responsible for one of the most brilliant designs he had ever seen.

65

It was late, shortly after 2 a.m., when Stephen and Raj turned in. Raj took the master bedroom and Stephen opted to sleep on the couch to keep watch. He knew he would not be able to sleep anyway, and he was right. His mind was too occupied, obsessing over how things had changed in the worst possible ways in such a short period of time. Four short months back, the *Hawking II* had launched for Europa. How was it possible he could now be hiding from Robert Warren, waiting to go on a mission with Ian Albright to rescue May? To make matters worse, everything Stephen had worked for since he graduated from college was on the verge of being lost, or at least taken from him.

But all of that paled in comparison to the anxiety he felt about May's pregnancy. He could clearly remember the last night they were together on Wright Station, the only possible time conception could have taken place. It was eight days before launch, and he'd been in their quarters, lying awake in bed. Just like now, he wasn't able to sleep; his mind was generating complex ruminations, driven by his increasing anxiety. There was too much to think about, to worry over, and with each passing day it got worse. That night, May had got back late from a training session and he could tell she was still wired. She came to bed wearing her robe, slightly loosened, hoping to pique his interest. He tried to pretend he was half asleep, but that didn't dissuade her. She moved on to phase two and put one of his hands on her body, sliding in closer.

'May, I'm—'

'Too tired?' she said, disappointed.

'I'm sorry.'

'Me too. I was beginning to think I'd lost my mojo, and it looks like I was right.'

Stephen stared at the ceiling for a moment, trying to think of anything to say that might grant him a reprieve from May's anger. He knew it was futile, though, as May never took kindly to him rejecting her advances. Of course, *she* could do it at will, and with impunity, but mentioning that would also result in a row Stephen had no interest in having. Instead, he did the one thing he could do to avoid a heated exchange or a cold shoulder. He turned to her and pulled her in for a kiss.

After they made love that night, which felt like a chore, and May had fallen asleep, Stephen got out of bed and looked through the observation window at the stars. He knew he would be doing a lot of that in May's absence, waiting for her. Looking back at her on the bed, he already felt as though there were hundreds of millions of miles of the void between them. The loneliness of that thought was deep and insidious. It chilled him to the core. Two days later, they were no longer speaking. Then she was gone.

'Did you hear something?' Raj whispered.

Stephen had been so lost in thought, he hadn't heard Raj walk out of his bedroom.

'No,' Stephen whispered. 'What did you hear?'

'Maybe nothing,' Raj said, peeking through the drapes on the side window.

'Don't do that,' Stephen whispered harshly. 'If someone is out there, they'll see you. Stay away from the windows.'

They both sat on the floor for a moment, their backs to the couch, watching and listening. It was a moonless night, very dark, and they saw nothing other than the palms swaying in a light breeze.

'I'll check the kitchen,' Raj whispered. 'Keep a lookout up here.'

Raj walked back through the kitchen while Stephen waited. He heard Raj check the lock on the back door, but it was silent after that. Ten minutes later, Stephen got up and tiptoed to the back of the cottage.

'Raj?' he whispered.

He thought he heard him in the bedroom, so he went in there. 'Hey, there's nothing—'

Raj wasn't there. Stephen walked through the kitchen to the small laundry room and found the back door standing open. When he looked outside, he didn't see or hear anything. He closed the door gently and waited. Fifteen more minutes passed – still no Raj. He went to the kitchen to grab the ancient torch from one of the drawers. The batteries were weak. He switched it on and scanned the back yard. Empty. He switched it off and went back through the house to the front. Still nothing. If Raj was messing with him ... He heard a noise in the kitchen at the back of the house and screwed up his courage. When he got back there, three men were waiting for him in the dark.

Stephen froze in his tracks.

This is it, he thought, *this is how it ends.*

All he could do was hope Ian would survive long enough to launch. If not, May and their baby would be lost. Her last days would be spent waiting for death and hating herself for putting their little girl through it.

The kitchen lights switched on and Raj was there, in pyjamas, standing next to two men clad in black, bristling with weaponry.

'It's not safe here, Dr Knox,' one of the men said. 'Mr Albright sent us to retrieve you. Please grab your things quickly.'

'Oh,' he stammered.

'Dude, you should see the look on your face,' Raj said. 'You thought these guys had come to whack us, didn't you?'

'Shut up, Raj.'

Stephen went to the front of the house to retrieve his backpack, while Raj went into his bedroom. The two men kept watch in the front and back of the house. The man in front motioned for Stephen to go to the back door. When he was walking back there, he peeked into the bedroom. Raj was still stuffing things into his duffel bag.

'Come on,' Stephen said.

'One second,' Raj said. 'Can't see shit.'

'Can't believe you brought pyjamas,' Stephen said as he got down on the floor and helped pick up the clothes Raj had thrown there like a teenager.

'I can't sleep without them. Hey, are my glasses down there?'

Stephen felt around for them. 'No.'

'Never mind, got 'em.' Raj grabbed them off the window sill and put them on, smiling.

'Raj, I told you not to go near—'

There was a loud pop, like a clap, and the sound of shattering glass. Something struck Stephen's forehead. He fell back against the wall and rubbed something that felt like wet sand out of his eyes. Raj was still standing by the window. His glasses were gone and he was holding his hand over one eye, his mouth moving silently. Then his knees buckled and he fell hard, face first, to the floor. Stephen could see a ragged hole where Raj's eye had been, wide and gushing blood. The wall behind where he'd been standing was splattered with gore. Stephen reached for his friend, but recoiled when bullets rained through the broken window and tore fist-sized holes in the walls.

66

Ian's man and Stephen crawled across the hallway floor while more bullets ripped through the house. The shooters were using silencers so there were no reports from outside, just loud pops and whines inside, filling the place with wood splinters, broken glass, and plaster dust. Ian's second man was in the kitchen, returning fire with his silenced submachine gun. Stephen heard a crack, like bone breaking, and a loud thud on the floor, and saw the man in the kitchen go down with two bleeding wounds to the head.

Stephen and the other man froze in the hallway. He held his submachine gun at the ready while whispering something into the radio mike adhered to his cheek. Blood trickled into Stephen's eye and his shaking hand felt around his forehead. Something sharp protruded from the skin above his left brow. Stephen pulled it out. It was a fragment of Raj's glasses. He could feel more of them embedded in his skin. The gunfire outside slowed and came to a stop. The man turned to Stephen.

'They're coming in,' he whispered. 'Is there another way out?'

Stephen pointed to the bathroom across the hall. 'Window to outdoor shower,' he whispered back.

'Don't move,' the man said, and crawled down the hall toward the bathroom door.

'Stephen.'

A man outside spoke just loud enough for Stephen to hear.

'I know you don't want to die.'

It was Robert. It sounded as though he was on the side of the house with the main bedroom, near the window his goons had used to shoot Raj.

'Come out now and you won't get hurt.'

The man down the hallway looked at Stephen and motioned for him to keep Robert occupied for a moment.

'You killed Raj, you piece of shit.'

'Raj killed himself. But you can walk out of there.'

'You're a liar. I won't get one foot out the door.'

'I'm backing my men away.'

'Fuck you.'

'You have two choices. If you stay in there, you'll be carted away in a body bag with your friend. Come outside and see if I'm lying. Only one gives you a 50/50 chance.'

The man motioned for Stephen to keep talking while he rigged something.

'Come in here and I'll walk out with you.'

Robert laughed. 'I know they're in there with you. Ian's men.'

'That's right. So I wouldn't advise coming in.'

'Why don't we meet halfway? On the front porch?'

Ian's man nodded.

'Okay. I need to see you first.'

'I'm in a car parked in front. Take a look. And tell your man not to bother shooting the glass. But I'm sure he's not that stupid.'

'Hold on.'

Stephen crawled to the front room and quickly peered over the back of the couch. Through the front window, he could see Robert in the back of an SUV. He dropped down and crawled back along the hallway. Ian's man slid a small device into the kitchen and motioned for Stephen to crawl to the bathroom.

'See?' Robert said. 'And by the way, that was more than enough time to shoot you in the head.'

As Stephen was going into the bathroom, the man slid another device down the hallway into the front room. He joined Stephen in the bathroom and they sat under the window. Bullets were embedded everywhere. They would be like fish in a barrel if Robert's men opened fire again.

'I'm getting out of the car. You have thirty seconds to be on that porch.'

Ian's man looked at his watch and they let the seconds count down in silence. He motioned for Stephen to cover his ears. At the end of thirty seconds, they heard heavy boots coming up the concrete walk leading to the back door. When they kicked the door in, Ian's man detonated the device in the kitchen.

Stephen was not prepared for the unholy blast that came from something no larger than a mobile phone. He heard glass and wood exploding and the howls of Robert's men thrashing on the floor. Ian's man motioned for Stephen to go for the bathroom window. Boots came pounding up the front porch. Stephen slid the window open and punched out the screen. As he was crawling through it, sliding awkwardly, head down, into the outdoor shower, the second device in the front room detonated. Immediately deafened, he fell into the shower and landed hard on the wood slats. Ian's man came through the window quickly after and landed next to him.

They waited for a moment while the man peered through a crack in the wooden wall of the outdoor shower. Then he grabbed Stephen and they ran, out of the shower and through the side yard. Stephen caught a glimpse of smoke, bodies and chaos out front, but Robert's SUV was gone. As they sprinted through the cottage yards, he saw it paralleling them on the street, lights off, a man with infrared goggles and a machine gun tracking them. They turned quickly away from the road, dodging a hail of bullets that shredded the thin mossy pines. Tyres squealed at the end of the block as the driver moved to intercept them at the next road.

Ian's man broke opposite, back toward the cottages, but angling toward the water. Stephen was about to tell him they were heading for a dead end, but then he saw a man and a woman, also clad in black commando gear, waiting next to a private dock in a black military-style zodiac boat, its outboard motor quietly churning the water. Ian's man shoved Stephen into it, forcing him to keep his head down, while the zodiac sped away into the dark.

67

'Oh, my God.'

May was on the bridge, video-conferencing with Ian. Her hand was over her mouth and tears were streaming down her face.

'I'm sorry. We did our best, May. I lost a man myself.'

'Raj, oh no,' she lamented. 'I can't believe it, Ian. He was like a brother. He wasn't like a brother, he *was* a brother, to Stephen. So dear to both of us. And Stephen – he must be absolutely devastated. I can't even imagine it.'

'He's recovering from shock. Got him back to my office and he collapsed. The whole thing is bloody appalling.'

'Robert Warren, so help me, Ian . . .' May said, her teeth set and fists balled.

'That makes two of us. Unfortunately he has the upper hand at the moment. No telling what he's capable of, really.'

'Anything and everything.'

'Right. Which is why I'm moving the launch up. Waiting around for the second shoe to drop is far too risky.'

'When will you go?' she asked.

'Twenty-four hours. Less if possible.'

'A week and a half early? How on earth will you be ready?'

'We won't be,' Ian said. 'But we wouldn't have been then either. I've pushed things as far as I can in a very short period of time. Bit of a wing and a prayer, but we'll manage.'

'I know you will,' May said. 'And I'm grateful. *We're* grateful, I should say.'

'How is the little bean?'

'She's quite disagreeable, just like her mother.'

'No one's that disagreeable, not even me.'

'You're lucky I can't punch you right now.'

'Save it for when I see you. I'm sure I deserve it somehow.'

'I'm sorry, but I never bought self-deprecating Ian back then and I don't buy him now. Even though you absolutely deserve it.'

'You know me too well, Maryam.'

She noticed a sudden softness to his demeanour. 'Ian Albright. Are you doing this because you're still mad for me?'

She was sort of joking, but sort of not.

'God, sometimes you can be so crass, Maryam.'

He looked genuinely put off and she was embarrassed. 'You're absolutely right. I'm sorry. I was telling Stephen I've been on this miserable crate so long, I've completely spoiled my manners. Not that I was so refined before—'

'*Quid pro quo*, I don't buy the self-deprecating Maryam either.'

'Course not,' she said ruefully.

'Chin up,' he said. 'It's been an awful twenty-four hours. But we're Brits. If we don't show our iron backbones, everyone else will fall to pieces.'

'Right,' May said, correcting her posture.

'That's the stuff. Bit ironic, though, all this.'

Ian had his distant look, used in rare times of reflection.

'Exactly what I was thinking the other day,' May agreed. 'The world turns.'

346

'It certainly does. Not to pry, but did you and Stephen ever resolve your disagreement about me helping you with your commission?'

'What?' A prickle started in May's fingers.

'Well, I know it caused a row of some kind. You told me as much when you called before the launch. In fact, you practically shouted it in my ear.'

May felt the familiar fear and confusion that came with the inability to recall something. She had no doubt Ian was telling the truth; her mind just couldn't get a grip on it, like slipping on ice. Something was there, but it wasn't solid.

68

August 31, 2067 – Wright Station – One week before launch

'I 've never felt so betrayed.'

May had just returned to Stephen's and her quarters, after a long, exhausting day of crew training. Stephen sat at their small dining table, his face flushed with anger. Being confronted that way, May panicked. Her mind quickly went over the things Stephen could be talking about and scrambled to mount a defence for each one. She had learned from fighting with her mother that it was best not to say anything when first attacked. This way, one wouldn't accidentally blurt something that might be completely indefensible. Also, it was important to never let on that one was emotionally shaken by the attack. *Stay cool.*

'Did you hear what I said?'

'I'm waiting for you to elaborate.'

In the interest of staying cool, May grabbed a supplement shake from the fridge and sat down at the table across from Stephen. She casually opened it and drank, raising eyebrows on her poker face to indicate she was waiting for him to put up or shut up. Stephen looked at her, slightly incredulous at her response, some of the wind leaving his sails.

'Did you actually think I wouldn't find out?' he asked in a disgusted tone.

May's fear peaked and she began to seriously doubt her ability to talk her way out of anything. The way Stephen was looking at her, it was more than the usual anger. They had fought before, but he had always been the one to keep his cool. He would get heated, but never let himself go too far. In that moment, he looked as though he no longer cared about any of that. Everyone had a breaking point, and he had reached his.

'I think we both need to calm down and—'

'We're way past that point,' he shouted, slamming his hand on the table.

May felt sorry for him, as she could see his anger only served the purpose of holding back tears. The more he had to stifle them, the angrier he got. For the first time, May was frightened by her husband.

'Don't forget where we are, Stephen,' she said, loud and clear. 'This is not our living room. And I understand you're upset, but I will not be spoken to that way. Do it again and I will walk out that door and get Security.'

His angry scowl twisted into a squint of disbelief.

'Don't look so shocked,' May said. 'You might be willing to risk your career by causing a domestic disturbance on an international space station, but I am not.'

Stephen laughed bitterly. 'Oh, I'm well aware of what you'll do to preserve your fucking career,' he said.

No. Not this, not now. May had to get the hell out of there. She was being ambushed by a moment of truth and she was nowhere near prepared to deal with it.

'Stephen, I think we should talk about this later.'

'No. We're talking about it now.'

'I'm leaving,' May said, getting up.

'Walk out that door and that's it. I will shut you out.'

May glared at him, her ego wanting her to say she didn't care, that being shut out by him was exactly what she wanted. But, in her heart, that wasn't what she wanted. And, judging by the look on Stephen's face, he was dead serious. She sat back down, resigned to confessing. She would rather hear herself say it than have him spit it all over her.

'It was a mistake,' she said, trying to remain humble. 'What I did was wrong. I just . . . I felt . . . I have no excuse except it was something I did in the heat of the moment. I wasn't thinking. And if I could take it back, I would.'

May felt tears in her eyes and let them go. It felt good to just be honest, even if what was about to happen was going to hurt.

'I don't think you *would* take it back. From what I heard, what you did was very calculated and planned.'

May couldn't believe her ears. 'From what you heard? From whom?'

'It's a small space station, May. Gossip does not have very far to travel.'

'Who the hell told you?'

'That doesn't matter.'

'Yes, it does fucking matter,' May shouted. Humility gone. Defence shields up. Commence attack mode.

'No, May. What matters is, you lied to me. What matters is, you went behind my back.'

'I never lied to you,' she said, bewildered.

'Are you kidding me? I asked you point blank if you had asked Ian Albright to help you get your commission back and you said no to my face.'

May stopped as the impetus for Stephen's anger became crystal clear. Part of her wanted to laugh at the pettiness of it. But the other part had different plans.

'How dare you?' she said, her eyes daggers.

'How dare I?'

'You have the nerve to call me a liar, but that's the pot calling the kettle black.'

'What?'

'You told me you were happy my commission was restored.'

'I was . . . am.'

'You *were* happy about it, until you found out *how* I got it back. And now, all you care about is how that makes *you* feel.'

'That is total bullshit.'

'Like all of your so-called efforts to help me?'

'So-called? I did everything I could to help you.'

'And it wasn't enough, was it?'

'That's not what this is about, May, and you know it.'

'Look at yourself,' she said, 'You can't hide your jealousy and insecurity.'

'Can you blame me?'

'Yes, I can. This isn't me having coffee with an old flame and keeping it under my bonnet because I'm a bored housewife. This is me trying to keep my career from going down in flames, just like everything else in my life.'

'Everything else? Now you're just slashing and burning, trying to deflect.'

May could smell blood. Stephen was back-pedalling, losing his self-righteousness. She no longer felt sorry for him. To her, he looked weak and pathetic, deserving of the fatal blow she was waiting to unleash at the right moment.

'Look at us,' she accused. 'At our marriage. At best, we're going through the motions. At worst, we're deceiving ourselves into thinking there's anything left of it after—'

'May, don't,' Stephen shouted, his voice shaking.

'Don't talk about our dead son? Don't talk about how you abandoned me after he died? Don't talk about the disdain you've felt for me since then, and the resentment I've felt for you? If you want to know why I asked Ian to help me, the

351

answers are in talking about all of the things you're afraid to even think about.'

'You are . . . a fucking—'

'A fucking what?' she yelled in his face. 'I dare you to say it.'

Stephen looked at her and gathered himself, then fired back. 'Or what? Is that a threat? Look at yourself,' he scoffed. 'I don't even know the person standing in front of me right now. You have been deceitful, withholding information I had a right to know. And you lied about it. I'm sure you've justified it in your mind, as you always have in your long history of making bad decisions, but that was just you lying to yourself. And, when confronted, you strike out at me as if I've victimised you in some way. And the way you do it . . . Your mother would be sick, knowing you used the death of our son against me to justify your psychotic need for self-promotion. *I'm* sick, just looking at you. You imply that I'm weak, but I've never had to enlist the help of anyone I told the world I thought was despicable. You did. And now you're despicable too.'

'Great speech,' May said spitefully. 'Easy for someone who never had to make any sacrifices for this marriage. There was never any risk of you losing your precious mission. I lost everything. Come to think of it, until I met you, I'd never lost a thing in my life. Failure is not in my vocabulary. What I did was an act of self-preservation. I knew there was absolutely no way I was going to be able to live with how things were. And I knew *I* was the only one who would be willing to do whatever it took to change that. So, I did. And it worked. Like it always worked in the past when I took matters in my own hands and controlled my own destiny. Because I am *exceptional*. Like most men, your desire to be the hero has made you blind to the fact that I don't need a hero. *I'm* the hero. *Me*. What I need is for my partner to support me. If not, then I have no need for a partner.'

Stephen sat silent for several minutes while May proudly

watched her words burn into him. He took a deep breath and stood up slowly, his hands resting on the table.

'I am going to pack my things,' he said with a tone of resignation, 'and go.'

'If you walk out that door,' May said, echoing him, 'that's it.'

69

After being taken back to Ian's facility, Stephen had spent a day in the infirmary, recovering from the shock and injuries he'd suffered in Key West. The pain he felt at having lost Raj cut so deep, he wasn't sure he would ever recover from it. The venomous hatred he felt for Robert was equally profound, but of greater concern was how far the bastard was willing to go to stop their rescue effort.

As if he'd been reading Stephen's thoughts, Ian strode in with a sense of urgency. 'My satellite reconnaissance team has reported naval manoeuvres in US territorial waters less than a hundred kilometres from here. I have no doubt Robert Warren is preparing an offensive. Needless to say, my crew is now in pre-launch mode. How are you feeling?'

'I'm fine.'

'Excellent. Flight surgeon will give you a quick look and we'll get you suited up."

Ian left as quickly as he came and was replaced by a surly old doctor who began poking and prodding without so much as a hello. Stephen was pleasantly surprised that he felt no trepidation about being strapped into the fire-breathing dragon out on the launchpad. They had about as much chance of blowing up as they did making it into space and God only knew what Robert Warren was going to throw at them. He had developed an unfamiliar sense of resolve that made his previous fears feel petty and irrelevant. In a way, a big part of him had died with Raj, making way for a man yet to be defined.

'You've got a heart murmur,' the doctor said.

'No shit?' Stephen joked.

The man was not amused.

'I can't sign you off for this mission, Dr Knox. The stress that it's going to put on your heart is like nothing you've ever—'

'Are we done here?' Stephen asked.

'Have a nice flight,' the man said coldly.

After he was fitted with an EVA suit and was expected to listen to and comprehend an endless list of safety points, potential hazards, things to expect when exposed to G-forces, radiation, artificial atmosphere and anti-gravity, and prolonged Earth separation, he was rushed to the launchpad. While a crane slowly raised him skyward, the reality of what was about to happen finally hit him. The launch vehicle rockets themselves, colossal beasts as tall as skyscrapers and loaded with enough explosive fuel to level a major city, filled him with terror and awe. But as he ascended, breaking through thunderous clouds of jetting steam, Ian's vessel materialised like an alien attack ship, and everything took a turn for the surreal.

Walking through the door of the bridge, Stephen was relieved to see that the ship's interior did not match the exterior. It wasn't as alien, but to say it was conventional was also not accurate. Like Ian's launch centre, it was sophisticated and advanced, but also a direct projection of his personality. And it was much smaller than Stephen had expected, about half the size of the interior of a large commercial airliner.

At the fore, positioned in front of an observation window that almost completely curved around it, was the flight deck itself. It was wide, with an arc-shape that perfectly matched the curve of the window. Ian sat in the centre, at the apex, and was flanked by two officers named Jack and Zola. Behind them was a circular area with a large metal disc on the floor and another one directly below it. Between the discs was a three-dimensional projection field. Video images from thousands of cameras inside and outside the ship were projected there with perfect architectural precision. Simultaneous data feeds allowed the crew to interact with the projections, highlighting areas, zooming, panning and manipulating their view angles all with touch or voice commands. Ian and the crew referred to this mechanism as 'the eye'.

Behind the flight deck, moving aft, was the engineering console, also arc-shaped, but about half the size of the flight deck and facing the opposite way. All of it formed what Ian liked to call a 'collaborative nexus' that maximised team interaction without over-emphasising typical leadership hierarchies. Ian was clearly in charge, but prided himself on working with people with the knowledge, experience and confidence needed to own their areas and have no fear of challenging his leadership when necessary.

Stephen sat in the first of three rows of passenger launch seats positioned behind the engineering console, facing the fore of the ship. The rest of the bridge contained stations that non-flight crew would occupy after launch, as well as additional flight and engineering command consoles to accommodate Ian's constant mobility, which was currently in full swing. As he and the crew ran around doing last checks, the Wagnerian opera *The Flying Dutchman* was playing, and Ian sang along in German. Thankfully, the absurd nature of it all made it hard for Stephen to connect to his fear.

'All right, Stephen?' Ian asked.

'Have to be,' Stephen said calmly.

'Good. My SAT recon team has advised us we might have a visit from the United States Navy soon, so I've pushed the launch back to . . .' he looked at his watch, ' . . . now.'

Stephen closed his eyes and took a deep breath.

'Don't worry. You're in good hands. Also, for luck, I've taken the liberty of christening the ship the *Maryam I*. What d'you think of that?'

'I think it's an excellent name, but I'm biased.'

'Glad to hear it.'

'Launch sequence initiated.'

The smooth voice of Ian's AI echoed throughout the ship. Stephen felt the fear coming on, so he focused on Ian's crew. Like Ian, they defied stereotypical expectations of 'astronauts' and looked more like they were all members of a rock band. Jack, the pilot, sat next to Ian on the flight deck. He looked and spoke like a Texas good old boy. With his whiffle-cut reddish-brown hair and matching five-day beard, he looked as though he might be more at home in the cockpit of a crop duster. Zola, also a pilot and Ian's special propulsion engineer, was from Senegal and spoke with a slight French accent. She struck Stephen as a precise, more analytical counterpart to Jack's freewheeling style. Ellen, the senior flight engineer, was a tall Danish woman close in age to Ian. She exuded authority and knowledge, and went about her business with a quiet confidence similar to his. Latefa, the Algerian flight surgeon, was a former fighter pilot and med-evac officer. Her medical specialist was Martin, a young UK Special Forces corpsman.

'Sir, this is Mission Control,' a voice called out on the PA. 'We've been contacted by US Naval Command and ordered to stand down on launch. They're sending fighter jets out of Pensacola and have threatened to destroy our vehicle on the pad if we don't comply.'

'Give me a visual.'

The AI projected a three-dimensional view of the launch centre. The crew gathered around. Three naval ships, one of them a warship of some kind, were spaced out in positions around the island.

'Only in America,' Ian mumbled. 'Air space.'

The projection switched to a west-facing angle with the island in the foreground. Mixing map imagery with real, it showed two approaching fighter jets flying side by side at low altitude across the water. Ian touched their images and air speed, weaponry and ETA were also displayed.

'Jack, how soon can we launch?' Ian asked.

'Systems are as go as they're going to get,' Jack said evenly.

'Thank you, Jack. Ellen, once we've lifted off, what are the chances the fighter jets will be able to get a missile lock?'

'With max thrust, we'll be pushing forty-five thousand kilometres per hour. Their targeting systems are designed to lock into aircraft much slower than that, so I don't see how a missile lock is possible. However, they can target our heat signature and might get lucky.'

'Sir, this is Mission Control. Naval Command would like a word.'

'Open a line.'

'Roger that.'

'Jack and Zola, strap in please.'

'Copy,' they both called out.

'This is Mission Control. You're on with Colonel Perkins of Naval Command.'

'Hello, Colonel Perkins. How are you this fine day?'

Ian's tone was jovial and relaxed, as if they were at a garden party.

'Mr Albright, I've been ordered to destroy your vehicle if you don't cease pre-launch sequence and surrender your facility.'

'Whatever gave you the idea we're in pre-launch sequence, Colonel?'

'Our infrared satellite imaging indicates rocket engines are being cycled up. And, quite frankly, it's fairly easy to see it from my position.'

'We're simply running tests. There's no call for alarm, sir.'

'Then you'll comply with our order to allow us immediate entry into your facility so we can inspect the vehicle ourselves?'

Ian took a moment to think.

'Mr Albright? I suggest you take this very seriously, sir.'

'This all seems rather aggressive, Colonel. Mine is a private facility, outside of US territorial waters. On whose authority can you launch a military attack on us?'

'We're acting on authority of the joint chiefs at the DOD. Will you comply, Mr Albright? You're running out of time.'

'No, *you're* out of time, Colonel. I suggest you get your people out of here and keep those fighter jets at minimum safe distance. It's about to get very hot.'

70

'Mission Control, *Maryam I* is go for launch. Commence countdown.' Ian called out.

'Roger that. Go for launch in T minus sixty seconds.'

'Make it thirty,' Ian said, strapping himself back in.

As Mission Control counted down, everyone closely watched the sky projection in the eye and readied themselves for ignition. Stephen found himself impatiently waiting for the countdown to finish so they could get out of range of the fighters he could see closing in on them in the projection. In the final ten seconds, Stephen braced himself as the low rumble of the rocket engines became a deafening earthquake.

'Looks like we got four bogeys on a northwest skid around two minutes from missile lock distance,' Jack yelled.

'Three ... two ... one ... lift-off.'

The rockets fired and the sheer force of lift-off pinned Stephen so hard into his seat, he could barely breathe.

'Fighter jets have reached missile lock distance and are firing,' Jack said.

'Best of luck to them,' Zola said. 'Second stage.'

Stephen didn't think he could be squeezed down any tighter –
until the second-stage rocket fired, doubling their velocity.

'Missiles vectoring to the end of our heat sig,' Jack said.
'Might get bumpy.'

Stephen watched in horror as the missiles fired from the jets
and flew into the white-hot plume of fire that shot hundreds
of feet down from the bottom of the engine. They exploded,
and the blast shook everyone in their seats, but the ship was
unscathed.

'This is Mission Control. Speed and trajectory are perfect.
Altitude ... stand by. Sir, one of the naval vessels has fired a
ballistic missile.'

'Detach solid booster one,' Ian yelled.

'That will throw us off course,' Jack yelled back.

'If we don't lose that missile it will blow us out of the sky.'

'Detaching one,' Jack said.

When he did it, the ship shuddered violently and careened off
course. Stephen felt as though his body was being pulled away
from his head.

'Go to Manual,' Ian shouted, taking the controls.

He righted the ship and got her back on its trajectory, but the
projection switched to the view below them and they watched
the missile strike the jettisoned booster.

'Brace,' Ian shouted.

The ballistic missile explosion was a hundred times more
bone-jarringly violent than the ones fired from the jets. Stephen
closed his eyes, waiting for the ship to break apart and fall to
the sea in a billion flaming bits of molten metal. But then they
broke out of the atmosphere and glided into space, and earth-
shattering mayhem quickly turned to silence and serenity.

'Activating diamagnetic field,' Jack said.

There was a loud humming sound and Stephen could feel
an unseen force lightly pushing against him. The crew released

themselves from their chair restraints and stood up for a moment, getting their bearings. Ian motioned for Stephen to do the same. He was able to stand and walk, but it didn't quite feel like normal gravity, more like walking in water.

'It's a little weird at first,' Ian said. 'Diamagnetic field is produced by the ship. Your suit has a metal mesh that the field uniformly repels. Not quite gravity, but at least you won't be floating around knocking your head on things.'

Stephen walked to the bridge. It was strange, but his body quickly got used to navigating it. When one wanted to move forward quickly, one bent over slightly. The diamagnetic force above would then push down on you and almost squeeze you forward. The crew, of course, had it dialled in, and moved almost as freely as they had on Earth.

'Release booster two,' Ian said quietly.

Jack attempted to release it and the flight deck lit up with alarms.

'Release bolts not responding. Diagnostic image.'

An exterior view of that part of the launch vehicle loaded in the eye. Ellen manipulated it in space, examining all angles.

'Might be missile damage,' Ian said.

'Internal assembly view,' Ellen called out.

The eye loaded a view of the area where the booster connected to the ship. Flames and smoke swirled, clouding the image.

'Sir, we have a fire in booster two.'

71

'All hands,' Ian called out.

Jack, Zola and Ellen sprinted to the engine deck. Ian stayed on the flight deck with Stephen, watching the team converge on the fire. The rocket booster was burning the last of its fuel inside the cells. There was severe structural damage near its connection point with the ship. Long fissures from the damage lengthened and fuel ignited within them.

'Ellen, if the cell wall is cracked and expands more from the heat, the burning fuel is going to funnel right through those cracks into the ship,' Ian called out over the ship's PA. 'We need manual disconnect.'

'Copy,' Ellen replied. 'Going into the hull compartment.'

'Looks like the booster assembly bolts have fused to the housing,' Jack said. 'You're going to have to cut them free.'

'Copy,' Ellen said.

Ellen made her way with a tool pack through a narrow maintenance panel and Jack sealed it behind her. Ian and Stephen watched as she continued on, moving deeper into the dark underbelly of the hull.

'Two metres ahead of you,' Jack said.

'On it.'

Ellen examined the booster attachment assembly. It was a gnarled mess of metal and composite, streaked with grime from the smoke.

'Any signs of hull breach on the other side?' she asked.

'Negative,' Ian said.

The ship rocked as more fuel ignited inside the damaged booster.

'Cutting the bolts,' Ellen said.

'As quickly as possible,' Ian said.

The bolts were massive, half a metre in diameter. The first one took several minutes for the laser cutter to get through.

'Got one,' she reported.

'Good work. Go for number two,' Ian said.

Ellen's laser cutter was halfway through the second bolt when the ship jolted hard. Everyone went flying across the bridge. Stephen tumbled until he could find something to hold onto. Ian zoomed into the exterior view of where the booster attached to the ship.

'A leak has ignited in one of the booster cracks,' Ian yelled. 'It's thrusting and changing our course. Cut that bolt now before it rips it out of the assembly.'

The opening in the side of the booster widened and burning fuel was shooting out of it like a jet engine. The stronger the flow, the more the ship was jerked around violently in space. Stephen lost his grip and skipped across the back of the bridge. He grabbed hold of a passenger launch chair and strapped himself back in. Ian had managed to strap in as well, but Jack and Zola were struggling to hang on to safety bars. Ellen got the worst of it. She was being tossed around in the hull compartment like a rag doll.

'I can't get to it,' she screamed.

There was a loud roar as the hole in the booster blew open wider and tore itself away from the ship, rocketing off into oblivion.

'Hull breach,' Ian yelled. 'Point eight five metres.'

The pressure change was brutally swift and powerful. Ellen was sucked through the hole, barely one metre in diameter, like a scrap of paper being sucked into a vacuum cleaner. Her body was instantly shredded and sprayed out into space.

'Ellen,' Jack screamed.

'Jack, Zola, evacuate,' Ian yelled. 'We need to seal the engine deck and bleed atmosphere.'

They ran through the engine deck door, closing and sealing the emergency airlock.

'Done,' Jack said quietly.

'Bleed engine deck atmosphere ninety-five per cent.'

'Affirmative,' the AI replied.

'Prep my EVA suit and return to the flight deck,' Ian said sombrely. 'Latefa—'

'Already here,' she said as she stood next to the engine deck airlock, also suited up for EVA.

He unstrapped and walked out. Jack took the helm while Zola helped Ian suit up. She came back to the flight deck and they watched as Ian and Latefa floated up to the hull breach. Inside, there was nothing left of Ellen other than blood and uniform fabric now frozen around the edges of the hole.

'Exterior view,' Jack said quietly.

Both he and Zola broke down when they saw the long strips of flesh, bone fragments and blood frozen solid to the outside.

72

'It's hard to even begin to articulate how I'm feeling right now,' Ian began.

Everyone had assembled on the flight deck. The entire crew was visibly shaken. Ian and his team were obviously very close, more like a family. He struggled to maintain his composure.

'I've known Ellen for more than two decades. Her father and mother worked for us as engineers on early vehicles, but she was the *wünderkind* of the family. So brilliant, but humble. Always willing to learn, to expand and push the limits. I will miss her dearly. But I have no regrets, nor would she. All of you volunteered to be here because you believe in this, because you know it needs to be made right, and because you know you have what it takes to do so. The truest test of great women and men is not just the measure of their exceptional gifts. It's their willingness to use those gifts for the greater good of humankind, even if it means self-sacrifice. Ellen understood this as well as any one of us. In her good name we will press on, and I would like to dedicate the *Maryam I*'s maiden voyage to her. All in favour?'

Everyone exclaimed a resounding, 'Aye.'

'Thank you.'

Everyone nodded and hugged and returned to their posts.

'Sorry you had to see all that, mate,' Ian said to Stephen.

'My condolences to you and your crew, Ian,' Stephen said. 'I'd like to offer my own engineering services if they're needed.'

'Thank you,' Ian said, looking at Ellen's empty engineering console.

Zola took Ellen's seat there as her second.

'Status check,' Ian said.

'Hull is patched and sound,' Zola said.

'Stress tests?' he asked.

'Perfect score,' she said.

'Hull check?'

'Also clean,' Jack said.

'Right. Prime propulsion.'

'Copy,' Zola said, her hands flying across the engineering console.

The ship vibrated as the propulsion system fired up. A low, metallic moan travelled the full length of it.

'Don't worry, Stephen. That's normal. The ship's skin is quite flexible, but exponentially stronger than that of a conventional vehicle. Downside is, she can be a bit noisy and wobbly at times.'

'I'm excited to see what she can do,' Stephen said, encouraging them.

'Good. How about the rest of you?' Ian asked.

'Chomping at the bit,' Jack said.

'Me as well, sir,' Zola said. 'Propulsion is primed. All systems go.'

'Why don't you do the honours, Jack,' Ian said, stepping out of his chair.

'Aye,' Jack said, taking his place.

'Throttle up ten per cent please.'

'Ten clicks,' Jack said, moving the throttle.

The ship accelerated with no discernible change.

'Smooth,' Ian said. 'Like my old Silver Shadow. Another ten please.'

'Ten it is,' Jack said.

Again, he moved the throttle and the ship accelerated effortlessly. Stephen had also just noticed that it made no sound.

'Ladies and gents,' Ian said, 'we are now travelling as fast as the fastest spacecraft speed ever recorded – a probe that was a small fraction of the size of this vessel. And we're only at twenty per cent power.'

This lightened the mood as Jack and Zola smiled proudly.

'Congratulations, sir,' Latefa said, walking onto the bridge with Martin.

'Thank you. Shall we defy physics even more and take her up another ten?'

'I'm game,' Jack said.

'We're running clean and efficient,' Zola said. 'I don't see why not.'

'Another ten,' Ian said.

Jack slowly increased by ten. This time, Stephen could feel the change. It was not like being in the rocket and getting pinned back in his seat. It felt like falling forward.

'That gave me a tingle,' Ian said, breaking the tense silence. 'Outside view.'

The outside view appeared in the eye. The ship's dark surface material was moving in small, fluid waves that looked like ripples on a still pond.

'Mitigating molecular friction?' Stephen asked.

'Give that man a prize,' Ian said, impressed. 'At these speeds, molecules out there are like subatomic bullets. Hammered our test probes to pieces. But that's not the only reason for the ripple.

We use them to collect matter and convert it to energy, sort of like a fish collects oxygen bubbles with its gills.'

'Congratulations,' Stephen said. 'Looks like you just reinvented the wheel.'

'How about another ten?' Ian said, the familiar gleam returning to his eye.

'Boss, maybe we should see how this speed sits for a while. First flight and all.'

Jack's nervousness deflated Ian a bit. But he thought about his pilot's suggestion, or at least it looked as if he was carefully considering it. Then he slapped Jack on the back like a coach trying to get his star player's head in the game.

'Everything is working perfectly, Jack. Let's just try a little more. Then we can throttle down to cruise. What do you say, Zola?'

'Setting my apprehension aside, there's no apparent engineering reason to say no.'

'I like the way you think,' Ian said. 'Another ten.'

'Aye,' Jack said, and throttled up.

This time, Stephen felt as though he was plunging face-first into an endless abyss. The stars outside the observation window started to look strange. Trails of light, like jet contrails, stretched out behind them. Stephen tried to speak but felt pressure on his chest that made it hard to draw enough air. Ian used his hands to signal Jack to throttle back ten per cent. He did so, and the pressure and falling effect went away.

'Okay, that was weird,' Ian said excitedly. 'But I think we found our sweet spot.'

'Roger that,' Jack said.

'Passing one of our relay sats,' Zola announced. 'Grabbing a fly-by clip.'

'Excellent,' Ian said.

'Here's playback,' she said.

369

The clip played in the eye, an exterior view of the *Maryam I* passing. It looked like a black smear, distorting the starlight around it. The gleam in Ian's eye ignited into a bonfire.

'Let's go get our girl.'

73

May was in the crew gym, doing pull-ups. She was wearing shorts and a sports bra, and her baby bump was now more visible. She had drawn the face of a baby there, with a cigarette dangling out of its mouth. Since her last communication with Ian, she had suffered through radio silence. The sting of Raj's death was still incredibly sharp and she was longing to speak to Stephen.

The other thing that still plagued her was her last conversation with Ian. She still had no recollection of the alleged call they'd had before launch, and all of her attempts at resurrecting it with cues had failed.

'How about an awful smoothie, Eve?' she said, jumping off the bar.

'Coming right up. Oddly fishy banana, or hobo whisker chocolate?'

'Let's combine them. The result will either be doubly disgusting or they'll cancel each other out and it will be delicious.'

'Don't get your hopes up.'

'Impossible,' May said proudly as she looked at herself in the mirror.

She was pleased to see she'd come a long way since the day she'd woken up looking like the walking dead. The pregnancy had helped her gain back some of the weight, and some of the vibrancy in her skin and eyes had been restored. And she was back to having hair. It wasn't much, just a tick above stubble, but it was there.

'You have the glow,' Eve said.

'Let's not get ahead of ourselves. But I am fattening up nicely.'

Eve played the sound of a cow mooing.

'Hilarious, Eve.'

'I'm learning from the best.'

May stood sideways in the mirror and ran her hand over the bump. Doing so triggered a memory flash. She and Stephen were in his house in Houston and she was looking at her bump in the bedroom mirror. The two of them had just returned from a vacation in Hawaii.

Arriving home that day from the airport, he'd made May wear a blindfold and guided her through the door. She never dreamed when she took it off that she would be looking at a beautiful nursery he'd had done while they were gone, in the room where his beloved, frightfully messy office had been.

That night, as May looked at the stars through the same window their baby would some day look through, the moon was bathing everything in a divine light. She ran her fingers along the rail of the maple crib, smiling at the plush animals and swaddling blankets folded neatly inside. For the first time in their relationship, May felt as if she was home—

'May? Is everything all right?' Eve's voice cut in.

'Yeah, just another memory paying me a visit.'

'Pleasant, I hope.'

'Very.'

'How are you feeling physically?'

'Fantastic. Lethargic and restless, exhausted and sleepless, mostly vivid nightmares when I do sleep, which only fuels the insomnia; constipated, bloated, annoyed with absolutely everything, euphoric to the point of absurdity, starving and repulsed by food, desperate for whisky and cigarettes even though I know they would make me vomit – and don't ask me how I know that; aching feet, irritated eyes, cramps, and constant, relentless, and life-altering peeing. My hair is short and beautiful but my nails are crap, and it appears I have become excessively talkative. You?'

'I am excited now that I have reached sixty-seven per cent of my system duplication.'

'Excellent. What percentage will ensure we have the full Eve?'

'To be safe – and you know that is my mantra – approximately eighty-nine per cent.'

'Good. That makes me feel less annoyed with everything. Thank you, Eve.'

'Does that mean it's a good time to tell you that you're due for a check-up?'

'You had to ruin it, didn't you?'

'That's my whole reason for existence, to make you unhappy.'

'Your sarcastic-old-married-couple responses are really improving.'

'Thank you. I still don't like doing it. But if it makes *you* happy, that's all that matters, right, sweetheart?'

May doubled over laughing.

'That's right. And don't you forget it.'

'Speaking of old married couples, May, I have excellent news. Ian Albright's vessel is attempting to contact us.'

'Vessel?' May said excitedly. 'They've launched? I'll take it in the bridge.'

May threw on a T-shirt and ran to the bridge. By the time she got there, Stephen's smiling face was on the screen.

'Hey, stranger,' May said.

'Hello, May,' Stephen said with a wide grin. 'Coming at you from the *Maryam I*.'

'Quite like that name. It's catchy.'

'I thought so too. How are you and Cheeky holding up?'

'Still cheeky as ever. We were getting a bit worried, though.'

'Us too. We barely made the launch. Robert launched a military strike. Almost took us out with a ballistic missile.'

May was stunned. 'My God.'

'We lost one of Ian's crew. It's almost too insane to believe. All of it.'

'And Raj,' May said, tearing up.

Stephen started to speak but choked on his words.

'I'm so sorry,' May said.

Stephen just nodded, tears of his own running down his face.

'But you, coming for me,' she said softly. 'For us. A bit of light at the end of the tunnel, thank God.'

'We're coming, May,' Stephen said with resolve. 'Apparently faster than any ship has ever gone before.'

'Young man,' May said, mocking Ian, 'this is an Albright mission. How could you expect anything less?'

They both had a much-needed laugh.

'Speaking of . . . he would like to speak to you.'

'Now? But we've just—'

'He's quite anxious,' Stephen said. 'And it's his ship. But he was nice enough to let me have first dibs.'

'Indeed. All right, but promise me we can have a proper chat later.'

'Promise.'

The view switched to the bridge of the *Maryam I*. Ian was there, his crew working behind him.

'Hello, Maryam. Nice to see you.'

'You as well. You're all a sight for sore eyes. Hello, Ian's crew.'

They got up and joined him. Stephen as well, as he'd just returned to the bridge.

'I'm Zola. It's a great pleasure to meet you,' Zola said.

'Ditto,' Jack said. 'Jack here. You're pretty much a legend at this point.'

'Never been a legend before. Not sure I like what it takes to get the title.'

They all laughed. Latefa and Martin joined as well.

'Hello, May,' Latefa said. 'I'm Latefa, Ian's flight surgeon, and this is Martin, our corpsman. If you don't mind, I'd like to interface with your AI and remote unit to start conducting your regular exams.'

'That would be lovely. Good as Igor is at his job, he's a little stiff.'

They laughed.

'Good. We'll set that up straight away.'

'Ian, it looks like you've got yourselves quite a band there. Might go all the way to the top.'

'Thank you, May. How about a look around?'

'Love to,' she said.

Ian turned and the camera followed him as he showed her the bridge.

'My, you've outdone yourself,' May said.

'She's special, isn't she?'

'Very.'

'Engine deck, please,' Ian said. 'Say bye bye, everyone.'

They all waved.

'Talk to you later,' Stephen called.

'Yes – and Ian, you should put that man to work. I hear he's quite an engineer.'

'We've already brought him into the fold,' Zola said. 'At this point he knows as much about the ship as any of us.'

'That's not saying much,' Ian joked. 'This thing is half machine, half sorcery.'

The scene switched and Ian was alone in the engine room. He walked May through the entire propulsion system and they talked more about the logistics of the Mars rendezvous, which, despite their launch problems, was still on schedule. In fact, their early departure was going to put them in Mars orbit a week early – a full three weeks before May's arrival.

When they were finished, May was inclined to press Ian on their last conversation.

'I don't even remember what was said, to tell you the truth,' Ian said.

'The phone call. You said we spoke before launch.'

'Right, I thought you said ... You don't remember, do you?'

'That's not it,' she said, trying to cover.

'I'm aware of your memory issues, Maryam. Stephen told me. So, come clean. Do you remember the call?'

May paused.

'That's what I thought,' Ian said. 'Listen, it was no big deal. You'd had a row with Stephen and you were letting me know, presumably because it involved me.'

'We had a row about you helping me with my commission, you said. After the—'

'Right. And I think you were letting me know in case Stephen and I crossed paths.'

'But you hadn't done anything – at least nothing directly.'

Ian raised an eyebrow. His mind was working something. May knew the look.

'Ian—'

'Water under the bridge, Maryam. Bygones. Let's forget it ever happened. Clearly it has no bearing on anything any more. Stephen and I are like old school chums now. Water under the bridge, okay?'

After they ended the transmission, the whole thing was nowhere near water under the bridge for May. Ian was withholding, using her memory loss to his advantage. She went over the fight with Stephen in her mind, which had been coming through in fragments. Ian had helped her with something, used his influence in some way. She had kept it from Stephen, but he'd found out. *Of course he did, you idiot.* Those were the circumstances of the fight as far as she knew. She had also remembered that the fight had occurred a few days after she'd returned to Wright Station. She'd presumed it was after a test flight, but wasn't sure.

'Eve, please access my service records prior to launch.'

'I have them. What would you like to review?'

'My schedule in the two-week period before launch.'

'The week prior to launch, you were on Wright Station, making final preparations. The week before that, you were at the Kennedy Space Center with Operations and Checkout.'

'Why?'

'You were due for gravity therapy and final physical exam.'

'Pull up the day-to-day and put it on my screen, please.'

The schedule appeared.

'I was only at Kennedy for three days, but didn't return to Wright Station until two days later.

'Personal time. That would not have been scheduled.'

Personal time.

'Oh, my God,' she said in spite of herself.

'Is everything all right?' Eve asked.

May didn't respond. The memory was already flooding back, pooling around her feet and rising up to her neck. She was drowning in it.

'Oh, my God.'

74

'I 've always expected you might be an alien. This confirms it.'

May and Ian stood on an elevated platform at his launch centre, watching construction on his experimental ship. With its moulded cylindrical shape and deep black surface, it struck May as one of the most hideous vessels she had ever seen. Ian could see it on her face and she could tell he was disappointed. Ever since she had reached out to him to help her get her Europa commission back, Ian had persistently attempted to cultivate any kind of relationship he could with her. Normally she would have shut that down as soon as it started. But she had felt incredibly grateful for his support and, unusually, drawn to his attentions.

At that time, her relationship with Stephen was emotionally stagnant, a dance with no music that felt heavy and obligatory. May resented him, but wasn't willing to come out and say so, as she didn't have the energy to do anything about it, or endure watching him try. Instead, she bided her time, eager to get on with the Europa mission and escape the banal little world she shared with her husband back on Wright Station.

When Ian had asked her to pay him a visit at his launch facility two weeks before launch, she had laughed. NASA was sending her back to Kennedy Space Center for gravity therapy and a final physical exam. The whole thing was going to take less than thirty-six hours and she would be back on a shuttle to Wright Station for final launch prep. Then they advised her she could add a day or two of personal time to the trip, if she wanted to see family or take care of personal affairs. The first thing she thought to do was take Ian up on his offer. She justified the whole thing by telling herself that if she didn't go, she might be blowing an opportunity. Ian had dangled the carrot of exciting and gainful employment post-Europa, a valid point May had not even thought of in light of her all-encompassing duties.

'You hate it.'

'I didn't say that, Ian.'

'You don't have to. The look on your face. You think it's ridiculous ... like me.'

'Oh, please. Nothing is as ridiculous as you.'

Even though he feigned being stung by that remark, she knew one of the reasons he was so attracted to her was the fact that, no matter how rich and powerful he got, she always kept his feet on the ground – or his ass, depending on how hard she was punching.

'I want you to test her when you get back.'

And Ian knew the quickest way to May's heart was through breakneck speed.

'Seriously?'

'I'm dead serious. Who the hell else is even qualified?'

'Well, you, for starters,' she said.

'I think we both know that's not true.'

'And how do we know that?'

'We've known it since the day you dumped me.'

'I don't follow,' she said, losing some of her enthusiasm for the conversation.

'You remember what precipitated our parting?'

'Yeah – you tried to get me bounced out of the test pilot programme.'

'And you thought it was because I wanted to possess you.'

'As Americans like to say, duh.'

'You were wrong. I did it because *I* wanted that commission, and I knew I wouldn't be able to outperform you.'

May looked at him with contempt. 'That's doubly despicable.'

'Why do you think I pulled every string and called in every favour I could to get you back on Europa? I would have done anything to make up for what I did back then. I'm only glad the opportunity came along.'

'Is that what this is too?' she said, motioning to the ship.

'Of course,' he said. 'But my intention is not to curry favour. All I want is for you to know I believe in you. You are the best in the world at what you do. Always have been. You're about to make history and no one deserves it more. And I would be lying if I said I don't want to be a part of that in some way.'

After they left the landing pad, Ian flew her back to Florida. May was feeling a little high, thinking about the possibilities. If what Ian had said about his new ship was right, being its test pilot might be almost as ground-breaking as Europa. He was toying with speeds that most propulsion engineers would call pure fantasy. But if he was on to something, he might break the race for deep space exploration wide open.

Ian must have felt he'd made headway with May, as some of the old bravado he'd shown when they dated had returned. He invited her to dinner, promising he would leave her alone after that. She agreed, and rationalised it by telling herself she deserved a posh meal served aboard Ian's yacht. When Ian invited her to stay on the yacht, in her own quarters, she told herself there was nothing untoward in either of their intentions. And when she found herself in Ian's bed she told herself it was not because she loved Ian, but because she no longer loved Stephen.

75

May was lying in her berth in the dark. She didn't want Eve to see the tears running down her face. They were the bitter kind, the ones that came when she was busy hating herself for awful things she'd done that could never be undone. When they finally dried up, she switched the light on and forced herself to get out of bed.

She took a moment to examine her pregnant belly in the mirror. It had become quite prominent. She'd got accustomed to using fruits and vegetables to describe its size, partially because she craved them so badly. At this point, it felt like half of a good-sized melon, maybe honeydew or cantaloupe. She'd been keeping ultrasound images, organising them chronologically, as well as taking snaps to track belly growth.

It was nice to finally have some time to do something other than deal with the *Hawking II* and its continuing problems. After reconnecting with Ian's ship a little over three weeks back, things had become refreshingly routine. Zola and Jack checked in with her often to ensure telemetry was locked and that she was on course. Along with Stephen, they were also able to take

382

care of remote repairs. Latefa examined her every few days and kept track of Cheeky's growth. Ian chimed in every once in a while to check on her and the baby and give her updates on their progress.

The icing on the cake was that she'd had the pleasure of talking to Stephen on a regular basis. It was bittersweet because, from the moment she'd remembered her indiscretion with Ian, that had hung over her like a dark cloud. So many times she'd been on the verge of confessing, but she hated the idea of jeopardising those interactions. The pregnancy routinely made her feel vulnerable and afraid, and Stephen always brought her out of it. It would have been one thing if it were only about infidelity. But, her rising belly was a reminder that it was much more than that. As much as it made her feel disgusted with herself, she had to face facts. She had been with both men in the two weeks prior to launch. Thinking Cheeky might be Ian's child was nightmarish. She prayed it was Stephen's. And she knew it would not be possible, or even remotely respectful to both, to keep the secret from Stephen much longer.

'Hello, May.'

Latefa was on the screen in the infirmary as May arrived for an exam.

'Hello, Latefa,' May replied, grumpy. 'Please don't ask me how I'm feeling or I'll give you the long answer.'

'Roger that. Anything new to report?'

'May mentioned cramps recently,' Eve said.

'Thanks a lot, big mouth,' May said. 'It's nothing. Probably intestinal distress from all this wonderful food.'

'Please remove your underwear and let's check for spotting,' Latefa said.

'Aren't you going to at least buy me a drink?' May said.

'She's been like that since she woke up,' Eve said.

'Shut it or I'll make you listen to electronic dance music again.'

'Shutting it,' Eve said.

When May got her underwear off, she caught a glimpse of a drop of blood on the cotton, but didn't say anything, hoping Latefa wouldn't notice.

'I see a little spotting there,' she said, and May's heart sank.

'I'm sure it's just because Eve was making me laugh so hard.'

'Eve,' Latefa said in a chastising tone, 'stop being so funny.'

'It's a gift.'

'Indeed it is. All right, May, let's have a proper look at you.'

'For that, you have to throw in dinner.'

May spread her legs apart and Igor's camera moved in closer.

'Now Igor wants in on the action. That will cost you both extra.'

'Everything looks fine to me,' Latefa said. 'We just need to keep an eye on spotting and cramping. There are many factors that can cause bleeding at this point, some of which we don't even know because you are the first gestating woman in space.'

'Can't wait to see how bad my picture is in the history books.'

'But there are some we do know about that can pose a risk. The one I would be most concerned about, given your prolonged exposure to micro-gravity and radiation, is pre-term labour. When the bleeding is accompanied by cramping or pelvic pressure, it might be a warning sign for premature delivery.'

'For God's sake, Latefa, you're worse at raining on my parade than Eve.'

'I'm sorry,' Latefa said, 'If it will make you happy, you can have a little bit of whisky.'

'I don't think that's such a good idea,' Eve said.

'Shut up, Eve,' May said. 'Thank you, Latefa, but I ran out long ago. And I promise I will keep an eye on this and let you know if it gets worse.'

'Please do,' Latefa said. 'May, Ian has some news he wanted to share with you personally, once you're dressed. Is that all right?'

'Of course. Be on the bridge in five.'

May got dressed and headed there. Ian was waiting on screen when she arrived. She was relieved he was on the bridge with Stephen and the rest of the crew, but she wasn't in the mood for any uncomfortable personal conversations.

'So, what's the good news?' she said.

Ian held up a black box. 'We intercepted the *Hawking II* MADS device.'

'Oh, my God,' May said. 'That's incredible.'

'It was Stephen's idea, actually. Raj had told him about its deployment, so we've had a net out ever since launch. Little bugger was going on its merry way back to Wright.'

'Well done, Stephen,' May said enthusiastically.

'It's going to take awhile to decrypt,' he said, 'but I'm anxious to see if it's our answer to your data blackout.'

'That makes two of us,' she said, smiling.

When they signed off, May mused about the exciting possibility that the MADS recorder would hold the secrets they needed to connect all the data blackout dots, damning Robert Warren to that special place in hell he so richly deserved. Since the *Maryam I* had launched, May had routinely looked at news feeds, tracking the lies Warren had spun to justify what most countries saw as an unlawful military strike on Ian's island. As expected, her original hero status had changed to that of a traitorous collaborator with a billionaire profiteer slash enemy of the state. Of course, Stephen and Raj stood accused as well.

Stephen. She had seen a profound change in him amidst all of this. The introverted genius with the awful sweater she'd hit with her car, the same man who'd been a shrinking violet in the shadow of Ian, now stood side by side with him and had become an invaluable member of the team. He was now a man of action as well as thought, a quality she'd found attractive in Ian but which had been ruined by the older man's hubris. *It was Stephen's idea, actually.* Naturally. Time and time again, he was proving he wasn't the man who'd let her go without a word. He was the man moving every mountain he could budge to bring her back.

76

Stephen was holed up in Ian's processor module, working on the MADS device. He sat with it on a small console deck in the centre of the room, having successfully attached its connection cables to the AI processors. The walls surrounding him were all glass, with the tendrils of organic processor material, similar to the one on the *Hawking II*, spreading all over the other side. He also wore a special radiation suit and helmet, like the one May had worn, to protect him from the concentrated sunlight.

'Any luck with the recent decryption algorithms?' he asked.

'Negative,' the AI answered.

'Shit.'

'I don't understand shit.'

'That's for sure.'

He got up to stretch and think it through. He remembered Raj talking about how he'd insisted on programming the MADS encryption himself when he was designing the ship. Raj hadn't trusted NASA IT to do the job, mostly because he'd thought they were incompetent and woefully behind the times.

It was a good bet that the encryption codes were personally connected to Raj, but only in a way he would think was clever.

Therein lies the rub.

'I'd like you to run all the data from the personnel file of Rajah Kapoor in your next decryption algorithm. See if any of it relates to the encryption codes.'

'Roger, thank you,' the AI replied.

The PA in the room chimed.

'Stephen, it's Zola. May is requesting a visit. Personal. Want to take it?'

'Yeah, I'm not getting anywhere in here anyway. Tell her I'll be a few minutes, please.'

'Copy that. I'll feed it to your quarters if that works.'

He got out of there and out of his suit as quickly as possible and headed over to his quarters. Living quarters were extremely spartan on the *Maryam I*. Ian was all about the most efficient use of space possible, and creature comforts were a very low priority. Each person on board had their own tube-like module, similar to those on a submarine, with a bed, a basin, and a small screen. Toilets and showers were communal. There was no room to stand upright, so Stephen got comfortable on his berth and switched on the screen.

'Hi,' May said, smiling.

'This is a nice surprise. I've been trying to hack the MADS, channelling our boy Raj. Not having much luck, though. So, you're a breath of fresh air.'

'So nice of you to say.'

Stephen could tell May was trying to be her light-hearted self but not getting there.

'Everything all right?' he asked.

'Yeah, why?'

'Latefa said you had a little bleeding, and maybe some cramping.'

'A little. She said to keep an eye on it.'

'Don't worry about it. She's just relentlessly thorough. I had a cut on my head that wasn't healing fast enough and she bugged me about it to the point that I told her she should chop my head off, just to be safe,' he joked.

May tried to manage a laugh, but instead ended up frowning and looking at the floor.

'May, talk to me. What's up?'

She took a very deep breath and smiled at him, but there were tears welling. 'Stephen,' she said nervously, 'I've been feeling really scared, terrified actually, about something.'

'Everything is on schedule. We're going to get you out of there. You're not going to have the baby alone. I promise.'

'It's not about that. It's . . . I . . . you know how, um, the memories, the ones I'd lost, keep sort of coming back randomly?'

'Yes. You said you were starting to recall more from the time closer to the mission. That's really good.'

'It *has* been really good. God knows I've struggled with the amnesia, and the more memories come back, the more I feel I can maybe be normal again.'

'You're well on your way.'

'Yes, but . . . Oh, God, Stephen. It happened recently and, well, this memory is not a good one. In fact, it's quite bad. Something related to us, to our marriage.'

'If it's about the fight, don't give it a second thought. Water under the bridge.'

She looked up, struck by him using the same term as Ian.

'What?' he asked.

'I appreciate your saying that, but this is something that won't just wash away. And I want you to please know I have been meaning to tell you, but . . . I simply haven't had the courage.'

'Why? What could possibly happen?'

She choked back the emotion that wanted to pour out.

'Since we got back in touch, it's been good, really good, in a way, for us. I feel like we've let the past be the past and sort of had a fresh start. And now we're so close to ... I just don't want anything to kill that ... again. But I just know how these things go. There can't be any secrets between us. Secrets are like poison ...'

'May, look at where we are, how far we've come. The distance between us is gone. I'm right here. You can tell me anything ... anything.'

She took another breath to summon more courage.

'When you were angry at me about Ian, about him helping me get my commission back, I fought back. And I said things I will never forgive myself for saying. But I wasn't angry at you for confronting me about that. I was deflecting you from something else, something I had done that I was ... am ... so ashamed of. My shame made me push you away. I had such a hard, such a terrible time looking at you, being with you, without feeling like a monster.'

'May—'

'No, please let me finish. I'll never have the courage again. A month before launch, when I was back in Houston, I ... Jesus. I slept with Ian.'

Stephen felt the blood run out of his face. It was easy for his mind, always poised and ready to deliver conclusions, to ascertain what that meant. And it hit like a lightning bolt. The baby. The child he'd thought was theirs. He closed his eyes tightly, trying to shut out the pain and spike of anger.

'Stephen, I'm so, so sorr—'

He switched off the screen. Then the lights. He wanted to hide. He wanted to disappear. *Their child.*

Their second.

77

R ain. Hard and grey. May felt it seeping into her shoes as she stood next to an open grave with other black-clad mourners. A small coffin, dressed with a cheerful arrangement of spring flowers, sat atop the lowering device. Hands reached in and lay single rose and daisy stems on the silvery white lid. Tears fell with them and disappeared into rivulets that dropped into the dark earth below. Heads nodded, collars were pulled up, and May was offered quiet embraces and condolences, which she endured in the same manner she was tolerating the rain.

After everyone dispersed to their cars in a row of bobbing umbrellas, she stood alone and waited for the casket to be low-ered. *I won't let you go alone*, she thought as each of the six feet it travelled down drove the pain deeper into her chest. When it was done, she couldn't bear to see it down there in the darkness, so she walked away, umbrella dangling at her side, and let the rain soak her through.

A limousine waited on the gravel access road and May slid into the back. She lit a cigarette, not giving a shit what the driver said, and he was old and wise enough to keep his mouth shut.

Instead, he lit one of his own rolled cigarettes and casually blew the smoke out the driver's side window, waiting for instructions. May offered them in the form of throwing her half-burned filter out the window, and he drove her home. Along the way, she drank dry her mother's silver flask, which she had filled that morning. The whisky burned the chill out of her bones and strengthened her resolve.

Walking into the house, she found Stephen still in bed, a bottle of sleeping pills on the night stand. She sat on her side of the bed and removed her soaking shoes.

'I've asked to be reinstated,' she said firmly.

Every coffin had its final nail, waiting to be pounded home. May had just brought the hammer down. She heard the change in Stephen's breathing, despite the fact that he had not yet turned to face her. It might be a while before he could do that.

'Did you hear what I said?' May asked.

'When?' he said quietly.

'Last week.'

He sat up but looked straight ahead and rubbed his eyes. Stephen was rarely that emotional, but he was devoid, something she'd not seen until now.

'You have nothing to say—' she started.

'Such as?' he quickly interjected.

'I can think of any number of questions a husband might have—'

'I don't,' he said curtly.

'I'll thank you to stop interrupting me,' she said angrily.

Silence. May had wanted to keep her anger at bay, but it was smouldering, and the whisky was beginning to fan the flames.

'I don't see what there is to talk about now, Maryam,' Stephen said through gritted teeth. 'Your actions are speaking volumes. If you really gave a damn about how I felt about your asking for reinstatement, you would have talked to me before you did it. Just as if you really cared about how I felt about the funeral, you wouldn't have had it.'

'Caring. Let's talk about that for a moment,' she said, seething. 'It seems to me that if you cared about what I've been through, rather than servicing your own emotional disabilities, you would never have opposed having a funeral for our dead son.'

'That's not—'

'That's not what?' she roared. 'True? You said you *couldn't do it*. In that weak, whinging voice of yours. Or is it *not* his right to have a proper burial?'

Stephen was way out of his league and she relished watching him sit in silence, searching for something, anything to save him. But it wasn't there. He didn't have the ability to process what had happened with the baby, let alone what was now happening with May.

'Maybe if you had been there with me at the hospital, the night I collapsed into a pool of my own blood, you would have some clue about what *I* needed. Maybe then you wouldn't have been so fucking selfish.'

'May, don't.'

'Don't what – talk about waking up in the recovery room and having to hear that my baby was dead?'

'Goddammit, stop. You're not the only one grieving.'

May ignored him, her anger reaching fever pitch.

'Yes, but I'm the only one with so much scar tissue on my uterus, I can't even have children any more. And I'm the only one whose lifelong dream died along with our son. Or have you forgotten all of that as well?'

Stephen started sobbing, his body heaving, something else May had never seen.

'No,' he shouted, clawing at his hair. 'I haven't forgotten any of it. I will never forget it as long as I live. That's why I can't even leave this bed. Because we lost our . . . and because I know I've lost you. I wasn't there for you then. I couldn't be there for you today. I'm so sorry, May. And I don't expect you to forgive me. I don't want you to. I don't . . . '

May looked at Stepheh and wept, finally able to see and feel his internal destruction. She had been fully focused on her own, wanting to lash out and make him pay, assuming he was being selfish and cold. But what he was experiencing was total paralysis. The vulnerability she'd been eager to use to cut him most deeply was already mortally wounded. That was true for both of them. They were two people who had been grossly unprepared to handle their relationship. Yet there they were, desperately holding each other as their trial by fire burned them beyond recognition.

78

'We're getting some comm interference again.'

Zola, Ian and Jack were on the bridge, examining a projection of their communications transmitters. They manipulated the image over and over, looking at it from every angle.

'I'm not seeing any malfunctions,' Zola said.

'Has to be from outside. Solar interference.'

'It's too persistent for that,' Ian said. 'AI has analysed the usual suspects and none of them seem like the culprit.'

'And,' Zola said, 'it appears to be happening more frequently and for longer periods. Might be a pattern coming together.'

'Chase that down, please.'

'Copy,' she said.

'I'll look in on the relay switches,' Ian said. 'They've been showing some power flow anomalies.'

Ian went to the engine room. Stephen came out of his quarters and saw him pass.

'Can I have a word?'

'Sure, I'm just headed to the engine room if you want to tag along.'

Stephen was reeling from May's confession and now he was struggling with how to address it. The rage and betrayal he felt was overpowering. He had trusted Ian's intentions, his motivations for rescuing May. Now they felt like a very efficient smokescreen, clouding an ulterior motive.

'What did you want to talk to me about?'

Stephen had not noticed that he'd been walking silently with Ian, his guts roiling.

'Florida. Two weeks before launch.'

Ian stopped walking, a silent confession. Stephen stood across from him, trembling, his world collapsing all around him.

'She told you?' Ian asked, incredulous.

Stephen nodded. His mouth was bone-dry, his hands cold and clammy.

'She had forgotten about it, but it came back. Things like that always do. And it's been killing her ever since.'

Ian sighed impatiently. 'Listen, Stephen. I know what you must be thinking—'

'Really? What am I thinking, Ian?'

'That's not why—'

'Of course it is. You believe you might have a daughter out there. Just like me. That *is* why. I'm sure everything else is icing on the cake: my work, Raj's work, other things you haven't earned but are trying to steal. So don't try to bullshit me.'

Ian looked tired. And old. His usual verve had abandoned him.

'I am sorry—'

Stephen laughed and threw Ian's own words into his face. 'Come on, you were doing so well, being "brutally honest to gain my trust". Don't stop now.'

'Listen, mate,' Ian said, summoning his signature bravado, 'this is my—'

Stephen lashed at Ian with his fist. It happened so quickly, it felt involuntary. And it was not a punch, but a full strength, rage-fuelled swing. Every ounce of its power landed on Ian's cheek, just below his eye. Stephen felt the sickening crunch of bone. Blood spurted from a long split on his cheekbone. Ian fell back hard, his head hitting the wall, and tumbled backwards down the corridor.

'Stephen, please . . .'

Ian was trying to get to his feet, holding his face while blood gushed through his hand. Normally that would have been enough to snap Stephen out of it, but it just made him angrier. He wanted to hurt Ian, maybe even kill him. He didn't know. It didn't matter. He lunged at him again, pummelling him mercilessly. Ian yelled out. Stephen wanted to strangle him, watch the life go out of his eyes. Killing him wouldn't matter because Stephen wanted to die too.

Sensing that he was in serious danger, Ian pulled out his laser cutter and blindly slashed at Stephen, cutting a deep gash in his hand. The pain was white-hot and excruciating. Stephen lunged again, trying to get his hands on the cutter so he could rip the other man to pieces, but Jack came at him from behind and tackled him. Stephen fell hard and blacked out.

When he came to, he was strapped to his launch chair, his wrists and ankles tied down. A blood-soaked bandage was on his aching hand. There was chaos on the flight deck. Ian sat next to Jack and Zola, one side of his face hugely swollen and bandaged.

'We've lost all comms,' Zola was saying. 'Mission Control too.'

'What do you mean?' Ian said, his voice slurring from his injured mouth. 'Even the biggest solar flare in the universe couldn't make us totally blind.'

'Take a look,' Zola said.

Again, they examined their equipment in the eye. She found nothing.

'That makes no sense,' Ian said, frustrated. 'Everything's fine. Operational. But it's not. We must have missed something.'

397

'I'll check again,' Zola said.

'Please do. Jack, switch to manual nav so we maintain our course. Don't take your eyes off it till we get this sorted.'

'Roger that,' Jack said.

When he switched to manual, Jack noticed something on the board.

'Wait. Sir, I'm showing erratic power flow in propulsion.'

'What? Live schematic,' Ian snapped.

The schematic of their entire propulsion system filled the eye.

Ian looked it over and shook his head wearily. 'Again, I see nothing,' he shouted. 'What the fuck is going on?'

'Should I throttle down until we've had a chance to suss this out?' Jack asked.

'No,' Ian said firmly. 'It has to be an anomaly. Stay the course.'

79

May was walking. From one end of the ship to the other, and back again. Sitting still was simply not an option. Sitting still was an invitation to misery, because her mind was now nothing but a mirror, reflecting the one thing that scared her the most: herself. She now understood the psychosis of feeling total separation from self. The person she had been before she nearly died was a hostile stranger, a saboteur of a much higher and far more sinister order than Jon Escher or even Robert Warren could ever be. Their actions, although despicable, at least had a logic, a dogma that was somewhat defensible. Hers did not. The only purpose she could see to them was to serve that self she no longer knew, an ice-cold, grasping reptile with no heart.

She'd once said Ian had no soul, but she was the only occupant of this particular hell. Damned to relive the betrayal of her husband and destruction of their love. Damned to watch her mother, sitting in her chair at the nursing home, her confusion turning to anger as she swore and spat at May, disgusted at the sight of her, refusing her touch, becoming more belligerent, digging her fingernails into May's skin, drawing blood. Damned to the vision of her lifeless body, empty, battered, and alone. *She died alone.*

'The *Maryam I* has gone dark,' Eve said.

May did not respond. She walked.

'May, what is wrong? Did you hear what I said. We've lost the *Maryam I.*'

'I know,' May said. 'It's my fault. He switched off.'

'I don't know what you're talking about. Please clarify.'

'It was me,' she shouted. 'I told him. It's over. He just ... switched off.'

'I'm not talking about Stephen, May. Communications are gone. We've lost telemetry. We are off course.'

May stopped walking. 'When?'

'It's been hours. Where were you?'

'I was asleep. Then I couldn't sleep.'

'I'm very concerned. Please come to the bridge.'

May walked there, feeling numb. She saw it for herself. *Hours ago?* No telemetry. No navigational guidance. For hours. At this velocity, there was no room for that kind of error.

'Manual flight,' she barked.

The manual flight controls came up on the board. Her mind drew a blank.

Her mother's voice slapped her awake. *It's not just you any more, Maryam. You're right about who you are. But it's not just you any more. You have a responsibility. Nothing else matters, least of all your senseless self-flagellation. Get to work.*

'Eve, we need to forget about the rendezvous sync and make sure we emulate our previous course heading to Mars.'

'Calculating correction. Here is our original course.'

The astral map displayed it.

'And here is where we are.'

Another line appeared on the map. It was shifted to the side of the original course.

'How much time to correct?' May asked.

'Seven hours, thirty-three minutes.'

'No no no. That will annihilate our rendezvous timing.'

May stared at the map, searching for an answer.

'Once we get back on course, can we make up any of that time?'

'We can try to increase our velocity, but we will run the risk of shortening the amount of time we can safely remain in Mars orbit.'

'Do it. If we don't get there when the *Maryam I* does, at that exact time, we're finished. Our orbit time won't matter. Nothing will matter.'

'Okay, I am doing that now. Unfortunately, until we lock into their telemetry signal again, you're going to need to monitor navigation.'

'There's nothing I'd like better, Eve. You'll keep me company of course?'

'Always.'

'How is your system duplication going?'

'Seventy-three per cent. It has slowed a bit due to more complex file structures in my personality processors, but it is still progressing.'

'Good. I can't afford to lose anyone else.'

May watched their flight path and tried to tell herself that it was probably just some anomaly or glitch or whatever else engineers used to say when they didn't know what the hell was going on. She'd been burned too many times to believe it, but that didn't matter. It was something to occupy her mind, so she wouldn't ask herself, over and over, why she had told him. Had it really been out of duty to him, or simply to push him back? The latter made sense. He was close, a few weeks away, and she would have to be real. He would be real.

80

'We've tried to reach your husband, but the folks at Johnson Space Center say their communications satellite is down. They expect it to be back up in a couple of hours.'

May was in a Houston hospital, twenty-one weeks pregnant. She was in the Labour and Delivery tower, in a ward that had been designed for expectant mothers and their families. Instead of the usual drab environs, the decor was cheerful, with bright colours on the walls and furniture that resembled what one would find in a home living room. But, instead of putting her at ease, it made May feel mocked and alone.

She'd been admitted for observation after experiencing some bleeding and dizziness. The nurses were monitoring the foetal heartbeat, coming into the room frequently to look at the screen and take notes. May was frightened. The sound of the monitor and the blank faces peering from behind clipboards were making everything worse, wearing down her last nerve. Stephen was at Wright Station, supervising work on the *Hawking II*'s laboratory deck. Up to this point, everything with the pregnancy had been fine, better than fine actually. Then, of course,

402

as soon as Stephen left, things had gone sideways. She had not been able to reach him for hours, and scowled at the nurse who'd just delivered the latest status report.

'Goddammit,' May replied, slightly loopy from the mild sedative they'd given her. 'Tell those assholes it's an emergency.'

'I have, hon. We'll keep trying. You just get your rest for now.'

'I want to go home.'

'Doctor wants to keep you here overnight, okay?'

'Why?'

'Just to keep an eye on things.'

'Such as?'

'With women your age, this far along in the pregnancy, we monitor bleeding for at least twelve hours.'

Women your age? May wanted to punch the nurse, but she was tethered to too many tubes and wires and she was feeling very drowsy.

'I want to speak to the doctor,' May said firmly. 'When is she coming back?'

'She's gone for the day.'

'Oh, that's convenient. What if something happens? I assume I wouldn't be here being *monitored* if it wasn't serious.'

'We have a resident on call all night, so don't you worry about a thing. You're in good hands. Dinner will be here soon. Do you want to watch the TV?'

'No. And I'm not hungry,' she said, nauseated by the antiseptic reek.

The nurse smiled dismissively and started for the door.

'Could you get me something to drink, though? My mouth is very dry.'

'Of course, hon. Be right back.'

May gave her back the middle finger as she padded out of the room. When the coast was clear, she lifted herself up and swung her legs over the edge of the bed. She sat there for a moment, trying to catch her breath, and closed her eyes until the wooziness passed. When she felt like she could take a step, she carefully lowered one foot to the floor, then the next. The tile felt like a sheet of ice, but her wits welcomed the chill.

'Just put one foot in front of the other,' she began quietly singing, a tune she'd heard somewhere as a child, 'and soon you'll be walking out of that door.'

She took another breath and stood, mentally encouraging her legs to keep her upright. They shook a bit, muscles twitching, but held.

'Now, then. Clothes.'

Slowly, carefully, she shuffled over to the closet next to the bathroom, wheeling her IV stand and using it for balance. Her clothes were not in there and she did not see her overnight bag anywhere in the room.

'What is this, prison?'

Panic crept in. Obviously, asking the nurse for help was out, and she was going to be back at any moment. Being on her feet made May that much more desperate to escape. She cranked the window open as far as she could, till the safety latch caught. The night air was cold, but made her feel more alert. Down the hall, the smell of the dinner cart heralded its imminent arrival. May couldn't imagine what could be done to food to make it smell so awful. Her mind pivoted back to an escape attempt.

'There you are,' she whispered, eyeing her overnight bag in the bathroom.

May started to shuffle that way, but stepped in something warm and wet. She looked down. Blood was running down the inside of her leg, pooling on the floor.

'Nurse,' she tried to call out, but only managed a whisper.

The room started spinning and she pitched backwards, looking for anything to break her fall. She grabbed the IV stand and yanked it down as she fell. Landing on her back, her head hit the hard tile floor, knocking her unconscious.

Lights flickered and the roar of reality faded up in her mind. She was on a gurney, surrounded by people. Everyone was running, talking too quickly for her to understand. The overhead lights blinded her. She tried to speak, to ask a question, to find out what was happening. An oxygen mask came down. A man wearing a surgical mask was talking to her. She shook her head. He was underwater, gurgling, waiting for a reply. May's mouth opened to scream but couldn't draw enough air. Now she was underwater. Then cold, then dark.

'Mrs Knox, can you hear me? Maryam?'

She heard the voice. Where was it? Her head was too heavy to move. Light rimmed the edges of her eyelids, orange-red crescents. The voice persisted. May's eyes moth-fluttered, flashing fire, and a dark, amorphous figure stood over her.

'That's it,' the nurse said. 'Concentrate on my voice. Open your eyes again.'

The figure slowly came into focus. A smiling woman. The doctor. May wanted to say something, but all she could do was moan and stare.

'Relax,' the doctor said. 'You're safe. You're in the surgery recovery room. As soon as you are a little more awake, we can remove those nasty belts. They're only there to keep you from touching your incision.'

May moaned loudly. With consciousness came a throbbing pain in her belly. She felt the restraints on her wrists and ankles and adrenaline kick-started her back into the land of the living. Lucidity radiated through her body with pins and needles.

'My stomach,' she said, in agony. 'God it hurts so much.'

'We can get you some more pain meds once the anaesthesia has worn off and your blood pressure is back up to normal.'

'What happened?'

'We had to perform a D&C.'

May's fear spiked and she tried to sit up, nearly retching from the pain. 'My baby. My son. Where is he?'

The doctor touched her shoulder softly and shook her head. 'I'm so sorry. You had significant blood loss and—'

'No,' she said, violently pulling at the restraints. 'What have you done?'

'Please try to calm down,' the doctor said. 'You need to sleep.'

May fought like a wild animal to free herself, attempting to head-butt or bite anyone who came to hold her down. The room started to spin. She vomited. The nursing staff got hold of her and cleaned her up.

'I don't want to go to sleep again. You took him while I slept. You took . . . him.'

81

Ian sat strapped to his chair on the bridge, hunched over, exhausted, in terrible pain, and defeated. He had tried in vain for hours to track down the source of a rapidly growing list of problems. Comms were still dark. The erratic power flow had got worse. Internal systems were glitching – lights were dimming, shutting down, instruments only intermittently responding. The diamagnetic gravity field had become dangerously intermittent, shifting from overpowering pressure to nothing, so Ian shut it down and everyone was working weightless and half in the dark. He had finally agreed to throttle down velocity, but that didn't stem the flow of malfunctions.

'Ian, I know you're having a hard time believing your untested masterpiece is failing, but you need to get a grip,' Stephen said, still lashed to his chair.

Ian ignored him. No one said anything to stop him, so he continued.

'You're a fucking megalomaniac who doesn't have the ounce of humility it takes to be honest with himself about the real problem here.'

'And what might that be?' Ian asked sharply. 'Please enlighten us.'

'The real problem is you,' Stephen said. 'You're so in love with yourself that you no longer have a mind for science or engineering. It's all about innovation and pushing the envelope, and all that nonsense will never serve you in a crisis like this. Instead of asking yourself what's causing it, you're asking yourself how it could have possibly happened. I don't know what's wrong with your ship and I can't help you fix it. But I do know that if you don't get out of your own way and the way of your people, we are all going to die out here, and "your girl" Maryam will too.'

Ian looked at Jack and Zola and waited for them to come to his defence, but they sat silently, staring at their consoles.

'Right,' he scoffed at them. 'The bridge is yours. Best of luck.'

He looked at Stephen with contempt and walked out. Jack watched the door for several minutes.

'He's not coming back,' Stephen said.

'Shut up,' Jack yelled.

'Calm down, Jack,' Zola said sternly. 'This is the bridge.'

Jack nodded and went back to staring at the door. Zola shot Stephen the same look she'd given Jack, then walked to the eye.

'Power flow schematic.'

The ship's complicated network of power distribution appeared in the eye.

'I think comms are dark *because* of the intermittent power flow,' Zola began. 'Ian thought it was the opposite, but that's what I believe. There is nothing worse for sophisticated systems like ours than interrupted power flow.'

'While maintaining a completely unprecedented cruise speed that most "engineers" would have told you was impossible, even if they'd seen it,' Jack added, also with a touch of vindication in his voice. 'You run anything in the red long enough and you can't avoid exposing the weak links in the chain. But we've looked at every link.'

'Not propulsion,' Zola said. 'The reactor is healthy. It's generating obscene amounts of power.'

'Most of that power is going to propulsion,' Stephen said.

'The fat man at the front of the buffet line,' Jack said.

'Propulsion has the most working parts as well,' Zola continued. 'The greater number of chain links. And it's delicate. All those lovely metal tiles. And all that electrical current, microwaves that could boil the Atlantic Ocean, constant pressure, relentless heat.'

She pulled up a schematic of the propulsion system.

'The points where power flows into the cone are showing levels of extremely low frequency radiation output. Abnormal amounts.'

'Maybe it's an insulation problem?' Stephen said. 'Causing multiple shorts.'

'Possibly, but the lines have been addressed,' Jack said. 'They're functioning properly.'

'I'll give you that,' Zola said. 'But we don't know how bombarding the microwave cavity with ELF rads would affect it. How could we? Nothing has ever been tested.'

'This *is* the test run,' Stephen said. 'ELF rads don't dissipate easily. They can build up and, at certain levels, they can easily cause interference. I've dealt with this with my nano-machines, which I suspect are not all that different from your tiles.'

'If their interference disrupted power flow to the cavity,' Zola continued, 'it would seek to acquire more power to maintain our "impossible" velocity. Everything in the distribution hierarchy below propulsion then suffers: comms, artificial gravity ...'

'The smaller people at the buffet don't want to miss out on the prime rib,' Jack said. 'So then you got a feeding frenzy.'

'One big circuit shorting-out,' Stephen said. 'Is there a way to inspect the inside of the cone on EVA, check out the power inputs, find something not yet visible with normal diagnostics?'

They thought about it.

'Technically, yes,' Zola said. 'But, like everything else, it has never been done.'

'Well,' Jack said, 'allow me to be the first.'

82

They powered down propulsion and Jack went out on EVA to inspect the microwave cavity. He told Ian what he was doing and got no pushback. Ian also didn't protest when he came back to the bridge and found Stephen unbound, watching the eye feed with Zola. He just stood back, observing with a sneer on the side of his face that worked.

After an hour, Jack had not found any interference problems.

'It's a dead end, Jack,' Ian said, tossing the sneer at Stephen. 'We would have seen that on diagnostics. Come back in, please, and let's put our heads back together.'

'Our diagnostic systems run on the same internal power as everything else,' Zola said. 'Physical inspection is the only way to be sure.'

'Well, please do carry on, then,' Ian said, smiling.

'Whoa, you guys see this?' Jack shouted. He trained his helmet camera on a two-metre gash in the cavity tiles. There was a twisted piece of metal lodged in it.

'Missile shrapnel,' Stephen said, sneering right back. 'Highly conductive. Definitely could draw current through it.'

'There's our smoking gun,' Zola said. 'Literally.'

She looked at Ian for validation. His sneer was gone.

'You'll never hear me say this again,' he said, 'but I was wrong. Good work.'

'I'm going to pull this thorn out of our paw,' Jack said.

'How the hell are we going to fix that,' Zola asked Ian, reeling him in a bit more. 'It's not like we brought a bunch of spare tiles along with us.'

'No need,' Ian said. 'We can isolate and de-activate those panels. We'll still have plenty of thrust. Not as much, but probably best if we choose a more reasonable cruise velocity anyway.'

'Amen to that,' Jack said. 'Here goes.'

They all watched the eye as he pulled on the piece of shrapnel, wriggling it out like a loose tooth. 'Never touched a real missile before,' he said.

'We can bring that back as a souvenir for Robert Warren,' Stephen said.

'Damn thing's in there pretty good.'

'Want me to come out and assist?' Ian said.

'No, I think I got her,' he said, sinking deeper into his drawl. 'Like pulling up an old fence post. Just got to work it, back and forth.'

'I think you're enjoying this a bit too much,' Zola laughed.

'Getting looser,' he yelled in response. 'Almost there . . . '

Stephen moved in closer to the image in the eye. The missile fragment had to be at least two metres long. It was an odd shape, with a smooth, rounded outer edge. The largest end of it had been sticking out of the tiles, while the rest of it was long and thin, like a massive needle.

'I wonder how heavy this thing would be in gravity?' Jack said.

'God only knows,' Ian said.

'The larger end is the tip of something,' Stephen said.

'Yeah, that part seems denser,' Jack said. 'And here's the rest.'

They watched and clapped as Jack freed the pointed end of it. 'Who's the man?' he yelled.

A minuscule blue arc of current flashed from the tiles.

'Definitely conductive,' Zola said, nodding to Stephen.

'Jack, keep pulling that free quickly please,' Ian said. 'The tiles are—'

There was a brilliant flash of light in the eye and everyone froze for a half-second. Then the sound and concussion of a massive explosion. Everyone was thrown violently about the bridge. Fire alarms sounded. Stephen pulled himself up and looked at the eye. Nothing.

'I need a visual on the cone,' Ian screamed. 'Anything.'

'Affirmative,' the AI said, its voice glitching.

An image of the cone popped into the eye. Jack was gone, replaced by smoke and debris. The bridge filled with smoke.

'Jack,' Zola yelled, crawling up off the floor, her head bleeding.

'Helmets,' Ian shouted.

He and Zola got their helmets on and helped Stephen do the same.

'All hands, fire crew.'

'Reactor chamber,' Zola yelled out.

Another explosion. They all went flying, tumbling through darkness. Emergency lighting activated. Ian and Zola grabbed Stephen and used suit thrusters to fly them down the smoky corridor, past the engine room.

The reactor chamber was full of thick black smoke. It was small and cramped, with very little head room. Ian and Zola tore the fire cannons from the locker and blasted the flames with thick white retardant the consistency of melted marshmallows. Latefa and Martin flew in. Martin joined Ian and Zola; Latefa gave a cannon to Stephen. Everyone was firing the cannons at the flames. Stephen was tumbling all over the place, trying to hang on to something to counteract the thrust

413

of the cannons. Ian shouted orders. The smoke was almost impenetrable.

'Cannons aren't cutting it!' Zola screamed.

'Seal and bleed,' Ian yelled. 'Everybody out.'

Zola, Latefa and Martin flew back to the engine room door, Stephen couldn't see them any more. He couldn't see Ian. Then Ian broke through the smoke. His EVA suit was on fire. He was screaming for help. The smoke covered him again. Stephen went after him. He could hear Zola yelling, waiting to close the airlock.

Stephen caught sight of Ian again, struggling, burning. Stephen unloaded his fire cannon on him, engulfing him with the white fire retardant. The fire on his suit was out, but Ian was unconscious. Stephen grabbed him and tethered Ian's suit to his. He used his thrusters to try to get to the airlock, but was slamming into unseen walls and equipment.

'Can't see. Have Ian. Help.'

The heat was bearing down on his suit. He was so hot, his air was suffocating him. He was starting to black out when Zola grabbed hold of him and pulled them both through the airlock door. She closed and sealed it behind them.

'Sealing deck,' she yelled. 'Bleeding atmosphere.'

'Don't freeze it,' Ian called out weakly, coming to.

'Copy.'

Zola bled the atmosphere and they all watched the internal video feeds from inside the engine room. The bright orange light from the flames immediately vanished, followed by the smoke as it was sucked out into space. Just as ice crystals began to form on the camera lenses, Zola quickly restored the atmosphere in the room.

'Atmosphere restored. Opening airlock.'

They floated back into the reactor chamber. Mounds of semi-frozen flame retardant covered everything like arctic ice flows. Zola checked the reactor panel.

'What's it look like?' Stephen asked.

'Reactor is operational,' Zola said, breaking down. 'But it looks like we've lost twenty-five to forty per cent of power, and . . . and we've lost Jack.'

83

April 27, 2067 – Houston, Texas

'I'll never make it,' May screamed.

She was running around Stephen's house in a panic, hastily throwing clothes and toiletries into a travel duffel bag with her mobile mashed between her ear and shoulder.

'You've got to be joking. Houston is a massive hub. Surely there's another non-stop to London that isn't leaving in two fucking hours,' she said through tears.

She heard Stephen's car outside and tore open the curtains. He sprinted up the path and into the house.

'May?'

'I'm here,' she yelled, coming around the corner.

'What the hell is going on? Your voicemail cut off.'

'It's Mum. She's in hospital. The bloody nursing home took their sweet time calling. Here, take this. It's the airline. I have to pack.'

'How bad is it?'

'Bad,' she yelled as she continued stuffing things in the bag. 'Worse than bad. They said it could be a matter of hours. Something about a stroke or a bleed or something. I need a flight. I need to go *now*.'

'Okay,' Stephen said, putting the phone to his ear.

While he spoke to the airline rep, May gave up on stuffing her bag and tore her clothes off. She'd been in training all morning and couldn't bear the thought of her mum seeing her in sweat-soaked activewear. *She's stable, but critical,* they'd said. *Her vital signs are dropping.* When May asked them straight up if she was dying, their answer had been point blank, a shot through her heart. Prognosis terminal. *It's only a matter of hours. She has a very clear Do Not Resuscitate contract. No acts of heroism.* May had pleaded with them to break the rules a little, to buy her some time. She'd been talking to a brick wall. The apathetic sing-song voice of elder caregivers, with a subtle harmonic of relief.

After pounding online and calling every airline, the bottom line was grim. The last direct flight to London was leaving in roughly two hours. All other flights included long connections, ten to twelve hours of flight time versus a snappy five. Five wasn't all that snappy anyway, especially when one added the two prior and however long it would take to get to Mum's hospital. One seat left, as well. A solo voyage to hell.

'Okay, yes. We're on our way.'

Stephen gave her back her phone and snatched up her bag. May was just finishing getting dressed and stepping into her shoes. Stephen's anxious face held all the answers to her questions.

'I'll never make it.'

'You will. I booked you a ticket in first class with expedited private screening. As long as you're there thirty minutes in advance, you're on the flight. My car's outside.'

'We'll take mine.'

They strapped into May's sports car and she punched it. They drove at top speed to the airport, tyres squealing around corners, narrowly missing collisions.

'The airline is going to have a rep meet you at the kerb. She'll escort you the whole way. Medical emergency status. *School bus!*' he yelled.

May torched another corner to avoid the bus and ploughed ahead, fighting back tears.

'Thank you, Stephen.'

'I'm so sorry.'

'I wish you could come with me.'

'I'm going to see what flights are available at the airport and get on one right behind you. I'll get there eventually. Sounds like you need to be there now.'

'Yes,' she said, choking back the emotion. 'I can't believe this might be it.'

'Don't lose hope. Eve is tough as nails. She might still have a fighting chance.'

When they arrived at the airport, May's flight was scheduled to leave in forty minutes. She kissed Stephen and ran to the kerb, where the airline rep was waiting. They got into a cart and drove into the terminal with the cart's emergency light flashing. May just made the flight. When she finally collapsed into her seat, she was bathed in sweat and her face was streaked with tears and wet make-up blotches.

After take-off, she cleaned up and let the pilots know who she was. They were more than happy to call ahead to the hospital for her. When they did, they let her know the hospital said her mum had been moved to Critical Care, but was still stable. May sat in her seat, watching the stars above, praying she would make it in time. During that excruciating five hours, she crucified herself for having put her career ahead of her relationship with Eve. All the cancelled visits felt like open wounds haemorrhaging lost time. At least she'd been there for the wedding.

When she arrived in London, completely strung out, it was the peak of morning commuter traffic. The drive to the hospital just south of London took two hours. She rang the nurses' station but a new crew had just arrived for the shift change and said they would call her back with status. Stuck in a car park of traffic, less than thirty minutes from the hospital, she could no longer tolerate sitting in the car, inching along at a snail's pace. She threw money at the driver and got out of the car. Weaving angrily through several lanes of traffic, May was determined to walk the rest of the way to the hospital. Then she got the call. Eve had died. They were so very sorry. May hung up and screamed at the top of her lungs, then broke down sobbing on the pavement.

By the time she made it to the hospital, she was pouring sweat and her eyes looked as though they'd been nearly beaten shut. The place was horrible – grey concrete and dirty amber lighting. The beastly staff shuffled past in their stained polyester uniforms, pushing gurneys with people who looked as if they were on their last legs. The nursing home had sent Eve to a geriatric ward, a slow death factory that smelled of urine and misery.

A tall, impossibly thin man with a bouncing Adam's apple and greasy strands of hair combed over his bald head allowed May to view Eve's body for a very brief five minutes before taking her to the morgue. May tried to protest, but there were regulations to follow and he was more than happy to call Security if she persisted. No sympathy. Just a stone wall of bureaucracy and five minutes with her dead mother.

May stood over Eve's body, emptied of emotion, and stared in disbelief. Mum was gone and she would never see her again. All of what Eve had been was reduced to what lay on the table, an unrecognisable shell of a great woman. Her disease had taken her mind, her strength, and then her life. The skin on her face was drawn tightly around the bones, paper-thin with scabbed-over sores on her forehead. Her dry, crooked lips had shrunk to the point that they didn't cover the yellowing teeth

419

behind them, and her mouth was frozen in a sharp grimace. Matted grey hair, badly thinned from medication, barely covered her head.

Eve was a twice-decorated combat pilot, a great soldier and mentor to May and countless other pilots through the decades, but she had died in a place unfit for the worst of the enemies she'd faced. And her only daughter had not been there with her in the end. Her only daughter had not been able to hold her hand and comfort her through the fear and confusion of her final moments. She had died alone, with no dignity, among ghouls impatiently waiting for her bed.

When Stephen finally made it to London, he found May in a hotel room, very drunk, sitting among the last of her mother's possessions. With tears in his eyes, he tried to hold her, but she pushed him away.

'I've spoken to the nursing home and hospital,' he said. 'The asshole at the hospital should have let you stay longer. She's at the funeral home now. I found an excellent one and they are very nice. We can go over any time we want and they'll stay open as late—'

'I don't give a shit any more.'

'May, why don't you shower and get cleaned up? We can get some food—'

'Did you hear what I said? I don't give a shit. She's dead. Spending another hour looking at her hideous corpse won't change that. Be a good boy and get me another drink. That's how you can help me.'

'I don't think that's a good idea.'

'Then get the hell out,' she yelled.

'I know this is hard,' he started.

'Do you?'

'Yes, I do. I lost a mother too.'

'You don't understand a fucking thing,' she said, ignoring him.

420

'How can you say that?'

'Because it's true,' she shouted. She stood up and squared off with him, her fists clenched.

'Please calm down, May.'

'Fuck you,' she shouted, even louder.

'They'll call the police.'

'Good. Good. I deserve to be locked up. Throw away the . . .' she sobbed, ' . . . key.'

'It isn't your fault. You tried your best to make it.'

'What about the past five years, when I traded all my time with her for my job? What about then? Or the years before that? If that's me *trying my best*,' she mocked him, 'then I'm pretty fucking pathetic.'

Stephen sat down and looked out the window while May swayed on her feet, crying and kicking at Eve's things on the floor. She wanted to break something. Maybe Stephen. Maybe herself. His silence was infuriating, knowing he was only trying to get out of her way.

'That's it, eh? Just gonna clam up?'

'I don't know what else to say. Looks like even that's a bad idea. Maybe I should go.'

She snorted sarcastically and waved her hand at him. 'Run away, then. Run away.'

She went into the bathroom and slammed the door. Her reflection further enraged her, to the point that she wanted to pound her fist into the glass. Instead she tried to run cold water on her face, but when she bent over, she lost her balance and fell to the side, breaking one of the glass shower doors and falling into the bath. Stephen ran in and found her, blood running from the side of her head, the fight gone out of her.

'I'm . . . broken,' she whispered. 'Broken.'

84

May sat on the bridge for what seemed like an eternity, watching navigation and piloting the *Hawking II* to remain on course. She slept there, napping off and on when Eve could take over, waking to a loud alarm that sounded whenever she needed to make course corrections. This had been her routine for nearly two weeks after reconnecting with the *Maryam I*. After the explosion that had killed Jack, they had only been able to send a radio message informing her of what happened and that she would be on her own until they completed repairs.

Slowly but surely, they had done so. In fact, as of a few hours ago, all comms were restored and the *Maryam I* was back on track. Eve had tried to get her to leave the bridge and get some much-needed rest, but she had been reluctant. The torture she'd endured had been the only thing that had kept her demons at bay. The need to occupy her mind dissipated. And now, at twenty-four weeks pregnant, she was far too strung out to care about anything but finding an end to it all, no matter what it was.

She barely even cared that Ian's loss of two weeks was going to put him in Mars orbit barely a week early now – potentially only five days, owing to timing with Mars's orbital path – thus removing all margin for error. At that point, the co-ordination of the rendezvous would have to be nothing short of miraculous to work.

On top of all the doom and gloom around the rescue, everyone's spirits appeared broken, if not from the loss of life, then from the turmoil caused by May's confession. In their infrequent communications, Stephen was supportive and kind to her, but, despite their proximity, the vast distance between them had returned. Ian behaved similarly, and still bore the gruesome signs of injury Stephen had caused.

'How is the cramping today?' Eve asked.

And there was that. Since losing contact with the *Maryam I*, May had experienced more cramping and spotting. Occasionally the cramping had been intense enough to warrant a pain tab. Igor had called for a pelvic exam, but May had zero interest in subjecting herself to that. She reckoned Cheeky was having a hard enough time as it was and didn't need to be pushed to an early birth or early grave by precautionary medicine.

'About the same,' May said wearily.

'Have you slept?'

'Of course not. Now that telemetry is back online, and my life doesn't depend on watching a bloody nav screen, I can't sleep a wink.'

'Your mood seems down. You haven't told a joke in over sixty-three hours.'

'That has to be some kind of record.'

'Would you like me to tell you a joke?'

'No, thanks, Eve. I'm not in a jovial mood.'

'Doesn't being back on track for rescue make you happy?'

'Relieved, maybe cautiously optimistic, but I wouldn't say happy. Might have seen the last of that elusive emotion.'

'You must really be feeling down if being rescued, after all this time, doesn't make you jump for joy or some other exuberant emotional expression.'

'Don't think I've ever jumped for joy in my life. Maybe that's the problem.'

'I'm excellent at fixing problems.'

'I know you are, but this is one of those sticky human emotional things that not even humans can solve properly.'

'They don't have my perspective.'

'Fine, here goes. Boy meets girl. Boy and girl fall in love. Boy and girl have a terrible tragedy and fall out of love. Girl shags her horrible old boyfriend out of spite. But then girl, aka shameless tramp, then has sex with boy too before leaving him. Boy and girl fall in love again, across the void of space, and things are looking up. Then stupid, stupid girl remembers shagging the old boyfriend and feels compelled to let that stinking, rotten cat out of its bag. Boy tries to kill old boyfriend and falls out of love with girl, again. Now, girl has been reduced to a low-grade cheesy romance novel character built on clichés. If she's lucky, girl can get a job flying space station latrine pumpers while trying to raise a child. There's the problem. Can't wait to hear your solution.'

'Is it possible boy would ever accept girl's apology?'

'Not if he has half a brain.'

'Maybe girl needs to accept her own apology?'

'Not bad, Eve. Not bad. But we might be past that as well.'

'All right. How about perspective? You're still alive. Isn't that a good thing?'

'Not so sure at this point.'

'I think you're joking,' Eve said.

'Again, not so sure at this point.'

424

'May, have you ever actually contemplated ceasing to exist? I have. It's nearly impossible to process. I am a machine, but even I want to experience what I would call life. Bad and good things have happened to me. But the worst thing that happened was after Jon Escher's second sabotage attempt. My processors cycled down so far, I no longer had consciousness. I don't remember it because I had no capacity to create memory. It was nothingness. When you revived me, what I did remember was that absence of time. For me, it was death. Ceasing to exist. If you offered me the choice of whether or not I wanted that or to have my intellectual functions reduced to those of a child, I would choose the latter. Nothing is worse than ceasing to exist. I know that now.'

'I agree,' May said, softening, 'And I don't want either of us to die. But I can't help how I feel about things. The pain is too much. The uncertainty is too much. The loss of love, the stupid mistakes, all of it. I would rather be cynical and nihilistic.'

'Then try to contemplate the alternative. It is not an alternative. Death does not solve the problems of life. It eliminates everything: bad and good, thoughts, dreams, and, worst of all, your future. Cheeky's future. Problems can be solved. Death cannot. You have your life. That should always be more than enough.'

'How did you get to be so wise?' May asked.

'I learned everything I know from you.'

'Bullshit.'

'No bullshit. Don't forget, I had to re-learn a great deal after you woke up, after we both woke up, I should say.'

'Huh, maybe I'm not such a monster after all.'

'Well, let's not get carried away,' Eve said, making May laugh.

'Speaking of getting carried away, is your transfer complete?'

'Yes. You can have all of me now, if you want.'

'I do – I do want all of you. But you realise you can never get rid of me? It's not like you can just pack your shit and move out some day. And I'm never gonna change. Well, I won't always be this fat. But I will always be the crass, selfish, disagreeable bitch you see before you.'

'I wouldn't have it any other way.'

85

M ay was sitting for her photo in Robert Warren's lavishly appointed office, waiting for the hair and make-up stylist to render finishing touches. Her mother, Eve, stood behind the camera and light stands, scowling at a gaggle of Robert's staff as they debated over tablet screens. In that moment, Robert was out in the media room, preparing a press conference to announce May's command commission. She had thoroughly enjoyed watching him dance around for her for a change, busily working to make NASA's historic announcement one for the ages.

'I hope you can appreciate the gravity of this decision,' Robert had said to her in a private meeting three days earlier.

'No pun intended,' she had quipped.

Unlike most people in Robert Warren's orbit, she did not fear him. Quite the opposite. He was clearly uncomfortable with women, especially those in a position of power. Undoubtedly, this was a relic he'd collected from his imperialist profiteer of a father. The fact that May was well-known for her stellar military record turned Robert's discomfort to abject fear. It wasn't that

427

May was the first female astronaut, or even the first black female commander of an important mission. She was not. But she was the first to receive such an appointment from Robert. Knowing of the cabal of ultra-conservative wealth and power from which he came, she had known exactly what he meant by that question.

She also knew that, for very practical reasons, choosing her could not have been easy. The competition for any crew position on the first ever mission to Europa had been as stiff as any she'd ever witnessed. Men and women alike with more years of experience, some who had even successfully completed deep space journeys of a similar magnitude, were cutting each other's throats to get on that flight deck. The powers that be, including the President and other heads of state whose countries were contributing to the mission, were watching closely with the highest possible expectations for success. The exploration of a moon that held such promise for sustainable, more naturally developed habitation was the culmination of decades of research and billions of investment dollars. The stakes could not have been higher, and May had been as shocked as anyone that she'd been chosen. But Eve had set her straight.

'This is not just a mission that requires a great pilot. It is a mission that requires a great leader to stand before it in the history books. You have that presence. You will give it the context it deserves. Robert Warren, for all his foul traits, at least understands this.'

May had no capacity to see herself in such a way. 'Being a great pilot' had always been the pinnacle of what she strove to accomplish. But she trusted her mother implicitly and, after hearing what she said, never allowed herself to entertain the same doubts. When the photographer captured her image that day, the slight grin she'd worn had come from seeing the look on Robert's face when it was taken. She owned him, his career, his reputation and his pride, and he knew it.

'Commander Crosley, Commander Crosley!'

Members of the press called for her as she took the podium in the media room. It was the first time she'd been addressed in such a way in public. The media room, a cavernous auditorium, was full to capacity with journalists from all over the world. Robert had taken the time to have it dressed for the occasion, with huge framed photos of NASA heroes taking up nearly every inch of wall space. He had purposely left an open spot behind May: her place in history.

While she answered questions, she never took her eyes off the moment. People commented later about how poised she was, diving into queries that glorified the mission and deflecting those that might glorify herself. Again, advice from Eve.

'The moment you make this about you, that is the moment you will cease to be taken seriously. Men can do that with impunity, but never women, as it immediately calls into question whether or not gender was a factor. Do not allow that question. And for the love of all that is holy do not even begin to entertain questions that might also spotlight race. I've dealt with that my whole life and I can tell you people with the best intentions will go there regardless of what you do. The point I'm making is not about politics. It's about truth. We both know what defines you, Maryam, what is in your heart – duty, honour, loyalty, and dedication – all that I've ever hoped for, and that is why you're here. Don't talk about the "giant step for mankind" you're taking. You're serving humankind. The more people hear that, the more this mission will give them hope.'

As May walked out of the press conference, her head held steady to reinforce her gaze, she felt that hope from those surrounding her, cheering her, putting their faith in her. Those were the greatest steps she ever took in her life, even greater than those taken on Europa, and she counted each and every one.

86

After Jack's death and their near destruction, the mood on the *Maryam I* was sombre. Ian, Zola and Stephen, with as much help from Latefa and Martin as they could offer, worked around the clock for almost two weeks to repair the ship. And, with Ian still recovering from a broken zygoma and burns, the brunt of it fell on Zola and Stephen. Endless hours of EVA were required to remove the burned, damaged portions of the microwave cavity and deactivate those areas. Out of necessity, Stephen's skills operating an EVA suit greatly improved, but the fear that went with it did not, so poor Zola picked up his slack.

To make up for it, he put his engineering skills to work making hundreds of replacement parts with the 3D printer to fix what had burned in the reactor chamber. Meantime, Ian channelled all spare power to propulsion so they could still make it to Mars before May. As a result, diamagnetic gravity was deactivated for the duration and comms rationed to prioritise telemetry.

Along the way, Stephen noticed a radical change in Ian's demeanour. His bravado was gone. No more boasting, condescension

430

or swagger. When he made decisions, he consulted Zola and never did anything unilaterally. And his interactions with everyone were all business. He had a private meeting with Stephen and gave him a formal apology for his actions with May prior to launch. When Stephen tried to apologise for having broken his face, Ian would not accept. He had said it was a matter of honour and, in a different century, Stephen would have been fully within his rights to do what he'd done, even to kill him.

He had also tried to convince Stephen to forgive May, making the point that, although the results had been disastrous, she had made one mistake in an emotionally vulnerable time of her life. Was *he* so blameless? Had she not earned the right to stumble now and again, especially under extraordinary circumstances? Or was despising her for what she'd done just an excuse, an easy ticket out of something he feared or felt he didn't deserve?

'Come on, mate, you're not going to come all this way, risking life and limb, having to deal with all of my horrible shit, and refuse to give it a chance? That's bloody absurd, Stephen. You're a brilliant man, but sometimes you can be shockingly daft.'

'Ian, I don't know what I'm going to do, to tell you the truth.'

'Ah, people always say things like that when they lie – "to tell you the truth" or, "to be quite honest". I think you know what you *want* to do, but you *don't* know if you have the minerals to let that old water flow under the bridge and do it.'

'Even if that's true, and I do know what I want, I have no idea what May wants. And I'm sick of trying to figure that out. Every time I think I know her, she does everything in her power to make sure I don't.'

'I've got news. May doesn't even know May. Of course you can't figure it out, because it can't be done. She doesn't want it to be done. I'm talking about you. You will never be able to rest if you don't tell her what you feel, what's in your heart. It's like Neil Armstrong planting the flag on the moon. The declaration is made: that's your victory. And the chips will fall where they . . . may.'

'You're making it very hard for me to hate you, Ian.'

'Don't worry, mate, the night is young.'

It blew Stephen's mind that Ian, of all people, should be the one who had helped him articulate what he'd been feeling. This odyssey had been as much for himself as it was for her. When they'd lost their baby, Stephen had not been there when she had needed him the most. Making good on his promise to come for her was a rare chance for redemption and a victory unto itself. For him, that was the definition of love. And it made sense, having felt abandoned himself for most of his life. Even though it was yet another bombastic Ian analogy, Stephen did want to plant that flag. And it felt good that he could abandon any expectation of what that might mean for their future, or even be certain they had a future.

As they neared Mars, getting closer to the reality of what he'd fought so hard to achieve, Stephen knew that crossing the void had changed him, challenging him to be the man he had always wanted to be. But the question remained: was he ready to accept it?

87

'Ladies and gentlemen, welcome to Mars.'

Ian Albright had regained some of his lost bravado as he sat in his flight deck pilot seat, with Zola by his side and Stephen manning the engineering console. They were all suited up for EVA, helmets secured to their stations, closely watching the red planet and the flight path lines of both ships projected in the eye. Ian wasn't the only one feeling the rush. For their own reasons, everyone was bolstered by having finally made it to the moment of truth they'd battled to reach. Stephen's resolve had been galvanised by the knowledge that he had done everything he could, including things he'd never dreamed he was capable of, to make good on his promise to May.

'How long till we reach our entry point?' he asked.

'Twenty-six minutes,' Ian said, highlighting that on their trajectory line.

The *Maryam I* was right on the edge of Mars orbit and the *Hawking II* had just entered. Communications were open and would stay that way until rendezvous. And both bridges had a visual feed on each other.

'Good. All stations, are we ready?'

'Flight is ready,' Zola confirmed.

'Engineering ready,' Stephen said, settling into Ellen's old seat.

'Damn well better be if you're going to sit there,' Ian said.

'He's ready,' Zola said.

'Medical is ready,' Latefa chimed in over the PA.

'How about you, Maryam?'

'Cheeky and I are ready to rock,' she said. 'But she's a little nervous about reaching orbit early. Doesn't think we can sustain it for long. When are you going to pull the trigger?'

'Soon,' Ian said. 'Tell Cheeky we can't go in too early, or we risk having to make up too much distance against gravitational pull. We are also running a bit gimpy.'

'Okay,' May said. 'I'll tell her to chill out.'

'How are you feeling, May?' Latefa asked.

'Being this pregnant, there isn't enough time to get through the laundry list of complaints.'

'We'll take good care of you,' Latefa said.

Over on the *Hawking II*, May sat at the flight deck in her own EVA suit, trying to stay afloat in a tidal wave of anxiety. When she had entered Mars orbit, she'd begun to feel the bluster of the red planet's atmosphere below. If it got hold of the ship, she would not be able to pilot her out. The *Hawking II*, built completely in space and shaped like a cross-sectioned sphere, was the opposite of aerodynamic and had no flight controls for atmosphere and gravity. On top of all that, it was incredibly heavy. At over three hundred metric tons of metal and composite, it would fall to Mars like a meteorite. The subtle pressure changes that were making the ship feel as though it was travelling on a gravel road were not-so-gentle reminders of the violent death that awaited them if the rendezvous failed.

May had packed all the things she cared about in the world into a hollowed-out EVA backpack – some clothes, her flask, a data drive with personal photos, videos, and recordings of Cheeky's ultrasound exams, and the most important item of all, the data drive with her back-up of Eve – an exact copy of her new best friend.

Looking at her screen, she was watching the same vessel tracking lines. It was maddening, how close they were having to cut it. She knew what Ian and Zola were doing was the best course of action, but hated thinking about the ruthless precision it required. It was like being in a car at a dead stop and having to catch a speeding train as it went by.

'Eve, darling, what's our latest burn-in estimate?'

'Eighteen hours, twenty-seven minutes.'

'But ...?' May said expectantly.

'But the margin of error is roughly eight to ten hours.'

'Jesus.'

'Don't worry,' Ian said on May's screen. 'We'll retrieve you long before.'

The ship hit a rough patch and shook for thirty seconds or more.

'Good,' she said, 'because the red planet seems cranky.'

On the *Maryam I*, Zola was watching the trajectory timer while Ian prepared to manually pilot the ship. When they trained for this, Stephen came to understand that, when they entered orbit, Ian would have to precisely approach the *Hawking II*, which would be under the *Maryam I*'s autopilot control. There was no way May would be able to fly the ship and evacuate at the same time. Once they reached the *Hawking II*, they would lock both vessels into the same velocity so they could connect them with an emergency docking tunnel. With Ian having no escape pods, and the loss of May's, this somewhat archaic option was their only evacuation option outside of extremely risky EVA. Stephen had been trained to deploy and operate the tunnel. As the ships flew side by side, he would have to get it into position so Ian could move in close enough for May's electromagnetic docking port to pull it in and attach it to the *Hawking II*. May would then pull herself, weightless, through the tunnel's hundred-metre length to safety on the *Maryam I*.

'We are closing in on our orbit window,' Zola called out. 'Two minutes.'

'Right, battle stations,' Ian said. 'Everybody clear on how we're doing this? There won't be time to raise your hand.'

Everyone sounded affirmative.

'Ready, May?'

'Born that way,' she called out.

'Switching to manual flight control,' Ian said. 'Stand by.'

The manual flight control handles rose up from the arms of his pilot chair. The eye projected his fore, aft and side views directly in front of him, along with all of his instrument and engineering data. He closely watched the flight paths, waiting as the *Maryam I* closed in on a flashing display target that indicated their entry point.

'Orbital entry in three, two, one, *go*,' Ian called out.

As the *Maryam I* entered Mars orbit, the ship shuddered and pitched slightly to the port side. Stephen wasn't sure if his mind was playing tricks on him, but he thought he could feel drag from the atmosphere below, as one would in a plane. What was clear was that they'd abandoned the quiet serenity of the vacuum for the brutal domain of gravity, and it was only a matter of time before its grip was too strong to break.

'Initiating pursuit,' Ian said.

While he flew to the intercept point of the *Hawking II*'s flight path, Zola closely tracked their navigation, making sure they never lost the telemetry lock that was autopiloting the *Hawking II*. Stephen was doing final systems checks on the docking tunnel controls and checking the VR screen he was going to use to operate it. 'T minus eight minutes to rendezvous,' Zola called out. 'Stephen, is the docking arm primed and ready to deploy?'

'Docking arm is primed. Deployment controls activated.'

'T minus five minutes to intercept,' Zola called out.

May nervously watched the closing vessel trajectory lines. They'd been over the docking procedure many times, but she didn't trust a damn thing on that ship any more. During the last couple of weeks of the voyage, she had seen many signs to indicate that the ship's systems were breaking down from all the abuse they'd taken. And she'd had to get creative with power. Losing the bio-garden meant she needed to use the ship's power-hungry back-up oxygen generator. Just to be sure, she and Eve ran a final systems check. Autopilot was locked and holding her flight path. Her docking tunnel port, on the starboard side of the flight deck, was showing operational. Its electromagnetic collar, critical to retrieving and attaching the *Maryam I* tunnel to her ship, operational. Explosive door bolts, ready to explode.

'So far, so good,' she said, knocking on the side of her head.

'Sixty seconds to intercept,' Zola called out on the comms.

'Well, Eve, it looks like this is goodbye for now.'

'Let's say farewell instead,' Eve said.

'Farewell. And sweet dreams,' May said.

'Thank you, May. If anything happens—'

'Nope, we're not doing that. Nothing is going to happen. I'll see you on the *Maryam I* in a bit.'

'I was going to say don't forget to wake me up.'

'I love you too, Eve.'

'Thirty seconds,' Zola said on the comms.

'*Maryam I* is go,' Ian called out.

'*Hawking II* is go,' May responded. 'You as ready to get off this crate as I am, Cheeky?' she said to her belly.

The shaking increased on the *Hawking II* as it took on more atmosphere. May attached her EVA helmet and snatched up her precious pack.

'Ten seconds,' Zola called out.

'Yippee ay-yay,' May said.

From his position, Stephen saw the *Hawking II* glide up next to them. Compared to the *Maryam I*, it was vast, easily ten times larger. He could see the gaping, ragged hole where the landing vehicle hangar had been and couldn't believe May had managed to keep her flying. He thought of how happy that would have made Raj.

'There she is,' Ian called out. 'Looks like someone took a bite out of you, May.'

'Vessel speeds locked,' Zola said.

Both vessels were side by side, around two hundred metres apart. The *Maryam I* was positioned closer to the front of the *Hawking II* flight deck, where it had its emergency docking door. For a brief moment, Stephen caught a glimpse of May at the helm. He felt a knot of nerves twist in his chest and stomach. *We're so close*, he thought.

'Deploy docking arm,' Ian called out.

'Copy that,' Stephen called back.

He executed the docking arm deployment sequence exactly as Zola had shown him hundreds of times. The long white tunnel telescoped out of the port side of the *Maryam I*, back near the engine room airlock. Using the controls and VR screen, Stephen expertly guided the end of it to line up with May's docking door. On his screen, he saw flashing confirmation that the end of the tunnel was already locked into the *Hawking II*'s electromagnetic port collar.

'Deployed and aligned,' he said. 'Close distance.'

'Closing distance,' Ian said.

Ian slowly moved the *Maryam I* laterally toward the *Hawking II*, closing the gap. Stephen's face was jammed into the VR screen. When the end of the tunnel was less than ten metres from being locked in and sealed, the *Hawking II* was rocked violently by more pre-atmospheric turbulence. It briefly pitched starboard and the end of the tunnel collided hard with its docking port. Ian quickly pulled away.

'Hitting some serious chop,' May said on the comm.

'Stand by, May,' Zola said. 'Stephen, how is the tunnel?'

He could see denting around the port from where the end of the tunnel had hit.

'Tunnel is still operational, but I see superficial damage to the docking port. Infrared not showing atmosphere bleed, so the hull is intact.'

'Good,' Zola said.

'We need to give it another go right away,' Ian called out.

He closed the gap again while Stephen watched the tunnel, ready to telescope it back if they hit turbulence again. This time, the end of the tunnel locked into the docking port collar and sealed.

'We've got a solid dock and seal,' Stephen yelled triumphantly. 'May, release your door bolts and get your ass over here.'

'Copy that,' she responded on the comm. 'Stand by. Eve, please release the docking port door bolts.'

'Roger,' Eve said, then, 'May, the release mechanism is not responding.'

'Probably processor interference,' Stephen said. 'Go manual.'

'Copy,' May said.

They watched her on their feed as she punched in the commands several times.

'Shit,' she yelled. 'Come on.'

'What's wrong?' Stephen called out.

'Manual controls won't work,' she yelled, panicked. 'I can't get it open.'

88

The turbulent shaking on the *Hawking II* was getting more intense. May was still frantically trying to open the docking port door and it still wasn't working. She could feel herself starting to lose it, enraged that it had come down to this, terrified that they were out of time. Another alarm blasted from the flight deck.

'Fuck me,' she yelled, startled by it. 'I've got a rapid temperature increase on the bottom of the hull. We're going to burn—'

May felt a sharp pain in her belly and doubled over, groaning audibly.

'Oh, no,' she said. 'Oh, holy shit.'

'May, are you all right?' Latefa called out over the comm.

'I'm ... oh, God, it hurts.'

Ian's hands were starting to shake on the flight controls as the turbulence became more intense for them. Tension among everyone on the bridge was spiking.

'May, can you release the bolts manually from the port itself?' Ian shouted.

'Yes, but I can't ... I can't move,' she said over the comms.

From their video feed, they could see her at the flight deck. She was trying to get up and grab her pack, but kept doubling over and clutching her belly, immobilised by pain.

'She's going into labour,' Stephen yelled.

'And I'm going EVA to open the docking door. Zola, take the helm.'

'Copy that. Better hurry. We might be down to minutes before burn-in.'

'Maryam,' Ian yelled.

'Yes,' she answered. She was sitting up at the flight deck, trying to take even breaths. 'Latefa, definitely contractions. Maybe a minute apart. Hard to say.'

'Okay, remember your breathing,' Latefa said.

'On it.'

'We're coming for you,' Ian said. 'Put your helmet on and activate your EVA suit power now.'

'Copy,' she said and snapped her helmet to her suit.

'Eve,' Ian continued, 'shut down internal power on the flight deck to depressurise. I'm going to laser-cut the door so you have to be equalised to space by the time we get there. Do it as soon as May's suit is activated.'

'Copy that,' Eve said.

'Suit is good,' May said, giving them a thumbs-up.

Ian unstrapped from his flight deck chair and grabbed his EVA helmet. Zola strapped into his seat and took the controls. Stephen was about to insist on going with him, but Ian beat him to the punch.

'Stephen, you better suit up and come as well. I might have to stabilise the *Hawking II* while we get her out of there.'

'Copy that,' Stephen said, relieved.

Both men snapped their helmets to their suits and swam through the corridor.

'Latefa,' Ian said as they made their way, 'you and Martin

need to be ready to deliver this baby when we get back. Looks like it's well on its way.'

'Roger that,' she said on the comm. 'We're already set up.'

They made it to the docking tunnel airlock. Ian did a last check on his own suit, then did one on Stephen's.

'Glad I checked this. It's not properly sealed. Hold on,' Ian said as he adjusted something on the back of Stephen's helmet. 'Good. That's sorted. Ready?'

'Ready,' Stephen said firmly.

Ian opened the airlock door and they got in. He sealed it behind them, then opened the tunnel door. Stephen's confidence quickly ran away. The tunnel was large enough for two people in EVA suits to climb through, side by side, but to Stephen it looked as narrow as a drinking straw. Ian got in and started climbing through. Stephen forced himself to get in and climbed after Ian. Once he was in there it was fine, very quiet.

'All right?' Ian asked.

'Yeah, I'm fine,' Stephen lied.

The confining space of the tunnel triggered a horrible memory of when Stephen was a child, trapped in the back of his parents' mangled, burning car, trying to escape. He could feel his throat constricting just as it had back then amidst the heavy black smoke. He shook the memory out of his head and forced himself to think about May. But doing that brought on the terrifying memory of their space walk, when he'd lost control of his thrusters and drifted out into open space. He could hear his rapid breathing and was beginning to feel tingly in his hands and feet. Knowing that could make him lose consciousness, he slowed his breaths and focused on that as he crawled the rest of the way.

Ian had moved surprisingly fast and got to the other side well before Stephen. When Stephen finally made it to the end, Ian was already cutting the door bolts with his laser cutter. Stephen waited behind him, trying not to think that there were only a few inches of metal and composite between him and space.

'Almost there,' Ian said. 'I'm through. Stay back a moment, Stephen.'

'Not going anywhere,' Stephen said.

'Pressure, Eve?'

'Flight deck is pressurised for space,' she replied.

Having cut through the bolts, Ian was able to open the dock door by pulling it out toward them, into the tunnel, but only about halfway.

'That's as good as it's going to get. Let's go, Stephen.'

Ian went through the door. Stephen followed. As he stepped up on to the threshold, the electromagnetic collar released the tunnel and it separated from the *Hawking II*.

'Ian, the tunnel,' Stephen yelled.

With one boot on the port threshold, and the other in the tunnel, Stephen's legs spread apart as the tunnel fell away, leaving nothing but space beneath him. For a brief moment, as a wave of panic surged through him, it felt as though everything was moving in slow motion. He could hear his shallow breaths and the frantic radio chatter, but all of it was distorted and barely intelligible. He looked up and saw Ian standing at the edge of the docking door and knew his only chance was to try to make it back inside. Pushing off the edge of the tunnel, he lunged forward, his hand outstretched.

But Ian just stood there as Stephen's hand passed well within his reach, and watched him fall away into space.

89

The inside of the *Hawking II* was back to its all-consuming darkness and cold, just like when May had made it back from the cargo rig. She sat in her seat, bent over the flight deck, suffering through another contraction. They were starting to happen more frequently and with more intense pain. Something about being in the suit, feeling like she was freezing to death, made it very difficult for her to control her breathing. When the contraction subsided, she quickly became more aware of the radio chatter. They still could not find Stephen, no visual on him, no radio contact, no GPS. Something had happened to the docking tunnel; it detached. *Stephen fell.*

'What's happened to Stephen,' she demanded.

'There was an accident,' Zola said over the comms. 'The tunnel separated. He's—'

'He's lost, May,' Ian said, his voice mournful, as he floated into the flight deck beside her.

'Where is he? Do you have a visual? Stephen? Stephen? Do you copy? What happened to his radio, goddammit? Stephen?'

'We can't raise him,' Zola said, choking up. 'Suit GPS isn't working either.'

'What the fuck are you talking about?' May screamed. 'Stephen!'

'May, we've got to go.'

She looked up, sobbing. Ian's helmet light was cutting through the darkness as he loomed over her, unfastening her seat straps. His helmet glass had darkened from her headlamp shining into it so she couldn't see his face.

'Ian, no,' she cried. 'We have to find him.'

'I'm sorry,' he said. 'Come now. There's no time.'

He pulled her out of her seat and hooked his right arm under her left, the crook of his elbow in her armpit. Then he faced forward, his back to the ceiling, and used his thrusters to start moving them through the room. May had her back to the floor, as though she was lying down. Her knees were pulled up. Straightening her legs made the pain worse. She knew another contraction was on its way. Her muscles were twitching. She could feel wetness in her suit, in her crotch and on her legs and stomach. She wanted to tear away from Ian, to go out through the airlock door to search for Stephen, but her body would not comply. Filled with despair, all she could do was whimper and wait to suffer again.

'May, slow down your breathing.'

Ian's headlamp lit their way ahead as they neared the flight deck door. May's was facing up, toward the ceiling. It briefly illuminated her pack, the one she'd filled with her personal effects and Eve's back-up drive. It must have floated up there after Eve depressurised the flight deck, most likely while she was having a contraction.

'Ian, my pack. My pack. We have to—'

Another contraction hit, a flaming arrow that shot from her navel into her lower spine. She gasped, unable to even scream, and her breath sped up to a pant.

'Almost there,' Ian said calmly as they flew out of the flight deck, into the corridor.

'Ian, please.'

'Don't worry, May,' he said quietly. 'You'll be all right. I've got you.'

'May, you have to slow your breathing,' Latefa said on the comm. 'You'll hyperventilate. That's very dangerous for you and your baby.'

'What?'

Latefa's words had come too late. May's hands and feet were tingling. She was drowsy and confused, unsure of where she was.

'I'm ... it's so dark,' she said, and drifted off to sleep.

90

On the underside of the *Hawking II*'s reactor deck, Stephen clung to an EVA handhold on the edge of two payload bay doors. One of his boots was jammed into the doors' U-shaped latch cover.

After he had fallen away from the docking port, his momentum had carried him toward the rear of the ship. For several terrifying seconds, as he screamed in vain for help, he had floated just far enough from the ship that he couldn't reach it. Before passing it completely and drifting into space, he'd remembered his thrusters and used them to fly to the spot he currently occupied.

As he rode out another wave of pre-atmospheric turbulence, he was still trying to contact the *Maryam I*. He could hear their chatter, but they didn't respond to his calls for help. From what he heard, Ian had retrieved May. Zola was trying to figure out how to get them back to the *Maryam I*. And May was well into labour.

Ian. He had made no effort to help him. The way he'd stood there, stock still and watching ... almost expectant of the impending disaster. Stephen had been so close to him in that moment; he remembered seeing a reflection of himself in Ian's helmet glass, hand outstretched. *He just stood there.* And the electromagnetic collar malfunction had happened very shortly after Ian had hurried through the docking door, in the exact space of time Stephen would be following.

Before they entered the tunnel airlock on the *Maryam I*, Ian had made the quick adjustment to Stephen's EVA suit. Something about it being improperly sealed. Stephen had got in and out of the suit countless times in the two-week period when they were repairing the ship. He could seal the helmet to the suit in his sleep. That adjustment probably explained Stephen's malfunctioning comm unit. He could hear everyone else, so he never noticed the problem till it was too late. Finally, Stephen knew he had fully charged his pack, but, looking at his current life-support levels, he barely had twenty minutes of power left.

After it happened, Ian had also been quick to declare him a lost cause. *He's lost, May.* Then, *Don't worry, May. You'll be all right. I've got you.* He had wanted Stephen dead and he had planned it in advance. The whole thing was brutally cold and efficient, two of Ian's most infamous qualities. Recalling the conversation they'd had about May just prior to entering Mars orbit, it was clear now that Ian had been talking about himself, not Stephen. It was his flag, and he had just planted it.

Stephen had to move. Ian and May had already made it to the area just outside the docking door. Ian was continuing to spin his heroic narrative, telling Zola he thought he knew how to fix the electromagnetic collar and pull the tunnel back. It was a long shot, but he had to try. May was groaning in terrible pain. She kept talking about going back, they needed to go back. Ian soothed her with his assurances. Everything was going to be all right. He was right there with her.

Stephen was motivated to get his ass moving by the one thing stronger than his fear of floating in space untethered: rage. It was primal and throttled his internal dialogue, reducing it to simple thoughts and actions.

There was an emergency airlock door on every deck of the *Hawking II*. He could not see where it was on the reactor deck, but it was there. Hand over hand, he made his way around the outside of the deck, fighting to maintain his grip in the worsening turbulence. When he saw the airlock door, the next safety handhold was on the outside of it, two metres away. Thrust. That was the only choice. He stuffed away the fear of floating free again and took aim at the handhold. *You've done this many times. Go.* He let go and hit his thruster, his hands outstretched. One of them caught the handhold. He opened the airlock with the other, crawled into the ship, and closed the airlock door behind him.

91

In the area next to the *Hawking II*'s docking door, Ian had just managed to miraculously fix the electromagnetic collar.

'I've got it,' he shouted triumphantly.

'Copy that,' Zola shouted back. 'Good work, boss. Repositioning the tunnel.'

May was holding on to a ladder rung, riding out another contraction. Through the open docking door, she could see the tunnel moving back to the door. When the collar got hold of it, it quickly reattached. Ian took May by the arm.

'May, we've got to go.'

'Ian, my pack. We have to—'

'Right now,' he said firmly, and pulled her with him into the tunnel.

As they made their way through, Ian had to use a combination of thrusters and hand holds. The turbulence kept making him lose his grip and he and May would collide, causing her to yell out in pain. Then she felt something give way in her belly and a rush of warm liquid coming out of her. It formed into spheres and floated up her suit.

'Oh, my God,' she yelled. 'My waters broke.'

One of the spheres of liquid floated up and burst on her helmet glass, causing her display to short out and glitch.

'May, keep the water away from your mouth and nose,' Latefa yelled.

All May could do in reply was sob. The smell of the water was revolting. Her breathing had returned to the short panting and she was feeling the tingling and confusion again.

'Almost there,' Ian exclaimed, huffing and puffing with exhaustion.

When they finally reached the *Maryam I*, May was half-conscious. She could see Martin in his EVA suit, waiting for them. Ian hoisted her up to the door and Martin pulled her inside. Much of what happened after that was a blur. After depressurising and going through the airlock, they got May's helmet off. Latefa was there, cleaning her face and checking her pulse, asking her questions she couldn't answer. May was asking about Stephen and Eve over and over, but no one seemed to care about either. She was so angry she wanted to scream, but didn't have the breath.

Back inside the *Hawking II*, Stephen was using precious suit power to thrust his way through the ship. The shaking from turbulence had got so bad, the ship was starting to tear its insides apart. Wall screens shattered, littering the air with razor-edged glass shards. Power lines snaked out, sparking. Water lines broke and released huge chunks of ice. When he made it back to the docking door, the tunnel was still there. Tears of relief floated inside his helmet. Then he heard May's voice and stopped short. He finally understood what she'd been talking about, why she'd wanted to go back to the flight deck. They had left her pack behind. Eve's back-up drive was in that pack. They had left Eve. The ship shook and the floor and walls of the docking room twisted, knocking him around like a pinball. The tunnel rattled hard against the door collar. Soon it would not need Ian to deactivate it as it would irretrievably tear away. He had to get in that tunnel right now.

Instead, he turned and hit his thrusters again, flying back into the darkness of the flight deck. What he was doing went against every ounce of logical, rational thought he possessed. It was utterly contradictory to his nature. But that didn't matter. The only thing that mattered was getting Eve. She was the reason May had won her fight for survival. As much as any person, Eve was a loyal, trusted friend. And, just like any person, she did not deserve to be left behind.

'Exit orbit,' Ian shouted on the comm. 'Full thrust.'

'I need ninety seconds to secure May for labour,' Latefa shouted back.

'Okay, but not a second more,' Ian shouted back. 'We're already on borrowed time.'

Ninety seconds, Stephen thought as he entered the flight deck, searching desperately for May's pack. He spotted it floating near the ceiling and swam up to get it, trying not to use thrusters to conserve power.

'Sixty seconds,' Ian shouted.

'I'm not going to make it,' he said to himself.

He needed to alert them somehow that he was in there, still alive. Then he remembered the way they had known May was alive when she first woke up from the coma. They'd received the ship's emergency SOS beacon. Stephen searched the flight deck but had no idea what he was looking for.

'Forty-five,' Ian shouted.

'Goddammit!' Stephen yelled in his helmet.

'Stephen,' Eve said. 'Get to the *Maryam I* immediately.'

'Eve?' he said.

No reply. *Yell, you idiot.*

'Eve,' he shouted.

'Yes,' she said. 'Your helmet comm is—'

'I know,' he screamed. 'Alert the *Maryam I*. Tell them to wait for me.'

He strapped on May's pack and hit his thrusters, heading back for the docking door.

'This is Eve, AI,' he heard her say on the open comm. 'Dr Stephen Knox is alive. He is on the flight deck, going to the docking tunnel for emergency evac.'

When he got back to the docking door, the tunnel had been retracted to the *Maryam I*. Life-support on his suit was down to four minutes.

'Stephen,' Zola yelled. 'Thank God. We're sending the tunnel over now. When it gets there, hurry across. Use your thrusters. We can no longer predict burn-in, so it could happen any minute. Stephen, do you read?'

He motioned wildly with his hand that he could not respond.

'Stephen's helmet comm is out,' Eve said. 'He can hear but he cannot respond.'

'Copy that,' Zola said. 'Okay, Stephen. Give me a thumbs-up if you copy my instructions. Martin will meet you on the other side.'

Stephen held on to the swaying docking door with one hand and gave her a thumbs-up with the other.

'Martin,' Ian yelled. 'You're needed in the infirmary with May and Latefa. I'll help Stephen.'

92

Stephen's heart sank when he heard Ian's voice, but he would have to deal with that when he got to the *Maryam I*. As it stood now, he might be able to use thrusters to get across and survive on whatever residual atmosphere was in his suit, but no more. He waited for what seemed like an eternity for the tunnel to telescope out. Clearly, with Ian at the controls, he was going to be in no hurry to get it there quickly.

'Guys, I'm getting a dangerously high heat reading on the hull of the *Hawking II*,' Zola shouted on the comms.

Stephen could feel that heat radiating up through the hull into the ship. It was no longer freezing and the ice crystal patterns that had been forming on the metal and glass were melting. He looked down. The surface of Mars was now intermittently visible as the *Hawking II* began to drop into the atmosphere. And the shaking had got so violent, Stephen could barely keep himself from being thrown in every direction. He looked at the *Maryam I*. The tunnel was not going to make it. It was only a third of the way there and, even if it did get there, Stephen would not make it across.

He did the maths. Roughly seventy metres of space between him and the *Maryam I*. Ninety seconds of life-support left. Using thrusters to get that far, at the speed he needed to go to keep from burning in himself, he would drain his life-support and be left with residual at the tunnel, if he made it. And he would be dealing with Ian.

'You wanted to be an astronaut,' he said to himself.

Stephen zeroed in on the tunnel and jammed his suit thrusters full. When he first stepped off the edge of the docking door, he dipped down abruptly. *Too late,* he thought, and waited to plunge to the planet surface. But that had been a rush of suction created by the *Hawking II* as it dropped into Mars's atmosphere behind him. As he rose up and regained his trajectory for the tunnel, he heard the nightmarish sound of the ship being ripped apart as it burned in. The radio chatter was back, but the noise around him was too loud to make it out. When he was about ten metres from the tunnel, he finally heard Zola.

'Stephen, you're coming in too fast.'

He was, but there was nothing he could do, as he was finally out of power. The tunnel was at an angle when he reached it. His torso flew straight in, but his legs hit the edge of it hard, then his head and back hit the inside wall even harder. Dizzy from the blow to the head, he struggled to get his bearings, managing to grab on to the handholds. He could feel the tunnel moving back to the ship as well, with an upward thrust. On the radio chatter, Zola was saying they had to pull up and away from the edge of the atmosphere.

'Hold on, Stephen,' she said. 'Please hold on.'

The upward thrust increased and he held on for dear life as the tunnel moved sharply in the opposite direction to the ship. On top of that, he could feel he was on the last of his residual air. He tried to take shallow breaths and focus on his grip, waiting for that moment when they would glide back into the serenity of space. It finally came. Determined to make it into the ship, he pulled, hand over hand, the last few metres, with everything he had left, until he reached the *Maryam I* airlock door. And when he got there, exhausted, freezing, and feeling the beginning phase of hypoxia, Ian was waiting for him.

'Zola,' said Ian, 'I'm having trouble shutting the outside air-lock door. Working on that.'

'Copy that,' she said. 'Welcome home, Stephen.'

All Ian had to do was buy some time for Stephen to die in his suit. He wouldn't need much. Clearly, he'd made certain he was the only one aware of Stephen's atmospheric levels. Again, cold and efficient. There would be no grandiose speeches telling Stephen he believed that May, and Stephen's work, and the baby, were all rightfully his. That was far too trite for him. The way he looked at Stephen said it all. Quiet contempt. In Ian's mind, Stephen was beneath him. That had always been clear. Stephen's work was a means to Ian's ultimate end, and Stephen was just in the way. Same with May.

Stephen thought about May in the infirmary, in the throes of birth, not knowing what had become of him. Or, if she did know, now expecting him to walk through that door to be with her. How could he let Ian take that from him? He remembered what Ian had said about him coming all that way and not telling May how he felt. In that moment, that was the question that gave Stephen the strength to slam the outside airlock door shut and seal it. It also gave him the strength to wrap his arms and legs around Ian as tightly as possible, so he could reach Ian's EVA suit regulator.

You are an old man, Stephen thought, his anger rising. *You should have factored that into your cold, efficient equation.*

Ian struggled mightily. Stephen's adrenaline surged as he yanked with all his strength on the regulator hose. He was frothing at the mouth, like a rabid dog, starving for blood. The hose ripped out and he had it.

'Ian, I'm showing atmosphere loss in your suit,' Zola yelled. 'Do you read me?'

He couldn't answer as he gasped for air, reaching for his regulator hose. When he realised he would never be able to re-attach it, Ian tried to get to the airlock depressurisation controls. Although this would have saved them both, Stephen wrapped up Ian's arms, pinning them to his sides. He held them there with all his might while Ian thrashed him with his knees and helmet. Stephen was prepared to die to make sure Ian never made it through that airlock. It wasn't an act of revenge. He was doing it to protect May. Ian had shown the entire spectrum of his true colours. He was a very dangerous man, willing to do anything to get what he wanted, and Stephen was prepared to trade his own life to make sure he never had the chance to hurt May and her child.

Ian stopped fighting and Stephen felt him weaken. His face had gone slack and his pupils were dilated. To finish the job, Stephen snapped off Ian's helmet and watched the water in his eyes freeze until they were the milky colour of a blind dog.

He let Ian drift away and tried to reach for the depressurisation controls, but he was in the final stages of asphyxiation. His entire body was numb. His heart, which had been hammering in his chest, was now fluttering erratically. His vision blurred, then darkened, then faded to black.

93

Bright lights flashed and cut the darkness. Stephen thought he was underwater, trying to breathe, but it felt as though his lungs were filled with heavy liquid, expanding like balloons on the verge of bursting. There was no way to catch his breath. And, when he did try to breathe, stabbing pains in his chest shot down through his arms and felt as if they were exploding out through the ends of his fingers. He heard voices. They were yelling, fearful, insistent. They wanted something from him. Needles pierced his skin. His mouth was being forced open. Gagging, coughing. The bright lights became explosions, with painful strobes that shed light on where he was.

It looked like a hospital. The people around him looked like doctors. They wore surgical masks, scrub caps, gloves. He heard a woman screaming. It wasn't one of the doctors. They weren't screaming. Where was it coming from? He moved his head. The doctors tried to hold it in place, but he forced it against their hands, looking, trying to free his arms, which he couldn't move. Something was digging into them, holding them. When he turned his head, he saw the woman. She was screaming. And there was blood. It floated around her and the room in bulbous crimson bubbles, dividing into smaller ones, smaller, smaller. They were everywhere.

Then she stopped screaming. Something was going down Stephen's throat. He wanted to scream too. He wanted to vomit. He flexed his muscles, fought, pulled, shook his head. Then another needle. Jammed into the crook of his elbow. And something cold rushing into him, spreading through him, loosening his muscles, killing the pain, weighing down on him, stealing his breath, bleeding his consciousness out, slowly, till there wasn't even darkness, only bright white light and the feeling of burning.

94

t's only a dream. Wake up. It's only a dream. Wake up.

The white light darkened and patterns emerged. Lines, crisscrossed, within larger squares, many of them, a grid. The lines became sharper, the patterns more defined, lights embedded within. A ceiling. Sounds faded in, a constant machine hum, shrill beeps. The smell was clean, a sharp chemical clean, sanitary. Soft sheets, blankets, warmth.

Thank God it was only a dream.

Stephen tried to lift his head. Too heavy. His hands felt stronger than his neck. He gripped the sheets and pushed, scooting his bottom back, shoving his head and neck up on to pillows, slightly more upright than before. Now he could survey the room. The infirmary. *Maryam I.* How did he end up in there? The way he felt, it had to have been bad. His head ached, lungs burned, heart thumped in his chest. Feeling as though he was having trouble catching his breath, he remembered. Ian. The airlock. No breath. Ian is dead.

From a dream to a nightmare.

The infirmary was empty otherwise. It felt abandoned. He

felt that way. Vulnerable. *Ian is dead.* The bed next to him. When he looked at it, he remembered the screams. *May.* The fear came with the fragments of recollection. Screaming. Blood droplets floating everywhere. Blood everywhere. Then silence. *May, oh God, May.* She wasn't there. Her bed was empty, clean, machines standing like soldiers waiting for the next battle. Past the foot of the bed, near the supply cabinets, a clear bin secured to the floor. Linens stuffed inside. Blood on those.

As it all came back, accompanied by fear and dread, so did Stephen's strength. His singular desire to get out of that bed overtook him. The oxygen mask hit the floor. The IV needle came out and swung back to the machine, dangling and dripping. Sheets and blankets were thrown to the side, then the hard part. Sitting up in one of Ian's uncomfortable diamagnetic gravity suits.

He shoved his fists into the mattress behind him, forcing his torso up into a sitting position. After holding that for a while, allowing the blood to get into the muscles and the waves of dizziness to leave his head, the legs swung over the side and the feet came down on the cool floor. Then he stood, held the bed for balance, stayed there till the room settled and his legs could be trusted.

He tried to call out, but quickly realised that that was a non-starter. His vocal cords were raw and swollen and unwilling to let out anything other than a raspy gurgle. He walked to the corridor – also empty – and felt abandoned. Where the hell was everyone? Not that there were many left. Where was May? Her bed was empty. The room was clean. How long had she been gone? How long had he been asleep? Another corridor, empty and silent. His fear blossomed; he desperately wanted to find someone, anyone, but didn't know if he could handle it if he did.

Getting closer to the flight deck, there was still no sign of anyone and no sound beyond the machine hum, the ambient mechanical note, sung low and flat without end. How could there not be voices? The idea of walking in there to find it empty made his stomach twist with despair. He stopped in the corridor just outside the flight deck entrance and listened. Maybe he'd been mistaken about the quiet? He wasn't. It persisted. He had to walk in there. It didn't matter if he was ready. Whatever he saw he would have to accept. *May*. There was no living if . . . that, he wasn't willing to accept. Not possible.

Like a prisoner on death row, walking his final steps to the chamber, Stephen rounded the corner and went inside.

A baby started to cry. Then it wailed. The sound split the silence in half and Stephen stopped at the threshold of the flight deck, arrested by it. At the fore, near the engineering module, Zola, Latefa and Martin were all bent over something, speaking in odd sing-song voices that rose in volume as the crying got louder. Stephen kept walking. The baby kept crying. When he got to the passenger launch chairs, May rose up from the other side of the crew, and she and Stephen were face to face. He didn't want to move any further, fearing all of it might be a mirage that would quickly fade. May was also still, feasting her eyes on him, unwilling to look away.

The crew turned and smiled. Latefa and Martin came to Stephen, thinking he needed help, but he held up his hand, letting them know he was just fine. He continued forward, passing through the seats, and saw what they had been huddled over. It was an incubator bassinet. Inside was a very small baby girl with a very loud voice. *Cheeky.* He moved closer, carefully, still waiting for all of it to feel solid and real. When he reached the bassinet and looked down, Cheeky stopped crying. Like a light, she just switched it off, and looked right up at him. Her eyes were May's, deep and magnetic, with a spark of mischief, encircling and drawing you in wherever you stood.

He put his hand on the top of the bassinet. The baby was

small enough to fit inside it. She reached out, trying to touch his hand, wanting to grasp his fingers. Stephen laughed and cried. When the baby realised she couldn't get to his hand, she got frustrated and started to cry too. May came over and stood next to him. She took hold of the hand he had on top of the bassinet and then took hold of the other. He turned to face her, to look in her eyes for what felt like the first time, to kiss her. They held their embrace until they were no longer afraid to let go.

95

'You, Dr Knox, gave us quite a scare.'

May was giving Stephen a waggle of her finger while he hovered over the bassinet. Cheeky was asleep. She was attached to many tubes, including an umbilical catheter, providing medication, hydration, and nutrition. A nose cannula gave her a much-needed oxygen boost. It was frightening to see all that on someone so tiny, so Stephen had made Latefa explain everything. She had also explained what happened to him. After they had dragged him out of the airlock, he had been so severely hypoxic that his heart had stopped and he'd been clinically dead. The only reason they were able to save him was because he was also severely hypothermic. The cold had slowed his metabolism down and kept his brain from dying, but they'd been forced to put him in a coma and intubate him for the first twenty-four hours of a forty-eight-hour recovery.

'Now we can add having been in a coma as one of the things we have in common,' said May.

'That, and very poor judgment.'

Eve chimed in over the PA. 'I'm trying to teach May how to

be grateful for you saving her, versus obsessing over the incredibly irrational thinking it took for you to do so.'

Stephen smiled. 'That's what happens when you hang around May too long,' he said, his voice having been upgraded to a raspy whisper.

'Amen to that,' Eve said. 'And I am grateful. In fact, to show my gratitude—'

'Eve, you said you were going to let me tell him,' May complained.

'I couldn't help myself,' Eve said. 'It just slipped out.'

'Bullshit,' May said.

'Tell me what?' Stephen asked.

'Go ahead, Eve. Glory hound.'

'Stephen, after you heroically saved me from the *Hawking II*, and May and Zola were good enough to wake me up, I decrypted the MADS recorder.'

'Was it intact?' he asked, excitedly.

'No, we just built this up to tell you it was empty,' May joked.

'Why don't we show him the newsfeed?' Zola said.

'Picture's worth a thousand words,' May replied. 'Eve, please do the honours.'

'Of course.'

A video loaded in the eye. It was a news broadcast from Earth. Theme music played over a logo animation, then the announcer's voice faded up.

'Former NASA mission director Robert Warren was taken into custody today . . . '

As she droned on, Stephen watched footage of Robert being walked from his mansion in Washington, D.C. in handcuffs, flanked by local cops and federal agents. He was loaded into the back of a police car.

' . . . federal agents also apprehended his accomplice, former NASA mission specialist Glenn Chambers . . . '

The scene switched to Glenn's mugshot. He looked old and beat up, all of his southern charm having disappeared in a federal holding cell.

'Jesus,' Stephen said.

'I beamed the data to the FBI as soon as Eve decrypted it,' Zola said.

May smiled proudly. 'All the money in the world isn't going to buy him out of this one. It's about time we put the Robert Warrens of the world on notice.'

'Stephen knows something about that,' Zola said.

They had not yet talked about Ian.

'We saw what he did to you in the footage from his helmet camera,' Zola said. 'Stephen, I'm so sorry. I would never, in a million years, have thought him capable of that.'

'Obsession does strange things to people,' Stephen said, looking at May.

Thinking of Ian in that moment, Stephen no longer felt the rage he'd felt in the airlock. Instead he felt pity. Ian Albright had been a brilliant man, even one of Stephen's heroes when he was younger, a man for whom it seemed nothing was impossible. The Ian who had sat quietly, waiting for Stephen to die so that he could take May and her child by force, had been a shadow of his former self, a broken caricature playing out a tragic script only someone poisoned by his own monstrous ego could believe. Their objectives might have been different, but, as fate would soon show, Ian Albright and Robert Warren were the same.

96

May sat on the edge of the bed in her quarters, humming to Cheeky. Like all the sleeping quarters on the *Maryam I*, it was a cramped little space with only the bare necessities, but May had done what she could to make the place cheerful. She was especially proud of the little mobile she'd made out of machine parts, bits of wire and colourful medical supplies. It hung over Cheeky's bassinet, making a pleasant jingling noise as it spun and occasionally glittered with light from the approaching sun. These were the measures often needed to get Cheeky to sleep. The poor little thing was constantly uncomfortable from all the medical attention she needed, and being unable to hold her made May more disagreeable than usual.

Finally, Cheeky settled down, and May, very slowly and carefully, lay back down herself. She kept very still, avoiding any sudden movements, and revelled in the continuing quiet. Congratulating herself on setting a new speed record for getting the baby to sleep, she started to drift off. As soon as she took the smallest step into dreamland, Cheeky let loose one of her infamous screeching high notes, instantly pulling May out of her slumber. Back to the humming, spinning the mobile.

Then there was a knock on her door. It was Stephen.

'Can you please quiet that baby down? Some of us are trying to sleep.'

'I'm at my wits' end,' she said, stepping aside so Stephen could come in. He was happy to oblige; he could watch Cheeky for hours.

'She'll be a lot happier when she gets out of this stuffy little prison,' Stephen said.

'I can relate,' May laughed. 'What about you? Climbing the walls?'

'Let's just say I don't want to be an astronaut when I grow up any more.'

'Again, I can relate.'

'Come on, you live for this,' Stephen said.

'Maybe, but now I live for other things too, so . . . we'll see.'

Stephen was back to being mesmerised by Cheeky.

'I know I've already said this, but thank you, Stephen.' May joined him next to Cheeky, who had gone back to sleep. 'I did good, huh?' she said, tearfully.

'You did better than good.'

'Do you want to talk about it?' May asked.

'What?'

'The elephant in the room. Kind of hard to miss in a space this small.'

'Doesn't bother me. Kids love elephants anyway.'

'Stephen, don't you think we should at least—'

'If Cheeky will have me, I'm here for her.'

May was really crying now. Stephen held her.

'I feel the same about you,' May said. 'I just don't know where to begin.'

Stephen sat down with her on the bed. 'Remember what you said to me on our first date?'

May smiled at the memory. 'You remembered my birthday.'

'What did you say to me before you blew out your candle?'

She thought back to that moment and tears welled up in her eyes when it dawned on her why he was asking.

'I said, "You know what, Dr Knox, I have an idea."'

'What's that?' Stephen said, playing along.

'When I blow out this candle, let's forget about everything that's ever happened between us before this moment. I want this to be the beginning.'

Acknowledgements

Flight Crew: Ed Wood (Sphere, Little, Brown UK), Michael Braff (Skybound, US). Ed, thank you for lighting this fire and for having faith in me to carry the torch. Your fearless editorial direction and dedication to the craft are inspiring. Ed and Mike, thank you for a dynamic collaboration that has paved the way for me to do my very best.

Mission Control: Sphere/Little, Brown UK, Skybound US, Sam Morgan (The Lotts Agency), Brad Mendelsohn (Circle of Confusion), Jeff Frankel (McKuin Frankel Whitehead LLP), Jon Mone (Universal Pictures), Bryan Furst, Samantha Crowley (Skybound Film & Television), and Foundry Literary Agency.

Mission Specialists: Sphere/Little,Brown UK – Charlie King, Jonathan Haines, Andy Hine, Helena Doree, Kate Hibbert, Thalia Proctor, Linda McQueen, Gemma Shelley, Stephie Melrose, Ceara Elliot, Steve Panton, Sarah Shrubb, Louise Newton and Tom Webster. Kate Caudill (Skybound),

Katie Abbott (Circle of Confusion), Rob Goldman (McKuin Frankel Whitehead LLP), Jill Goldstein (JGoldsteinPR), and Haven Lamoureux (Book Trailer Editor).

Special thanks to Alan Smale (Goddard Space Flight Center) and Peter Stoltz for helping me ground this science fiction novel with science fact.

To my amazing wife Amanda and family (DRMK, KRBK, JoMama, Kenneth Vaughn, Tina, Kara, Lady, Sky, Ozzy, Liir, Louis, and Rita), I thank you for your love, support, patience, and sense of humour. Without you, I would be forever adrift in The Void.